Outstanding praise for the n

How I Stole Her I

"A hilarious and compelling story abo payback. Liz Ireland has created a cast c are deliciously twisted and yet completely sympathetic. From downtrodden diva Alison Bell to the serial adulterer Pepper Smith, you can't help being pulled into their tangled web. Wickedly clever one-liners, outrageous abuses, and a page-turner of a story make *How I Stole Her Husband* a must-read for chick-lit fans."

—Jennifer Coburn, author of *Reinventing Mona*

"*How I Stole Her Husband* is a wonderfully written, often hilarious story of a young woman's journey from all-around discontent to hard-won acceptance of life in all its crazy splendor. Alison Bell is the most likeable heroine I've met in some time—charmingly down-to-earth, sometimes painfully self-aware, and just a little bit desperate to make something of her life. How she plans to pluck herself from the depths of poverty to which she imagines she's sunk, how she re-discovers the love of her life and how she recovers triumphantly from the havoc he wreaks makes for an utterly absorbing read. Liz Ireland takes a clever concept and raises it to an unexpected level of sophistication. Don't miss this book!"

—Holly Chamberlin, author of *The Summer of Us*

Three Bedrooms in Chelsea

"The three-girls-in-the-city formula gets an extreme chick-lit makeover in *Three Bedrooms in Chelsea*, an amusing sexy read."

—Lauren Baratz-Logsted, author of *The Thin Pink Line*

"The sexy singles occupying *Three Bedrooms in Chelsea* are heart-warming, funny and unforgettable. Liz Ireland has created an absolute delight!"

—Patti Berg, author of *I'm No Angel*

Charmed, I'm Sure

"Captivating! *Charmed, I'm Sure* is an enchanting blend of hex and sex! A rollicking romantic romp that will make you believe in magic.

—Stephanie Bond, author of *A Whole Lotta Trouble*

When I Think of You

"Fresh and funny!"

—Jennifer Crusie, *New York Times* bestselling author of *Bet Me*

"A fresh, fun, comic romantic tale."

—*Rendezvous*

Books by Liz Ireland

HUSBAND MATERIAL

WHEN I THINK OF YOU

CHARMED, I'M SURE

THREE BEDROOMS IN CHELSEA

HOW I STOLE HER HUSBAND

Published by Kensington Publishing Corporation

How I Stole Her Husband

Liz Ireland

KENSINGTON BOOKS
www.kensingtonbooks.com

KENSINGTON BOOKS are published by

Kensington Publishing Corp.
850 Third Avenue
New York, NY 10022

All Kensington titles, imprints and distributed lines are available at special quantity discounts for bulk purchases for sales promotion, premiums, fund-raising, educational or institutional use.

Special book excerpts or customized printings can also be created to fit specific needs. For details, write or phone the office of the Kensington Special Sales Manager: Kensington Publishing Corp., 850 Third Avenue, New York, NY, 10022. Attn. Special Sales Department. Phone: 1-800-221-2647.

ISBN 0-7582-0837-5

First Kensington Trade Paperback Printing: March 2005
10 9 8 7 6 5 4 3 2 1

Printed in the United States of America

How I Stole Her Husband

Chapter 1

I never would have guessed how many people read a sleazy tabloid called *New York Now!* until a complete stranger spat on me. There I was, minding my own business, my arm stiffly extended with fingers snapping impatiently to flag down a cab, when an arc of saliva hit my cheek with a warm, sickening splat.

"Slut!" a woman yelled. As if the warm slime on my cheek weren't insult enough.

She had obviously read the paper. Though how anyone could recognize me from the grainy picture that scurrilous rag printed, I'll never know. I might not be Paris Hilton, but I usually have one chin, not five. The *Post*'s snap was much better—me looking heavy lidded and saucy in sable—but that didn't appear till the day after the spit incident.

Don't write off my assailant as just your garden variety Manhattan lunatic, either. She was a fifty-year-old lady swathed in raw silk and a Hermès scarf and carrying a Bendel's bag. When you're labeled ***NAUGHTY NANNY!*** by a newspaper, even a crappy one, you attract high-end spitters.

That was a difficult day. Even in New York, where weirder things than this happen on the street on an hourly basis, it's hard to recover your dignity after wiping a glob of some stranger's body fluids off your cheek. I was already jittery back then for a lot of different reasons—I think it's fair to say I was going through a rough patch—but being used as a human spittoon just about nudged me over the edge.

At any rate, anyone without a jot of empathy could understand how I ended up stealing an eighteen-thousand-dollar coat after that.

Or maybe they couldn't. It's still hard for me even to understand.

Sometimes, when I sit back and take a deep breath, it's hard to figure out how any of this happened. What's easy to figure out is when.

The time: Six months ago.

The place: A dentist's office in Dallas.

Not long before, I had been laid off from my job answering phones at a local travel magazine. Prior to that, I had been let go from another company where I was proofreading real estate ads. I was not setting the world on fire. At twenty-eight, I was still hovering in the cold and rubbing two sticks together.

And wouldn't you know. Everything seems bleak, and then you get a toothache.

So there I was, installed in a dentist chair, waiting for a filling to set and fretfully flipping through the latest copy of that pointless glossy, *Definitely Dallas*. I was combing the want ads, hoping that there would be something available at the magazine itself. Though pointless, *Definitely Dallas* was a venerable city institution, available in every hotel room in town and as ubiquitous in doctors' offices as *Highlights*. Surely someone there needed phones answered or something proofread?

They didn't, apparently, but one ad that caught my eye looked even better. In fact, it looked so good that at first I thought it must be a mirage.

> Live-in nanny needed. Dallas couple seeks caring female who loves children to help look after adorable girl, 3½. Must be dedicated, responsible, creative, flexible. Opportunity for relocation to NYC or London! Generous compensation! Excellent references req'd. Bilingual a plus. Call 555-0201.

Quick like a bunny, I ripped off my bib, sprinted out of the dentist office, and called the number on my cell phone from my car. I didn't even wait for the Novocain to wear off. The crunch was on. I'd been unemployed for two months and had my credit card refused at Safeway the night before while I was attempting to buy deodorant and a week's supply of ramen noodles. Poverty had even forced me to downgrade from a porcelain filling to silver, and how I was going to afford that when the bill arrived, I had no idea.

To be frank, my life wasn't supposed to be like this. I had not been sufficiently prepped for financial woe.

Here is my dirty little secret: I used to be rich. A daddy's girl. A pampered only child. Even when my dad lost all his money after I graduated high school, I still had assumptions of forthcoming unmerited reward. When I graduated from college, I landed an incredible job and expected to be a millionairess by the time I was thirty-five. (In other words, I was naive.com.)

Now I was twenty-eight, and the most money I'd ever made in a year was when I was twenty-three. I had netted more from my allowance when I was fourteen than I had working temp for the past three months. My income, with the exception of that one anomalously prosperous year, had been dropping precipitously from childhood forward, and now was in a total free fall. I was on the fast track of downward mobility.

With money problems came other difficulties. I started suffering from insomnia. My social life had tapered off considerably. My best friend had moved to New York, and another friend had married, promptly produced a child, and become maternal and dictatorly. A few acquaintances I suspected were just avoiding me. I could hardly blame them. "Nobody wants you when you're down and out," sounds cruel, but it does have its logic. Too much bad news (and ramen noodles) makes people uncomfortable. The week before I had seen an old work acquaintance turn ill-at-ease when I sang the praises of a new salon I'd found that featured twelve-dollar haircuts.

And of course there were acquaintances—the ones who had

known me in my flush younger days—who I was careful not to put myself in the path of.

So there I was. A poor friendless insomniac with bad hair. The kind of person I certainly would have avoided myself, had I been in any position to be choosy.

What I really needed was a miraculous rescue. A new life.

That classified ad was the change I needed. I felt it in my bones.

Those two tantalizing words, *generous compensation*, lodged in my head, where they gamboled about like fat furry puppies. I wanted this job. I had to have it. It was perfect! I was so ready to be generously compensated. Creativity, of course, was a slam dunk for me. I had practically been the drama queen of my high school. (Now I pictured myself putting on festive puppet shows and throwing together prize-winning Halloween costumes.) Dedicated? Of course I was dedicated . . . or I was certain I could be, if I knew what the hell I was supposed to be dedicated to. And I was bilingual—almost trilingual, if you counted the smattering of Spanish I had learned off of *Sesame Street* when I was a kid. *¡El cielo es arriba!*

I was pumped. And frankly, it's not in my personality to stay pumped for more than a few minutes, so I had to call right away, before I could think of the million and one reasons I would probably fail at being a nanny in the unlikely event anyone was demented enough to give me the job in the first place.

"I'm calling about the nanny position," I told the woman who picked up the phone. "My name is Alison Bell."

"Oh. Just a moment." Over the line, I could hear the efficient shuffling of paper and the whir of office machines in the background. "Have you worked with children before?"

"Yes, I have," I said, not entirely lying. "I worked as a teacher for one school year."

Actually, I had only lasted a few months, having quickly learned that substitute teaching has nothing to do with teaching and everything to do with crowd control and extreme survival technique. (Attention TV moguls: Substitute teaching has major untapped reality-show potential.) Luckily, given the bureaucratic nightmare that was the Dallas Independent School

District, I'm sure this woman would never be able to find out that I had been a total failure and barely escaped with my life. If she called DISD, they would probably only give her the date of the school year I worked. And who knows? I had never received a notice that my sub license had been terminated. The powers that be might even think I was still out there somewhere, standing in front of a class of hostile glassy-eyed adolescents, or running for my life down some long, long hallway.

"Oh—excellent," the woman piped in.

I was encouraged. "Since that time, I have had a few jobs in publishing, but working with children is what I find most fulfilling."

"How old are you?"

Could she ask me that? I had thought there was something about age discrimination. "Twenty-eight."

"Married?"

"No, I'm single."

"That's good. This is a live-in position, you know."

I'm *so* single, I wanted to say. *Extremely* single. Live-in position meant that, on top of generous compensation, I would have free rent. That thought alone made me dizzier than the prospect of a dream date with Mark Ruffalo.

"You have a college degree, then?"

"Yes. From North Texas State."

"And when would you be available—"

"Any time! I could start tomorrow!"

"—to meet Mrs. Smith?"

I winced. *Really should not cut off the interviewer, Al.* "Mrs. Smith?"

"The Smiths are the family you would be working for. Their little girl is named August."

"Oh. Then you're . . . ?" For some reason, I thought I had been speaking to my potential employer.

"I am Mr. Smith's secretary. I have been doing phone interviews, just to screen out entirely inappropriate candidates."

And here I was, slipping through the net!

"You wouldn't believe the number of calls we've received—and from some people with no qualifications whatsoever."

I clucked my tongue. The crust of some people—trying to get my generously compensated job.

"I would be free to meet her at her convenience any time this week." I took a breath, realizing that too much freedom just made me sound like a slacker queen. "Though mornings work best for me." Employers always seemed to like those up-and-at-'em types. "I'm a morning person."

"Mrs. Smith can meet you tomorrow at eleven at her home." She gave me the address and some basic directions, which I didn't need. The Smiths lived in Highland Park, my old stomping ground.

I practically floated the rest of the way home. This was *my job*. I knew it. In a few months I would be packing up to relocate to New York or London! My dream! It was all I could do not to pace around my dirty apartment pumping my fist in the air. I needed to high-five with someone, so I called my friend Jessica, who was living in New York.

"I've done it," I told her. "I found a way to get out of Dallas! New York, here I come!"

"Excellent! What happened?"

I told her about my nanny job. I had to go into details, because the details were so great.

But really, I should have known better. Although Jessica has many wonderful traits, loyalty being tops among the many, she also happens to be one of those cautious types. Okay, paranoid. It's not just that she sees a cloud behind every silver lining, she actually sees the puddle that cloud will create, which will freeze over outside the stoop of her apartment and that she will then have the bad fortune to step on. This, in turn, will be the cause of her spending a Saturday morning in the emergency room and stumping along on crutches for two months thereafter. She is my own personal Cassandra.

Sometimes her fears can be useful. She grew up in Dallas and could tell you how to get practically anywhere in the city without having to make a left-hand turn.

Jess, of course, had reservations about my new job. "Al, are you sure taking care of a three-and-a-half-year-old is for you?"

I hadn't really been thinking about the kid. I was too

wrapped up in generous compensation. And relocating! "How hard can it be?"

"Don't you remember subbing? You hated that."

"I didn't *hate* it." *Disliked it intensely*, perhaps. *Was rendered suicidal by.*

"You spent a month afraid to crawl out of your bed," she reminded me. "And when you did finally manage to mentally tunnel out, you were a maniac. Remember jujitsu?"

It's true, during that period of my life I sort of snapped. I became obsessed with self-defense, until I read a story in the paper about a guy who was a black belt in karate, who got shot at a 7-Eleven. One of my less laudable characteristics is that I'm easily discouraged.

But talking to Jessica, I was still feeling buoyant. "This is totally different. This is a tiny girl. Pre-hormonal. Her motor skills haven't advanced to the point that she can handle heavy weaponry."

"Uh-huh. Did you ever babysit?"

"No."

A snort. So much for high fives. I was beginning to feel a little uneasy.

"Oprah ran a story a couple of months ago called 'Kids Who Kill,' " she said. "Did you see that?"

"They killed their nannies?"

"I don't remember anything about nannies, but I'm sure it could happen. Or think about all those grown-ups who go berserk. Mothers drowning babies in bathtubs . . ."

Oh, Lord.

"But I *like* kids," I insisted, for once in my life refusing to yield to pessimism. To answer Jess's skeptical guffaw, I added, "In theory, at least."

"This kid isn't going to be a theory. Everybody loves adorable little kids in Jell-O ads, but real kids aren't like that."

"*Hello?* I never said I was Bill Cosby." I wasn't ready to angst about nitpicky details, like how good with kids I was or wasn't. "I'll have money, and I'm going to be moving. Those are the important things."

"So you'll move with this family, and then you'll quit?"

What kind of person did she think I was? "Of course not—not until I feel like I've earned my keep."

Then I would quit.

"You'll feel stuck," she predicted, "like an indentured servant."

"No, I won't."

"We'll see."

She didn't sound convinced, so we moved on to pleasanter topics, like stuff we would do when we were finally living in the same town again. Or at least when she visited me in London. We had attended North Texas together and had been roommates for a year. Afterward, I had gravitated back to the city I knew best, while Jess had surprised everyone by taking off for the Big Apple, where she answered phones by day to pay the bills and played cello in a small group—the Hoboken String Quintet, or some such thing. It wasn't the New York Philharmonic, but I envied her. She was happy where she was.

Maybe I would be happy soon, too. After years in Dallas, most of them bad, not to mention sleepless, I really felt I needed a new start in a new town. New York or London would do me fine. I wasn't going to be particular.

That morning I woke up at two, as usual, to wrestle with insomnia. But on this night I was full of plans, not worries.

I arrived at the Smith house ten minutes early and had to park down the street and wait in the car. I stared at the house, a hulking faux Tudor with a semidetached three-car garage and an immense front yard rolling away from it that was manicured within an inch of its life. The grass was so green and clipped so short it looked like artificial turf. (The Smiths' monthly water bill was probably higher than my rent.) An old pecan tree leaned off to the side, but it was hard to imagine it actually producing pecans or doing anything so ill mannered as shedding leaves. No doubt there was a gardener on hand to scoop up the leaves the moment they sullied the ground.

It was a gorgeous, luxurious house, but not out of place on

the street, which was lined with homes in various architectural styles but all of equal size and inflated value. Highland Park was the section of Dallas where the rich rich folk traditionally lived. I had lived there back when my family still had money, when private schools and housekeepers and cars that cost enough to support a middle-class family for a year were things I took for granted. Now when I drove through places like this, I felt an unhealthy mixture of smug contempt—*the waste of money!*—and salivating envy. *Was there anything more delicious than wasting money?*

Ever since college I had been avoiding this neighborhood, but now I felt like kissing the expensively landscaped ground. I was the prodigal daughter. Sure, I had suffered some bitter travails. I hadn't been able to keep my Neiman's charge, or stick to a decent manicure/pedicure regimen. In college I had denied my roots and refused to rush. But now I was coming back to my people.

At exactly two minutes till eleven, I pulled my car up in front of the house and got out. *Home!* I practically skipped up to the doorway. I wasn't going to consider the possibility of not getting the job. This was my job, my house, my golf-course lawn.

At least until I moved to London or New York.

A stout Latina woman answered the door, gave me a disapproving shake of her head, and showed me to the living room. The house was silent as only large old houses can be, the kind of silence in which you can hear your own watch ticking. You couldn't detect the whir of the air conditioning, though the cool, tomblike temp let you know it was on.

Even though I was used to places like this from my greener years, I couldn't help gawking. The house was laden with treasures—eighteenth-century tables and Tiffany lamps and modern art-glass vases. It was all jumbled together with studied carelessness, including a framed original Buster Keaton one-sheet print for *Sherlock, Jr.* that I coveted immediately. A sprawling Persian rug on the floor took up as much square footage as my entire apartment.

If a kid lived here, she was probably only allowed in this

room on Christmas mornings, for a photo op. I wondered if I myself would be spending much time here. Probably not. But I could handle that. I was so prepared to be a mere appendage to all this wealth.

The purposeful clickety sound of size-six heels on the marble of the front hall came toward me, and I turned toward the door, shoulders straight, smile in place, ready to grovel, in a dignified way, in order to secure this job.

When Mrs. Smith wheeled into the room, however, my shock was such that I'm sure the smile melted right off my face. My stomach flipped wildly as recognition struck, and my armpits started to flood. For a moment I actually felt faint.

I knew this person. Had known her practically all my life, but not as Mrs. Smith. She was *Pepper McClintock.*

I hadn't seen Pepper since I was eighteen, on graduation night 1993 at the Bramford Preparatory Academy for Girls. Pepper had delivered a short speech that night, which was expected of her as secretary-treasurer of our senior class. It was her duty to inform the school that the class of 1993 was leaving the school a perpetually bubbling art nouveau–style water fountain.

I remembered the speech because I was one of a smaller faction of my class who had voted to give the school a line of magnolia trees. That proposal had gone down in defeat to the powerful water-fountain faction, headed by Pepper, and it seemed to me on graduation night that she was practically gloating as they wheeled that damned water fountain in on a dolly to be presented to the headmistress.

It wasn't just about the water fountain. During our senior year, Pepper had become my nemesis. First she had won the role of Madge in the senior production of *Picnic*, relegating me to a much lesser role. Then she had the nerve to steal my boyfriend of six months, leaving me to go stag to my own senior prom. Unforgivable.

In fairness I should probably mention that during that prom, and on the night of graduation, Pepper had been wearing a neck brace, and that it was sort of my fault that she had had her little accident. It *was* an accident, although naturally there was a lot of speculation at the time whether I had actually engineered the whole mess. Especially since I came out of it with a relatively minor sprain.

As I stared at her slack-jawed face now, I thought about seeing her at that prom, neck stiff in its white foam casing, dancing with Spence . . .

Spence *Smith*.

And now she was . . . *Mrs. Smith*?

Blood started to drain out of my head, leaving me woozy. Her last name couldn't just be a coincidence, could it?

At that point, I really didn't think it was possible to be any more mortified than I already was. To be caught interviewing for a nanny job with a woman you went to high school with—whom you outscored on the SAT by two hundred and fifteen points—was bad. Very bad. BP girls just didn't become domestics.

But to realize that this airhead from high school who had snagged your boyfriend *still* had him—and was doing spectacularly well—was beyond embarrassing. I wanted the earth to swallow me up, but the sumptuous Persian rug beneath my feet refused to cooperate.

Why had I ever thought I could do this? Especially in Highland Park, where I knew people. I should have sensed danger . . .

Pepper's face contorted into a series of expressions ranging from shock to disbelief to glee. She settled on glee—who wouldn't?—and then threw out her arms. Her body bounced, causing a jangle of silver and jade jewelry, and she ran toward me with childlike enthusiasm. "Al! Al! Al!" She gave me one of those sorority hugs that required minimal body contact and continued to squeal. "Little Al from BP! I wrote your name down but it didn't click! I *can't* believe it!"

"I can't either," I mumbled, willing my pulse to come under control. It was racing now, in the way that a deer's would race when finally kicking in to flee a predator. I needed to get out of there, but I couldn't think of a way to escape gracefully.

"Sit down, for heaven's sake!" she gushed, as if I had just dropped by for a social call. I had a hard time adjusting to her volume, which seemed higher than anyone I had spoken to in years. And her enthusiasm, which was too over-the-top to be sincere, yet somehow struck a chord with me.

And then I remembered. This was the sort of geeked up excitement we all used to use with each other at school. The tonal equivalent of air kissing.

"I'm so glad to *see* you!"

I'll bet she was. I had gained twenty pounds. She, on the other hand, seemed to have diminished by even more than that. When last seen, Pepper had possessed a layer of baby fat that had melted away in the intervening years, leaving nothing but a sinewy husk, a perfect couture hanger.

I gazed desperately toward the door. "Oh, I—"

"*No*, you *have* to sit down and have a drink with me. A real drink." She dashed over to the door, still clickety-clicking excitedly in her Jimmy Choos. "Marta! Could you bring us some Bloody Marys, please? *¡Gracias!*" She hurried back to me. "Sit, sit, *sit!*" she commanded, practically pushing me onto a sofa before perching onto a chair opposite. "I haven't seen you in *forever*. Nobody has. You should have been at the tenth reunion! Everybody was all, 'What's happened to Al?' Everybody said they hadn't been able to find you—and now here you are!"

"Here I am," I repeated.

She leaned forward. "Al, I was *so sorry* to hear about your dad."

"Oh, well . . ."

She cut me off with a dismissive wave. "There's no need to be embarrassed. Believe me, with Spencer working in investment, lately it seems everyone's had it rough."

Spencer. It wasn't a coincidence. I felt like I had swallowed lead.

"Sometimes it's like *half* the people we know are in Club Fed," she said.

I couldn't figure out what she was talking about. "My dad didn't go to jail."

She drew back, surprised. "He didn't? But I heard he went bankrupt."

"No, he went broke the old-fashioned way. He paid off all his creditors and then shut down the business."

"Oh!"

My father had run Bell Office Machines, a business he had inherited from his father. The company had raked in the dough after World War II, but my father was not a good businessman and had stubbornly resisted the computer era. By 1994, the company could have changed its name to Bell Office Dinosaurs. He shut it down and sold off all his business property and the old family house in Highland Park. Now Dad lived on the small ranch he bought in East Texas during the good times. He didn't ranch anything except weeds, but he was able to live on a little interest and fancied himself a country gentleman.

"I see." Pepper's tone suggested that she had just lost all respect for my father. No doubt it was better to go to jail than actually repay people you owed money to. At least when you came out of jail you wouldn't be *poor.* "That must have been really difficult for you."

"Not too bad. I switched colleges, of course."

"Oh no!" she commiserated. "And you were so psyched about going to Stanford!"

"Reed."

"Right! I knew it was one of those left coast places."

"I got a great education at North Texas."

"*Of course* you did." She patted me on the knee even though she sounded unconvinced. "You were always such a brain."

The woman named Marta huffed into the room with the Bloody Marys. "I made them weak. It's only eleven o'clock."

Pepper shot her a look then smiled sweetly. "I'll take another one, then. You can get right on that."

Marta squinted at her resentfully, turned, and walked out.

Pepper bent toward me as she handed me my drink and whispered, "She thinks she's *my* nanny."

I sipped politely. It *was* a disappointingly weak drink. I could have used something stronger. Actually, I could have used a cyanide caplet.

Pepper downed half of hers in a sip. "I can't wait to tell

Spencer I saw you!" She was bouncing in her chair; jangling again. "You remember Spence, don't you?"

I almost fell off the sofa. Did I *remember* Spence? Was she some kind of a nut? Could she have forgotten . . . ?

She laughed. "*Of course* you remember Spence. You guys went out for a while, didn't you?"

"A little while." I fumed.

Six months! I wanted to scream at her. He'd been *mine*.

I forced my lips to produce a reasonable facsimile of a smile. "Where is Spence?"

"Taiwan. He's *always* traveling. Leaves me here to do everything."

Yeah, like dealing with all the domestic support staff. Must be rough.

She chuckled. "It's a good thing I know how things were back then, or I might be jealous."

"How things were?" I asked. "How were they?"

She waved a hand. "Oh, you know. Kids hooking up right and left—total hormonal madness. It's not like anything back then actually meant anything."

I felt myself gasping, but I couldn't actually form any words. For one thing, it probably wasn't kosher to blurt out to someone that, actually, you had been in love with her husband. And for another, I had thought along similar lines at the time.

"*Anyway*," she said, leapfrogging this uncomfortable topic, "I'm *so* glad to see you, you can't believe. Ugh! I've just been interviewing so many people for this job. Teenagers, mostly. I think you're the first adult who's walked through that door in days. Like, duh, do I really want to give my daughter over to some gum-chewing adolescent to raise?"

I blinked at her. Was she implying that I was too old?

"Oh—and one *really* ancient lady came by. The sweetest old thing, bless her heart, but she was just *a mess*. I think she was already in the early stages of Alzheimer's. She kept talking about how she would teach August to knit." Pepper doubled over, hooting with laughter. "August is three!"

Tomorrow she'll be hooting over my *interview*, I thought, paranoia ramping up to full throttle. I darted another longing glance at the door.

"At least I know I can trust you," she said. "And you're so smart. And bilingual." She tilted her head. "You are, aren't you?"

Suddenly I wasn't so sure. Not that it mattered.

She squinted. "French, right?"

I nodded.

She sagged with relief. "That's good. Spencer and I really wanted a person who could speak French, but we didn't really want to have an actual French person living in the house. You know what I mean?"

I nodded again.

"A couple of people who answered the ad have been Spanish speakers, but that's *not exactly* what I meant by bilingual. I mean, sure, Spanish can be useful, but we wanted something more European."

Spain no longer counted as Europe, apparently.

"Without having to have an actual European in the house?" I guessed.

"Exactly!" Any sarcasm that might have just happened to seep into my tone sailed cleanly over her head. "We wanted to find someone with *values*," she explained. "That's why we wanted to find a nanny here, who could move with us. Can you imagine trying to find someone to look after a child in London?"

"I don't know . . . I've heard of English nannies before. Didn't they sort of invent them?"

She eyed me sagely. "Believe me—the days of Mary Poppins are long gone. To get somebody like that now, you'd have to unload your child's trust fund. Can you imagine? Or—oh, Lord!—New York City! I wouldn't like to have to hire someone there. You hear all sorts of stories just about people trying to get reliable dog walkers there."

"I'm sure it's difficult everywhere."

"Oh, sure—but New York City! No telling what kind of *freaks* I'd have to interview to find somebody halfway decent."

My skin was beginning to break out in the crawlies.

"But we know you're a BP girl, so now our worries are over!"

I was starting to feel sick. The moment I had recognized Pepper, I had known that there was no way I could take the job, even if it was offered to me. I had enough hang-ups without having to live in a situation that reminded me just how short of my goals I had managed to fall in life. And the longer Pepper yammered on, the more cemented became my decision. *A nanny? Had I been insane?* No way did I want to deal with this crazy woman who was convinced that I was one of her. A Dallas Brahmin.

Married to my ex-boyfriend.

She had to be nuts to think that I would even consider it. Surely she knew I was just sitting here talking to her out of politeness.

"Of course I can't commit to anything just now," I said.

"Of course not! You'll want to—Oh!" she cried, startling me. "I'm seeing Phaedra this afternoon. Remember Phaedra?"

As in an old science-fiction movie, I felt as if I were flailing against the spiraling background, trying not to be sucked back in time. Phaedra had been Pepper's best friend through school.

They were *still* friends?

"Phaedra married Skip. Skip Honeywell? I'm sure you remember *him*." I didn't. "Anyway, they got divorced. It was very sad, because they had *three* little ones. All boys, too—what most guys *dream* about! But Skip cheated on Phaedra with about six different women, so she'd have to be a real doormat to put up with that."

I mumbled an agreement.

"And anyway, he left her." Pepper sighed. "Phaedra really went berserk for a while."

I shook my head. One hated to think of someone named Phaedra going berserk. Especially when there were children involved.

She leaned closer, relishing every word. "Joined AA *and* flirted with becoming a Christian Scientist, if you can imagine. I worried she was going to turn into a real wacko. But then she met this really nice man named Flint Avery who's, I dunno, some sort of genius at marketing or something, and now she's almost back to normal. Except that she doesn't do drinks before dinner *or* take Advil."

"My goodness." I hadn't realized AA let you opt for an after-dinner-only option now. That certainly would make the whole program more appealing.

I considered whether it would be too soon to make my escape.

"I know!" Pepper exclaimed, as if I'd just agreed with her about something. "Personally, trying to get by in this world without Paxil and a little Vicadin seems too brutal for words, but you can't argue with success. Phaedra's been living this spartan existence for almost a year and a half and she *looks* great. We went to a spa in New Mexico together last month and just had a blast."

I looked at my watch and expelled a sigh of regret. "Shoot! I have this appointment at noon . . ."

Pepper's eyes flashed open. "But you can't go yet. You have to meet August!" She jumped up, clearly expecting me to follow suit.

"Oh, but . . ."

"You *have* to," she said. "I already told her we were having a visitor, though of course I didn't know then who you were going to be. She'll be so excited when I tell her you're an old school friend."

I had my doubts, but I couldn't think of a polite way to refuse to meet Pepper's kid. So I followed her crisply bustling figure up through the hall and up a flight of stairs, down another series of hallways, until we reached, at last, August's suite. She was in her playroom, which was amazing. The walls were a pale mint green, and an artist of some skill had been brought in to copy the original Pooh illustrations. The furniture was all modern and painted in Necco wafer colors, with a few Pooh motifs scattered here and there. Tigger hopped dizzily across the front of a little wardrobe. A honey jar with bees buzzing around it was painted on the door of the television cabinet.

The television was on, and loud, and right now some commercial for processed cheese sticks was blaring at us.

Pepper swept into the room. "August?"

A small blond head peeped over the top of a miniature sofa. "Mommy!" she yelled, as if she hadn't seen her mom in weeks.

The kid was unbelievably cute. She could have been in a Jell-O commercial. White-blond hair that frizzed into a sort of punk Shirley Temple look. Big blue eyes. Black lashes. She was dressed in little Gap clothes, denim overalls and a pink T-shirt underneath. When she saw her mom, she hopped off her sofa, ran crashing into Pepper's knees, and peeked up at me with shy hostility.

"This is Alison," Pepper said. "Can you say hello? Your mommy and Alison went to school together."

August's small fist went straight to her mouth.

"She's shy!" Pepper mouthed at me.

I bent down, remembering suddenly that I had come prepared to win over my small potential employer as well as her parent. That seemed so long ago now, before I was ambushed by Pepper. "Hi, August. I have something for you." I reached into my pocket and brought out a small lime sucker. I glanced up at Pepper. "Is it okay?"

"Just this once, sure. Say thank you, August." August's fist wrapped around the sucker, which went back directly into her mouth, plastic wrapper and all. As I stood up, a finger puppet accidentally on purpose fell out of my pocket. It was a happy frog with dangling legs.

"Oh! I forgot I had the Hopster with me!" I stuck the frog on my index finger and proceeded to do a little vaudeville routine that delighted Pepper, but frankly seemed to spook August a little. She wound herself more tightly around her mom's leg.

When we left the nursery, Pepper was all praise for my clunky kid technique. "You are *so great* with August! You wouldn't believe the people who've been through here. Some of them have obviously never even been around kids before, and yesterday some girl came here with a whole set of Disney DVDs to bribe her with! Can you imagine? Of course August *loved* her."

Damn. I didn't even know how to bribe a three-year-old. Talk about inept. *Finger puppets?* What did I think this was, 1972?

Not that I wanted this job. I absolutely didn't.

The strange thing was, Pepper was acting as if it were a given that I had it, when before, when we were going up to August's suite, she had been treating me more like a visitor than a potential employee. Maybe this was just an old-school-chum courtesy, to let me think that the decision was up to me. When we both knew what the decision would be.

As we walked back downstairs, she started giving me instructions. "Now, we always call her August. No nicknames. Spencer's parents are always calling her Augie and it just drives me insane." She flicked me a look that spoke volumes about the state of in-law relations in the Smith household. "They know I don't like it, too. You can be sure of that."

"August is such a great name," I said.

"I think so. Of course we named her that before the world and its wife started naming their kids August," she added bitterly.

"I didn't know." I tried to think of kids I'd known with the name of August and came up with . . . none.

"Puh-leez!" She rolled her eyes. "Of course, the way people are popping out kids these days, no name's safe anymore."

At the door, she gave me another of those weightless hugs of hers. "I'm so glad you showed up!"

"Well, I have to . . ."

She waved away my mumbled hesitation. "I know. *Think it over.* Of course you do! I'll give you a buzz tomorrow. How about that?"

"Sure thing."

"It was *just great* to see you Al."

"*Just great* to see you, too, Pepper."

I got out of there as fast as I could without actually running.

Chapter 2

The first time I ever met Pepper McClintock was at her fifth birthday party. My parents met her parents at a fund-raiser for the art museum, so I somehow ended up on Pepper's guest list. Because Mom wanted to make a good impression, we went to the toy store and picked out a beautiful Steiff panda bear for Pepper's present. By the time we got to that party I was in love with that panda and feeling a little tearful about having to give it away.

The McClintock house was amazing. It took me a while to realize it was actually a private residence and not a public park. There was a western theme to the party, and a huge, fourth-of-July-style banner proclaimed the backyard to be PEPPER'S DUDE RANCH. For the party her parents had brought in a Ferris wheel, and a giant inflated mattress for kids to jump on, and, most incredible of all, ponies. A whole herd of Shetland ponies for kids to ride, plus four men in cowboy outfits to lead around the kids who were too chicken to ride on their own. The serving maids wore cowgirl dresses.

It was stunning, like having your very own three-ring circus in your backyard. For the first time in my life, I experienced a sensation of tightening in my chest, and dry throat. My temples even throbbed a little. Why couldn't this be *my* backyard? (All I had was a single swing, attached to a tree branch.) Why couldn't it be Alison's Dude Ranch?

When I was introduced to Pepper, she grinned at me, showing her perfect line of tiny baby teeth. She was, by the way, adorable. Little and cute, with long blond hair and a flouncy Dale Evans–style split skirt and vest with rhinestones that my Mom later whispered to my Dad had cost a king's ransom. I didn't know what a ransom was, but I was impressed by the fact that some king was doing without his ransom so that Pepper McClintock could wear fancy white culottes. When they hoisted Pepper up on one of those Shetland ponies, she looked like a movie star.

Me, I hadn't heard about the western theme. Mom had never said that there would be horseback riding—she probably had barely glanced at the invitation. I was wearing my scratchy old dress leftover from Easter, and I didn't feel comfortable, much less cute.

I was looking up at Pepper's majestic figure—loathing her already, I'm afraid—when she spoke the horrible words that started the trouble between us. "She's got *cooties*!"

The kids around me erupted. Girls screamed "eeeeeeww!" and ran, and boys whooped. (Some of them ran, too.)

I was taken aback. . . . Maybe I'd let a sheltered existence, but I didn't even know what cooties were. I spotted Mom standing amid the line of mothers on the periphery, laughing and not paying much attention to the kids. I ran over to her and yanked on her arm like it was a bellpull. I could smell that grown-up fragrance of Worth perfume mixed with white wine when Mom bent down so I could whisper in her ear. "What's cooties?"

Her brow pinched slightly. "What?"

"*Cooties.*"

She laughed throatily. Marge Bell was never one to tie herself in knots over the little bumps in the road of my childhood. "Oh, Alison, I don't know. Don't be silly. Go back and play."

I dug in the heels of my Mary Janes. "Do I have them?"

"No," she said. "If one of the little boys or girls said you did, you just ignore them." She sent me a meaningful look. *Mingle*, the look said. *Don't embarrass me.* "Now go play."

I skulked off, unsatisfied. How was I supposed to ignore

Pepper? She was the center of attention. And to think—I was giving her my panda!

I hated Pepper.

It wasn't just the cooties, either. I couldn't take it all in. For *my* last birthday party, which had been a pretty damn big deal, we'd had a balloon artist. At the time, having a man make a dachshund out of balloons for me and my friends had seemed like unbelievable fun. I'd felt so cool. But this. This was beyond anything I had ever imagined.

And the house was huge! A palace. I got lost twice looking for the bathroom, and ended up in what had to be Pepper's bedroom. What I discovered there astounded me. There, propped on the bed, was a whole menagerie of stuffed animals. I counted to five (my limit) more times than I could count. And right there, in the center of them all, buried amid all that wealth of plush toys so that he was almost forgotten, was *my* panda bear.

I went running back to the party, completely confused. Could it be Pepper had opened the presents already?

But no, when I returned to the long table where the cake was, my present was still there, wrapped. So I took what I decided was the only logical course of action. I picked up the wrapped gift and started walking toward our car. I was ready to leave.

My mom saw me and attempted to head me off at the pass. I explained to her that Pepper already had a panda bear, and that I wasn't about to give her mine. Especially after she had told everyone that I had cooties. I mean, let's face it. I didn't owe her anything after that.

Mom eyes darted nervously toward the other adults. A few had noticed that I had demanded we leave. (Actually, I might have been yelling.) "It's your present to Pepper, Alison," she explained reasonably as she sank her nails into my shoulder blades. "You have to give presents at a birthday party."

"No way," I said, holding tightly to the present.

"Alison . . ."

"She *has* one already. I saw it!"

"Maybe it will make a friend for the other panda, then. You

want to be a good girl and give your hostess a present, don't you? That's the right thing to do."

I had learned all about charity. I knew that you were supposed to give to the needy and not blubber when your parents donated your broken Barbie's Dream House to the toy drive. But giving pandas to the wealthy was an entirely different matter. It stretched the bounds of philanthropy. "She doesn't need it as much as I do!"

Mrs. McClintock was heading for us now, and Mom looked frantic. "Alison, give me that box!"

A short tug-of-war ensued, which I inevitably lost. I started screaming. Soothing words were spoken to me as I cried in outraged gulps. Someone brought me a milkshake. I threw it at a maid. Mom finally yanked me by the arm and told me that if I did not settle down this instant I was going to have to go home before I had any cake or a pony ride.

I twisted out of her grasp and bolted. But instead of running for the house, I ran toward the ponies. Some evil force had taken hold of me; I no longer felt any kind of restraint. I could barely hear my mother shrieking at my back. I had my eye on one thing: Horse shit.

I hadn't heard of cooties but I wasn't a total ignoramus. I knew from stepping in it at my cousin's house just how awful it was to come in contact with horse poo. Or any kind of poo. It marked you. It was probably even worse than cooties.

I picked up a big handful of it off the ground and streaked across the lawn toward Pepper. Before any adult could grasp the true horror of my motives, I came within striking distance and lobbed my missile straight at Pepper's chest.

Direct hit!

A loud gasp went up, followed by delighted shrieks and howls from my contemporaries. Pepper burst into tears and stood immobile with that big blob on her Dale Evans vest.

When things calmed down, I was forced to apologize—to Pepper, to her mother, to the maid—then dragged away from the party in shame.

Pepper and I met many times after that. We attended the same elementary school, the same confirmation classes at the

Episcopal church, and of course the same high school. In all those years, the horse poo birthday party episode was never mentioned. Occasionally I wondered if she had forgotten it entirely, or was just lying in wait for the right moment to seek her revenge.

She never did retaliate. Not officially. Even when she stole Spence she denied any horse poo connection. If you can believe that.

But I think it's safe to say that my relationship to Pepper was never what anyone would call smooth.

Chapter 3

I spent the afternoon after my interview with Pepper on my couch, eating Kellogg's Sugar Pops straight from the box. It was the only thing snackable left in the apartment. I felt wrung out, as emotionally drained as if I had been watching *It's a Wonderful Life*. Except this was my life, and it wasn't wonderful, not by any stretch of the imagination. I whiled away three hours just thinking about what ifs: What if we hadn't gone broke . . . what if I hadn't been such a flake . . . what if I hadn't stayed in Dallas and gotten stuck . . . what if I hadn't lost Spence all those years ago. . . .

Try as I might, though, I couldn't see any upsides, any hidden wonders or Capra-esque payoffs amid all the missteps and screwups. My life would have made a very bad Christmas movie, I decided. There would be no angel, no miraculous rescue. When I jumped into the freezing river I would simply have to sink like a stone and drown.

For a while I tried to read a magazine, but the only one in the apartment had Gwyneth Paltrow on the cover. Some things you should never do when your self-esteem is at low ebb. Like buy M&Ms in two-pound bags. Or crawl out on the ledge of a tall building. Or read one more damn article about Gwyneth Paltrow's fabulous fucking life.

Witnessing Pepper McClintock's fabulous life had been punishment enough. God, she'd looked good. No, she'd looked *rich.* She was living in the land of plenty, of platinum charge cards and domestic staff and spas.

I couldn't believe I was being eaten alive with envy this way. Until the age of eighteen, I'd had Pepper's life. We had been the Bell family of Highland Park. Our lives bore all the earmarks of perfection, Big D style. Dad was a businessman, and Mom belonged to clubs. *Definitely Dallas* had done a feature about us, including a posed picture of the three of us in front of the fireplace, with me in a taffeta party dress sitting on Dad's knee, and Mom in some kind of late seventies Bob Mackie glamour outfit. We had a sprawling two-story stone house, took incredible vacations, and attended benefits that were covered on the society page of the *Dallas Morning News.*

All my schooling, from Montessori up, took place at private schools. I never stepped foot in a public library until after college. Discount stores were completely off my radar until my teens, when my girlfriends and I would lark off to Target (Targee!) to go look at all the cheap stuff.

Those were the days.

After I went to college, my family imploded. Dad's business seriously tanked. I guess it had been just barely limping along for years, but nobody discussed mundane stuff, like the fact we were on our way to pauperville, with me.

The summer after my high school graduation, my mother started taking weekends away. When my dad's difficulties worsened, Mom bolted. She ran away to Houston to be with a very rich (and married) man named Murph Tripton. By that time I was already at college. Dad flew to Oregon and told me. He also confessed that he really couldn't afford the tuition at Reed anymore, so the next semester I transferred. North Texas was a lot cheaper, and I wanted to be closer to Dad, anyway. He seemed so alone.

He seemed so pathetic, actually. As did our entire situation.

It wasn't like I was destitute, but I began to see that, without money, without everything perfectly in place, the flaws stand out in relief. My dad, always so tall and dashing in his custom-made suits, seemed to thin out both in body and spirit, as if the stuffing had actually been kicked out of him. Without my mom there to remind him what he usually liked to eat, he dithered over what to order in restaurants. He'd always been quiet, but I had never imagined my dad as a ditherer—never. And I was amazed when he told me he had wept in frustration one night because he didn't understand how to use the washing machine. ("Who thought of a thing like that, with a knob you have to turn *and* pull out? Does that make sense?")

After a while, I no longer wondered how we could have gone broke. The puzzle then became how anyone with my family's genes could ever have gotten rich in the first place.

Mom didn't completely disappear from my life. Her maternal instinct kept sputtering on, like one of those twenty-year-old Chryslers you're amazed to see still out on the road. She loved to pop up on me, unannounced. At my dorm in college, say, or Saturday morning when I was back in Dallas on my own. It was as if she wanted to catch me off guard so I wouldn't have time to summon all my anger.

And I had a lot of anger stored up for her. She had abandoned us. She was an adulteress, a home-wrecker. I was pissed.

Her blitzkrieg tactics usually worked, though. She always took me by surprise. And once I was faced with her, I never could get as mad as I wanted to be. I would huff or fall stubbornly silent, but there was something about her that made me pity her too much to just out-and-out scream at her. Her hairstyle kept changing, and her clothes got brighter, younger looking. Sexier. Her mouth curved up perpetually now in a bright nervous smile.

Murph was rich, and even though Mom wasn't his wife yet, she obviously had sporadic access to money. She would bring along odd stuff to bribe me. One day it might be some expensive, tart-smelling dusting powder from Neiman's; another day she would present me with a hamster in one of those cages that was all colored plastic tubing. She didn't seem to know whether she wanted to treat me like a confidante or a five-year-old.

We were all the same people, yet in one short year we went from being fabulous Bells to just another screwed-up broken home. From the social register to Jerry Springerland in one leap. I was too old to earn much sympathy from anyone as a child of divorce, of course. Technically I was an adult of divorce; most people in my peer group had gone through this particular trauma already. My sophomore roommate was already working on her third stepmother; no one was going to fall in step with my pity parade.

There was no one for me to talk to, to commiserate with. I had no siblings, and at that point Dad was still trying to figure out the washing machine, and Mom grew prickly and defensive every time I brought up the subject of her defection.

"You don't understand," she'd tell me.

That's what she always said. Once—the time she brought the hamster—she added, "You probably won't understand for years."

"I'm too young to understand adultery?" I asked, watching the little fuzzball try to burrow into a corner in his plastic cage. I knew that feeling. If only I could have nestled myself in sweet-smelling pine shavings and not come up except to consume a few pellets. "Do you think I don't go to the movies?"

"You might think you're old enough to understand everything in the world, but you aren't."

"I know you think I'm a baby whose affection you can buy off with gifts of fuzzy rodents, Mom, but I'm nineteen. *Nineteen*." I made it sound as though that number carried with it the wisdom of the ages. "And what's not to understand? You cheated on Dad just as he happened to be going broke. End of story, end of family."

"There's more to it than that. People have reasons . . ."

"Stop, you sound like Woody Allen."

Mom laughed. *Laughed*, I swear. "There's not one of us who won't behave badly before it's all over, Alison."

Comments like that nearly drove me over the edge. "Where would this world be if everyone shared your Lucrezia Borgia philosophy?" I screeched.

"Exactly where we are," Mom replied. "It's a dog-eat-dog world out there, in case you haven't heard."

I fell onto the bed. It was hopeless. How I could have sprung out of this woman's womb was inconceivable to me. We were from different planets.

Mom's visits grew less frequent through my twenties, until she was mainly popping up via postcard. Mom and Murph traveled a lot, and the perky missives I received were always guaranteed to raise my blood pressure. ("You wouldn't believe the smell of this place!" she wrote me from Agra, when she was visiting the Taj Mahal.) Most of the time I didn't care if I never saw her again.

Still, my hard knocks came late, and were relatively buffered as hard knocks went. I didn't know the taste of government cheese. I didn't have to pole-dance my way through college. I took out a few loans and learned to my horror that credit meant that something has to be *paid back*. Back then I realized I could go one of two ways: Mom's way, or what I considered the honorable way. I still had a few rich friends. There was a part of me that wanted to cling to what I could, to try desperately to seduce some business major before I officially became a nobody.

Instead, I adapted my philosophy to fit my student loan debt. I told myself that money had never meant that much to me anyway. And it hadn't. (Why should it? I'd always had it.) In my own private school way, I'd always been a nonconformist. A rebellious free spirit in a trust fund world. I learned to look with a sort of benighted amusement on unreformed rich people, especially the women who went from Daddy's care to a hubby's care without a stint of independence in between.

Pepper was one of those women. You could tell it just by looking at her. She was twenty-eight and still had the pampered skin of an eighteen-year-old, a condition that could only be achieved through constant tending. Her tiny figure shrieked personal trainer. But mostly you could see it in her eyes, which showed no sign of worry. She had never been harrassed by a boss. Never been late for a deadline. Never been fired.

Never been involuntarily unemployed.

I had *so* wanted that job. I felt as if it had been yanked away from me, bodily, like when a thief runs past you and snatches your purse. I was left spinning. I still felt breathless, humiliated, defeated. Of all the people in all the world . . .

Pepper McClintock!

Had Spence lost his mind?

That was the real heartbreaker. Spence Smith had *married* her. Why hadn't I heard this?

Because, of course, I had avoided anything to do with Bramford Prep since my family's fall from financial grace.

Spence and Pepper probably told people that they had been high school sweethearts, but that was just such a joke. Spence Smith was *my* high school sweetheart.

I met him the fall of my senior year in high school, at one of those dorky meet and greets that girls schools sometimes have. A mixer in the school cafeteria, with all the tables moved into storage for the night. A DJ was hired for the evening, no doubt to play exhausting dance music by the Romantics and David Bowie and all those people that seemed so over with by then. Being a senior, I was very cool toward the whole enterprise. But of course there were going to be boys there, so you had to go. You could sneer, but there was no question of skipping.

Besides, I had an agenda.

When I spotted Spence, he was doing a freaky dance move, crouched over his shuffling feet and snapping his fingers like a character in a Peanuts strip. It was so geeky and over the top that you had to be impressed. It wasn't often that a guy so good looking would make such a wacky spectacle of himself. I couldn't help laughing, especially at the way his purported partner, Larissa Halliday, kept backing away from him. By the end of the dance they were practically on opposite sides of the room, which suited me fine.

I didn't wait for an introduction, but zipped right into Larissa's spot. "You're terrific!" I blurted out at him before the music had even stopped. "I'll bet this cafeteria hasn't seen moves like that since the salmonella incident three years ago."

To my relief, he laughed. When he stopped moving he was even better looking. He had a crooked smile, dark brown eyes, and that short dark hair with the longer bits on top that sort of flopped into his forehead. A sweetheart, really.

We had that awkward moment of introducing ourselves, yelling over "La Isla Bonita," which I was trying not to pay much attention to because I had finally shaken myself free of the Madonna spell after concluding that she was, you know, another totally bogus eighties corporate icon. I told Spence—shouting into his ear—that he looked like John Cusack. Okay, maybe I was projecting a little. I happened to be in love with John Cusack at the time. But Spence really did sort of look like him. Kind of hunky and geeky both. I went on to scream at Spence that I bet he was an actor.

He drew back, surprised. And of course, flattered. Everybody is always flattered when you say that they seem like an actor, which I suspect shows how few people know actors personally.

"You mean you've never been in a play?" I asked, astounded.

He shook his head. "Not if you don't count anything where I appeared as a pilgrim or a shepherd."

Such modesty! I simply had to pull him aside and tell him what he was missing. Specifically, the chance to costar in Bramford Prep Rep's upcoming production of *Antigone*, for which I was stage manager.

When I was in high school, theater was my bag. My aunt had even given me a little sequined tote with the comedy/tragedy heads on it in sequins that said *Theater Is My Bag*. (Which I promptly tossed into a drawer with an embarrassed shudder.) In high school, our guidance counselor always told us to have a passion, some activity that would look good on a college application next to all the compulsory volunteer work the school made us do. My designated passion was theater.

Usually I believed the point of theater was to be *in* the show, but you didn't have to be Madame Cleo to predict that this Greek thing was going to be a train wreck. I preferred to bow out. (The year before I had big roles in *The Miss Firecracker Contest* and our all-girl production of *Waiting for Godot*. I could afford to be magnanimous.) The production in the winter, *Picnic*, was the one I had my eye on. I'd spotted the movie version of it on the shelf at the video store, so I figured it had to be better than some saga about a Greek chick trying to bury her brother. Still, I had volunteered to help in *Antigone*, and part of my job was scaring up male cast members. I wasn't sure whether this cut-rate John Cusack was really ideal to play Creon, the king of Thebes, but beggars couldn't be choosers.

Plus it gave me a great excuse to give Spence my phone number.

The shock was that he called me back. I mean, I liked Spence right off, but I had buttonholed quite a few guys at that party—guys who in my desperation I exclaimed were dead ringers for Dennis Quaid and Brad Pitt and even, God forgive me, Robert De Niro—but most of them, once they understood the motive behind the flattery, took to the hills. Extracurricular activity at an all-girls school might sound almost pornographically appealing to teenage boys at first, but the moment they realized it required parading around in a sheet in front of a bunch of papier-mâché pillars, their enthusiasm evaporated.

Which is why I was all the more impressed with Spence. And grateful. The drama director, Ms. Crouch, had been giving me grief that very afternoon for not finding a Creon yet. (Never mind that *she* was the genius who had picked a play with a prominent male lead.) I was terrified of screwing up my stage manager job. There's no relationship more dysfunctional and sick than one between a student and a teacher she's dependent on for good college recs.

The situation was getting desperate. We had already been reduced to casting short-haired freshmen girls as guards. Ms. Crouch was threatening to bring in her erstwhile love interest, the school's bald, buck-toothed lacrosse coach, to save the day when Spence called me at home. I could have wept. He was rescuing me.

"The part is yours," I announced. "You start Monday. Rehearsal at six thirty."

He laughed. "Whoa, that was simple. What if I told you I stutter when I'm nervous?"

"I'd say that if you'd read the script, you'd know that no one would be awake by the time you came on stage anyway."

"The second act?"

"No, the second scene."

"In other words, you don't think this will make me a star."

I replied, flirtatiously, that in my book he was already a star.

He groaned. "Too easy! Would you mind talking me into it? Say, Saturday night?"

From the moment he rattled up in his seventy-nine Monte Carlo for our date, I was impressed. The last boy I had gone out with more than once, Robert, had a new BMW convertible that he'd been given for his sixteenth birthday. He seemed to think he had arrived; no more mountains to climb once you owned a Beemer. After I got over that junior prom hump and didn't need a steady, I had decided Robert was unbearably smug and upper middle class and not worth my time.

Spence's love for his metal heap was more palatable, especially since I knew his dad was a super-successful corporate attorney. Spence was like a guy who could have adopted a champion pedigreed Old English sheepdog but had opted for the shaggiest mongrel at the pound. I commented on the Monte Carlo's vintage look and he beamed at my appreciation. "Yeah, it's almost a classic. And it runs, too." He added under his breath, "Usually."

We only stalled once on the way to a restaurant, a joint called Twist's on Greenville Avenue where a lot of SMU students hung out listening to Green Day and Poi Dog Pondering as they consumed burgers and lots of things with melted cheese. It was election year and we talked self-consciously about politics. Our parents were Republicans—I didn't actually know any adults who weren't, except maybe a couple of teachers, who didn't really count because they led such pathetic lives anyway—but we were both considering heresy.

Well, Spence wasn't even just considering. "I'm voting for Clinton," he declared boldly.

"You're eighteen?" I asked, envious. He was an adult! And voting Democratic. In Dallas. It sounded so radical, it almost made me want to clasp hands with the cheese eaters at the next table and belt out some old Bob Dylan songs. (If I had happened to know any of those old grandpa tunes, which I didn't.)

But Spence's declaration did give me the feeling that he was different—a real independent. He wasn't even going to wimp out and vote for Perot, who was the protest vote of choice for

Dallasites, since he was from Texas, and rich. Spence wouldn't just follow the herd.

(I was big on being different then. I was dying to get a tattoo, like several other girls in my class had.)

As it turned out, Spence wasn't much of an actor; then again, Bramford Prep Rep wasn't exactly the Great White Way. And there was camaraderie in being involved in a genuine thespian disaster, which is what our *Antigone* was. That much was apparent from the first rehearsal. It wasn't the actors' faults. It's really hard for professionals to make Greek tragedy gripping. When you're dealing with a bunch of teenagers—who, let's face it, have a tentative command of modern English even at the best of times—asking them to speak English that simulates the rhythms of ancient Greeks is begging for trouble. From the moment the lights went up, it was as if a sedative spray was emanating from that little stage.

But we had a hell of a cast party at my house after opening night.

That was where Spence and I shared our first real smooch. Actually, it was really like dry humping on the floor of my bedroom. This was the precursor to the night a few weeks later when I lost my virginity by the Smiths' swimming pool. Among my friends, I was one of the last holdouts, but even though I was completely inexperienced, I knew instinctively that Spence was one of those guys I shouldn't let pass me by. And sure enough, even on a chaise lounge with a stiff waterproof cushion, even in November weather that was really too cold for outdoor trysting, even serenaded to the tune of a crackly portable radio playing "We Are the Champions" in tribute to the late Freddy Mercury, Spence got the job done in impressive fashion. He was sensitive, surprisingly expert, and very well endowed.

There was a sort of frantic sweetness to it all that carried us through Christmas and on into that second semester of senior year that seemed like an eternity galloping by. Everything was earth-shattering and ridiculous. One minute it seemed like high school would never end, and in the next I would harbor the tiny hope that it actually wouldn't. For a few short months

I had that breathless, luxurious feeling of simultaneously wanting to hold tight to something and fling it away.

I couldn't wait to graduate, to get on with my real life, but I hated the thought of leaving all my friends, especially Spence. He was already accepted early admission to Vanderbilt, a place I had no intention of going, no matter how much I liked him. And I liked him a lot. He was one of those great guys who doesn't mind just hanging out, and likes all your friends (but not too much), and looks hurt if you don't order dessert after dinner.

Occasionally, especially after we'd had furtive sex at one of our houses, trying to ignore the signposts of babyishness trailing around our bedrooms, Spence would talk about the future. As if we, as a couple, were going to be sharing it.

"Won't it be great when we have spring breaks together?" he would ask. "We can arrange to meet somewhere really great—Europe or someplace."

He always liked the idea of traveling. And he had taste. I liked that about him. He wasn't one of those boring guys who dreamed of spring breaks on the coast and life as a *Girls Gone Wild* video.

Still, his musings could make me uncomfortable. Wasn't the whole point of going off to college to meet *new* people? Sure, I loved Spence, but I didn't want to tie myself down. I had cut my teeth on *Forever* by Judy Blume when I was twelve. I knew these high school things always ended. I was romance savvy.

When it came to our relationship, I cast myself in the role of the grown-up. The sophisticate. But it wasn't always easy.

On Valentine's, he took me out to Café Pacific and in the middle of dinner handed me a little box. My heart skittered when I looked down at it. It looked like a ring box. But . . .

When I opened the box, I was relieved to see that there was no diamond solitaire. He hadn't gone too far off his rocker. But the box was from Tiffany, and the heart-shaped locket was ringed with stones that looked pretty real to me. I opened it, and laughed. He had put my senior school picture on one side, and his picture in his makeup as Creon in the other. He looked slightly dazed in his greasepaint.

"I don't know what to say," I said, half-quipping. It was the nicest present a boy had ever given me.

"You're supposed to say that you'll wear and cherish it forever," Spence said. Then his expression changed to a sincerity that made me squirm. "I wish you would, Al."

I could never figure out if he were more emotionally advanced than I was, more in touch with his emotions, or just needier. You would have thought *I* would be the needy one. Spence had this tight-knit family who all worshiped each other, while I was the only child of a marriage that, had I been paying attention, I could have seen was faltering.

"I love you," he said.

We went home and drank a lot of champagne that night. Too much. We ended up in my parents' hot tub way past the time they could have come back from whatever party they were attending. He kept talking about plans. "I hope we have a house like this someday."

That did it. If there was one thing I was sure I didn't want, it was my parents' life. Especially the sprawling house in the old neighborhood. The oppressive materialism of it all. What I really wanted was to live in a cool apartment. A loft, maybe. It would be one of those places where artsy people drifted in and out. Kind of like the Factory updated with the cast of *Reality Bites*.

"There's a lot ahead of us," I told him. "You don't want to get too serious."

"But I feel serious," he said. "Don't you?"

"Sure, I feel that way now. But we have to face facts. These high school romances never last."

"So what are you going to do? Get your diploma and dump me?"

I laughed. But somewhere in the back of my mind, a worry nagged. What *was* I going to do?

I probably took him for granted, but it was a busy time. It seemed every time I turned around, there was another deadline looming. Hurdles to leap. College applications, term papers, midterms.

Picnic finally came around. I had already secured Spence his spot as Hal, the sexy drifter. I was really looking forward to being on the stage with him, especially when I read the play and realized we'd be sharing a lot of scenes, even a kiss, together. But when auditions for the female parts came along, my little dream was derailed. There were nontheater kids in the auditions, including a few seniors who had never even taken a drama course. One of these was Pepper McClintock, and I grew increasingly horrified as Ms. Crouch seemed to focus on *her* for the role of Madge. It took me all of thirty minutes to realize what Ms. Crouch was up to. She was casting *unknowns*!

During the break after the first hour, I sidled up to Ms. Crouch and subtly asked what the hell she thought she was doing handing the best part of the year to somebody who had never even walked across a stage before.

"Isn't Pepper wonderful?" she exclaimed, as if she actually thought I would agree. "I admit I was skeptical when she told me she was going to audition, but I'm just thrilled. *Thrilled.*"

"You talked to Pepper about this already?" In that case I was sunk. These teachers always seemed to love the students who sat in their offices and *talked*. (Got talked at, was more often the case with our blowhard faculty.)

"Yes, she came to my office last week. She said she had seen the Kim Novak movie and wanted to be in the show. She said Spence looked exactly like William Holden."

"William Holden!" What a little weasel. He looked nothing like William Holden. She had the wrong movie star entirely. "She said that? I mean . . . she mentioned Spence *by name*?"

"She said she thought he was great as Creon. She saw the play three times. Did you know that?"

Three times? But Spence had sucked. What the hell was going down here?

"I think they'll look terrific together," Crouch said. "Look at the stage directions. Listen to the dialogue. Pepper *is* Madge."

I should have known it was hopeless from the moment I read that Madge was "almost painfully pretty." I hadn't really been thinking about that, or the fact that I would have been ridiculous swanning around a stage moaning about how I was tired of everyone telling me I was beautiful, which tiresome Madge does all through that script. I hadn't been thinking of anything except the fact that this was my last play at Bramford and of course I was going to get something juicy.

During the rest of auditions I scrambled. I smacked gum and did my best to be the tomboy little sister, Millie. I could have won a Tony for my reading of old-maid schoolteacher Rosemary's "Marry me, Howard" speech. I even did a pretty good reading for the mother character, if I do say so myself, though I shuddered at the prospect of having to do a matronly part.

But when the cast list went up the next morning after assembly, I hadn't been assigned the part of Millie, or Rosemary, *or* the boring mother. I was listed as Mrs. Potts, the neighbor.

Mrs. Potts! I was staggered. Mrs. Potts was sixty and hardly had any good lines at all. The doddering old woman part was something I assumed would be foisted off on a freshman.

Ms. Crouch greeted me in the hallway, where I was accepting wry congratulations from my fellow cast members and wiping egg off my face.

"Congratulations!" she chimed, blinking earnestly, as if she didn't really know I would be upset. "What do you think?"

"Mrs. Potts?" I asked, trembling with the effort not to make a scene. "I didn't even read for that character."

She lifted a finger and poked it into my sternum. "That's because I *knew* you could do it. Millie and Rosemary are plum roles, but they don't require the skill that making a woman like Mrs. Potts come to life will require. *You've* got that skill, Alison." She beamed at me with teacherly pride which at that moment I could only interpret as malicious.

"Lucky me," I muttered.

Not that I was bitter or anything.

Spence was really great about it. He took me out and plied me with tacos until I was sane again.

Well. Sort of sane.

"I can't believe she gave my part to that skank ho!" I exclaimed.

Spence laughed, but I could tell he was a little worried. After all, he was going to have to pretend to be in love with this skank ho. "Is she that bad?"

"Bad?" That was a hoot. "Pepper McClintock? Wait till you see her! She thinks she's such hot shit. Her father owns half of Dallas or something. He's a *banker*," I added, as if that explained it all. "The place they live in is like a palace."

"Not like the shantytowns where we live," Spence said. He was from University Park, a stone's throw from me.

"Okay, but this place . . . you wouldn't believe." I had to tell him about the birthday party. And once I got started, I also felt that honesty required me to confess that during our first meeting I had thrown horse shit at Pepper in her sparkly Dale Evans costume.

Spence was amusingly appalled. "And you criticize *her*?"

"I apologized," I said. "Besides, these people are, like, totally beige."

Beige was my word of the moment for everything stultifying and awful about our bourgeois world.

"I guess that translates to 'non-poo-throwing.' "

I rolled my eyes. Maybe I shouldn't have told him about that. He would never let me forget it now.

"Just watch! At the first rehearsal she'll show up in a Polo shirt, white jeans, and *penny loafers*." I stuck my finger down my throat for effect. "I think Pepper was on crack the day they announced that the preppy look was over. She must have a closet full of knit Ralph Lauren shirts in every hue and stripe. Every out-of-uniform day she wears the same damn thing. I mean, how completely insecure can you be to have to wear your own little uniform on out-of-uniform day?"

I was going for a sort of modified grunge look myself back then. I sweated through the winter in a wool flannel shirt I'd found in my dad's closet (an old Christmas present from yours truly that he had never worn) and I'd had this awesome black-blue rinse done on my hair. One of my friends had given me an earcuff for my birthday. *In Utero* had been on my Walkman for months, and I really wanted to get to the Pacific Northwest, where it was all happening. That's why I wanted to go to Reed College.

That, and I'd heard they didn't actually give you grades there.

"Sounds like Pepper dresses like my sister," Spence said. "All the women in my family are those traditional preppy types."

"No one related to you could be this awful." I gulped down the heel of a taco. What is it about greasy meat that makes a person feel so much better? "Oh! And just wait. She'll manage to squeeze all the people she knows at Hockaday into the conversation, first thing." Hockaday was the only school in town snootier than mine. "Makes you wonder why she didn't go there—like, maybe her parents didn't know any Hockaday board members to bribe."

His eyes glinted with humor. "You BP girls are just one big family, aren't you?"

One big family. That was what the headmistress was always telling us. *"The BP family will be a part of you all of your life."*

It was the kind of BS remark I loved to snigger at. But if I'd had a crystal ball to see into my future, I wouldn't have been laughing.

Chapter 4

When I woke up in the night after my interview with Pepper, insomnia had nothing to do with it. Someone was pounding on my door.

I cranked up one of my eyelids and aimed a bleary glance at the clock. Eleven thirty, the extra-big red digital numbers read. Unbelievable! Some nut was pounding on my door at eleven thirty. I grumbled my way out of bed and shrugged on my robe. This was what came of cheap apartment complex living. Drunken neighbors tormenting you—and not even having the courtesy to wait till the middle of the night to do it. Creeps. Had they no consideration for the unemployed? Didn't they know I had to be up worrying in two and a half hours?

Peering through the peephole, I saw only air where I expected an unruly drunken idiot to be.

"Who is it?" I shouted through the door.

"It's me. Pepper."

I looked again, focusing downward, and discovered her standing on my doormat. I was so surprised, I was speechless as I opened the door.

She marched right across the threshold and tossed her Kate Spade purse on my old Pier One chair, the kind that looked like a rattan satellite dish with an oversized cushion disk imposed on it. From her manner you would have thought she had been there a million times. As if she were one of those endearing sitcom neighbors who was always popping by in the middle of the night. My own private Kramer.

Something had her agitated. She turned to me, hands making nervous fists at her sides. "I have *got* to talk to you, Al." She looked like she was about to go ahead and spit out whatever was so damn important, then stopped herself. "Do you have something to drink? Something with alcohol—or a San Pellegrino will do in a pinch."

Unbelievable. A woman could walk up to the second floor of a vinyl-siding-clad apartment unit called the Cedars, where the only cedars were sad half-brown twigs in weedy pots, and demand cocktails and designer fizzy water.

But come to think of it, I also suspected this encounter was probably going to require a strong belt of something. "No on the San Pellegrino, but let me see what I can manage in the way of alcohol."

I went to the galley kitchen, pulled out a bottle of vodka, and started making screwdrivers. Or whatever you would call vodka mixed with Dole Pine-Orange Banana juice, which was all I had on hand. While I worked, Pepper plopped herself down next to her purse. The ugly chair swallowed her; she looked like a perfect little pearl in a disgusting gray oyster. But those BP manners hadn't left her. Like a model uninvited guest, she pretended to be charmed by my crappy apartment.

"What a fun place you have!" she exclaimed, looking at the souvenir Stonehenge ashtray Mom had brought back from England the last time she made a swing through town. "You must have one of those fabulous single lives."

I added several more glugs of vodka to my drink. "Actually, it's pretty dull." I could have tried lying, but what was the point? She was sitting right in the inner sanctum of my schlubdom.

She chuckled. "Tell that to an old married person!"

I gestured around my apartment, with its stained gray wall-to-wall carpet and acoustic tile ceiling. "This isn't *Sex and the City*. It's not even *That Girl*." My life had become about as unfabulous as it could get. And now Pepper was a witness. My mortification was complete.

Her brow furrowed as her gaze alit on a dried out rubber tree plant next to my outdated television, which obviously didn't have a DVD player attached to it. I didn't even have cable at that point.

I handed her her drink in a Taco Bell *Lord of the Rings* glass with that blond Elf hottie on it. "How did you find me?"

"Luckily you left your address and number, or I never would have. Is this part of town even Dallas anymore?"

"It's Addison . . . sort of," I said, a little embarrassed to be so far up the toll road from the fashionable folk.

At the same time, I couldn't entirely hide my annoyance. She *did* have my number. My next question—*"So why the hell didn't you call first?"*—remained politely unspoken.

She downed that drink I gave her in one gulp. "Mm, that's good. Is there any more?"

What the heck. I handed her mine. She made quite a dent in that, too. Something was definitely gnawing at this woman's brain.

When she was done coating her nerve endings with alcohol, she looked up at me gravely. "It wasn't till after you left this afternoon that I started thinking that maybe you'd feel weird about taking the job."

The job? Could she actually believe that I was thinking it over? If so, she was probably also waiting for Peter Cottontail to come hopping down the bunny trail, or for Andrew and Fergie to get back together.

"I mean, maybe you wouldn't want to work for me," she said, "because we went to school together."

"I never . . ." My words petered out quickly. What was the use of lying? She was honest enough to say it outright, so I might as well be, too. "Well, yeah. It does sort of make me feel funny."

She stood abruptly, sloshing vodka and Pine-Orange Banana on the stained carpet. I began to wonder if she'd had a drink—or a few—before she came over. "But it shouldn't! It *ab-so-lute-ly* shouldn't."

"Look, it's not that I'm embarrassed," I lied.

"It's no comedown to work with children."

"I think taking care of children is about the most rewarding work there is . . ."

Pepper automatically made a "here-here" noise like you might hear watching the British parliament on C-SPAN. "I totally agree."

"But I made a personal pledge I would never take a job with family or friends, and I really do think I should stick to that."

She sank back in her chair. Amazingly, she appeared almost hurt. "But it's not like we're really friends."

On that point, I couldn't contradict her.

"And neither of us has that much to do with Bramford Prep anymore, so you don't have to worry on that account." I sputtered, but she waved off my incoherent objection. "Oh, I know, I know. I go to reunions and all that. But it's not that big a deal. And Phaedra's my bud, but you know Phaedra. She barely made it out of BP, anyway."

I was having a hard time following. Did the fact that Phaedra made lousy grades make her any less of a blabbermouth? Was I supposed to care what Phaedra thought anyway?

Well. As a matter of fact, I supposed I *did* care. A lot. Phaedra, and Larissa Halliday, and Missy Irvington, and all those other plaid-skirted phantoms from my past that I had been avoiding all these years. I felt sort of foolish for doing so now. What was I but a big fraidy cat? I had been running, hanging my head, just because I wasn't rich and leisured anymore. But what had *they* been doing with *their* lives?

Looking at Pepper at that moment, slightly drunk, with dribbles of Dole Pine-Orange Banana on her slacks, I didn't feel particularly intimidated. So she was rich. Big deal.

I lifted my head. "The most important consideration is August." Suddenly I was T. Berry Brazelton.

"Of course," Pepper chimed. "August is my primary concern, too."

"All the rest is ancient history."

"Totally ancient history," she agreed. "It's been a long time since I thought about all of that—you know, senior year, and the neck brace . . ."

"That was an *accident*," I said. "I want you to know that. I swear."

"I totally believe that," she said. "No matter what Phaedra still thinks. And despite all the pain and embarrassment it caused me, living with that neck brace did wonders for my posture."

I nodded furiously. "You're like a flagpole." She was.

"Anyhow, it's all forgotten. Water under the bridge. And the fact is, you would be great. It's like I was telling Phaedra—you're *just* the type of person I would want raising my daughter. I mean *helping* to raise her. You're one of us."

I felt like we were running in a big circle. "I know, but . . ."

"And the thing is, with all these big changes ahead, we want August to feel some sort of continuity. If we end up in New York, which looks most likely, there could be shuttling back and forth, and you know how confusing that could be for her."

New York. Frank Sinatra started singing in my head.

Stop, I commanded that voice.

"We'll probably have a big place, so you don't have to worry about being squeezed."

A big place? In New York? Billy Joel. "New York State of Mind."

"And you'll always have privacy, I can assure you. I'm not one of those snoopy employers. I know one woman who has her whole house under surveillance. I think that's sick."

Tony Bennett was crooning "Autumn in New York."

"And August really *loved* you. She's incredibly shy with strangers, but I could tell there was a bond there. You should have heard her when I said we were coming to visit you."

The soundtrack abruptly came to a halt. "She's here?"

"Uh-huh. Right outside, in the car. She's asleep."

"*In the car?*" This was unbelievable. "Aren't you supposed to, like, watch her?"

"It's okay. The car's locked, and it's not at all hot outside now that the sun's down."

She spoke as if August were a Pomeranian.

At my insistence we went outside, where Pepper's Jag was

taking up two spaces next to my Ford. Sure enough, in the back seat, August's white-blond head peeked out from under a black leather jacket. She held in her arms a cartoon plush toy shaped like a fish.

"See?" Pepper said. "She's fine."

The weirdest thing happened. I felt this odd tug. *A bond.* Especially when I glanced back over at Pepper, who was leaning back against her car and staring up at the stars. She reminded me a little of my own mom, I realized. And if that was even a little bit true, I had some idea of what August was in for.

"I'd better chauffeur you guys home," I said.

"Nah," Pepper said, reaching for her keys. "I can drive."

"I'd feel better if you let me," I insisted. "I can get a cab back here."

"See?" She laughed, relenting. "You're a perfect caretaker!"

I threw on jeans, locked up the apartment, and got behind the wheel. It was the first time I had driven a car this nice since I was a teenager. I had forgotten how quiet Jags were. I had forgotten that rich smell of real leather upholstery. I had forgotten the thrill of simply cherishing something because it was a best-in-class luxury.

I remembered now.

Pepper called a cab from her cell phone, so a car would be there to pick me up when I got to her place. When she hung up, she turned to me and smiled. "If it makes any difference, I was going to up your salary a little. The last girl we had wasn't . . ." She lowered her voice, as if there might be a spy from the INS hiding in the glove compartment. "Well, frankly, she wasn't exactly legal, so of course we weren't going to pay her what we would pay a real person."

She quoted me a figure of two thousand a month, plus room and board. Which seemed astonishing to me. If I spent no money for a year, I would have twenty-four thousand dollars! Amazing. Especially since the work . . . well, it wasn't actual work. I mean, not in the mind-numbing repetitive clerical sense of the word. Sure, substitute teaching had been bad—traumatic, even—but this was different. Totally different. This would be like hanging out with a kid at home.

I remembered my own childhood spent mostly sitting in front of the television watching a succession of cartoons, soaps, afternoon talk shows, and sitcom reruns. We had a housekeeper who looked out for me, but what had she done, exactly? Made sure I didn't track mud around the house and fed me canned tomato soup at lunchtime. I could handle that. Easy.

For two thousand dollars clear per month—plus a ticket out of Big D—I could definitely handle it.

I tried not to let my greedhead attitude show in my face, but I'm not sure how successful I was. "Can I get back to you tomorrow, Pepper? There's someone else I was speaking to . . ."

Despite not wanting to look overeager, I did feel hesitant. Doubts were trying to make themselves be heard over Frank Sinatra's siren song. Why had Pepper come here in the middle of the night? Why not just wait till morning? Why the in-person appeal?

Did I really seem competent to her? That was a boost.

Maybe working for her wouldn't be so bad after all.

Maybe I could actually go through with it.

Oddly enough, it wasn't until hours later, when I was back at my apartment, lying in bed and staring sleeplessly at the ceiling that I remembered that neither Pepper nor I had mentioned word one about Spence.

"Would you entrust Jason to me?"

I asked this question of my friend Nola. Jason was the tiny sun around which Nola circled, the proverbial apple of her eye, so I knew she would give me a straight answer.

Plus, if there's one thing I've noticed, it's that my married friends take pride in being brutally honest with me. For my own good. They really want me to know the mistakes I am making that will totally fuck up my chances in life. They love to point out the things I'm doing wrong, wrong, wrong, and more importantly, what blueprint I need to follow to have a life just like theirs. Never mind that I don't particularly envy the lives of these married folk.

I didn't envy Nola, who was married to an incredibly dull

engineer named Steve, but I wanted to know if she would hire me as a nanny. Because no matter how much I wanted to take Pepper's job now, I still felt unqualified. True, I was probably better prepared to take care of a child than a woman who would leave a kid asleep in the back of a car in the middle of the night, but that was setting the bar pretty low.

Nola gasped. "Jason? *My* Jason?" She goggled at me like I was some pathetic single creature who had gone round the bend and was actually asking her to cough up her child. "Why would you want Jason?"

As if.

The cherub in question was in the next room watching some very loud television show that featured bad MIDI music. Unfortunately, he was singing along, so it sounded like he was in the kitchen with us. This was probably the farthest away from her son Nola ever got. Letting him sit in a room alone was a big step for her. I mean him.

"I'm not suggesting you actually give him to me. I just wondered whether you would think I would be any good at child care."

She deflated in relief and took a big swig of coffee. "You mean babysitting? I'd be thrilled! Steve and I haven't been out to a movie in—"

"I mean, would you hire me as a nanny?"

She blinked. "Steve and I can't afford a nanny."

I had to remind myself that I was dealing with a mind that had clocked extensive time in front of *Teletubbies*. Maybe it wasn't entirely her fault if her neurons weren't firing on all cylinders. "I've had a job offer," I explained. "As a nanny. I'm asking you if you think I should take it."

She laughed, then double-checked to make sure I was joking. When she saw that I wasn't chuckling along, her jaw dropped. "Someone wants to hire *you* as a nanny? Who? Who would do this?"

"A family named Smith in Highland Park. They're very wealthy, and they might actually be relocating, so not only would it be a big career move, it might actually mean a relocation for me, as well. So I want to consider whether I have the right stuff before I start on so many changes."

Of course what I really wanted at that point was for someone to talk me into it. I figured I could count on Nola for this. Eventually. She wholeheartedly embraced her position as mother not only to Jason, but to me and probably countless others as well. If I ever needed a good scolding or talking-to, Nola was my girl. Also I sometimes got the feeling that she was terrified I would end up homeless and want to use her spare bedroom.

She sipped more coffee, her lips pursed. "How much money?"

I provided the details, whereupon she set down her coffee cup and gave it to me straight. "Of course you should take it. Are you crazy? This would be a good setup for you. It's about time your luck changed!"

"There are some drawbacks . . ."

"You need the money. And free rent! What could be so bad about that?"

"It's not the money. It's my employers. I know them."

"So? What person doesn't get a job through connections at some point in her life?"

"I went to school with this person."

"So?"

"I hated her."

She bit her lip. "Oh."

"And I dated her husband."

Nola cocked her head. "Dated, or *dated*?"

"*Dated.* In fact, he was the first guy I ever *dated.*"

"Oh, no."

"It's not a huge deal . . . I mean, I'm completely over the guy . . ."

She got up and refreshed our cups, and all the while, her brow was pinched in that worried Mrs. Cleaver way. Probably she was thinking about that spare bedroom. Finally, she was ready to make her pronouncement. "You've got to take the job, Al. It's the responsible thing to do. Even though it might be a bit awkward at first, I don't see that should color your thinking too much. I mean, imagine how awkward it will be for *her*!"

Nola *would* take the wife's part.

She was just gathering momentum. "And think what good experience it would be! People are always looking for good child care."

"I thought people were always looking for *cheap* child care."

She nodded. "That too. You'll never be rich, of course. But I don't guess you ever expected to be."

Never be rich. The words felt like a knife plunging into my stomach, then twisting.

All of a sudden, my skin felt clammy. *Never be rich?*

I had never really thought about it before, but if you could never expect to be rich, never even hope for it, what was the point? Wasn't that the American dream . . . the possibility that through some miracle, a few million dollars just might end up in your bank account, to be taxed at an enviably low rate? That was *my* dream, at any rate. Not that I had ever spelled it out explicitly, or taken steps to make it a reality. I had spent so long just expecting it as my due, I was still in readjustment mode.

But Nola was so right. Once I decided to toss in my lot as a nanny, I would never amass serious wealth. Time to squelch my inner Warren Buffet.

"I guess you're right . . ."

Nola's eyes sparkled. Somehow she always seemed happiest when she was handing out unpleasant truths. " 'Course I am!" she crowed, ignoring the fact that I was now sagging over my coffee mug, dispirited. "Now where are these people moving to?"

"Oh . . . probably New York," I said gloomily.

"New York? That would be fantastic!"

"Right. Being poor in New York would be even better than being poor in Dallas."

She clucked at me. "You won't be *poor*. Or at least, not very. Anyhow, you'll be making *something*, which is a big step up from where you are now."

Ouch. I had to remind myself that this was what I came here for. A little of Nola's straight talk. But Miss Bossy was really feeling her oats today.

"And don't you have a friend in New York?"

"Jess lives there."

She frowned. "Oh, that's right." Nola didn't approve of Jess. They'd only met once, but it had only taken once for her to pronounce her a hopeless flake. "But Steve's brother, Finn, lives in New York! You'll have to look him up."

I'd heard her talk about this guy before. He was practically a saint or something. As if being Steve's brother weren't reason enough to avoid him.

"He'd just love to meet you. In fact, he'll be visiting here in a few weeks. I'll be able to introduce you. Break the ice."

"Is he still doing social work?" I seem to remember her nattering on about the man ladling out soup, or some such activity.

"Yes, he loves it. He works with homeless teens."

Oh, God. Could there be anything more grim?

Not that I didn't have any humanitarian impulses. They just tended to be a little muffled when it came to actually pressing the flesh. Especially with teenagers; I had an uncomfortable history with them.

"Steve and I spend almost as much time worrying about Finn as we do worrying about you," Nola said. "Except Finn's trouble is that he's such a workaholic. I'll bet he hasn't had a girlfriend in years."

Couldn't wait to meet him.

"Well, there's a chance that I won't ever make it to New York," I said. "Who knows?"

"That would be a shame. I know how you've been wanting to get out of Dallas."

Notice she wasn't bemoaning the fact that she would be losing such a good friend. But I understood. When we'd worked together, we had been lunch-hour inseparables, but we hardly saw each other that much anymore.

A crash coming from the next room sent Nola springing to her feet.

"You should take the job, Al. Definitely. In fact you should call up this moment and beg them to let you start tomorrow."

She shouted back to me as she disappeared from sight. "You never know how long it will be before another person offers you anything!"

That, unfortunately, was the truth.

Coming out of Nola's, I felt that I would be a complete washout if I didn't beg Pepper to take me in. She made it seem as if I should offer to work for half the price just to cement my position. So I was pretty sure I would take the job.

Then I talked to Jess, filling her in on the pertinent details.

"Forget about it," she said. "This instant. Let it go. I've given the whole nanny thing some thought, and I'm sure you'll be miserable. You'll have the kid's mother nagging you all the time, and nanny cams watching your every move."

"Pepper says she's not into the spying thing. And it pays more than I thought. And they'll move me to New York for nothing," I reminded her.

"Right! If Miss Rich Bitch doesn't scratch your eyes out when she finds you ogling her husband."

"I'm not going to ogle him. For heaven's sake."

"You told me he was an old boyfriend."

"But I'm over him. Completely."

"Uh-huh."

"Do you think I'm some kind of a nut? What kind of person pines for her high school boyfriend for ten years?"

"Have you found anyone who you liked as well since?"

"Unfair question," I said.

"Why?"

"Because high school boyfriends always have a sort of glow about them."

"Not mine. The only time Stuart Slatkin glowed was when he overapplied his Clearasil."

"I just mean that we cut them slack because they're only half-formed. You assume they'll improve with time. And if they don't, it doesn't matter because you're not there to see it."

With older males, of course, it was a different story. This is one of those things they never warn you about. The older people get, the weirder they become. Some time around twenty-five, bizarre habits begin to set like cement. And the hell of it was, as the pickin's grew slimmer, I was growing pickier. A deadly cycle. But with experience, and many time-curdling dates, came wisdom. I started developing a list of definite *don't dos.*

Don't do strip-mall comedy clubs.

Don't do mosh pits, folk festivals, or open-mike poetry nights.

Don't do movies where exploding cars outnumber lines of dialogue. (Sometimes difficult to know in advance.)

Don't do NASCAR.

Spence arrived in that halcyon time in my life, before I had started my don't-do list.

"But Spence was different," I said, sighing. "He didn't have any outstanding flaws."

"Uh-huh, he was perfect. Except that he dumped you without warning."

Jess knew all about that, because in college every time I had a few beers I would inevitably moan about my great lost love. Sometimes I'd moan about him even without the beers.

"I've thought of another reason you don't want to be a nanny," Jess said. "*Jane Eyre.*"

"She was a governess."

"Same difference."

"I like Jane Eyre."

Jess grunted in disgust. "She was a *wimp.* She kept saying she wasn't, but she was. She was Mr. Rochester's beck-and-call girl, even after he let her be embarrassed by his bitchy friends at a party. Even after it became clear that there was a violent pyromaniac in the attic. Oh, she was big on rationalizations, but let's face it, the woman was a doormat."

"But she ran away when she found out he lied to her," I argued. "She resisted."

"Some resistance! She went running back the first chance she got, when he finally disposed of that wife of his."

"The wife died in a fire. It wasn't his fault—he tried to save her."

Jess clucked at my gullibility. "That's what *he* said. It always seemed fishy to me. And how did Jane react?" Jess's voice became high and flutey. " '*Reader, I married him!*' Like we're supposed to be glad she wound up with that jerk."

Jerk! I nearly fainted. "Would you rather she wound up with the boring missionary?"

"She should have taken the dough she inherited from her dead aunt, hopped on the first coach to London, and rented an apartment."

"You're the first person I've met who didn't love that book," I muttered. You never could tell about people, I supposed.

"Hitchhike to New York," Jess advised. "You'd be safer."

"Hitchhike, she tells me!" This from the woman who once refused to let me drive her places because my make of car had a low crash-test rating on an auto safety Web site. Now she thought I would be safer thumbing rides with potential serial killers than taking a job as a nanny with Pepper McClintock Smith.

"Al, I've known you since college. You'll be torturing yourself, putting yourself around all that money. It's like dropping a recovered junkie into a poppy field."

"I was never that bad. Money never meant that much to me."

"You were the only kid in our crapola dorm with a *Swedish* stereo system. And do you remember how you felt when you totaled your little Saab convertible and could only afford a used Ford Escort to replace it?"

"Okay."

"You *wept*."

"Okay, okay."

I sighed. I hadn't expected Jess's advice to completely counteract Nola's. I needed a friend I could use as a tiebreaker between the two of them. It looked like I was going to have to use my own judgment, which was always risky.

But what could I do? I needed the job.

And deep down, I longed to be around all that money.

And to see Spence. Just see him.

Chapter 5

When I got a load of my new nanny digs, all my doubts disappeared. True, I was being housed above the three-car garage, which just screamed servant class. I'd seen *Sabrina.* But this garage apartment was the nicest place I'd ever lived on my own. It was so posh, when I got a load of it I actually gasped and twirled around as if I'd arrived in fairyland. Three rooms with polished oak hardwood floors, furnished with an eclectic mix of antiques. ("Just cast-offs," Pepper let it be known.) An Italian tiled bath with a shower that had three jets and a water-massage feature. Even the kitchenette had Viking appliances and granite counters.

I was still sweaty from moving boxes. My furniture—what little there was of it—was squeezed into inconspicuous corners or put in storage in the garage below. I had balked at the idea of having a furnished apartment when Pepper told me about it over the phone. *Furnished rooms* smacked of musty bedsitters in boarding houses or sleazy hotels. But now my little qualms made me want to laugh. I would have been just as happy at that moment to take all my things into the backyard and build a bonfire.

That would have felt great, actually. A completely fresh start.

"The people who owned the house before we did used this as a mother-in-law apartment." Pepper, who was not sweating, laughed. "They must have liked their in-laws *a lot* more than I like mine."

Only then did it occur to me that these in-laws she was speaking about were Spence's parents. His father I vaguely remembered as a well-dressed, very busy guy who smoked a lot of cigars, but his mother had been so nice to me. She'd sent me a silver pen set for graduation, even after Spence had dumped me, and now I felt a knee-jerk allegiance to her.

"Do you think you'll be happy here?" Pepper asked.

Her tact astounded me. She had seen the dump I was living in. She must have known that I felt like kissing her feet. "It's better than I could have dreamed!" I gushed, wishing I could shower and change so I could greet my new life with the respect my apartment merited.

"Great." She called attention to the gift bag she had been holding all this time. It was a little Saks bag with a bow on it. "August wanted to bring you something, to welcome you." She glanced around, frowning. "Where did August get off to?"

"Behind the door," I said.

Pepper had brought August with her to be part of the greeting committee, but the minute August got a look at me, she had darted behind the door and remained in hiding ever since.

Pepper put her hands on her hips. "What in the world are you doing back there?"

August turned her back to us and pressed her nose against the wall, reminding me of the old-fashioned punishments teachers used to mete out. Only this was self-inflicted. She looked as if she believed she could disappear if she just stared at the wall hard enough.

"I'm not August," she said.

Pepper's long-suffering look clearly indicated this identity confusion was a recurring source of irritation between them, like battles over broccoli at the dinner table. "Of course you are! At least, you were the last time I checked." She reached over and took hold of her daughter's shoulders, turned her, then marched her right up to me. "There. Why don't you give Alison your gift?"

For the briefest of moments I flashed back to a certain birthday party, and a fear shivered through me. What if this was all an elaborate revenge scheme? I probably flinched as August dutifully held up the Saks bag; I half expected a load of poo to come flying out at me.

"Mommy got you soap," August said.

I peeked into the bag with that sort of mimelike facial exaggeration that novices use with kids. But when I started pulling all sorts of Estée Lauder bath products out of that bag, I really did get excited. Foaming bath gel, bubble bath, powder, and eau de parfum. All full size. Even a new loofah sponge.

"Thank you so much!" I cooed. "Really," I told Pepper, "this is so nice. I love this stuff."

She shrugged off my display of gratitude, but I could tell she was pleased. "It was all August's idea. She wanted to get you something."

"Thank you, August," I said, though August was completely distracted by something behind me.

"Just our way of welcoming you to the Smith madhouse!" Pepper exclaimed, laughing breezily.

I stood up, slowly. I felt awkward bringing the subject up, but it seemed equally weird not to broach the master of the house. "Is Spence here?" I asked. "I'd like to say hello."

"He's just *dying* to talk to you, too," Pepper said. "He's *so* excited about your working for us. Unfortunately, he's in Hong Kong just at the moment."

"Daddy's in Hong Kong!" August shouted, suddenly interested in the conversation.

"That's right." Pepper lowered her voice and added, eyeing me pointedly, "She *always* misses her Daddy."

The words seemed to imply that this was some weird emotional tic. I wasn't sure how to respond, but in the next moment I realized that an answer wasn't necessary.

"Well!" Pepper said briskly. "I'll leave you to it. Are you sure you don't mind having August with you while you unpack?"

The words jolted me. I thought August was just coming over to greet me. I didn't know my job had officially started. I looked at August and my stomach tightened. I had to start sometime, but I suddenly felt like an aerialist being asked to work without a net.

"Of course you don't!" Pepper said, laughing. "You two are probably going to be old buds before dinner. August was just *dying* for you to move in so she could come play."

"Oh . . ."

August looked completely disengaged from us, actually. And I had a million things to do. How was I going to accomplish anything while I was looking after a kid?

Especially since I had no idea what looking after a kid entailed . . .

I smiled at Pepper. *Don't let them see you sweat*, the old saying went. "Sure! Terrific! Dinner is . . . when?"

"Whenever you feel like making it," Pepper said, heading for the door. "I just like Pepper to be bathed and ready for bed by eight."

Bathed? That was something I hadn't contemplated.

Then again, I hadn't thought about being a Wolfgang Puck to the pint-sized, either.

"Okay, great!" I shouted after Pepper's retreating figure. With a backward wave, we were dismissed.

August had managed to climb up on my Pier One disk chair and was perched on it, staring around the room curiously, swinging her chubby legs and studiously not looking at me.

"Would you like to help me unpack, August? I sure could use some help."

She remained a completely unresponsive lump.

"August?"

"My name isn't August."

Right. Time to get this little matter straightened out. "What is your name then? I'd like to know what to call you."

"I'm Miss Spider." The bland contempt in her blue eyes conveyed that I should have known as much without having to be told.

O-kay. Obviously I was dealing with some kind of crazy arachnophilic kid. I hoped to God she wasn't a bug collector. I wasn't very fond of bugs. Spiders, roaches, ants . . . no sir, didn't like 'em.

But my shaky grasp on child psychology gave me the hunch that I was supposed to play along with these little games. "Are you a big black scary spider?" I said in a loud syrupy voice that I didn't quite recognize as my own. I sounded like one of those readers in the children's circle at noon story time at the public library.

August didn't respond.

"Are you Charlotte?"

Her forehead pillowed. "Who?"

"Charlotte, from the book *Charlotte's Web*. Have you read that?"

No response.

Maybe she was just a generic spider. How the hell was I supposed to know? I tried to put the subject of names behind us and spur her to action. "All right, spider, come help me put things in the kitchen. Would you like to do that?"

Her legs stopped swinging and as she stared at me, she transformed from a pale lovely cherub into a quivering tyrant with the hue of a red hot. "I'm *Miss* Spider!"

I was almost afraid to speak. I didn't want her to start crying, but though her eyes were bloodshot, creating a startling contrast with the blue of her irises, I realized she was not in danger of bursting into tears. She was just one seriously pissed-off kid.

I passed the next hour under August's watchful, semihostile gaze, rushing from room to room, not wanting to let her out of my sight. Responsibility began to weigh down on me as any number of heart-stopping scenarios played through my mind. What if she left the apartment and fell down the stairs? What if she wandered out to the backyard and drowned in the swimming pool?

"Would you like a Coke, August?" I asked her, hoping to make staying in one place sound appealing to her. Not that she had seemed interested in moving a muscle so far. She was still on that chair.

No answer.

Too late, I remembered. "Would you like a Coke, Miss Spider?"

"Miss Spider doesn't drink Coke." She flung herself onto her back and began to walk her feet around the rim of the chair cushion until she was practically upside down. Her hair hung in a blond cascade off the edge. I guessed this was spider behavior.

"That chair looks a little like a spider web," I said, still in my saccharine adult-to-child voice.

"No, it doesn't," she said.

She continued to hang upside down, and I continued to fretfully go through my boxes, unloading clothes that didn't seem worthy of their surroundings.

My predecessor had left a few things. An old T-shirt. Socks and a few laddery hose wadded in the top drawer of a bureau. A severely diminished wedge of Lava soap on the soap dish. In the kitchenette there were condiment bottles and a dusty can of Underwood Deviled Ham. (Did anyone actually eat deviled ham, I wondered, or was it manufactured specifically to take up space on shelves?) A few books were lying on the bookshelf in the living room. I scanned the offerings, which were heavy on the self-help titles, although there were some romance novels in there, too. A few often-read copies of Danielle Steele's oeuvre stood next to *Stress!* (The title was written in broken letters that brought to mind an earthquake.) There were a few titles with dainty covers of flowers and cameos, with inside flyleaf art of bare-chested men in tight breeches holding women in various stages of swooning. The last book on the shelf was *Recognizing Depression.*

Maybe those books should have signaled something. Maybe a screaming realization should have dawned, like the moment in *Silence of the Lambs* when the girl in the pit sees the bloody fingernails left by her predecessors in the walls. Those titles should have sent me shrieking out of that apartment for dear life.

Instead I wondered what kind of pathetic person had been

living there, shrugged, and shoved the books aside to make room for my haphazard collection of old college texts, pilfered library books, and as-yet unread bestsellers.

What must have been hours later, I jolted awake, gasping and panicky, to the sound of a car engine turning over and the late afternoon sun slanting through the venetian blinds right into my eyes. It took me a moment to register where I was.

Had Pepper left? I pushed aside the copy of *Recognizing Depression*, which I had dozed off reading, and jumped to my feet in time to see her silhouette in the passenger side of a red Land Rover that was pulling out of the drive.

Of course I realized that she wasn't beholden to tell me her comings and goings . . . but I had sort of expected she would.

I woke August, who grumbled and swayed in the Pier One chair like a hungover leading lady trying to pull herself together before a performance. "I'm tired!"

Her lungs were certainly up and running. My ears still needed to adjust to kid volume. I was always amazed that such big noises could emanate from such small bodies.

"Once we eat and get your bath taken care of, you can go to bed."

"I don't wanna go to bed!"

Try that on for logic.

I tugged August off the chair and she stumbled after me out the door. I locked the apartment—I was under strict orders to keep every outside door locked at all times, since a robbery had occurred down the street two years ago—and hurried down the stairs. August was not in such a hurry, however. She held onto the railing and clomped down one stair at a time, stopping occasionally to puff out an exhausted breath. Even this late it was broiling hot outside, and I grew impatient to dash back into air conditioning.

"Come on, Miss Spider, let's hurry along."

She glared at me and continued her agonizingly slow descent. Once she had finally conquered the staircase, however, she ran ahead of me to the side door of the house. When she stood on tiptoe and twisted the knob, she screamed, "Hey! It's locked!"

I nodded and searched through my new set of keys for the side door key. I still had never been in the kitchen. And what about Marta, the maid? Would she still be in the house? I hoped so. She might be able to help me rustle up dinner for August.

Maybe she would even make the dinner, I thought with greedy hope.

When I finally fumbled the door open, I walked ahead of August, trying to give the impression that I knew what I was doing.

"Hey!" she screamed from the door.

"Let's get dinner," I said, not stopping.

In the next second, a piercing shriek blared out, about ten times more loudly than a car alarm. I whirled in confusion, then remembered that the house was wired with motion detectors. I rushed around, trying to remember where the alarm controls were. When I found the box, I goggled at the keypad cluelessly. *What had Pepper said to do?*

August was standing next to my legs, her hands lifted over her ears, elbows sticking out. She started screaming. Now my ears were full of shrieking alarm *and* shrieking child.

My clothes felt damp with sweat as I stabbed at buttons, trying vainly to remember the codes Pepper had told me about in her quick walk-through of the house. *Shit, shit, shit!*

Amazingly, after a few wild tries the blaring stopped, and I was just left with August's shrieks. I put her hands away from her ears. "The noise has stopped!" I shouted over her bleats. I was breathing hard, as if I'd just run around the block. "It's over."

This seemed to satisfy August, who listened to the silence with a cocked head, then skipped away.

Since I should have listened to her warning about entering the house, I decided to follow her. Sure enough, she led me to the kitchen. The room was a much larger, better-stocked version of the kitchenette in the garage apartment. Granite counters, maple cabinets reaching all the way to the ceiling, Sub-Zero fridge. There was a large island in the middle of the room, with copper pots and skillets hanging off a rack above. I wasn't sure if those were usable pots; they looked as though they might be there for purely decorative purposes. In fact, the whole kitchen looked as if it might be purely decorative, like a show kitchen you would find in an ad in *Gourmet* magazine.

Where to begin? Obviously Marta had left and I was all alone here, like a marooned astronaut. It took me a few moments to get my bearings and adjust to the new landscape.

Where was Pepper? It still seemed strange that she would just run off and not say anything. The gleaming counters and smooth stainless-steel plane of the refrigerator revealed no note of explanation, no "back in a flash!" reassurance.

"What would you like for dinner?" I asked August, who was attempting to scale up the sides of a chrome stool.

"Not hungry!"

At least she was talking to me, or yelling at me. "You have to eat dinner."

She gave the statement several moments of serious consideration, then brightened. "Macaroni and cheese!"

"Good answer." That was one menu item I was pretty sure I could handle. I started searching through cabinets, which were overflowing with food. Cereals, canned goods, boxes of mixes. Dizzying assortments of condiments, every type of snack cracker under the sun, bottled water, soda, liquor . . .

But no blue box of macaroni and cheese.

Damn.

"Do you have macaroni and cheese often?" I asked August as I peered into a cabinet that revealed only high-end glass Tupperware.

"Uh-huh. Mary-Saul makes it for me." I nodded. I knew that Marisol was my immediate predecessor, the depression queen. "So did Julie."

I had no idea who Julie was, but I got the idea. Mac-n-cheese had been made in this house. Often. I went through the cabinets again, and what I saw caused my heart to sink. The pasta shelf. Elbow macaroni. These people had been making macaroni and cheese *from scratch.*

I pulled out the crinkly plastic bag and steeled myself for the chore ahead. It couldn't be too hard, I thought. You just boil some pasta and throw in some milk and cheese. More time consuming than the Kraft route, for sure, but there would be a certain satisfaction in making something wholesome for my charge.

Or so I told myself as I grated a hunk of medium cheddar I'd found in the fridge. I grated off part of a knuckle and hopped around the kitchen shouting *fuck! fuck! fuck!* between sucked in breaths of pain, until I saw August's big blue eyes pinned on me, whereupon I reached back to some pre-elementary corner of memory and shouted *fudge! fudge! fudge!* Which only made me feel more foolish.

By the time I had drained the macaroni and dumped everything into a saucepan, I realized that a mistake had been made. Or, if not a mistake exactly, a miscalculation. The milk and cheese weren't forming a sauce. The milk was turning a Cheeto-orange, but remained stubbornly sloshing around the bottom of the pan while the strips of cheese adhered to the pasta like cheddar leeches.

August stood on her stool and peered into the pot. "Eew!"

I turned up the heat.

"Watch out, you might fall," I warned, pressing her back down in her seat, out of view of the pot. "This will taste great—just you wait."

The doorbell rang.

"That's the door!" August trumpeted helpfully.

"Stay there," I told her. "I'll be right back."

It felt weird going to answer the door in a stranger's house. What had happened to Pepper? Was she just going to leave me here all alone all night?

When I tracked down the front door and swung it open, a cop stared down at me. He was middle-aged, a bit on the pudgy side, his jowls clean shaven. And he wasn't smiling.

My guilt response kicked in immediately. Obviously, I had

been found out . . . but for what? The only terrible thing I had done lately was scream fuck in front of a four-year-old.

"Are you having trouble here, ma'am?" he asked in a heavier-than-average drawl.

"Trouble?"

"AAA Alarm called us that you were having an emergency."

I sagged with relief. "Oh! That. That was just me being stupid. I'm new here."

He seemed to be looking beyond me, peering into the foyer. Maybe to see if I had company . . . or an accomplice . . .

"I'm the nanny," I explained. "I just started today and I didn't know how to work the alarm system. When I came in from the garage, I tripped it off."

"I see."

"My name is Alison Bell." I thought he might want to write that down for his report.

"Uh-huh."

He wasn't writing anything down, so maybe there would be no report. Or . . . was he waiting for me to crack? For me to break down and shout "*All right! I did it! I killed them all—for God's sake stop staring at me!*"

"Okay, Miss Bell. Be more careful next time. These false alarm calls take up a lot of our time."

"I'm very sor—"

Before I could apologize, or relax in the assurance that I was not going to be dragged off in handcuffs, another alarm went off. This one sounded different. It was more whooping than shrieking. More like a submarine siren you might hear in an old war movie than a car alarm.

"What the—?"

Before I could turn, the officer brushed past me. "Smoke!" he hollered.

Sure enough, there was dark smoke billowing down the hallway. Had my macaroni and cheese caught fire? *Omigod. August!* My pulse kicked into high gear, and I wheeled back toward the kitchen, nearly mowing down the cop in the processs. August was right where I'd left her, eyes wide even in the haze, as if she couldn't quite believe what was going on.

Never in my life had I been so glad to see someone sitting upright. I scooped her up and ran outside. "Stay right here!" I instructed her, forgetting that was exactly what I had said the last time, when I left her in the burning room.

Back in the kitchen, the officer had turned off the gas jet and was using the fire extinguisher on my macaroni. White powder plumed around us. It was overkill, but I couldn't say I blamed him.

"I think that'll do it," he said, once he'd discharged what appeared to be the entire contents of the canister.

I searched for the oven vent and turned it on. "Thanks."

"Don't mention it—it's what we're here for." He looked me over, as if doubting the story I'd given him earlier. "You say you're taking care of the little girl?"

I nodded. "This is my first day."

"Maybe your last," he said, chortling.

After he left, I opened all the kitchen windows, letting the hot humid air displace all the cold smoky air. Then I brought August back in. She took one look at the kitchen and dragged the back of her hand across her face. "I'm hungry!"

The kitchen was a wreck. I had to get this place tidied before Pepper came back. I dragged in a chair from the next room and put August on it. A box of juice from the fridge seemed to calm her down a little. I started cleaning frantically. Another half hour had the place sparkling except for the charred pot soaking in the sink. Now I needed to get it dirty again to make dinner.

I got down another pot.

"Use the zoom machine!" shouted August, causing me to jump. I had been so busy and she had been so quiet that I had forgotten I was being watched.

"Zoom machine?" I asked.

She pointed to a microwave almost hidden from view in its own recessed cabinet. "Mary-Saul uses the zoom machine when she makes macaroni!"

Oh, God. My knees went weak on me. Could it be . . . ?

I went to the freezer and opened it with something like

dread. And there it was. A little stack of Stouffer's packages. I banged my head against the stainless steel.

I was an idiot. An incompetent. A nincompoop.

I yanked out a box, unwrapped it, and tossed it into the microwave. Ten minutes later I was hovered next to August as she twiddled macaroni on her fork. I suddenly felt hungry myself, but I couldn't eat anything. I didn't feel worthy.

I wished August would eat something, though. She seemed more intent on examining her food than consuming it.

"I'm tired."

"Just eat. Then bath, then bed."

Her mouth turned into a pout, which looked like the start of something bad. I remembered seeing a drawer that had peanut butter energy bars in it. "How about a peanut butter treat?"

She swung her head toward me and nodded.

I had one unwrapped in a flash, and she devoured it. The macaroni and cheese ended up in the garbage disposal.

We went up to August's suite and I poured a bath with lots of bubbles, which seemed to please Miss Spider. She frolicked in the tub and let me scrub her hair down, no problem. But when she got out, she wrapped herself in a towel and took off running. And then she disappeared. A frustrating twenty minutes of hide-and-seek ensued, and then she suddenly gave up. She traipsed back to her bedroom and was docile as I yanked a nightgown over her head. She slipped under the covers, and I nearly felt like weeping with relief. It was over.

"Story!" she yelled before I could make my escape.

"What story?" I asked, looking at her bookshelf.

"Miss Spider!"

I stared at her. "Huh?" It hadn't occurred to me until that moment that Miss Spider was a real character. Or rather a real fictional character.

"Miss Spider's Tea Party!"

"Okay, okay."

I don't think I had read a story aloud since I was in first grade, but I did my best. It helped that the story seemed really cool—bugs not wanting to accept some spider's invitation to tea. I was sort of into it, but halfway through I looked up and August was completely zonked.

This time I did sigh. It was over. One day down.

I eased the book silently shut and was heading for the door when someone appeared, startling me.

Pepper put her fingers to her lips. "Is she asleep?" she whispered.

I was nodding when suddenly August bolted up in bed. "Mommy! Mommy! Alson made the alarm go off and it was *so loud!* And then there was this big fire in the kitchen and the policeman came and sprayed stuff all over! And then Alson made me dinner but I wouldn't eat it so she gave me candy! Then I ran all over the house with no clothes and she couldn't catch me!"

Pepper laughed. "Wow! Sounds like you two had a great night!"

August pouted and let out a series of little hiccups. "I miss Mary-Saul. When's Mary-Saul coming back?"

"We'll just have to see," Pepper said, tucking her back in. "Good night, baby. Kisses."

"I'm Miss Spider." She flopped over tiredly, turning her back to us both.

Pepper shrugged her shoulders at me and led me out into the hall.

The minute the door was shut, I began sputtering out explanations. "I'm so sorry about the alarm . . . and the fire . . ."

Pepper lifted up her hands and waved them at me. Her eyes were bright. "Forget about it! Happens all the time. I hope the police didn't give you a hard time. They're always so pissy when the alarm goes off by mistake. But I'm like, isn't that part of their job, to check on things like that? What else are we paying such outrageous taxes for?"

"It was okay," I said. "But I wasn't sure when you were going to be back."

"I went out with Phaedra." Pepper yawned and stretched. "I'm about to pass out. It's Leno and then bed for me."

"Yeah, me too." Except for the Leno part.

"Good night," she said. As I hit the stairs she stopped me.

"Oh! August is playing over at her friend Alexandra's tomorrow."

"All right." I really did feel tired. "Is there anything you would like me to do?"

She blinked at me. "You have to take her there."

"Oh. Right." I cleared my throat, attempting a recovery. "I meant, do you want me to stay at the house while she plays, or is there anything else I should be doing?"

"No, you'd better stay and watch her." She lowered her voice. "Mimi, Alexandra's mom, is such a slacker parent. She's never around, and even when she is—well! I wouldn't trust this new girl she hired for Alexandra *at all.*"

Just because I was bone tired didn't mean I could actually sleep. God forbid. At two am, as usual, I was bolt upright in bed, squinting at the unfamiliar darkness around me. The very silence of the neighborhood after my years of proximity to a main traffic artery was distracting. How did people manage to sleep with all this *quiet*?

Every time I closed my eyes I kept hearing burglar alarms, or seeing that policeman laughing at me. I felt like such a loser.

But you did it. You made it through one day.

Well, half a day.

That's something, isn't it?

As milestones went, half a day on a job wasn't exactly pat-yourself-on-the-back time. But at three am I finally was able to convince myself that I should take heart. I had weathered a few storms and had managed to sidestep doom. Things could have been worse. (If the house had actually burned down, say . . .) If nothing else, I assured myself as my eyelids finally grew heavy again, I had discovered that my employer wasn't exactly going to be watching me like a hawk.

The electronic strains of Beethoven's Ninth jangled me out of sleep. I sat up, gulping in air. My cell phone. After a moment of groping in the dark for it, I located it on the nightstand and murmured a sleepy request to be left alone.

"Alison!" my mother trumpeted. "Did I wake you up?"

I flopped back down on my pillows, groaning.

"I did, didn't I?" she asked.

"It's the middle of the night here."

"Is it? I had no idea."

"Then why did you ask me first thing whether you'd woken me up?"

"I'm not sure," she said, losing interest in what time it was, or how I was. "Anyway, *guess* where I am."

"I don't know."

"Guess."

I turned over and muffled a scream by sinking my face into my pillow. The phone I just left on the pillow by my ear. Mother started croaking out her rendition of the love theme from *Moulin Rouge*.

"Now guess," she said.

"Tokyo."

"I can't hear a word you're saying, Alison. Is someone there strangling you?"

I lifted my head off the pillow. "I should be so lucky to have another person in bed with me."

"What a thing to say to your mother!" she said, relishing playing the shocked parent. "Anyway, you're so ridiculous. You've got scads of boyfriends."

One way my mother dealt with uncomfortable facts was simply by denying them. Or deciding that the opposite was true. I hadn't had a steady boyfriend in years, so she preferred to think of me as a mad party-girl. Irritating as it was, I have to say that it seemed to work quite well for her. It soothed her mind and gave her a good character to slip into conversations with friends ("My unbelievably popular daughter!"). But when she talked about me this way to me, it always took me a moment to adjust to being fictionalized.

"I'm at the Ritz in Paris," she told me. "It's heaven. Oh, I wish you were here! You'd really love it."

For a moment I had a vision of myself sweeping through a magnificent lobby on the arm of someone good looking and French. The dream evaporated as soon as I realized that I didn't have anything nice enough to wear to the Ritz. I hated to be underdressed, even if it was just in my imagination.

"Motel Six is more my speed now, unfortunately," I told her. "Are you calling just for funsies, Mom, or is there anything in particular you wanted?"

"Just calling to see how you're doing, of course."

"I'm fine," I said. "I got this new—"

Before I had a chance to blurt out the news about my employment, my move, my hopes for the future, Mom added, "Also I was wondering if you'd seen Murph."

The words I had been speaking dropped into the vacuum of lost thoughts. I couldn't quite believe what she was asking. "Murph?"

"Yes, my husband."

As if I didn't know who Murph was. "Isn't he with you?"

"He was," she said. "But he seems to have disappeared. Have you heard anything there about him?"

"Well, no."

"Have you been watching the local news?"

"No, I've been busy and . . ." I gulped. *Local news?* "Mom, why would Murph be on the local news? Did he win the lottery, or murder someone?"

She laughed. But it was a brittle laugh—not comforting.

"Are you in trouble?" I asked.

"Heavens, no! I've still got my American Express. I doubt the Ritz will kick me out for weeks yet."

"I wasn't referring to how you were fixed for money. I meant . . . is everything okay between you and Murph?"

A nervous chuckle trilled from her continent to mine. "Of course! Why wouldn't it be?"

"Mom, you just said you had lost your husband. Look for him on the local news, you said."

"Oh, well, I'm sure it's just temporary," Mom replied blithely. "He probably got restless with all my shopping. You know how men are. I just thought that since he's practically a celebrity there, you might have heard him mentioned . . ."

Murph wasn't a celebrity, except in the way very wealthy people are. They pop up in photo collages of charity fund-raisers in glossy magazines, and on the fringes of spreads about political fund-raisers.

"I haven't seen or heard anything, but like I said, I've been really busy lately."

"That's good!" she said brightly. "It's good to be busy!"

"Are you sure you're okay, Mom? Is there anyone you'd like me to call?"

"No, no, no! Everything's just fine here. This is actually Murph to a T. That's what happens when you marry a man with his own jet, Al. They tend to zoom off at the oddest moments."

"I wouldn't know about that."

She laughed. "Sure you don't! All those people you know are probably swimming in cash."

"Well, actually . . ."

"Wait till you see what I got you in Paris!" Mom exclaimed. "You'll *love* it."

"Oh. Great."

"I've got to go now, honey. I'm going to the opera this evening. *La Traviata* again, but what the hell. At least it's a toe-tapper."

I laughed. "Sure, the heroine dies of consumption, but it's got a good beat and you can dance to it."

"What are you talking about?" I guess *American Bandstand* hadn't been her thing. "Oh well, never mind. Have a good evening. For Pete's sake get out and have some fun!"

"It's three am here," I reminded her.

"Good heavens!" She sounded surprised. "You should be in bed."

I tossed the phone back on the nightstand and stared up at the ceiling, stewing. My mother was a nut. Calling me up in the middle of the night to ask about her missing husband, then telling me not to worry about it! And then not even bothering to ask how I was . . .

Of course, if I were abandoned at the Ritz, I would probably be a little self-absorbed myself.

What had happened to Murph?

I never had warmed up to that guy, but I'd never been

around him much. During the divorce I had sided squarely with Dad . . . still did, even though Dad had also found someone. He had fallen in love . . . or in something . . . with a dog groomer named Darla down in East Texas. It was an odd match, my courtly old-fashioned father and this leathery middle-aged woman who said things like "that chaps my grits." It seemed like a desperation match, and I felt sorry for my dad. They were married and now Darla washed dogs in a portable building in back of the house. She was awfully nice to me, but for some reason I felt awkward visiting. I don't think Dad feels comfortable having me see him with this new woman. He's so prim. Part of him probably still feels like he's betraying those original marriage vows.

But I never visited Mom. Never. And Murph never seemed eager to have Mom bring me down to Houston so we could be one big happy family. In a way, that was logical. Mom was the third Mrs. Murph Tripton, and I believe there were at least six children sired in those earlier marriages of his, so Murph probably was glad to keep additional family obligations to a minimum. Mom was so eager to please Murph, to keep her hands on him and his money, I'm sure she traveled the path of least resistance when it came to her family. I was sacrificed so that husband number two wouldn't feel threatened.

But now I was up angsting over the man's whereabouts. That in itself was worth about another hour of sleeplessness.

Chapter 6

I awoke to a peculiar buzzing that wasn't a doorbell and wasn't an alarm clock. My eyes blinked open and I pivoted around in a tangle of sheets, trying to pinpoint the source of the noise. My gaze alighted on a small box next to a potted Christmas cactus on a pedestal table just out of reach of the bed. A dim light flashed every time I heard the buzz.

I skimmed out of bed, inadvertently hauling the sheets with me and winding them around my ankles, which caused me to mince like a geisha girl toward the box. Up close it looked like a square speaker with three buttons at the bottom marked *call*, *talk*, and *listen*.

I pressed *talk*. "Hello?"

Nothing happened, so I pressed *listen.* A maniacal giggle came out of the box. "August?" I shouted. The box fell silent.

When I pivoted towards my clock, the time registered. Almost eight thirty. *Whoops!* No one had given me an exact schedule, but I assumed that I was supposed to be over at the house before now. With the theme from *Moulin Rouge* still in my head, I performed my morning ablutions in record-setting time and hightailed it over to the big house.

Marta was in the kitchen, casually wiping down the gleaming counters.

"Good morning," I said. She swung around to look at me, but didn't say anything. "Have you seen August?"

"That's not my job."

Great. "Have you seen her?"

"No, and I got here forty-five minutes ago. And I had to take the bus."

"When does she have breakfast?"

"Fifty minutes on the bus."

I repeated my question.

"When you give it to her."

"What about Pepper?" I asked. "Is she up yet?"

Marta looked at me as if I'd lost my mind. "Mrs. Smith never gets up before ten."

"But August has a play date today. With a friend named Alexandra? Do you know her?"

"Maybe."

Terrific. While Marta was deciding how much info she felt like parceling out to me, I ran upstairs to see what August was up to. She was wearing a lavender sweatsuit with pink hearts and was planted on her little couch in front of some glaringly bright kid's show with the volume turned up to an earsplitting volume. Was three and a half years old too young to introduce the concept of aural degeneration?

"Hi, August!" I yelled.

No response.

Not this again, I thought, my heart sinking. Taking a deep breath, I marched over to the television and jabbed at the volume button until the noise level was more reasonable. All the while I felt like a cartoon of an authoritative adult. "Wouldn't you like to have breakfast, August?"

She stared right past me.

"Miss Spider?" A hint of a plea stole into my voice.

Nothin'.

"You have a play date this morning with your friend Alexandra," I said. "You wouldn't want to miss it, would you?"

August puffed out her cheeks and then exhaled. She picked up her remote and flipped off the television, then hopped off the couch and stomped toward the doors. I followed her, amazed that my implied threat seemed to be working and she was headed downstairs. She made a beeline for the kitchen.

"Marta, Marta!" she said, flying at the maid's sturdy legs. "I'm soooo hungry!"

Marta stared at me with raised brows and told August to sit down at the little glass table in the corner. "Alison will get your cereal for you."

There was a dizzying array of cereals to choose from. Cold cereals, hot cereals, instant oatmeal. Boxes of unappealing bran concoctions and Special K stood fortresslike next to Crayola-colored boxes of pure sugary crap.

I hadn't eaten yet, and my own stomach rumbled when I saw the box of Peanut Butter Capt'n Crunch. It had been years, but I felt nostalgic for the sweet styrofoamy taste and the plowed-up feeling it left in the roof of your mouth. Also, I hadn't eaten yet.

"How about Capt'n Crunch?" I asked.

"Golden Grahams!" she yelled at me.

That seemed like a lackluster choice to me, but I did as commanded and emptied a bunch in a bowl and sloshed some milk on it.

"Too much milk," she said when I set the bowl in front of her.

"It's fine," I said.

She ignored me and sat back stubbornly in her chair. I got up, drained the milk into the sink and started over. This time I let her pour the milk. The carton slipped out of her hands and fell to the floor, causing a white flood across the tile.

Marta let out a stream of Spanish curses while I dove for the paper towels. I wasn't about to let her make an attempt to clean up after my mess. Still, she came and stood right over me while I tried to mop it up with squares of Bounty. For a moment I half expected her to boot me with her Naturalizers.

"Mackie," she said as I hovered on my hands and knees. "The little girl's family name is Mackie. She lives over on Beverly. It's not far."

That scrap of kindness almost brought tears to my eyes. "Thank you."

It was after ten already by the time I was tugging August

out the door toward my car. Continuing in her usual cooperative mode, she was digging the heels of her Keds into the pavement and screaming something completely incomprehensible at me.

A door banged behind us, and to my shock, Pepper came flying out the door in her nightgown and bathrobe.

"Where are you *going*?" she shouted at me.

I pointed to my car, parked on the street. "I'm trying to get August to Alexandra's. We're running late this morning."

She laughed. "*That's* okay. Good Lord, things are so disorganized over there! But you can't drive in *your* car."

"I can't?"

"You don't have a car seat. You'd better take the Hummer."

I stood stock still. "Hummer?"

She handed me a set of keys. "I know! It's crazy! We used to have an Esplanade for the family stuff, but it got hardening of the arteries or something last spring. Or really I think Spence just wanted a Hummer, and I refused to give up my Jag and he would *die* before selling his precious Porsche . . ."

My mouth was hanging open. I couldn't help it. Spence had a *Porsche*? And a Hummer? I still imagined him rattling around in his old Monte Carlo.

Of course he was rich, he probably thought nothing of buying whatever vehicle he wanted . . . but his choices seemed so ostentatious. So un-Spencelike.

"It's easy to drive," Pepper assured me, obviously mistaking my motionless disbelief for panic. "It's just a little large."

It was a boat. I loaded August in and backed out of the driveway feeling as if I were ready to storm through a bombed-out city. Which seemed all the more incongruous since there was a Wee Sing CD blaring over the speaker system.

I got to the Mackie's at ten fifteen and at first glance I could see what Pepper was warning me about. As I was pulling into the driveway a little girl burst out the front drive and was nearly squished by the Hummer's massive wheels. She was pulled away just in the nick of time by a Hispanic girl who appeared to be fifteen, tops. I turned off the engine and mentally braced myself for a morning of chaos. Now I was going to have two little kids to take care of. No way this teenager would be of any use.

I helped August out and she ran over to Alexandra, dragging her pink Barbie backpack on the pavement behind her. The two girls whooped with delight to see each other and held hands as they ran toward the house.

"Hi, Pilar!" August yelled as she ran past the Mackie nanny.

"Hey, girl. Who are you today?"

"I'm Dora the Explorer!"

The two girls shouted an anthem about a backpack and disappeared inside.

I was still standing outside, amazed. How had Pilar gotten that vital information out of August?

Pilar came up to me. "Are you the woman they hired to replace Marisol?"

I nodded, introducing myself. Maybe this woman was some kind of nanny prodigy. "August changes personality every day?"

"I guess. It's always the first thing I ask her. A sort of who-are-you-this-time game." She looked at me, concern beetling her brows. "Are you okay? You want a little tea, maybe a snack?"

That sounded so good. I still hadn't eaten. But I remembered that I had a job. "Shouldn't we watch August and Alexandra?"

"Oh, sure," she said, as if it were *no big deal.* As if she were assured of being in control. I was in awe. "They'll probably dance to Alex's *Wiggles* video all morning."

"What?"

"Just follow me. I've got fresh banana bread in the kitchen."

She did, too. Homemade. As I tucked into my second slice, I wondered if Pepper really thought Pilar was disorganized, or whether she just didn't know what the hell she was talking about. Probably the latter, I decided.

Lucky for me.

"**I** so suck at this."

"At what?"

"At being a nanny."

Jessica sighed in that *I told you so* way that I always thought was a little unfair, coming from her. I mean, she was always telling people so. If you were constantly throwing out warnings, odds were that you would manage to predict a few catastrophes correctly. "It's only been a few days."

"I know, I know, but I haven't slept. I've got this crazy little *Three Faces of Eve* kid to deal with. I never know from day to day whether she's going to be Miss Spider or Scooby Doo or a toilet paper roll. She lives in her own little world, and I mean *her own*. She's got a suite to herself and wakes me up by speakerphone, and I think she sees her mom for a few minutes every day, about as often as I do. And the maid has it out for me most of the time, I'm driving around Highland Park in the equivalent of a Sherman tank, I still can't sleep, and my Mom seems to be marooned at the Ritz in Paris."

"Wow."

"I'm overwhelmed."

"I meant wow about your mom, not you."

No one cared about my problems. I was beginning to doubt whether I would have, either, if they didn't belong to me. My problems always seemed to lack zing. "There are worse places to be marooned."

"Has your boyfriend come home yet?"

It had been so long since I'd had anything resembling a boyfriend that the question startled me. "Who?"

"The master of the house. Your new employer. Mr. Rochester." Jess was certain there would be a romantic *Jane Eyre* scenario blossoming between Spence and me.

"For heaven's sake, *don't* call him my boyfriend. He hasn't been my boyfriend for ten years now. That's ancient history."

"Mm. Where is he?"

"Taiwan. Or no, Hong Kong."

"So you haven't seen him *at all*?"

Now that I thought about it, that did seem a bit odd. "But he's one of these frequent-flyer husbands, I guess."

"Uh-huh. Either that or that crazy Pepper woman has his body hidden in the basement."

I let that statement pass. "Anyway, he must be so different from what he was when I knew him. I mean, he's this high-finance type now—the kind of guy who buys a Hummer—and when I knew him he was just a sort of schmucky teenager with a bad car and blemish worries."

"I thought you said you really liked him."

I sighed. "I did. But it was just a high school thing . . ."

My words trailed off and a dollop of silence hung on the line, then Jess broke into an off-key rendition of "The First Cut Is the Deepest."

"Stop!" I exclaimed. What was it with people singing to me on the phone lately? "The man is *married.* You know me, Jess. Cheating is awful, the worst. I'm not a prude, God knows, but I don't have a lot of respect for husband snatchers."

"It's that old fear of turning out like your mother. It happens, you know. Sometimes there's just nothing you can do about it. I've noticed lately that I have all these tics that used to annoy me when my mom did them. Like clicking my teeth when I'm trying to remember something."

I had actually heard her doing that. It *was* annoying.

Suddenly I had to fight off the horrible certainty that we were all doomed to become duplicates of our mothers.

"I think homewrecking is a family tic I can overcome if I'm careful," I quipped. "And in any case, I couldn't have a relationship now if I wanted one. Adulterous or nonadulterous. With anybody."

"Why not?"

"I'm too damned tired."

"**P**haedra's coming over," Pepper announced from the doorway.

August and I swung toward her. We had been absorbed in *The Little Mermaid*, and now I had to press *pause* so that we wouldn't miss a moment. August had seen the movie a million times, but this was my first time and I think I was falling in love with that little singing crab.

"Oh," I said. "Great."

"She's bringing Arthur, Riley, and Skip."

"I thought Skip was her ex-husband."

"Skip Junior, I meant. He's her oldest."

August moaned and dove under a couch cushion.

"You wouldn't mind looking after them for a while, would you?" Pepper asked me.

I stared at August's bottom half sticking out from the cushion. She flailed her legs and made muffled growling noises.

"It'd be, like, a *huge* favor," Pepper said.

I nodded. I was sometimes amazed at how hands-off and polite Pepper was toward me. Cordial. "Sure. No problem."

I have to admit, though, that a little part of me stung at being relegated to child care while two of my old classmates were going to be socializing downstairs. But *c'est la guerre*.

"Is there anything you need me to do?" I asked.

"Nah! I'll let you know when they get here."

She left, and August reemerged from her hidey hole. The first thing she did was eject the video, put it back in its case, and return it to the video drawer. I was always impressed at how good she seemed to be at getting things done, how independent she was. Her little friend Alexandra didn't even know how to turn a television off and on. On some days, electronics gave me a hard time, and I had twenty-four years on August.

Right now she stumped around the room, grabbing up beloved toys. At first I thought she was tidying up and I was going to commend her for being so thoughtful. But then I realized her behavior was almost frantic, like a medieval chatelaine preparing for a siege. She tossed her valuables into her bedroom with life-and-death urgency.

"Don't let them into my room!" she said to me.

I smiled indulgently, trying to calm her down. "No one will go in your room unless you want them to. That's your space."

She gaped at me as if I were a moron. Downstairs, the front door opened and voices sounded in the hallway. August shrieked and streaked into her room, slamming the door behind her.

In the next moment, a tidal wave of little boys hit the room. There were three of them—ranging from August's age to perhaps seven or eight for the oldest one—which was amazing, because they seemed like a whole herd. They were just a screaming blur, and within seconds I had been brained by a Hot Wheels car.

"Boys!" I worried I was bleeding. "Let's settle down. Boys!"

"*Boys!*" the oldest one sneered, in imitation of me. "*Boys!*"

One of them made a farting sound that reduced the other two to extravagant braying laughter. A football was produced and thrown, whizzing by my head by a hair and then just missing August's cute lamp.

"*Hey!*" I shouted. "Watch it! You nearly knocked over the Pooh lamp!"

I should have known better. They stared at me slack-jawed for a moment, before the middle one said, "Poo?" He turned to the conspicuously shut door. "We're sorry we nearly ruined your poo, August!"

"August!" the youngest taunted. "Come out, August!"

"AugustSeptemberOctoberNovember! Come out!"

As if the scenario weren't nightmarish already, they started to whine. "Come out and play, August!"

"Yeah, August, don't you like us?"

Her forbearance was astonishing. She didn't make a sound. My nerves were already unraveling. I started flashing back to substitute teaching and was afraid I was going to start trying out my half-remembered jujitsu.

"*Quiet!*" I screamed.

They swung away from the door, and I suddenly felt like the mother gazelle who sacrifices herself to distract the pack of hyenas from her young.

"Settle down this instant or you will have to go sit with your mother and Mrs. Smith and not move a muscle until they're finished talking. Understand?"

Amazingly, they seemed to.

The little one stared up at me, suddenly angelic. "Can we watch television, Miss . . .?"

"Alison."

"Alison, can we watch television?"

"I'm hungry," another piped up.

"I know August has movies!"

"August, can we watch some of your movies?"

Nary a peep came from behind that door.

I eyed them warily. Could I trust them to sit quietly in front of the television while I ran to get snacks?

More to the point, if I didn't let them watch television, what was I going to do? I had no blueprint for entertaining three thuggish little boys. I was a hostage to them, and they knew it.

"All right," I said. "Sit down and I'll put a movie in for you. What would you like to watch?"

"*Jurassic Park!*"

"In your dreams," I said. "Try something Disney."

"That's baby movies!"

I pulled out a copy of *Sinbad.* August had confided to me that she didn't like that one anyway.

"That's the worst movie ever!"

"Yeah!"

"Would you like me to take you down to the living room so you can sit with the grown-ups and not say another word?"

Three heads hung down.

I put the DVD in the player and stepped away. "I'll be right back," I said.

Of course it was a mistake. *Of course.* Any fool could see that. But at that moment, I wasn't just any old fool, I was the grand Pooh-Bah of fools. And I was in way over my head.

By the time I got back with a tray of boxed juices and cookies, the scene was horrifying. August was standing on top of the entertainment center—how had they gotten her up there?—with her eyes squeezed closed and her hands over her ears. She was screaming. The other kids were jeering at her and pelting her with Fritos. Where had the Fritos come from? The floor was covered with them, as if there had been a corn chip blizzard.

"*Outside!*" I don't know where the angry yowl came from, but once it was out of my mouth it made perfect sense. These just weren't indoor children.

When they turned to me I pointed toward the door. "Down

the back stairs and out to the yard. You can play football but *stay away from the pool.* Now!"

With supremely happy grins on all of their faces, the three boys scooped up the football and then scooted by me, grinding Fritos dust into the carpet with their Nikes. I heard them clattering down the back stairs. Though how they could clatter when the stairs were carpeted was beyond my comprehension.

August was red-faced and barely hanging on to the tears standing in her eyes. "I hate Arthur!"

Just Arthur? I was amazed. I hadn't been able to differentiate a single personality. They just seemed like one despicable mass of bullying to me. But maybe when you were a kid yourself the differences stood out clearer. Like the way fish could tell each other apart.

I lifted her off the entertainment center and handed her a box of juice. She looked so beaten, I nearly cried for her. These were the parts of childhood you forgot about . . . if you were lucky. The icky parts. "Go on in your room and try to take a nap."

"Okay," she said in a quavery hiccupy voice. She slammed her door behind her.

No doubt there was some serious post-traumatic stress going on in there.

Unfortunately for me, I was still in the middle of the battle.

I went down the back way and out the door. The boys were tearing across the yard. Still, they seemed slightly less horrifying in the great outdoors than they had inside. Their destructive power seemed diluted by more space, and they were just high-spirited kids. It was the kind of scene that would bring a smile to your face if you were driving by a park and saw a bunch of little boys frolicking. Two of them had gotten their hands on badminton rackets, and now they were running around swinging them at each other.

I fell into a lawn chair and sucked down a box of juice myself, waiting for my heartbeat to slow and my anger to die down.

Through the gate, I looked out and saw a large Lexus SUV in the drive. It took me a moment of staring at it to realize what it was that was worrisome. That first night when I had seen Pepper drive off in the red Land Rover . . . she had told me that was Phaedra's car. But obviously it wasn't. Unless Phaedra had more than one vehicle at her disposal. Which wasn't unlikely, really.

A few seconds later, I heard the sound of heels against the deck. I looked up and saw Phaedra coming toward me. It was undoubtedly her, even though I hadn't seen her in a decade. She had the same tawny skin, the same sharp cheekbones. Her hair was still straight and fine and hung down long, although the brown was now streaked with a dark coppery red. She was a knockout. You would never think this woman capable of having given birth to the three monsters in the yard. She wore a flippy flirty skirt that showed off toned legs, and her ropy arms jutted out from her bright orange sleeveless blouse.

"Hey there, BP girl!" she said, swirling a mixed drink of some kind in her hand.

I guess her early drinking rule had fallen by the wayside.

I jumped up. "Hey!" More air hugs.

"Look at you!" she said, giving me an up-and-down stare.

Here is where I felt self-conscious. I was not overweight, exactly, but neither was I fashionably slim. I was soft and unmuscled. I wore a pair of jean shorts and a Hawaiian shirt—a goofy outfit, but practical and a good spill-hider. My sandals were workmanlike slides, unlike the slim high things she perched on.

I immediately envied her look. Her outfit.

Occasionally I wished one of my friends would turn me in to that awful *What Not to Wear* show, so I could get the five thousand for new duds. Yes, they would make you look like a frumpy fool, but for a shopping spree maybe it would be worth the humiliation.

So far my friends hadn't gone to bat for me, obviously. Maybe I needed to trade them all in for a more sadistic set.

"I can't believe it's you," Phaedra said. "Look at you!"

I wished she would stop looking at me, actually. "How have you been, Phaedra?"

"Not so bad. I was up and down there for a while, but who

hasn't been?" *In your case, more up than down, obviously*, her eyes said. She grinned.

"Right."

"I *can't believe* you're working for Peps."

"Me neither."

"She says you're a whiz—just great with August."

As if Pepper would know. Pepper was usually home for about an hour or two a day. She went out every night. "August is a sweetheart."

Phaedra rolled her eyes. "Isn't that the truth!" She cast a glance at her offspring, who were letting out howls as they tackled one another. "They never stop, do they?"

"They're very high-spirited," I replied diplomatically.

"You should try living with them. It's a wonder I ever found a man who would take me on with those three little hooligans in the bargain. Luckily, I found somebody rolling in money, so he could afford to soundproof half the house." She smiled. "Pepper's mixing drinks inside. I'll bet you could have one if you asked."

Her slightly condescending tone made me bristle. "I'd better not. I'm on duty."

"Oh, that's right."

"Do you have a nanny?" I asked.

She shook her head. "I used to, but after the divorce, I decided I wanted to take a more hands-on approach. Actually, the most incredible thing happened to me. When I went to my therapist for the first time, she asked me to think of five words to define myself, and the first thing that came to me was *mom*. I burst into tears right on the spot! I realized that nurturing was integral to my personality, and I had been denying myself. Depriving myself of my own children."

Would that we all could have been deprived of the little monsters.

"They're only this age for such a short time, you know?" she remarked.

I nodded. *Thank God.*

"Of course, girls are easier." She shook her head ruefully. "Peps is such a lucky bitch, but try telling her that."

Pepper didn't think she was lucky? I felt myself straining toward Phaedra, wanting dirt. Don't ask me how I managed to hold my tongue.

"Well, I guess nobody appreciates what they have, do they?" she asked me, her dark brows arching slightly. In the sunlight it appeared that even her brows had copper highlights. I wouldn't have put it past her.

"I guess not," I agreed.

"Just when she was going out of her mind after the whole Marisol episode, *you* walked in."

I stared at her. Something told me this was leading somewhere. What was the *Marisol episode*? I had noticed that Marta seemed to go rigid every time mention was made of my predecessor; I guessed they had had a falling out or something. But now I wondered if Marisol had been fired.

"Poor Peps! She was all ready to look a gift horse in the mouth."

"Really," I said.

"Well, *you know*. I guess it was sort of awkward for you both. What with Spence and all."

Bingo. I smiled. "When I answered the ad, I had no idea who the Smiths were," I confided.

Phaedra cackled. "I figured! Peps was so freaked out. She wasn't sure."

Freaked out? This was news. "I didn't even know that Spence and Pepper had gotten married."

"God, you really have been out of the loop, haven't you? Well! That would have given Peps some peace of mind to know you were so completely in the dark. She wasn't sure."

So Pepper was worried I had spun some kind of weird revenge fantasy? That I had some Machiavellian plan to undermine her marriage? "Ten years is a long time. I hadn't really been keeping up at all."

"Exactly what I told her. And after ten years—well, what were the chances that you were some kind of psycho coming back to snatch Spence from her?"

"Right," I said.

She laughed. "You can thank me for your job, FYI. I don't

know if she ever would have screwed up to go visit you that night if I hadn't intervened."

I gaped at her.

"That's Peps. Ever vigilant." She took a step forward. "Especially when it comes to that marriage of hers. You know how that goes—when the boat leaks, you better be handy with a bucket. You gotta bail out or bail, as my lawyer used to say."

Pepper's marriage was leaking? I practically turned red in the face with all my pent-up curiosity. Which of course was exactly what Phaedra wanted.

Phaedra was the kind of friend who actually *would* turn someone in to *What Not to Wear.*

She wagged a long red fingernail at me. "You were almost bailed overboard, sugar bun. I told her to see reason."

"What did you advise?"

She shrugged. "Nothing specific. I just asked her what she was so afraid of." She gave me another once-over. "I guess when Peps calmed down once she looked at the situation squarely and realized she was safe."

The implication being that it was unlikely that I would ever be a threat to any marriage.

It would have been very bad form to appear stung, to acknowledge that I had just been insulted. Instead I tried to dig for more info. "I sure like your Lexus."

She rolled her eyes. "You can have it! I'm sick to death of the pokey old thing. I want something snappy."

"Like a Range Rover?" I asked.

She looked at me as if I were crazy. "Hell, no. Like a flashy Saab convertible." Her head snapped around, toward the boys. "*What the hell are you doing over there?* Are you playing badminton with a frog?"

I pivoted and gasped. Sure enough, some poor creature was airborne, headed for a racket. My eyes squeezed shut. I couldn't watch.

"*Arthur!*" she bellowed. "You hit that frog and I swear you'll never see your PlayStation again! *Ever!*"

Arthur dropped his racket, and the other two boys, heeding the warning, went innocently limp. Pepper appeared on the patio, her cell phone attached to her ear but obviously too curious to see what the ruckus was about to stay away. Somewhere in the yard, a very nervous frog hopped to safety.

"Come on, boys. We're going home!" Phaedra turned to me, smiling sweetly. "It was *so* good to see you, Al."

"Good to see you, Phaedra," I said.

"I can't wait for Spence to get back!" she added, laughing. "Who you calling, Peps? The boyfriend?"

Pepper snapped her phone closed, and glared playfully at Phaedra. Then they laughed and went inside.

I stared after them, my breath coming in heaves. How do you like that? All Phaedra's talk about Pepper being vigilant about her marriage. And yet Pepper was cheating on Spence with a Range Rover.

Chapter 7

"So what do you think of Pepper?" I asked Spence after our first rehearsal of *Picnic*. "Wasn't she as awful as I said?"

He looked noncommittal, but then he wasn't the kind of guy who was into trashing people. Which was admirable. Irritating, but admirable.

"I think she might be a little shy."

"Shy!" I nearly coughed up a bite of cheeseburger. "*Sly*, I believe might be a more accurate description. Did you hear her cozying up to Frau Crouch?" I did my best simpering impression of Pepper. " '*Miss Crouch, how on earth am I going to make an audience believe* I'm *the prettiest girl in town?*' She wasn't just fishing for compliments, she was reeling in marlins. How pathetic was that?"

"She was just being modest."

I snorted. "Please! Crouch told me point blank the girl *begged* her for the part . . . that she has some sort of Kim Novak complex."

"She didn't say that," Spence said.

"Okay, not in so many words," I allowed. "But she did wheedle her way into the production by cozying up to Crouch. And now she puts on this humble act. It's sickening."

"She's just nervous."

"Of course! She'd have to be brain dead not to be. She can't act her way out of a paper bag. And of course, she's not *that* pretty. I mean, c'mon. Didn't I tell you that she was going to show up in that ghastly getup? She always looks like some eighties sitcom throwback."

Spence said nothing. Just thoughtfully dipped a french fry in some ketchup.

I sucked on my chocolate shake. "Not that I'm jealous of her or anything."

"No need for you to be," he said.

I leveled an apologetic stare at him. "I feel so bad for getting you into this."

"Don't be. I volunteered."

"What are we going to do about that hair of hers?" I muttered aloud. "Did you see the way she keeps flipping it over one shoulder and then another? Like a shampoo commercial. I wouldn't care if she fell on her face, of course, except I have to be up there on that stage with her."

"Maybe once we get our lines memorized . . ." Spence said.

Poor guy, I thought. *Trying to be so brave.* "She had no business auditioning. I don't know if you caught it, but Pepper has completely rewritten history. '*Miss Crouch just begged me. Said she'd had me in mind for Madge all along.*' I wish I had a tape recording of what Crouch told me so I could expose her publicly."

Of course I had not told Spence of Pepper's multiple viewings of Antigone, or that she thought he was the reincarnation of William Holden. No sense giving him a swelled head.

"You believe Ms. Crouch?"

"What?" I asked. "Of course."

"But you hate her."

"I don't hate her."

"You complain about her all the time."

There was no arguing with that. "Okay, but why would she have lied to me?"

"To make you feel better for not getting the lead part."

I scowled. "I'd rather play Mrs. Potts any day."

Okay, that was major sour grapes, even though I was sort of getting into the little old lady thing. I wanted my Helen Potts to be feisty, but with a touch of pathos. I sort of saw her now as the conscience of the play. I envisioned people making comparisons between me and Jessica Tandy, which, natch, wasn't as good as being compared to, oh, Michelle Pfeiffer or somebody like that. Anyone under the age of ninety, say.

Also, I was facing a makeup challenge, which was fun, but worrisome. To tell you the truth, I was beginning to think theater was just a big pain in the ass. A lot of work and stress for very little payoff. I was definitely going to switch my major in college to something like English or history, where you weren't always being badgered by nutty drama teachers and staying up nights worrying about lighting gels.

Spence raised his brows at me, obviously unconvinced by my Mrs. Potts proclamation. But then he shook his head. "Yeah, I guess you really wouldn't have made a good Madge."

I was a little offended by this. "What do you mean?"

"Nothing." He shrugged. "Just that you don't care about . . . how you look."

I really didn't have an argumentative edge here. No one would have called me a fashion plate. At that moment, I was still wearing my plaid school skirt, only with an entirely different and unmatching red plaid shirt over it. I had recently cut my dyed raven black hair into Bettie Paige bangs, which seemed edgy at the time but didn't quite work for me. I just didn't have the bone structure to handle all those right angles.

"But Pepper's got that sort of soft, feminine look about her." Spence's eyes went a little dopey when he said this, which made my throat hitch. Involuntarily, I fingered the locket I wore around my neck. "She's got an unself-conscious grace."

All I could think to say to that was, "Huh?"

He seemed to snap to a little. "I mean, she's just what Madge should be. A normal, pretty teenager."

"A yawn, you mean." I could not believe this. He was actually talking as if he *liked* her. But that was crazy. Pepper was so totally the opposite of what I was. . . . Spence couldn't be interested in her. If he was, why on earth would he have ever asked *me* out?

I tried not to let the questions get to me. What did any of this matter, anyway? What Spence and I had was just one of these high school things, I told myself. Next year I would be in Oregon and Spence would be in Tennessee.

But when I had to sit in the audience during a rehearsal while Spence and Pepper kissed onstage, it felt as if my whole body clenched into a fist. I sank into a C shape and watched the proceedings, praying that I didn't look as red-faced as I felt. It wasn't just the jealousy that got to me, either. When a Red Cross person lectured to our health class during sophomore year, she said that, when you had a heart attack, it felt as if an elephant were sitting on your chest. At the time, the comparison caused me to burst forth with a blast of inappropriate laughter. But honestly. How are people supposed to relate to that description? How many people have had an elephant sit on them?

As I watched Pepper and Spence, I wasn't having a heart attack, but there was an elephant sitting on my chest. Maybe they should have told us that having a heart attack felt just like losing a person you didn't realize you were in love with until it was too late.

Or was it too late?

The next morning, I knocked on our school guidance counselor's door. Miss Bowes had been responsible for getting three generations of BP girls into college, and she looked it. Her crisp suits and Nancy Reagan hair couldn't hide the weary bags under her eyes, or mask her irritation when she peered through her bifocals and saw me nervously approaching her desk. "Is there something I can help you with, Alison?"

"I want to see about applying for late admission."

If I had asked her to put a camel through the eye of a needle, she couldn't have been any more exasperated. Her hands plunked down on her bony hips. "Good heavens! I thought we had you squared away with Reed. Has something happened? Do you need to stay closer to home?"

"Not really. I just decided I want to go to Vanderbilt."

"Vanderbilt," she said flatly. "You're kidding."

"I think it would be a good choice for me. I'm sorry I didn't think of it before, but there has to be some way to beg my way in, don't you think?"

She sank down into her chair. "What are they doing at Vanderbilt these days, offering cash gifts to shilly-shallying seniors?"

I had no idea what she was talking about. And in any case, she could hardly accuse me of shilly-shallying. "I'm not a slacker, Miss Bowes. I got all my applications in on time," I reminded her.

"Yes, to every college, apparently, except the one you now swear you want to go to. Any points you want from me for punctuality, Alison, have been lost to carelessness and indecision."

This was what exasperated me about school. These nut-job administrative types had a cow whenever I wanted to do something just a little bit out of the ordinary. They were always having fits about paperwork, about getting all the blanks filled in and everything stamped on time, so they could file me away and forget about me. Surely when it was my life, my happiness, and my future at stake, I could be forgiven for being a little rattled. "I just . . . changed my mind."

"You and how many others!"

I blinked at her. "Excuse me?"

"Pepper McClintock was in here just two days ago, asking me to get her into Vanderbilt."

August needed a swimsuit. Actually, she had a swimsuit—a sort of retro blue and pink striped one-piece with daisies appliqued on it. It was drop to your knees cute, but August couldn't stand the thing. She practically went into hysterics every time I took it out of the drawer.

It wasn't the suit. I knew enough about psychology to figure that out. It was swimming that terrified her. She was one of those kids who spent the entire swimming lesson weeping at the side of the pool rather than stick one little toe in that water. And I was the one who was bearing the brunt of her hysterics, because Pepper had announced to me that "our project" for the summer was to teach August to swim. So I was to take her to swimming lessons.

Which was actually more like taking her to a thirty-minute scream-therapy session.

I used every trick I could think of to get her into that water. I tried reason, reminding her that the swimming pool was just a big bathtub, and she didn't mind taking baths, did she? She shouted at me that the water was green here, and that she didn't want green stuff on her face.

I cajoled and bribed. I offered gifts untold and unlimited trips to her favorite ice-cream store.

No dice.

The shame tactic didn't work, either. August didn't give a damn whether everyone at the pool was staring at her, or thought she was a baby, or considered her a rank coward. When it came to not getting her face wet, she was determined to go it alone, to be a rugged individualist.

What's more, the problem of the swimming lessons was causing our relationship—already tenuous at best—to deteriorate. After the third try at taking her to the pool, she announced that she hated me and wanted me to go home. (Home, I guess, meant somewhere farther away from her than the garage apartment.)

When we got back to the house that afternoon, she went running straight to Pepper, weeping. Pepper was in her dressing room in front of a cosmetics-laden table, trying to style her just-washed hair.

She went out every night.

Not that I was bitter or anything. Only she couldn't have been going out with girlfriends *all* the time. Like Phaedra, I also couldn't wait for Spence to get back. I couldn't believe she gallivanted around town like this all the time. What kind of marriage was this?

None of your business, I was constantly having to tell myself.

Pepper, as soon as she had pried August away from her silk shorts outfit, looked up at me with startled blue eyes. "Are you still having problems?"

"Oh, just a little . . ."

"I hate Alson!" August wailed, throwing herself at her mother. The wetness of her cheeks in contrast to the dryness of her hair and cover-up made me feel like an utter failure.

"Why don't you go with Alison to your room now, honey," Pepper said, patting August dismissively on the shoulder. "Mommy has to go visit with friends. You wouldn't want to make me late, would you?"

"I hate Alson!"

Pepper looked at me, laughing and rolling her eyes. *Kids say the darnedest things!*

I took August's hand and dragged her mid-tantrum over to her suite. I did everything I knew how to calm her—I let her change into her favorite clothes (jean shorts and a Veggie Tales T-shirt her mother despised), sat her on her couch with a Martinelli's sparkling grape juice and cheddar goldfish, and popped in a movie. *The Little Mermaid.* There seemed to be no limit to the number of times she could watch the damn thing.

August accepted my help without acknowledging me in any way.

I sat in my chair, trying not to feel resentful. I knew August wasn't yet four and didn't understand words like *hate.* I knew I was supposed to be her nanny, not her best buddy. I knew it wasn't Pepper's responsibility to make my life any easier.

But give me a break. Would it have killed her to take my side? Maybe tried to explain again to August why she needed to learn to swim?

I was so tired. I still wasn't sleeping, only now I was being awakened at seven in the morning by the intercom. Day by day, I was fraying, falling apart.

I must have dozed off in my chair, because the next thing I knew I looked up and August was gone. That crab was back on screen. I jumped up and looked in the bathroom. No sign of August. Damn.

I slipped my feet into sandals and skidded downstairs. "Have you seen August?" I asked Marta.

She looked at me. "What happened? You fall asleep again?"

"I just looked away for a second . . ." But I'm sure my red-stained cheeks gave me away.

She went on dusting the mantel. "She hasn't been down here."

I was halfway up the staircase again when I met Pepper on

the way down. She was all dolled up, with Ungaro perfume wafting ahead of her. "Oh, there you are!" she said. "I was just talking to August."

"I just looked away for a second . . ."

Ignoring my babbling, she fiddled with something in her purse and brought out a card. A MasterCard. "August wants a new swimsuit. You can take her shopping this afternoon. There's a store in Highland Park Village I like, or go to North Park if you have trouble."

I was trying hard not to gape. A new swimsuit? The one she owned now had never touched chlorine.

"She wants a green suit, preferably with a mermaid motif."

She did? This was news to me. For some reason, it always shocked me when Pepper knew things about her daughter that I didn't.

"She swears that if she's a mermaid she won't be afraid of the water," Pepper explained.

Uh-huh.

"I think it's so cute that she wants to be a little mermaid, don't you?"

"Uh-huh." I looked down at the card she had given me. "Won't there be a problem . . . maybe with the signature . . . ?"

"Don't worry about it," she told me. "I'm sure they won't make a fuss over it."

By the time August and I set out on our shopping expedition, it was two o'clock and blistering hot outside. Even though the Hummer had been stowed away in the dark garage, it was stifling in there. August immediately began to whine. I turned on the air full blast, which immediately made me feel clammy and feverish.

The store in Highland Park Village, once I had found it and squeezed into a parking space and a half, didn't have anything mermaidish. I tried to cajole August into trying on a yellow suit.

"Green!" she shouted at me.

"August, please . . ."

She looked at me. "I'm not August!"

"*Ariel*, then," I said, taking a shot in the dark. It didn't work. She wandered off, and when I followed her and took her hand, she started yelling at me. "You're not my mommy! You're not my mommy!"

God only knows what had brought that on.

As I tugged her toward the door, the saleslady looked at *me* as if I were some kind of a nut, and very possibly a kidnapper. "I'm the nanny," I mouthed as I pushed through the door.

But I have to say she didn't look convinced. I would spend the rest of the afternoon checking my rearview for police cruisers.

The Hummer, which now had been sitting in the sun for twenty minutes, felt like a giant kiln on the way to the mall. August's face was red and her hair stuck to her temples in wet hanks. "I want ice cream," she said.

"Maybe after we've bought your suit . . ."

Not the thing to say. She started crying, and rather than argue, I turned up the radio to try to drown her out. The oldies station was playing the tag end of "Gypsies, Tramps, and Thieves." "Listen, Ariel! This is what they played on the radio when I was your age!"

No response.

Next came David Lee Roth singing "Pretty Woman," which offended me on so many levels, I felt my face going as red as August's. First, the Roy Orbison version was better in every way. For another thing, this was hardly an *oldie*. It had been playing while I was in junior high school! It was the music of *my* life, not some old geezer's. Were the airwaves of our country being taken over by ten-year-old program managers?

I was about to punch the button to snap the radio off, when I looked back and saw that August was pumping her legs in time to the beat and humming along. Enjoying herself. Damn. She would probably grow up thinking this was a classic. I shuddered.

At the mall I managed to park near a spindly parking lot tree. I got out the stroller and was trying to snap the contraption open when August started whining again. "I wanna walk!"

I looked at her doubtfully. "This is a mall. It's huge."

"Walk!"

I was such a pushover. "Okay, hold my hand."

For hours we crawled from store to store, stalking the elusive green bathing suit. August had very specific ideas of what was green. She didn't want lime green, or anything verging on aqua, or a deep forest green. She wanted eye-popping fish green. Preferably, she informed me, with something shiny on it.

The mall wasn't crowded, but when you're walking with a toddler, it feels as if the whole world is rushing around you in a blur while you pick your way through groups of teenagers and around brusque businesswomen bleating into cell phones. August would wear herself out, whereupon I would carry her until she started thrashing impatiently. She hated being treated like a baby.

I hated being treated like a punching bag. I should have brought the stroller, of course. My first mistake.

We finally wound up in a store I of course had never in my life been in. It was named Precious Little Things . . . which was apt if you were approaching the title from a price-tag angle. Sticker shock city.

And what did August like in this store?

Everything.

She who had been my pint-sized naysayer all afternoon, my diminutive companion from the land of *Nyet*, was now primed for a retail bender. When she eyed a stuffed dalmatian dog near the entrance she broke away from my hand, and I don't think I ever truly got her under control again. She wanted to try on white flared jeans and taffeta party dresses, she wanted a backpack shaped like a swan and made with real feathers (that somehow made me think of Bjork), and she wanted a pair of teal cowboy boots. I was ready to tug her out of there before we both went insane, when suddenly we both sighted our Holy Grail: a green bathing suit with shiny sequin rows shaped to resemble fish scales.

August's eyes flew open and her arm jutted out in a full-throttle point. "It's an Ariel suit!"

It was awfully close, I had to admit. It was a two-piece,

which I wasn't sure Pepper would be wild about, but the top wasn't so much a bikini top as a sequined sports bra. And it came with accessories! A sequined swim cap that Esther Williams would have been proud to wear, water wings, and little green swim fins.

Anyway, it didn't matter what I thought. August was enraptured. Once the cap was on her head, she refused to take it off. Even checking out, I had to lift her up so that the clerk could scan the price tag dangling Minnie Pearl–style off August's scalp. I was so relieved, I forgot to worry as I handed over the MasterCard.

"Can we get ice cream now?" August asked, already on to her next objective.

"Sure." It felt so good to have this ordeal over with. Maybe the right outfit really would persuade this cat to get into the water. At any rate, she wasn't screaming that she hated me. That in itself felt like a triumph.

No wonder so many parents tried to buy their kids' love. It worked.

"What flavor are you going to get?" I asked her.

"Banana mousse supreme!"

At first I wasn't sure I had heard her right. This was no flavor I had ever heard of. Yet she seemed perfectly sure about the wording. "Where—?"

The clerk interrupted me. "Ma'am?"

I popped to attention and smiled at her. "Oh, yes?"

"Your card . . ."

"Do you need to see my license?" I swallowed back panic. God, what was I going to do in case she wanted ID? Would they let me forge Pepper's name anyway?

"No, we don't. But you might want to try another card? This one has been refused."

My jaw dropped. This was one worry, oddly enough, that hadn't crossed my mind. "Refused!"

"Yes ma'am. I'm sorry."

Naturally I was accustomed to having cards refused, but those were *my* cards, not cards I had borrowed from rich people. I felt as if some kind of cosmic joke were being played on me.

The clerk waited expectantly for me to pull out another credit card.

August was waiting, too, staring at me bug-eyed in her sequined swim cap. She couldn't have known what was transpiring, but she obviously knew that her purchase was hanging in the balance. No way was I going to be able to tell her that she couldn't have that bathing suit.

The cost of the suit, plus the cap, waterwings, and flippers, was $110.79. I knew pulling out my own credit card would bring nothing but another refusal. Out came my checkbook, so rubber laden it could have doubled as a basketball. I smiled at the clerk as I wrote out the check. Luckily, she didn't seem to notice that the name on the check was different from the one on the credit card she'd just handed back to me. She took my license information, but didn't put my number through to Check-rite. Thank God for small favors.

On the other hand, I was now stuck for $110.79. My bank account hadn't had that much money in it in months.

"What's the matter, Alson?" August asked as I carried her out of the store.

"Nothing."

"I want ice cream."

"Oh. Right." I was already worried about that check. "Where is that place?"

It turned out the ice cream store was directly below us, but August's sense of direction wasn't fully developed, so we wandered down practically every massive mall artery before I finally tracked it down. August insisted she wanted a double cone of banana mousse supreme, which seemed like a tall order for a person whose body mass seemed smaller than some cats I'd met in my time. On the other hand, who was I to argue? In times of stress, I could polish off a pint of cherry Garcia in one sitting, no problem.

When we got back out to the parking lot, I regretted not trolling for a better position while parking. Plus I had left the mall by the wrong door, so it was quite a hike through the broiling sun to get to the car. Waves of heat rose from the pavement, and the air choked you with that hot asphalt and exhaust smell. Sweat trickled down my back.

August seemed heavier than she had before, and I had to hitch her up on my hip several times.

"Alson?" she moaned when we were halfway to the Hummer.

"Yes?" I asked, distracted. My mind was still fixed on that check.

"I feel sick."

She was sort of damp looking, and greenish. "Are you fevery sick?"

"I feel all throw-uppy."

My footsteps sped up considerably. "We'll get you right home."

"Alson?'

I was practically running. "Yes?"

Her response was a stream of vomit. What appeared to be a day's worth of food was immediately transferred from her innards to my shirt. It was all I could do not to drop her like a hot potato. I barely managed to set her down before I started hopping around and flapping my shirt. I had one measly Wet One in my purse, but it was like trying to clean up the Exxon Valdez oil spill with a washrag.

August was crying. I took her hand and hurried her to the car. "We'll be home soon, sweetie."

She hiccuped, causing me another moment of fright.

I was in danger of erupting myself; I had to keep gulping to stop myself from doing my own Linda Blair–type turn. Nothing this revolting had ever happened to me. In the hot car, I stank of regurgitated banana.

Speed limits be damned. I gunned it all the way home.

August was still whimpering in the backseat; she grew especially agitated as I pulled onto her street. In fact, she began hopping up and down in her car seat. I was wary now of her making any sudden jerky movements.

"Daddy! Daddy! Daddy!"

"Your daddy is in Taiwan." Or Hong Kong. Pepper never seemed clear on that.

She never seemed to care, either.

"Daddy!"

I screeched into the driveway and pulled into the garage. Sure enough, there was a car that hadn't been there before. A Porsche.

Oh, damn.

"Daddy!" she screeched impatiently.

I jumped out of the car and made short work of getting August out, too. Was there any way to sneak her up the back way, where no one would see us? I wasn't what I would consider overly vain; still, is there a person alive who would opt to meet their high school boyfriend while sporting a gallon of vomit on her chest?

I was too late, though. As I was hustling August toward the house, Spence appeared near the garage. August ran toward him and flung herself at him in a kind of filial ecstasy. "Daddy! You're home!"

"Augie!" he cried joyfully.

He bent down and gave her a long hug, then swung her up so that she was perched high on his hip. After a few moments, his nose twitched, as if he had picked up a putrid smell.

That would be me.

He turned to me and his mouth broke into a broad, devastating smile. "Alison!"

"Hi, Spence," I replied.

Not so slowly or subtly, that big beaming grin of his faded and his gaze trailed down to my chest . . . and not in an admiring way. My T-shirt was sticking to me. "My God!" he exclaimed in disgust. "What's happened to you?"

Chapter 8

I had begun to think of Spence as just an occasional talking point, not really part of the household. Yet here he was, in the flesh, and damn it if he didn't look good. Damn good.

Damn.

I had thought so often of the time I had told Spence he looked like John Cusack, which I had known at the time was an exaggeration, that I had actually begun to think he *did* look like John Cusack. But he didn't! His face was more angular; it almost did a Dick Tracy right angle at his jaw. How had I forgotten that?

Or maybe he had just changed. Was that possible? Could a person become more angular? He had also lost that adolescent stoop to his shoulders, which made him appear taller, more solid. And like a lot of rich guys, he had that air of being buffed and polished. It didn't hurt that he was in a dark gray suit that was snappy as hell. It didn't so much as hint at having just endured a plane ride. With it he wore a midnight blue tie over a blue shirt, *not* something old Spence would have done, so he had obviously received some fashion counseling in the past decade. Usually only Europeans looked this good. He could have done a photo spread for *Esquire* right then and there.

And there I stood, in shorts, sweaty, with regurgitated ice cream plastering down my front. "August had a little too much ice cream and excitement," I explained, trying to get away, or at least get downwind.

August had undergone a complete recovery. The kid was glowing. She had Spence in a headlock, and even while we spoke peppered him with questions. "Did you miss me, Daddy?" she asked. "Did you bring me anything?"

"What do you think?" he asked her back, kissing her on her sweaty temple, where a lock of blond hair peeked out from under green sequins. Then he smiled at me. "If you want to go change, I can haul the monkey into the house."

Picking up on the reference to herself in that sentence, August squealed with delight. "I'm not a monkey!"

"Who says?" he asked, swinging her up on his shoulders.

I have to admit, seeing him with his adorable daughter in his arms caused a tug in my chest. Something about grown men being at the mercy of little kids can do that to you, if you don't watch out. I was normally not one to be swayed by Hallmark moments, but this one caught me off guard.

I was turning to go, but he stopped me. "You'll come back over when you're done, won't you?" he asked. "In fact, come to dinner with us. I'm dying to catch up."

I hesitated. Should I accept a dinner invitation his first night back? I wasn't quite sure it would be appropriate. He probably needed some downtime. Family time.

There would also inevitably be awkwardness over the fact that he was the employer and I was the employee.

Oh, get over yourself. What was I supposed to do? Hide in the shadows? Play Jane Eyre for the rest of my life and keep my head bowed as I sat inconspicuously in poorly lit corners?

"Are you sure you wouldn't like some low-key time at home now?" I asked.

"This will be low-key." He added, "I wouldn't have asked you if I didn't mean it."

"All right." It was practically August's dinnertime now, though I worried over whether she should actually eat anything. *Precisely why you should go to dinner with the family*, I told myself. *To look after August.* That was all the rationalization I needed. "I'll be back over in a flash."

"Good!" He sent me a friendly wink.

That simple little gesture, that wink, seemed to put jet packs in the heels of my sandals. It lifted me up. For the first time in days, I felt completely awake. Almost hyperalert. I flew up the stairs to my apartment, full of thoughts of trying to get myself cleaned up. I could use that new expensive soap Pepper had given me. And what was I going to wear?

It wasn't until I was standing in the shower being pummeled by water that a little voice of reality squeaked in my ear. *Cool your jets, Alison. It's just dinner. With the guy you work for.*

Who just happened to be the guy I used to be crazy about.

We waited for Pepper. And waited.

While we lingered, expecting her to pop up at any moment, I served sparkling apple juice to Spence and August by the pool. August ran around in her sequined swim cap, repeatedly telling her father she was a mermaid. Only now she was also wearing the little Chinese outfit he'd brought back for her, a silk pajama suit embroidered in pink and green with a Mandarin collar. She absolutely adored it.

The sequined swim cap–Mandarin ensemble made me laugh. "It's *Dangerous When Wet* meets *The Good Earth.*"

Spence laughed, too. "She definitely gets her flair for fashion from her mom. And I mean that in a positive sense."

"No way," I said. "Look at you—Mr. *GQ.*"

His gaze met mine, and I realized that was probably not a good thing to say. I mean, it would have been okay, except that I really did think he was hot. Anyone would have. Luckily, I could hide the flush creeping across my face by focusing on August.

She romped around the backyard, telling us to watch her roll over, swing, and go down her slide. We sat in the shade of the porch and indulged her and talked between stunts. There was so much we didn't know about each other now. And yet we parried, not quite wanting to come right out and ask probing questions.

"What a cool watch!" I said, looking over at the gold standing out on his tanned wrist. "It looks like an antique."

"It was my granddad's. He willed it to me when he died."

"I'm so sorry."

His smile faded. "It's been a while now. How are your parents?"

"Great!" I said automatically. Then I backtracked. "Well, divorced."

"Oh."

"But that was years ago," I said, feeling foolish for swapping misfortunes with him. "Around the time my dad got out of his business."

"I heard about that."

There was a pause in the conversation, as there always was when the subject of going broke came up. As if people feel the need to mourn all that lost money with a moment of silence. "Dad lives in East Texas now. He remarried."

"And your mom?"

My mom's the type of person who calls you in the middle of the night to tell you she's misplaced her husband. I hadn't heard from my mom since that phone call. The one time I had tried to track her down, the man at the desk at the Ritz said she'd checked out. "Oh! She's the same, only more of a jet-setter than she used to be."

"She was always a character."

"Mm!" Even after all those years, it was hard for me to cut her any slack. I smiled stiffly. "She's something, all right. How about some crackers?"

I ran and got us something to eat while we waited to go out to eat. It was almost seven now. Much longer on an empty stomach, and August was going to be fussy. She might turn fussy anyway, just because it was getting late.

"Pepper didn't say where she was going to be, I suppose," Spence said when I came back out, almost as if he knew the answer.

"No, she didn't."

He looked lost in thought as he munched on a Triscuit. Did he suspect anything? I felt an almost instinctive urge to cover for Pepper. Don't ask me why. It was that troubled expression on his face, combined with that natural impulse to make excuses for someone who was screwing up.

And what did I know about Pepper's personal life, when it came right down to it? Maybe I had pieced it together all wrong. I was just going on hunches and innuendo from Phaedra . . . hardly a reliable source.

"She's probably out with Phaedra," I went on. "They hang out together a lot."

He rolled his eyes. "Tell me about it!"

Apparently I'd touched on a sore spot. "Phaedra's looking good."

"Why shouldn't she?" he asked. "She doesn't do anything."

O-kay. Don't talk about Phaedra.

"Of course Pepper's the one who looks *really* great," I piped up. "I couldn't believe it when I saw her."

Spence downed the last of his apple juice as though it were a whiskey. Then he sent me a long assessing look. "You're the one who surprised me."

I never expected you to go to flab, I half expected him to say.

He didn't, though, bless his heart. "I thought your hair was black."

Okay, it was not an outrageous compliment. It wasn't, "You're looking better than ever." "I dyed it black in high school," I confessed.

"Really? I had no idea."

"You thought raven black was natural?"

"Yeah, why not? Raven's a hair color, isn't it?"

"To Clairol, maybe."

"But some poet referred to raven-black locks, too." His brow creased. "Burns, right?"

"I can't remember," I replied. "But I'm impressed that you do."

He grinned. "Okay, then it was definitely Burns."

August was beginning to fade. "I'm hungry!"

He turned to his daughter. "Tell you what, Augie." I noticed she didn't make him guess who she was. "We're going to order a pizza. What do you say to that?"

"Yay!" August did a jumping-up-and-down dance. "Pepperoni! Pepperoni!"

"Would that be okay with you?"

The question startled me. After just two weeks of living around Pepper, I had forgotten what it was like to have my opinion consulted. In fact, I had just assumed that whenever someone said "we" were going to do such-and-so, it really meant that *I* would do it. I had fully expected to be the one calling in the pizza order. Yet Spence had already pulled a cell phone out of a hat and was headed for the house, I assumed to look for a phone book.

When he reached the door, he turned back to me. "It looks pretty."

I met his eyes guiltily. I had been checking out his butt. (*Nice.*) "I beg your pardon?"

"Your hair. It's prettier now."

"Oh!" I straightened bolt upright in my metal patio chair. "Thank you . . ."

He was already gone again.

I tried to appear calm as I watched August. She had collapsed on her back on the grass, and was drawing circles in the blue sky overhead with one outstretched arm. It wasn't an activity that begged for collaboration. She was off in her own zone.

So was I. I knew I shouldn't give a flimsy little compliment too much weight. A lot of guys liked to flirt once they were married, because they felt they had a buffer. They knew that you knew that you couldn't take them seriously.

Unless he wanted to be taken seriously . . .

I squinted at the patio door. Spence wouldn't be that way. He was a good guy. Look what a great dad he was to August. She was crazy about him.

Goddammit, where was Pepper? If she were here, I wouldn't

be sitting around wondering whether I should get fluttery about her husband telling me my hair looked good. You would think that after her husband had been away for weeks and weeks, Pepper would want to be here as the reception committee. Or maybe Spence hadn't told her he was coming. But how could he not tell her? Pepper ran around with a cell phone practically attached to her ear, and he had one, too.

I sank down in my chair. Their lack of communication wasn't my problem. I wasn't going to give it another thought.

Yeah, right.

"Did Pepper know you were coming home today?" I asked the moment he reappeared.

He sighed. "I was able to catch a flight a day early."

Just like that. He got bored in Hong Kong and just headed home. Amazing.

And he didn't call his wife?

Puzzlement must have been written all over my face. "I thought I would surprise everybody," he explained.

"Score! We're surprised."

He laughed sheepishly, and for that second I saw a little more of the teenager I'd known. The Spence who didn't look entirely sure of himself. It was a relief to see him shed a little of his master-of-the-universe mantle. I felt more comfortable, even though seeing him that way caused a regretful hitch in my chest.

Not that it mattered. I might dither all I wanted about Spence's marital status, but for all I knew he was a contented family man. And why shouldn't he be? He had a great life. An incredible house. An adorable daughter. As for his wife . . . well, who was I to say?

Anyway, he probably never thought about other women anymore.

"I guess you have a whole flock of boyfriends," he said.

I jumped. Then I emitted a high, shrill laugh. "Oh, right!"

What a thing to say to me! It was the kind of comment my mom was always tossing off. I think it made people more comfortable to think of women in their twenties battling off men like girls in old Jane Wyman movies than the reality, which was far more grim. Funny how single women in their forties were all assumed to be sitting alone in their apartment with an overweight cat watching *Law and Order* reruns, but until then, it was supposed to be nothing but fun and games. At least to the people who weren't out there.

The weird thing was, Spence sounded like he meant it. As if he actually believed I was a swinger.

Maybe it made sense that he thought that way. He hadn't been out there. He had been dating or married to the same woman since he was eighteen. *Eighteen!* Practically an infant. How often did that happen nowadays? It seemed quaint, a throwback to the days when people entertained themselves with sing-alongs to "A Bicycle Built for Two." And it explained how Spence could believe the rest of us were living in a hedonist fantasyland.

For the next hour, we ate pizza and talked more about ourselves. It wasn't intimate conversation so much as the getting-to-know-you chatter you have with coworkers when you start somewhere new. Spence gave me his resume—a series of promotions that led to ever more impressive banking jobs. He used to love traveling, he said, but that was when Pepper used to go with him, before August. These days he found he wanted his family with him, which is why his fingers were crossed for a relocation. He wanted to go to a new city and stay put. He worried he was missing watching his daughter grow up.

From what I had witnessed in the past two weeks, that was true. Then again, sometimes it seemed to me that Pepper was missing watching her daughter grow up, and she was living in the same house with her.

I outlined my own work history for Spence—a tidied version, of course, skipping the horror of substitute teaching and any mention of being fired. My dot-com year, I played for laughs. All that money! The hubris! I made it sound as if I had subsequently embarked on a mad romp through the work world and had burned out on office life. I was "still searching" for what I wanted to do with my life, I told him, but I felt good where I was now. Caring for his daughter, I said, was the most fulfilling job I had found thus far.

After I had finished this monologue—a minefield of fabrications, omissions, and positive slants on dubious motives—his gaze met and held mine. His lips were curved in a wry smile. "Yeah, you certainly looked fulfilled when you were getting out of that Hummer this afternoon."

I couldn't help laughing. It was easier now that I'd taken a shower. "That was a work hazard I hadn't anticipated."

"All joking aside, Al, we're lucky we found you. Although I suppose it would be more truthful to say we rediscovered you."

I stared into his eyes for as long as I could before my cheeks felt fired up. I hoped I didn't look like a moon-faced idiot, which was how I felt. It couldn't have been love at first sight, obviously; but was it possible to fall in love at first memory? Because that's what this felt like. Like all my memories of being young and hyperenergized and in love for the first time were foaming up again. The night felt warmer, not the oppressive heat that I usually associated with summer, but like a cozy blanket around us. I felt like laughing, like dancing, like getting out an old Hole CD.

But I was frozen in my chair.

From inside, I heard the slamming of a door and the quick clicking of Pepper's heels. She was yoo-hooing like mad through the house, but Spence didn't answer. Both of us remained immobile, with our eyes locked.

Pepper slid open the patio door and clipped out, arms outstretched. "Spence! My husband was home, and I didn't even know it!" She went up behind him and crooked an elbow possessively around his neck. "What the heck are you doing here?"

He gestured to the half-demolished pizza box. "We dined without you."

"Darn it all!" I caught a whiff of minty alcohol breath; she had obviously had a snootful. "I was out with Phaedra! Why didn't you call me?"

"I did," Spence said, a little curtly. "Your phone wasn't answering."

"Oh." She let go of him and slid into an empty chair. She cut a glance over at him. "Are you sure you tried?"

"Of course I tried. Check your phone. You must have turned it off for some reason . . ."

Her laugh was an easy cross between breezy and brittle. "I believe you, I believe you!" She looked over at me. "Spence is always so prickly after long plane rides."

"Am not."

"Are so! How long *is* it from Hong Kong, honey? Twelve hours?"

Spence looked . . . prickly. His jaw was clenched and both hands were gripping the arms of the lawn chair, like he was posing for the Lincoln Memorial. "Eighteen."

It was amazing what a difference two minutes could make. All the nostalgic romance had been sucked out of the air. Yet this fraught atmosphere had a vague whiff of nostalgia about it, too. I hadn't felt tension like this since I was a kid, sitting at dinner between my parents.

Phaedra had said that this marriage was a leaky boat, and if this was Spence and Pepper's idea of a reunion, I could see what she meant.

Pepper shook her head at me. "You can't blame a guy for being a little cranky after eighteen hours, can you?"

Spence slapped a hand down on the table, and the pizza box hopped in surprise. "I'm not cranky!"

We both blinked at him wordlessly. Then, when I dared move, I glanced over at August, searching for an escape. She was conked out on a chaise lounge, a victim of too much shopping, excitement, and pizza.

My voice sliced uneasily through the air. "Bath time!" I stood and picked up a grumbly August, not even bothering to coax her into walking with me. I wanted out of there. When she figured out that she was being carried away from the action, she immediately started protesting. "I wanna stay up with Daddy!"

He and Pepper were still having a glare-down. "You have a message on the answering machine," he told her in a low voice. "Phaedra called at six. She said she wondered why you weren't picking up on your phone."

"Oh!" Pepper exclaimed casually. "That's an old message, then. I met her after some shopping."

Even though she didn't bat an eye, she still had the look of a woman whose alibi was unraveling.

"On the message, Phaedra said she was going to call Colby."

Colby? My ears perked up. Was this the boyfriend Phaedra had mentioned?

Give Pepper credit. She never flinched. You had to look deep into those eyes to see panic. "Phaedra's such a ditz!" she exclaimed. "I don't know why she thought *I* would be over there, though Colby's been hanging around here often enough."

"Oh?"

She smiled. "He's taken quite a shine to our Alison."

At the mention of my name, I jumped. I was almost worried that I would drop August.

"And who can blame him," Pepper said. "Doesn't she look great?"

Spence stared up at me, his lips a pensive line. "Great."

I stood there with a smile frozen on my face.

Pepper squinted at me. "I think you've got a date with Colby tomorrow night, right, Al?"

Spence was still looking at me. August was staring at me, too. I felt like an actor in a scene in which all of the other players had forgotten their lines and were now forcing me to improvise. I wanted to stick to the script. *Just the nanny! Haven't had a date in months . . .*

Or, if I was forced to make something up, I wanted to come out with a righteous indictment of Pepper's trying to involve me in her scheming, cheating ways. What a scene that would have made! It could have ended with Spence sweeping me into his embrace. *"Come on, Al. I should have stuck with you all along!*

But all eyes were focused on me, and I was having trouble thinking of any words at all. So I took the path of least resistance. "Right," I agreed.

"No way," I said. "I won't do it."

"Please?" Pepper sounded so pitifully girlish, I almost ex-

pected her to add pretty please. With sugar on top. "It's just one night."

I couldn't believe I was even in this position. I had been so shocked, though, I hadn't known what to say. I hadn't wanted to out Pepper in front of her husband; I didn't want to be responsible for the crash and burn of a marriage. I mean, I know I'm not a saint. But I'm not evil.

Pepper, on the other hand, apparently was. "Oh, don't look at me that way," she said. "It's not what you think."

"What is it, then?"

"Colby's just a friend. Really. And actually, I was going to drop him because he's been getting all sorts of wild ideas. He's decided he's Valentino. But believe me, I'm not interested."

"He's the guy in the red Range Rover?"

She seemed surprised. "Yeah."

"You go out with him a lot."

"Well, so what? I hate sitting around the house. You've seen yourself how much Spence is gone. I'd go out of my skull sitting around watching television, or whatever it is I'm supposed to do. You've got to help me out, Al."

"Why?" I asked. "Okay, you lied to Spence. I did, too. Can't we just leave it at that?"

"But now he expects you to be going out tomorrow night."

"Okay, I'll lie again. I'll say I called it off."

"C'mon, Al. Even Colby agreed to do this."

"He must be insane."

"He is."

"Terrific—sounds like a fun night ahead."

"That's why I want to dump him. And it's not like you have to do anything much. Just let Spence see Colby coming and going. Just to deflect some of the heat. You understand."

The longer I hesitated, the more Pepper's eyes began to narrow until finally they were pinpricks of blue boring into me. "Unless there's some real reason why you don't want Spence to see you going out with Colby."

The statement startled me. That was just it! I *didn't* want him to see me going out with anyone. Wasn't that sick? For some reason, I wanted to play the celibate devotee. I wanted him to see that I was still available.

There was something very wrong with that. Very, very wrong.

I sighed. “Oh, all right.”

All the anger gushed out of her. She practically clapped her hands with glee. “Oh, thank you, Al! I’ll make Colby take you out somewhere nice. Believe me, I’ll never forget this.”

“Believe me. Neither will I.”

Chapter 9

I wanted it to be a big surprise when I got into Vanderbilt, so I didn't tell anyone that I had applied. Not even my parents. Certainly not Spence. Also, I have to admit that a part of me knew what I was doing was wrong. I fancied myself a budding feminist, not some bubblehead who would backburner her own vision so she could traipse after her high school boyfriend.

But what else was I supposed to do? Pepper McClintock was chasing him! The boy needed protection.

Of course I had to tell the people who were writing me college recommendations that I would need their services once again; though this time I refused to use Ms. Crouch. I was sort of begging Vanderbilt to let me in, which was irritating since Reed had already accepted me with open arms, and I had to come up with a new essay that I explained why I had such a Tennessee jones all of the sudden. Something that didn't involve going insane with jealousy at seeing my boyfriend passionately kissing Pepper McClintock every night.

Of course, that kissing was just stage stuff. I was a professional enough amateur to see that Spence was just doing what he had to do. Poor Spence really didn't have a choice. And I bore a certain amount of responsibility for our predicament. Hadn't I been the one to rope him into Bramford Prep Rep?

Spence and I were still going out. Nothing had changed . . . well, nothing that couldn't be explained away by the fact that we were both really, really busy. Sure we weren't seeing as much of each other outside rehearsals compared to before, but on top of *Picnic*, there were a million things to do. As May and graduation approached, everyone and her dog was having some kind of a party or dance. Not to mention, I still had to pass all my classes, and I had this awful government term paper to write—twenty yawn-inducing pages on the impact of third parties on American politics. With footnotes.

Third parties had sounded like a great topic when I picked it in the fall, but now that I was up to my ears in Populists, Bull Mooses, and Ross Perot, I realized that I had made a fatal error. I mean, twenty pages was a lot of pages to fill talking about *losers*.

Long story short, there wasn't a lot of time for hanging out with Spence and, you know, introspecting together.

One night in early May Spence was driving me home from rehearsal. We weren't talking, but not because we were mad or anything. I was probably thinking about what the hell I was going to wear to the senior prom, or else Free Soilers, and who knew what Spence was thinking about. It sort of unnerved me that we could drive along in silence like this and think nothing of it. I swear it sometimes seemed like we were already turning into my parents.

Then something jangled my consciousness. We *weren't* driving along in silence. I realized there was a mosquito buzz of pop music in the air—Phil Collins—and I aimed my attention to the radio with the intention of swatting it off. My hand stopped midway, however, when I saw that this wasn't the radio. This was a *cassette*. I nearly lost it.

A cassette indicated a willful desire to hear "Sussudio."

"What's that?" I demanded. As if I didn't know.

He shrugged. Defensively, as you might have guessed. "Just a tape."

Too ashamed of himself to say the so-called artist's name aloud, you'll notice.

I picked up the little plastic case with my fingertips. "Who are you consulting now for your musical taste? Casey Kasem?"

"Oh, come on," he said. "It's just music."

"It's elevator music! It's beige!"

He nearly ran a stop sign. "Who are you to talk? At your house the other day you were listening to the soundtrack from *Paint Your Wagon*."

"That's Lee Marvin," I said. "Lee Marvin is always bad ass. Besides, listening to musicals falls under the umbrella of eclectic. This is just . . ." I shivered. ". . . *Top 40!*"

"God, do you have to be so judgmental all the time?"

I jerked toward him. "Judgmental? Me?"

"You've got an opinion about *everything*."

"Well, of course. You're supposed to, unless you're a jellyfish or something."

He snatched the cassette cover away from me. "Forget it. It's not mine anyway."

That I could believe. He had all sorts of unfortunate friends. "Whose is it?"

"I borrowed it from Pepper."

I swear it was almost like my fingertips were burning. "Pepper! What is she doing giving you cassettes?"

"I just took it out of her purse the other night and forgot to give it back."

I sank down in my seat.

Okay. This was no big whoop. I could deal. It wasn't like he could completely ignore Pepper. None of us could, unfortunately. At least not until this damn play was over.

"Pepper!" I muttered. "Can you believe she hasn't memorized her part yet?"

Bitching about Pepper was my latest enthusiasm. Whenever I felt anxiety, I could shoot my mouth off about her and get instant relief. It was like an asthmatic sucking on a bronchial inhaler. "The poor stage manager will probably have to be feeding her lines to her through every performance." I was very sympathetic to stage managers after *Antigone*.

And though only myself and a few other disgruntled players seemed to notice, Pepper was lousy. She read all of her lines in the same flat Valley-girl-goes-Dallas twang. She just didn't get the most basic concepts of theater, like projecting, or not letting that blond curtain of hair hang over her eyes, or stage blocking. We had marked off the stage with masking tape to denote where all the set pieces would be, but she was oblivious. She was constantly sticking her head through walls and making exits through large pieces of furniture. Most of us would roll our eyes, but not La Crouch and Spence. Oh, no. Judging from their reactions, you'd think Sarah Bernhardt had been reincarnated right there at Bramford Prep Rep.

"She's got a lot of lines," Spence said, gunning through a yellow light.

I decided he wasn't defending her so much as just being naturally chivalrous. "You had yours down weeks ago."

"She'll get the hang of it. It's her first play."

"I wouldn't overestimate her. Maybe you haven't noticed, but Pepper's not exactly the brightest bulb in the chandelier."

He didn't say anything. Just kept his eyes on the road.

I really was worried about him. He was obviously going through that thing where you become overly attached to the other actors in the play you're rehearsing. It's like Stockholm syndrome for actors. That happened to me at drama camp once. I totally had the hots for this guy who was playing George to my Emily in *Our Town*. I even made out with him by the couch in the student lounge one night after curfew. It wasn't until camp was over and I met him once for a movie that I realized that he was a complete drip *and* bore a scary resemblance to Kirk Cameron. The magic was gone before we even settled into our seats at the multiplex.

You really had to guard against that kind of thing. You had to be able to see the other person for what they actually were, not who they were playing.

I decided to nudge Spence along a little in his recovery process. "Did I ever tell you about the time in history when we were studying the Depression and Pepper asked whether Herbert Hoover invented the vacuum cleaner?"

Granted, that had been in fifth grade. But it was a true story.

Spence's brow pinched. "Who did invent the vacuum?"

I hadn't anticipated that question. "I have no idea. But I know it wasn't Herbert Hoover."

"Maybe it was one of his relatives. It's not that common a name."

"You're missing my point. My point is—"

"Gerald Ford, for instance."

I did a double take. "What?"

"Ford's a pretty common name, but if she had asked if Gerald Ford had invented cars, she wouldn't have been too far off base. He was part of that family."

"Yeah, but—"

"Not that Ford actually invented the automobile."

"But see, Pepper wouldn't have asked if Gerald Ford was related to Henry Ford, she would have asked whether he was related to Indiana Jones."

Spence looked at me, frowning. "Why would she do that?"

"Harrison *Ford*."

"That's stupid."

"I know, that's what I . . ." I hate it when you have to explain a joke. It just makes you feel like an idiot, and sure enough, that's how I felt. "But this had nothing to do with Ford, or automobiles. That might have been different. I mean, *vacuum cleaners*. Duh!"

"Or Teddy Roosevelt being the inspiration for the teddy bear," Spence went on. "That's a true story."

I was practically tearing my hair out. "You so don't get it. She's a numbskull. When we were in comparative religion together, Pepper asked the teacher *where* Islam was. Like it was a country or something."

Spence chuckled. Not the reaction I was hoping for.

"I mean, the girl is a real idiot, when you come right down to it."

He darted a look of irritation at me. Irritation. *At me*. "Oh, come on."

"She is!"

"Because she didn't know who invented the vacuum cleaner? Which, for all we know, was actually invented by a man named Hoover who was related to Herbert Hoover?"

"Forget vacuum cleaners!" I said. "I'm sorry I ever mentioned them. My point is that her brain just isn't saddled up and ready for action. You must have noticed that. Plus, she's a little devious, if you want my honest opinion."

"Devious? She's the most upfront person I know."

That flabbergasted me. "Pepper? You've got to be kidding me!"

"Well . . . I think she's fundamentally honest. And she's got a zest for things that I really admire."

Zest!

"Take this play," he said. "Look at the way she's tackling that challenge. She's never been on a stage before."

I sank down in my seat. "You don't have to remind me of *that*."

He slowed down in front of my house, practically caressing the steering wheel. "I don't even think this is really her type of thing at all, yet you can tell she just loves coming to rehearsals and embracing this new challenge."

Loved embracing my boyfriend, more like. How could he be so naive?

"Just tonight Ms. Crouch was telling her that she was a natural."

I guffawed. "Like Crouch would know talent if it whomped her upside the head! Not that she doesn't pride herself on being some prep-school Svengali. It's so pathetic! The other day I heard her telling Pepper's friend Phaedra that *she* should have auditioned."

"I like Phaedra," Spence said.

My jaw nearly came unhinged. I might have squeaked out a wounded-animal bleat. "When did you meet *her*?"

"After rehearsal the other night. When you skipped rehearsal to do your Bull Moose research."

"Let me guess. Phaedra *just happened* to show up and you guys went out after rehearsal."

"Well . . . yeah. We went out for ice cream."

Ice cream! How wholesome! Everybody in school knew Phaedra was practically the Ecstasy queen. Now she felt some all-consuming need to go out with my boyfriend for milkshakes!

"Pepper's had it in for me since we were five," I grumbled.

Spence gaped at me. "What?"

"Horse shit, remember?"

He burst out laughing. "Are you still chewing over some fight you had when you were five? That's totally fucked up."

It was, I knew. But it was the only explanation I could think of for why Pepper McClintock would be stealing my boyfriend.

"You should just forget all about that," he said. "Pepper has."

The words were a knife in my back. "How do you know?"

"She told me."

"You were talking to Pepper about me, and the horse poo party?"

"Well, yeah."

"Behind my back?"

"Well, I've been with her so much lately . . . we have to talk about something."

"What did she say about me?"

He shook his head. "Nothing."

"If she mentioned that party, she must have said *something.*"

"For your information, *she* didn't mention it. I did. She didn't really remember the incident, or you even being at her fifth birthday party."

She *didn't remember*? "Of course I was there. What a liar!"

"I'm telling you, she didn't remember it. She laughed when I told her, though. She thought it was a funny story."

"A story?" I shrieked. "But it happened! She knows it happened."

"C'mon," he said. "Don't be jealous."

I practically levitated out of the passenger seat. "Jealous?" I shrieked. "Me? Of Pepper? Why should I be jealous?"

His face screwed up and he looked at me as if I were crazy. As if I had just asked an insane, off-the-wall question. "Because she got your part in the play."

I froze. *The play?* Did he really think that was what this was all about?

"What?" he asked.

I laughed. "Nothing."

"What is it, Al?"

I shook my head. What a babe in the woods! He had no idea what he was dealing with. He was really going to need me to keep an eye on him.

I wasn't proud of my behavior in the following weeks. I took to rushing home the moment the last bell rang at school so I could check the mail. Every day that I didn't get a letter from Vanderbilt, I died a little. During this time, I had my first bout of chronic insomnia. I stayed up nights worrying, then I dozed through school, ran home, then dragged off to rehearsal tensed up and sleep deprived. I was a mess.

The only thing that kept me going another day was when I detected that Pepper had also not heard from Vanderbilt . . . or if she had, she had been rejected. (Nobody ever talked about rejections.) I was pretty sure she wouldn't get in, seeing as how she was lower in class ranking and SAT scores than I was. I'd heard she was having to use family influence to get her into North Texas State, which was a place most people at Bramford Prep used as a backup school.

I wondered if she would even tell Spence when she didn't get in. Then I wondered how I could find concrete proof that she didn't so I could tell him myself. I sort of dreamed of that moment.

Even though I was completely focused on college, my schoolwork started to slide. Really slide. Not that it really mattered. Most teachers were slacking off at this point, too, except one. Mr. Garbely, the government teacher. He held everyone's graduation in his hands, but I just couldn't work up much enthusiasm for my government paper, which was late. Garbely finally called me to his office for a conference, to talk about the first draft deadline that I had missed.

"Is there a paper, or is this just a phantom you're working on?" he asked me.

He was so snarky. One of those bitter sarcastic teachers who probably regretted not getting their Ph.D.s.

"There is a paper," I told him. Which was true. It was in my bedroom at home, in the garbage can.

"Are you going to keep me in suspense, Miss Bell, or am I ever going to be allowed to view this elusive document?"

God, he was tedious. "I just have a little more research to do . . ."

"Your note cards were supposed to be turned in already, Alison."

"Yeah, I know, but you know, like, I thought of something really great that I wanted to put in at the last minute."

He threaded his fingers behind his head and leaned back in his squeaky teacher's chair. I hated when teachers stared at you this way, as if they were deciding whether to believe you or not. They always suspected you of bullshitting them.

As it happened, at that moment I was bullshitting him, but why should he have immediately jumped to that conclusion?

"Can I ask what this bombshell you want to drop is?"

I was so tired, I had a hard time sitting up straight, never mind thinking. But at that moment, a stroke of genius occurred to me . . . or, if not a stroke of genius, something that at least would shut Mr. Garbely up.

"I'm going to interview Ross Perot," I said. "In person."

Garbely gaped at me. Just to see the shock on his face was worth any trouble I worried I would suffer later on. And I was pretty sure there would be trouble.

"Perot? When?"

"Next week," I said without batting an eyelash. I might have been getting a C in government, but I hadn't made A's in Drama One, Two, and Three for nothing.

It wasn't till I was out of Garbely's office that I started feeling a little shaky. I mean, what was I going to do if I couldn't get my hands on Ross Perot? I was pretty sure he was in Dallas, but where? How on earth was I going to hunt him down? And even if I could find him, there was a snowball's chance in hell that he would want to talk to me, some nobody at a second-rate girl's school. I was so screwed.

That night was a big disappointment. There was no letter from Vanderbilt and the show was rehearsing scenes I wasn't in, so I had to make up some lame excuse to go to rehearsal.

Crouch did a double take when I came in, as did all the actors slumped around the stage. This was the last week of rehearsals, and everybody was pretty sick of *Picnic*. "What are you doing here?" Crouch asked. "I didn't put you on the callboard."

She called the dry-erase board on her office door the callboard. So pretentious.

"Scene crew," I said, off the top of my head. "I was wondering if I could join the scene crew."

She squinted at me. Scene crew was something only desperate, stagestruck freshmen actually wanted to do. Besides, the set was almost built, and I have to admit it looked pretty good. It consisted of muslin flats representing two houses, with window cutouts and even little window boxes attached. I wouldn't have called it realistic, actually, but it was better than most of our productions.

There was no reason on earth I would want to join scene crew the week of the production, so I had to make something up. "I was thinking if we had a platform behind Mrs. Potts's house, I could play that one scene from the second story. It would give the staging a little more dimension."

Crouch looked impressed. (It didn't take much.) "That's fabulous!" she exclaimed. "Only I don't have time to work on that tonight, Alison. I will call a special scene crew for lunch Friday."

I lingered at the door, throwing surreptitious glances at Spence and Pepper. They were standing over in a corner by themselves, which of course made my jealousy flair. Never mind that their standing together might have had something to do with the scene being rehearsed. "I could stay late and tell you about it," I suggested to Crouch.

"I can't stay late," she said. "I'm jazzed about this idea, though! Excellent thinking, Alison! A-plus!"

"But maybe if I just stayed and looked at the blocking . . ."

By now, all the rest of the cast members, including a few who looked like they would have done anything to be at home watching *Melrose Place*, were glaring at me. And Spence was staring at me as if I had lost my mind.

Maybe I had.

"You can go now," Crouch told me firmly when she noticed I hadn't moved. "We'll deal with it on Friday."

"Yeah, but—"

"Okay!" She turned to her players. "Let's take it from Rosemary's entrance."

"You don't know Ross Perot, do you?" I blurted out.

Someone onstage laughed.

"What?" Crouch turned on me, her brow wrinkly with annoyance. "No. Why?"

"I need to talk to him for my government paper," I said.

She folded her arms at me. "Alison, this is a *rehearsal*. We leave schoolwork outside those doors." She nodded toward the doors behind me. No doubt wishing I would exit through them.

"I've met Ross Perot," Pepper piped up. "He's a good friend of my family's."

Spence gazed at her with nauseating admiration. "Really?"

I wanted to gag.

She nodded.

"I voted for him," Spence said.

I screeched. "You *what?*"

"Alison . . ." Crouch said. "I think you'd better go now."

I slunk back home, stewing. Ross Perot? Why would Spence lie about something like that? But he had to be lying to someone—me or Pepper.

Oh, I needed to keep an eye on him, all right.

When I got to the house, I actually stuck my arm up the mail chute to make sure an envelope hadn't gotten stuck in there. It really was odd that I hadn't heard from Vanderbilt. It had been weeks and weeks! And stuff did get stuck in the mail chute sometimes.

My dad came wandering in and saw me this way. "What's going on, hon?"

I straightened immediately, nearly dislocating my arm in the process. "Hey, Dad," I said. "Do you know where I could find Ross Perot?"

"I don't think you'll find him in that mailbox."

I chuckled along with him. "No, seriously. It'd be a big help if I could talk to Ross Perot. Do you know anybody who knows him?"

My dad was such a sweetheart. He actually stood there thinking about it. "I might know somebody on the business council who knows him."

My dad belonged to all sorts of business organizations in those days. "It would be fantastic if I could talk to him, just like for five minutes. It's for school."

"Well, I'll see what I can do."

He was such a great dad. Even though I knew there was probably nothing he could do, he was so earnest.

"Everything okay?" he asked.

I looked into his eyes and saw worry there. I also noticed lines in his forehead where I hadn't seen any before, and a sort of crunching of his shoulders toward his ears. I assumed he was concerned about me. What else would he have to worry about?

"Yeah, everything's fine." I thought for a moment about asking him if he was okay, too, but I decided against that. Dad never talked about himself or his problems. We weren't that kind of family.

He headed for his study, and I went up to my room to worry and watch *Melrose Place*.

Two days later I was snoozing through third period English (I mean, did it really matter now if we read *The Mill on the Floss*? Wasn't it a little late to be cramming literature into our heads?) when my name was called over the intercom system. I jerked awake.

"Alison Bell, you have a message at the front office."

The whole class swiveled in their uncomfortable seats to ogle me. In all my years at that school, my name had never been called on the speaker before. It was startling.

Mrs. Westerbury eyed me, too, and the alarm I saw in her eyes panicked me. Had somebody died?

"Go check on your message," she said, releasing me. It was almost the end of class anyway. "Take your things."

I grabbed my books and sprinted for the office, filled with

trepidation. All I could think was that my dad had had a heart attack. He'd seemed so haggard lately.

When I got to the office I was practically trembling with dread. The school secretary reached into a cubbyhole and took out a pink slip.

"Ross Perot called," she blurted out before she'd even handed it over.

I went limp. "He did?"

Go, Dad!

I looked down at the message. *Can meet you on the fourth at eleven o'clock.*

"Wow," I said.

The fourth. That was tomorrow!

What the hell was I going to say to Ross Perot?

As it turned out, I had a lot to ask him. I even begged out of a run-through tech rehearsal early so I could go home and try to weed out questions. When I had called and talked to his secretary, she had informed me that I would only have fifteen minutes in the presence of His Jug-earedness, so I was going to have to choose carefully. I also ran out to an all-night drugstore to buy a little tape recorder, so I would have a lasting record, if not to give Mr. Garbely, then to hand down to my grandchildren. They would think I was so with-it, so politically aware even as a teenager!

I thought about majoring in political science in college. Or maybe journalism. Maybe I could be the next Diane Sawyer.

The next Diane Sawyer overslept on the day of the interview, but decided to skip morning classes. Who cared? School was almost over anyway. Besides, I wanted to give myself plenty of time in case I got lost downtown. At the appointed time, I was standing in front of Ross Perot's secretary, fumbling with a package of AA batteries I had bought at the last minute for the tape recorder but hadn't put in yet.

"I'm Alison Bell," I said.

She turned her blank expression on me. "Who?"

"Alison Bell," I repeated. "I spoke to you on the phone yesterday. I made an appointment to see Mr. Perot on the fourth at ten o'clock."

A lightbulb finally clicked on behind those eyes. "Oh!" she exclaimed. "The McClintock girl."

The mention of that name made me jump. Was Pepper trying to get an interview with Ross Perot, too? That little weasel!

"No, my name is Bell. Alison Bell."

The secretary pursed her lips at me. "I only meant it was as a favor to Buck McClintock that Mr. Perot agreed to see you."

"Buck McClintock?" I practically shrieked. That was Pepper's father. The banker.

Pepper was responsible for getting me this interview? Why?

But of course the reason was clear to me almost immediately. That snake. She had done me a favor to make herself look generous in Spence's eyes.

"Yes, of course," the secretary said, burying herself into a dayrunner the size of a desk encyclopedia. "But that was for June fourth, not today."

I felt like the woman was sprayhosing me with bad news. No Ross Perot interview. Plus I owed Pepper a favor.

"But I graduate on May 29." Then I added, muttering, "Well, I'm supposed to."

There was the small matter of that government term paper. I was so screwed.

The secretary couldn't have looked any less interested, except for one detail. "Are you saying that you need to cancel your appointment?"

I admitted that was probably the case, and watched with dismay as my name was crossed off. Now I was going to be beholden to Pepper for nothing.

I went to school and was staggering toward fourth period when Crouch stopped me in the hall. "Lunch!" she snapped at me.

I had no idea what she was talking about. My head hurt. "Huh?" I was too tired to form words.

"We're having a special scene crew at lunch to build your platform. Such a terrific idea! I hope we can get it done in time for dress rehearsal tonight. I invited faculty."

I grunted.

But at lunch there I was, wielding my hammer. The plywood structure we nailed together looked rickety, I must say. But we were prep school kids, not carpenters.

"I have never been so wasted," one of the girls recruited for scene crew said. Her name was Jade and the other girl's name was Devon. I barely knew them, except for the fact that they had worked stage crew on *Antigone*, too; they were freshmen.

Devon looked a little green around the gills. "Me neither."

"What happened?" I asked. Yes, they were freshmen, but freshman gossip was better than nothing.

"You missed it," Devon said.

"What?"

"The cast party at Pepper's."

"*Cast party?*" I hadn't heard anything about a cast party. Last night? I could feel my voice looping up in hysteria. "Cast party?"

"Yeah, after you left early, Pepper invited everybody to her place. It was wild! Half the people were skinny-dipping in the pool."

"Skinny-dipping!" I practically shook the girl named Devon by her skinny little shoulders. "Did Spence go skinny-dipping?"

Her eyes bugged, and she shook her head. I sagged with relief. Then she added, "That is . . . I dunno, really. He and Pepper sort of disappeared."

Her companion nodded. "Yeah, after the first thirty minutes, nobody saw them."

How I made it through the rest of that afternoon, I'll never know. I was in a rage, and I was tired, and I was really, really hurt.

At the end of the day, I saw Crouch one more time, winging nervously through the hallway. "Go get some rest!" she said. "Big night tonight!"

"Hmph." I had hardly thought about the dress rehearsal since lunchtime.

I made it home and drooped through the front door, only to be confronted by my mother. "Alison! Look!"

She swooped down on me with an envelope.

"It's from Vanderbilt!" she exclaimed. "You didn't tell me you had applied there!"

But instead of being angry about my secrecy, she seemed overjoyed. She and Dad had never been wild about my going to Reed. They worried it was going to turn me into a hippie or something. I tried to explain to them that no one who had been raised in Highland Park could become a hippie even if they wanted to. That would require thorough deprogramming and longtime retail deprivation.

But even though Mom was thrilled, I stared at the rectangle in my hand in utter shock. Mom was so out of it. Even after a year of watching me deal with college stuff, she didn't realize that when colleges accepted you, they sent you an information packet, with forms that you needed to return. They didn't send you a thin envelope with a letter inside.

This was a thin envelope. Very thin.

I didn't even bother to open it.

Mom followed me halfway up the stairs, chirping at my back. "And here I thought you were all set for Reed. But this is wonderful! My friend Midge went to Vanderbilt. She pledged Tri Delt. I'll bet she would have written a wonderful recommendation for you! Kathy Fry went there, too. You know her! She met her first husband there. She's a Kappa. She'll be so excited to hear you're going."

"I probably won't be," I said, taking one stair at a time. "In fact I probably won't be going to college at all. I'll have to study for my GED because I failed my government term paper because of Ross Perot."

"What?" Mom asked, frowning. "Ross Perot?"

"It's no big deal."

"What is GED?" she asked.

"Never mind."

She blew out an exasperated breath. "Why do you get so moody? Even when good things are happening. I'd think you'd be happy!"

"Tech rehearsal tonight," I muttered before I shut myself into my room.

The show must go on. Even though I knew that this was probably the last show I would ever act in, I still held to that corny old motto. I gathered up my little makeup box (a fishing-tackle box assembled at drama camp one summer) and headed back to school. In the girl's bathroom near the cafeteria that we traditionally used as the women's dressing room, I was the second person there. The first was the sophomore playing Millie, who was a nervous wreck.

"I've got a zit!" she shrieked. "What am I gonna do?"

"You're supposed to be playing a teenager," I reminded her.

"The school paper's going to be taking pictures tonight." From the tone of her voice, you would have thought the *New York Times* was coming.

Like I cared. As far as I was concerned, the world had ended. I slopped on foundation makeup and started sculpting old lady lines with an eye pencil. I had practiced this weeks ago, but now I dragged the lines on half-heartedly. I struggled to get my gray wig on. It was way too tight, and it made me look like Vicki Lawrence in those old Mama's Family skits on the *Carol Burnett Show*.

At that point, Pepper breezed in. She didn't have much makeup to worry about, since she was just supposed to be pretty. Grr.

I wondered if she expected me to thank her for setting up an interview with Ross Perot . . . a month too late to do me any damn good. I still couldn't believe she had thrown a cast party the minute my back was turned.

"Hey, Grandma!" she said to me, slapping me on the shoulder as she passed.

Everybody laughed.

I was strapping the foam padding onto my hips. My fat suit. I seethed.

Crouch breezed in not long after. "Fifteen minutes, ladies!" She flicked a glance at everyone, one after the other. "Deborah, try to cover that pimple a little better. Margaret, you're just the perfect Rosemary! And Pepper—you look beautiful!"

"Thanks, Ms. C—and thanks for the recommendation," she said. "It worked!"

I nearly dropped my drooping prosthetic boobs. "What?"

Pepper beamed at me. "I just got my acceptance letter from Vanderbilt!"

There were squeals of congratulations. My head was spinning. *I was rejected while Pepper was accepted?* How could that have happened? *How?* Was God taking an extended coffee break up there, or what?

Our stage manager poked her head in. "Places!"

Backstage room was tight, so I had to crawl up to my platform before all the other actors started crowding in backstage. I didn't get a chance to tell Spence to break a leg. I did get to tell Pepper, though I really wanted to tell her to break her neck.

I was too beaten down to have my usual stage nerves. I hovered on the platform, already sweating in my costume, and stewing. What had I done wrong?

Pimply Millie took her place onstage, and the lights went up. The audience clapped.

"Really?" I heard Spence whisper.

He was right below me. I craned my head around, and saw who he was talking to. Pepper, naturally. She was nodding and grinning.

And then, to my utter horror, their heads came together. Not in a stage kiss—they weren't even on stage. They were in the wings, out of sight. And this was a real kiss. With tongue.

I felt ill. My face grew hot, my skin clammy. I was sick and yet I couldn't help craning over the side of my platform to get a closer look at the disgusting display. Did they not realize Pepper had a cue coming up? Did they not realize I was there, just above them, watching?

And then I remembered . . . *I* had a cue. I remembered because the stage manager poked her head around to hiss at me. But when she did, she bumped into the young lovers. Pepper sprang away from Spence, hitting the two-by-four that connected the beams supporting my platform. The Mrs. Potts house began to sway. In my panic, I grabbed my side of the flimsy muslin flat that the front of the house was painted on. Which was a grave mistake. Instead of just sending the platform crashing down, I brought half of the set down with me.

My only consolation was that both myself and the house landed squarely on top of Pepper. And, in the department of poetic justice, my doctor said that it was probably the padding on the fat suit for Mrs. Potts that saved me from getting a lot worse than a sprained arm.

Chapter 10

I wasn't well for this date with Colby—if you could even call this twisted compulsory charade a date—and as I prepared myself for it, I didn't even bother to try to psyche myself into thinking I would have a good time. I mean, how much fun could you have with your employer's paramour? For mood music while I dressed, I passed over party sounds in favor of a Chopin CD Jess had sent me. The Funeral March was on it, and in that spirit, I threw on a black knit dress and as little makeup as I could get away with. Par-tay!

My phone rang, and praying for it to be Colby with a cancellation, I lunged for it. It was Nola. "Are you bringing wine?" she asked by way of greeting.

I frowned. "When?"

"Tonight."

How did she know I was going out tonight? And why would she think I would take wine out on a date?

Then I remembered. The get-together for Steve's brother! Flynn, or whatever his name was. I glanced over at my calendar and started gnawing nervously on my lower lip. Shit! How could I have forgotten?

"You forgot, didn't you?"

Shit! "No . . . no . . . I was just about to call you."

She let out a long-suffering sigh. "Al, I've told Finn all about you. He's just dying to meet you."

"Then you couldn't have been truthful," I joked, trying to buy some time.

"Stop being so negative about yourself," she said. "Now what's going on over there?"

"It's this big mix-up," I explained. "I could kill Pepper."

"You have to work."

"No—that's the worst part! I have to go out with her boyfriend."

"Her *boyfriend*?"

"I know, it sounds awful." I gave her the Cliff's Notes version. "Pepper swears she's not sleeping with this Colby character . . ."

"Oh, for pity's sake!" Nola was always mercilessly tough when it came to dealing with other people's problems. "Tell her where to get off."

"I can't do that. She's my boss."

"And did she hire you to be a beard?"

"No, but it wasn't like I signed a contract. I'm sort of at her mercy on this. If I don't do it—if I just walk out now—not only will she fire me, but her husband will realize that she was lying and I'll be a little bit responsible for the bust-up."

"That is *sick*," Nola said. "Do you want me to give this woman a call? I would just love to give her a piece of my mind."

That Nola. There were occasions when it was really great to have someone so motherly on your side. The trouble was, she really *would* call Pepper. You had to be careful with her.

"It's okay—only I feel bad for squirreling out on you."

"Well, never mind," Nola huffed. "It's not all your fault, I guess. It's that screwy job you took! Why?"

"Because you told me to."

"Hmph!" I could hear her drumming her fingers, thinking. "Okay, tell you what. Finn's in town till Sunday. We'll have dinner tomorrow night. Will that work for you?"

"Yeah, that'll be good."

Pepper had told me to take tomorrow night off, anyway. She and Spence had some kind of big dinner planned.

I hung up and returned to my closet. A shoe decision still needed to be made. I was just trying to gauge how much heel discomfort I was willing to put up with when the doorbell rang.

The clock read a quarter past seven. He wasn't supposed to be here till seven thirty. I padded cautiously to the door and opened it.

It was Colby, all right. We hadn't been introduced, but I knew it was him. He was just the sort of guy you would expect Pepper to fool around with—he had reddish-blond hair, one of those stocky, muscled builds, and fair skin overly tanned from too much time on the golf links. In high school, he would have been the kind of guy to toilet-paper your house the night before you went on vacation. The kind of guy who would get a DUI and then get his record expunged after his daddy went to the courthouse and raised hell.

He charged right across the foyer, nearly mowing me down. "Jesus Pete! I thought I was going to have to wait out there forever!"

Granted, I wasn't expecting much in the way of enthusiasm from this guy. But this was beyond.

I must have been gawping, because his face twisted in annoyance and he snapped his fingers in my face. "Hey, Helen Keller, you have a bathroom?"

Quaking with anger, I pointed.

He turned on his heel and sped into the bathroom.

I grumped back to my bedroom, practically slamming the door. *No way. Forget it. Uh-un.* If Pepper wanted me to cover her ass, she should have at least have the decency to sleep with someone halfway civilized. And what did I owe Pepper anyway? What the hell was I doing?

I tried to calm down. At least knowing I was going out with this beast made my shoe decision a snap. He didn't rate more than a low platform with a comfort sole.

I came out of the bedroom just as the toilet flushed. A few moments later, Colby emerged, looking calmer. "Phew! Sorry about that. Had Mexican food for lunch."

I gaped at him.

He sighed. "You do talk, don't you?"

I nodded.

"A blue streak, I can tell." He gave me an up and down look. "Are you ready?" The way he said it translated to, "Is that really what you're wearing?"

I grinned. "Uh-huh."

"Okie-doke, then," he said. "Let's get this over with."

As per Pepper's instructions, our first stop was the big house. I was supposed to make a show of having left my wallet in August's room . . . just so Spence would be forced to see that, yes, I actually was going out with this asshole.

I passed by the living room, where Spence and Pepper were sitting miles away from each other, watching a baseball game on ESPN. August was lying across Spence's lap, half asleep. It was the first time I had ever seen her in this room. "I forgot my wallet!" I barked.

Pepper jumped up. Surprise, surprise. "*Did* you?"

I could hear her making extremely loud small talk to Colby even when I went up to August's room.

When I came back down, August ran up to me. "Where are you going, Alson?"

"Dinner." It was a better answer than *The fifth ring of hell.*

"Can Daddy and me go with you?" she asked.

For weeks I had been craving a night out with a real adult. This evening, I realized, didn't qualify. I wished I could take August up on her answer.

When we got into his Range Rover, I sighed. "That August . . ." She was a heartbreaker.

Colby nodded, misunderstanding. "Yeah, kids are annoying, aren't they?"

He made a burning rubber sound as he pulled out of the drive. At the stop sign, he flicked on the AM radio. "You listen to Rush?"

"I'm a music person," I said, answering with what I thought was diplomatic restraint.

I don't know why I bothered. It wasn't like anyone was listening. "You should hear this guy. He's almost as good as Rush."

No Rush Limbaugh, I silently added to my don't-do list.

I slanted a glance at my face in the vanity mirror; it was

frozen into a mask of dread. *How long* were we supposed to stay out?

Colby drove to a steak house. "This is okay, isn't it?" he asked when we were seated, when it was obviously too late to ask for my preference.

"I don't usually eat that much beef," I said.

"Oh, well, they'll have something you can eat," he said. "Shrimp cocktail or something. Everybody has to cater to the vegetarians now."

I was going to point out that a vegetarian wouldn't eat a shrimp cocktail, but what was the point? "I'm not a vegetarian, exactly."

Colby didn't appear to be into nuance. "You people are taking over the world."

"Who?"

"Vegetarians."

"Really?" I asked, staring around the room, where every table seemed to have the equivalent of a small cow cooked up on plates.

Out of irritation, I ordered the pasta primavera. Colby ordered rib eye.

"Pep didn't tell me that you were some kind of feminazi."

She didn't tell me you were a Neanderthal throwback, I wanted to add. "I don't consider myself a feminazi."

He laughed. "Right. None of you people do."

"I think reasonable people can disagree without calling each other names."

"You're calling yourself reasonable?" He shot out his hand to flag down our waiter. "Scotch and water." He looked over at me as an afterthought. "You want something?"

I shook my head.

"You might want to rethink that decision," he said. "I have a feeling this is going to be a long meal."

I ordered a vodka tonic. He was right about it being a long meal. We were there for an hour and a half, which seemed more like a month and a half. After ten minutes of sputtering conversation, we basically gave up trying to communicate and just shoveled food into our mouths.

"Pepper told me you were sort of a pill, but I didn't think it would be this bad," he said over a hunk of pecan pie. Frankly I couldn't understand why he would bother with dessert. I was dying to get home.

I laughed. (I was a little drunk. One vodka tonic had led to another . . .) "Like I would want to pattern myself after Pepper."

"You could do worse," he said.

"Right. An adulteress."

His lips twisted. "Nothing like a broad who throws *Masterpiece Theater* words at you."

"Nothing like a man who still uses the word 'broads,' " I shot back.

"Anyway, what's Pepper supposed to do? She's lonely. It's not like that husband of hers is a saint."

I sat up straight. "Spence?"

He stared at me through heavy, hooded eyes. "That's right. Do you think he's all alone in Hong Kong for weeks on end?"

"He travels on business."

"Baloney. He might be on business, but dollars to donuts he's got some Asian spices sizzling on the side."

The man was nauseating. "Not necessarily," I said.

"You don't know much about men, do you?"

"I know they're not all alike."

His brows raised. "Got the hots for your employer, Nanny?"

I bridled. "He used to be a good friend of mine."

"Right! Pepper told me he was boning you back in high school. It's a pretty wacko setup if you ask me."

"It wasn't—I mean it's not—" I shut my mouth. No sense arguing with this coarse fool.

He chuckled at my discomfort. "Anyway, it's not like you're the first nanny Spence has had a thing for."

My mouth popped open.

"Haven't you heard?" Colby asked. "He was caught *in flagrante* with the last one. Not that I blamed him. *She* was hot."

"You're lying," I said.

He shrugged. "Suit yourself."

"If you don't mind, I'm ready to go home."

His chuckle was irritating. "Look at you. All hot under the collar."

"I've just had enough of this sham date."

"That goes double for me." He stared at his watch and heaved a long breath. "Unfortunately, we still have two hours to kill. I promised Pepper I wouldn't have you back a minute before eleven o'clock."

"This is completely twisted."

"You're telling me," he muttered. "We can go to a movie. *In for the Kill* is playing around here, I saw. I wouldn't mind seeing that."

I dug my fingers into my palms. An explosion movie. What could be better?

Then again, who cared? Explosion movies were one of my dating don't-dos, but this was hardly a date. This was an endurance test.

The next morning Pepper was down early, and in a really crabby mood. Marta shot me a warning look as I entered the kitchen. I have to admit, I was a little stunned to see Pepper there. She hardly ever hung out in the kitchen and rarely showed her face anywhere before ten. Yet there she sat in her bathrobe with a sour look on her face, hovering in a C-curve over a cup of coffee and the paper. You would have thought she was the one feeling slightly hungover from vodka tonics.

The question on my tongue—"Where's Spence?"—I wisely decided to swallow. I had heard his Porsche backing out of the garage this morning. One thing to be said for living over someone's garage: you knew the comings and goings of the house. You just had to guess the details.

Marta usually looked askance at my stealing cups of coffee before going upstairs, but this morning she was feeling generous. Or maybe she just didn't want me to leave her alone with Pepper and that scowl. Suddenly she was Alice from *The Brady Bunch*. "There's coffee," she practically singsonged to me. She even opened the cabinet holding the coffee mugs, as if I didn't know where they were.

So much friendliness almost scared me away.

"Sit down and have a cup, Al," Pepper said, just as I was about to make my escape.

"But August . . ."

She waved a hand, dismissing my objection. "August is up in her room watching that Boobah show. I don't know how anyone could stand that so early in the morning! Why do the British keep sending over these irritating children's programs? Do they hate us?"

I stirred half and half into my coffee. "What I don't get is who thinks of this stuff. All these alien creatures in eye-popping colors and the repetitive songs. It's as if the children of the world are sitting around being entertained by shows dreamed up in drug rehab clinics."

I would have been happy to talk about Boobahs some more, but Pepper had more predictable matters on her mind. "So how did it go last night?"

I shrugged. "Okay . . ."

"How was Colby?"

A pig, I wanted to say. "He was fine."

"He's such a sweetheart. I wish he weren't so nuts about me! He doesn't have a dime, of course."

"I thought he was a lawyer."

"He is! A great lawyer. He handled Phaedra's divorce for her." She sighed. "The trouble is he's such a scamp. He blows it all on vacations, and gambling. Isn't that nuts?"

I agreed that it was.

"He's the kind of man who'll decide to stop wasting his life when he's about fifty. Then he'll find some twenty-year-old to marry him and have three kids and act like family life is the greatest thing in the world."

I responded with a moment of silence to mourn the as-yet-unborn Mrs. Colby.

She eyed the paper in front of her. "I hate men. They're all a bunch of controlling jerks." She was perusing the tiny space that was still roped off for the society section. The rich and famous were relegated now to one half page below the fold, wedged between the horoscopes and the lawn service ads.

"Look at this," she told me. "Here's an example. This is just un-fucking-believable!"

I craned my head so I could see. Instead of the usual photo from some gala event or another, there was a picture of a woman in a sequined leotard. "What's that about?"

"Some old geezer from Houston has run off with a Cirque de Soleil bendy woman! Apparently it's a big scandal down there. The press is having more fun than they've had since Anna Nicole Smith left for Hollywood."

I clucked my tongue. "How old is he?"

"Sixty!"

"Sixty's not that old."

She pointed again at the picture. "Too old to keep up with an eighteen-year-old bendy woman."

My eyes popped. "She's eighteen?"

"That's *his* story. Of course he's married."

"How did he even meet this woman?"

Pepper laughed. "Who knows? The paper said he dug her up in Paris. I guess anything can happen in the city of love!"

Just that one word, Paris, caused my blood to run cold. *Oh, no. It couldn't be!* I was almost afraid to look. "What's this guy's name?"

She bent her head. "Lipton or Tipton or something."

"Tripton!" I exclaimed.

"Right." She frowned at me. "How did you know?"

"He's my stepdad."

Good gossip apparently achieved what caffeine could not. Pepper's eyes blinked open, and she finally looked fully awake. "Oh . . . my . . . God. You are *kidding* me!"

I wished. "No."

"Does your mother know?"

"She must! I heard from her a little while ago while she was in Paris. She didn't know where Murph had gotten himself off to."

"Now she does, I'll bet."

"Now the whole world knows . . ."

I almost uttered the phrase I never thought I would ever in

my life say. *Poor mother.* I swallowed it instead. If ever anybody had it coming to her . . .

But to have the breakup be so public! Not to mention so bizarre. Being left for anyone would be a blow. But a Bulgarian bendy woman!

"The paper says she does a backbend and then twirls hula hoop–like metal rings with her feet," Pepper said. We eyeballed the photograph more closely. "She can swing hoops with both feet at once like that. Isn't that amazing?"

I groaned. "No wonder Mom didn't want to go into details over the phone."

"Something like that's really humiliating," Pepper agreed. "Especially for a woman of a certain age. Though of course nobody likes to be made a fool of."

"But what did *she* do?" I asked, feeling outrage welling in spite of myself. "Murph is the fool. He's the geezer frolicking with the Bulgarian rubber band."

To my surprise, she tossed the paper away from her in disgust. "Oh, I know it! Isn't it irritating? And your mom is *so nice*, too!"

I practically choked. "Huh?"

"She is, I remember her. She was really beautiful, and had this husky voice. Am I right?"

"I guess . . ."

"I always remember looking at your mom and thinking that she was just the type of person I wanted to have as a friend when I was grown up."

Perhaps this was the source of my mother-daughter conflict.

"I'm *sure* she would never let herself go," Pepper said. "She's probably spent years and years keeping herself toned and firmed up and fabulous, am I right?"

"Right."

"But does this old idiot, this Murph Tripton, appreciate it? No! He runs off with some circus tart."

Put that way, it did sound pretty sad. Except that at one time, *my mom* had been the tart Murph had run away with.

Because of her, some other woman had been left sitting alone wondering what the hell had happened to her life.

"What chance does anyone have?" Pepper practically wailed. "All the cards are stacked against women. It really pisses me off."

I cleared my throat nervously. "Well, it's not like *you* have to worry."

She glared at me, but it didn't feel like anything personal. She was just glaring at the world in general. "Everyone has to worry! That's the trouble with the whole damn setup. You can never just *relax.*"

Now I knew why Marta didn't want me to leave. Pepper seemed, well, crazed. As if she were already gazing into the maw of a brutal middle age of Botox and abandonment.

After an interminable minute, she snapped to and laughed. "Oh, well! The more publicity there is, the more sympathy your mom will get. That's bound to help her in the settlement."

"Settlement?"

"Divorce settlement. I hope she has a good lawyer. She does, doesn't she?"

"I don't know."

"You should have her call Colby."

"Oh, right." *When pigs fly*, I thought.

"He's a real whiz. He'll take that jerk for everything she can get."

The idea of another divorce made me sick, and I really hadn't had much to do with the first one. I hadn't been involved at all, really, except through listening to my mom talk about what a pain it all was. Not so much her divorce from my dad, but Murph's from his first wife. At the time, my mom seemed more stressed out about Murph's divorce than about her own. And of course, in that divorce there had been a definite villain, who, according to my mom, was the prior Mrs. Murph. (She was so *grabby.*)

"What a mess," I said.

"Oh, screw it!" Pepper pushed back from the table as if this was all about her. As if she had just undergone some trauma. "I can't stand all this stress. I'm going to spend today at the day spa. I'm sure they can squeeze me in. Don't you ever feel like you'll just die if you don't get a full-body mud wrap?"

"All the time," I said.

"It's *so* good for you." She glanced over at Marta. "That's what I gave Marta for her Christmas present last year. She loved it! Didn't you, Marta?"

What was Marta supposed to say? "It was great."

Pepper looked at me and smiled. "Maybe I can get that for *you* this Christmas!"

I might have managed to mumble some sort of enthusiastic reply.

"I'm sure they'll have good spas in New York."

That perked me up. "New York?"

She nodded. "Can you believe it? Spence dumped that on me last night. We're going to be moving after all."

She didn't sound completely happy about it. Whereas I was suddenly floating. New York! It was like a dream. Not to mention, I was stunned that I had actually made the right decision. It looked like this dumb job was actually going to pay off.

"Aren't you glad?"

"Glad?" she repeated, her voice arcing in distress. "Would you be glad if you had to move across the country, where you were going to have to scrounge up new friends, new everything?"

Actually, I'd be thrilled. I was thrilled. But I could see Pepper was having problems. Probably wondering how she was going to come up with a new squeeze. "It's like *Meet Me in St. Louis*," I said.

"What?"

"That movie. The whole thing centers around the fact that Judy Garland and her sisters don't want to leave St. Louis and move to New York. I never understood that."

"Well I do! I don't understand why Spence's bank couldn't have an office somewhere cool, like LA." She sighed. "Oh, well. At least he'll owe me for this. Big time."

* * *

It was August's swim day, which was usually traumatic. For one thing, I had to squeeze myself into a swimsuit, this tankini thing I had bought three years and ten pounds ago. My job on swim day was to stand in the water, shivering and miserable but pretending I loved it, and try to convince August the water was fine. So far, of course, it hadn't worked.

On swim days I always had to steel myself to face her, and the fight to get her into a swimsuit, and the angry swim teacher who would always glare at me in her racerback Speedo as I, dripping in defeat, led my weeping but otherwise dry charge away from the pool at the end of the lesson. Like it was *my* fault that August wouldn't be coaxed into the water. Obviously the failure was hers, though would she admit it? No, she would just point to all the other kids frolicking in the water like little otters, as if that were somehow proof of her abilities as a swim instructor and my failure as a nanny.

At the appointed time I went back up to August's room, prepared to do battle, but she was perched on her couch, resplendent in her mermaid costume, singing merrily along with a *Mr. Rogers* rerun. A plush towel was neatly folded into a square at her side. She'd even managed to inflate her water wings and had them puffed up on her arms.

"Ariel!" I exclaimed. "You look fantastic!"

She stopped swinging her legs, stopped singing, and turned her head. "My name," she announced, as if I were mentally deficient or perhaps just blind, "is *August.*"

"Oh." No sense pointing out inconsistencies as long as she seemed to have her act together. I was getting ready to coax her downstairs when she punched the television off with the remote, hugged her towel to her chest, and hopped off the couch.

"It's time to go!" she exclaimed, rushing past me.

She was excited all the way to the swim center and kept up a constant tuneless variation on "It's a Beautiful Day in the Neighborhood." She kept running her hands over her capped head, reveling in the feel of the sequins.

"I'm going swimming!" she exclaimed.

Could it have been the outfit that made the difference? Maybe she was clothing confidant, or she actually did think she was a mermaid. Speedo woman looked in disgust at the busy, sparkly ensemble; for a moment I expected her to refuse pool admittance to anything sequined. Yet she had to give credit where credit was due when she noted that August didn't seize up, clamp her eyes shut, and start shrieking the way she usually did at the first whiff of chlorine. She plunged right in, then coughed and paddled around in her water wings, her head arched out of the water with regal care. Of course she ignored everything that the swimming instructor told her, but this was still progress. No one was complaining except one kid who inadvertently got whacked in the leg by an emerald green fin.

At the end of the lesson I made sure August made it out of the pool okay and then slogged up the steps. As I was just about to streak for my towel, an incredible cry went up.

"*Daddy!*"

August was running toward Spence like a green lightning bolt. Grinning, he held out his arms and actually let her wriggly wet body collide with his very expensive suit. I would have been amazed if I hadn't been so mortified. Right now every other thought in my head was crowded out by the awful knowledge that I was dripping wet in an outdated too-tight tankini that made me look like some sort of potbellied Dr. Seuss creation.

He looked up at me and grinned. "Hi!"

"Hi," I said, scooting toward my towel as fast as I could. "What are you doing here?"

"Daddy's taking me to lunch!" August yelled at me.

"You might want to dry off first," I told August, taking her hand. "We'll be back in a jiffy."

Spence frowned. "You're coming too."

"Oh, but . . . I've got the Hummer . . ."

"That's okay. I'll drop you back here afterwards."

"Oh, but . . ."

His gaze met mine. He was smiling. "Am I really going to have to twist your arm? You used to eat like a trucker."

My stomach did an uncomfortable flip. Funny how being told that you were a glutton could sound so sweet. "I still do."

"Good! I know just where we should go."

"Well, okay . . ."

August was tugging on my arm as if she were a husky and I were a sled. "Come on!"

In the dressing room I changed as fast as I could, taking a little more care than usual with makeup. Even after rinsing off in the shower I smelled like chlorine, but there was nothing to do about that.

Not that I was trying to impress anyone. It would be nice to talk to Spence, and I did want to ask him about New York. But it wasn't like I was trying to be a seductress. I would have fallen on my face if I had tried. Sometime in the past month I had turned into one of those women who carried little sandwich bags of Cheerios in my pockets so I could calm an impatient three-year-old at a moment's notice. I wore walking shorts and sensible sandals. And I always hauled around a tote bag of supplies—juice boxes and coloring books and Wet Ones.

"Where are we going?" I asked when we were all wedged into the Porsche.

Spence grinned secretively. "Just a little place I know."

It felt so weird to be in a car with him! Did he feel it too? And not even in old Monte! "What happened to your old Monte Carlo?"

He groaned. "I totaled it in college. Totally totaled it. I skidded and hit a highway barrier, then got smashed from the back by a truck."

"That's terrible!"

"Walked away without a scratch," he said. "But when the police arrived they thought I was in shock because I just stood there, white as a sheet, staring at my poor crumpled car. I had to convince them that I didn't need paramedics. I was heartbroken."

I felt a pang of heartbreak myself. I could remember that car and his silly pride in it so well. In its own way it had more flair than the thing we were driving around in now. Spence hadn't wanted to drive the Hummer; I had the weird feeling that he wanted to show off his snazzy sports car, but there was something completely unimaginative about a rich guy in a Porsche. "What on earth convinced you to get a midlife crisis car?"

"You think I'm too young to have a midlife crisis?"

"The key word would be *mid*life. Most people these days hope to live beyond fifty-six."

"Most people these days don't get married when they're twenty-two. I got a head start on my adult headaches."

Headaches. Hm. "You and Pepper got married right after college?"

"We graduated one month and then eloped the next."

Curious. August was just three. So it wasn't as if they *had* to get married. I wondered what the story was.

Not that it was any of my business.

He could see the calculations going on behind my eyes. "False alarm," he explained. "Take my advice—first go to the doctor, then run off and get married. Or not."

I flicked a glance at August, who was installed in a car seat we had squeezed in the back, and was glad to see that she wasn't paying the least bit of attention to us.

"Not that I regret a thing," Spence added.

"No, of course," I said. Saddling himself down with a superficial, cheating woman with the temperament of a twelve-year-old . . . what was to regret?

Spence zipped onto Greenville Avenue, and we drove past the Whole Foods and my old favorite Chinese joint. "But you see, in ball-and-chain terms, I'm practically forty. I earned this Porsche."

"I like the Porsche!" August interjected.

"You're my girl, Augie," Spence said with a smile in the rearview.

Something about the smile that stretched between them like an invisible cord made my heart squeeze. He *was* still a nice guy—probably one of those fathers who would slip gum into your school backpack and whoopsie-daisy you onto his shoulders when you most needed it. My throat tightened, and I aimed my gaze out the window just as Spence pulled up to a small brick building.

"Remember this?"

"Twist's!" I exclaimed. It was the place we had gone on our first date, which had become something of a hangout for us.

"What's this?" August asked suspiciously.

He turned in the seat and started unbuckling her. I had to flatten myself against the passenger window to avoid brushing up against him. "This is a place I used to come with Alison." He glanced over at me. "Back when we were frisky young things."

I'm sure my cheeks were pink. I actually had to look away, pretending interest in the dull blond brick facade.

"What's frisky?" August asked.

"Happy," Spence said, catching my eye.

His phone rang and he took it out of his pocket. As he spoke in a businesslike tone to some unnamed minion, I hurried August inside and grabbed a table. I tried really hard not to think about being frisky or happy, but unfortunately, I felt both. I had first-date nerves, and this was nothing like a date. Nothing.

Twist's felt like a nineties time warp. The walls were painted in the same deep colors of purple and green that they had been back in school, and there were local concert posters along the wall. It had been a long time since I had thought about Rage Against the Machine. Then again, maybe not long enough.

The Rolling Stones were playing when Spence joined us. "I'm sorry about that. It seems so awful to take a call when I'm with people who have nothing to do with my work."

"It's okay," I said. "You can't help it."

He smiled appreciatively. "It really drives Pepper up a tree."

Score one on Pepper, I thought, unable to resist giving myself a high-five. Mick was singing "Start Me Up," and I hummed along happily for a bar.

"I guess you would call the Stones *beige*," Spence said, reminding me of my old annoying self.

"Geezer rock sounds better with every passing year."

We ordered Cokes and a heap of greasy food.

"What about New York?" I asked. "This morning Pepper mentioned . . ."

"Next month," Spence said in a clipped shorthand. His manner made me suspect that August hadn't been fully vetted on this subject yet. "We're going."

Even though moving had been part of the ad I answered, moving *me* hadn't been mentioned since. I wasn't quite sure how to bring it up. I thought carefully as I twisted a cheese fry loose from a basket.

"You always said you wanted to go there," Spence told me. "You should be happy."

I felt the tension deflate from my body. So that was it, then. "Yes! I'm very excited."

"Good," he said, as if that was that. "I want you to be. I want you to stay with us for a long, long time."

"Oh, I . . ."

He laughed at my discomfort. "Don't worry, I'm not going to make you sign a lifetime contract."

I chuckled listlessly. This didn't feel entirely right, yet I couldn't say that it was wrong, exactly. Oh, maybe an advice columnist would screech at me for sneaking away with my married ex-boyfriend to our old hangout. Maybe Jess would be telling me that all sorts of bells and whistles should have been sounding off in my head. But the way it had unfolded thus far, everything seemed logical. He was just being a little nostalgic.

It was *nice* to know that he hadn't forgotten that we had been happy once. That I wasn't just some sexual stepping stone in his adolescence. To me, he had certainly been much more than that.

"And now I have another reason for wanting to go to New York," he said.

"What's that?"

"To get you away from Colby."

I tried to shrug casually. "Oh, him. He's just a . . . well, someone to go out with. That's all. I haven't dated much."

Spence shook his head. "He makes me sick. I always thought

he had designs on—" I widened my eyes and nodded meaningfully at August. He took the hint. "Well, you know."

Guilt, guilt. In that moment I could have happily strangled Pepper. How could she not appreciate what a fantastic guy she had snagged? How could she jeopardize her marriage for someone like Colby?

And Colby had made up stories about *Spence's* infidelities! Talk about pot-kettle-black. To think that he had criticized Spence—and worse, that I had almost believed him—was revolting.

Spence aimed a lazy smile at me, and my stomach fluttered. "Do you remember the first time we came here?"

I nodded. "The first time we went out."

"After the dance," he said. "Remember that dance?"

"That stupid mixer. You were the lousiest dancer I had ever seen. I was in awe of you."

"Pepper would never dance with me in college."

"No guts. She obviously has low tolerance for public humiliation."

He laughed, then eyed me long and hard. "I can't believe no one has snapped you up yet. Of course, if you go out with lame jerks like Colby, that would be one explanation."

"I don't, usually." I really didn't want to talk about Colby . . . or even any of the guys I'd really dated. What was the point in going through the list of lame relationships that usually barely limped past the three-month mark? "I guess I'm just sort of a loner type."

"You always were. Self-sufficient. Independent. Opinionated."

He made me sound like some granite carving of a pioneer woman, which was exactly the opposite of the feckless wreck that I actually was most of the time.

"I used to admire you for that," Spence said. "I guess I always felt insecure."

"Most high school kids do."

"But you were so sure of what you wanted. Remember? I wanted you to go to Vanderbilt with me, but you weren't having any of it. You wanted to go to Reed and study the fine arts and travel and have all sorts of adventures."

I sucked miserably on my soda. "It didn't quite work out that way."

"I've thought about you so often over the years," he said. "Wondering what you were doing, and what if . . ."

What if *we* had stayed together and gotten married and produced an adorable little girl like August?

My insides felt as if they would turn to mush. I couldn't take it. I splashed my Coke as I slammed the plastic glass down. It beaded along the top of the waxy polish of the wood tabletop.

"Uh-oh!" August yelled, delighting in seeing an adult make a blunder.

Uh-oh was right. I busied myself trying to sop up the spill. My brow furrowed in the effort I was expending, trying to send shut-up vibes to Spence. It wasn't that I didn't want to hear what he was saying. Just the opposite. I was lapping it up like porridge, and I probably would have asked for more if August hadn't been there.

Thank God she was there.

But Spence didn't seem to have any qualms about singing the praises of the Alison Bell of old, even if I had qualms about listening. "You were always giving out advice!" he said, still strolling down memory lane. "I sometimes wonder what would have happened if I'd heeded even a little of it."

"I was just bossy. It's the only-child thing."

"No, it turned out, in a lot of ways, you were right. I think you were pretty good at reading people, even then."

He was referring to all the things I'd said about Pepper. Obviously. I should have listened to Jess. I never should have taken this job. He was going to be my undoing; how was I going to be able to resist falling in love with him, when I was already halfway there? He was going to be Rochester to my Jane. Maybe it wouldn't end up as *Reader, I married him.* Maybe it would just be *Reader, I slept with him.* But that was worse! I knew his wife, and she wasn't a madwoman (not certifiably, anyway) and she wasn't locked away in an attic (unfortunately).

But did I get up and walk out then? Did I tell Spence that we should change the subject? Oh, no.

"What do you mean?" I asked.

He shrugged. "You were always making dramatic pronouncements about things. Remember what you said that one time? 'These high school things never last,' you said. Maybe you were right."

"Oh, that was just . . ." Wait. I had been talking about *him and me*. But that's not what he was thinking about now. He was thinking about himself and Pepper.

I saw the waitress coming at us and nearly jumped for joy. "Look! Here come the cheeseburgers!"

But Spence seemed oblivious. He didn't stop speaking even as the waitress handed us our plates. "Maybe what you should have said that these high school things *shouldn't* last. That there was no way we wouldn't outgrow each other. That nobody in his right mind would fall in love at eighteen and stay in love for the rest of his life."

"Are you hungry?" I asked August in a cheery voice completely at odds with the mournful mood at the table.

I shot a meaningful look at Spence before bending over with frantic eagerness to secure several napkins around his daughter's person. *Shut up*, I tried to communicate with my eyes. *At least in front of August.*

He had to be crazy, going on this way.

Crazy, or very, very sad.

Chapter 11

August didn't mention lunch all afternoon, but the moment she saw Pepper come through the door, she launched herself at her. "Mommy, Mommy! Guess what? Me and Alson and Daddy went to lunch and it was just like old times!"

Pepper, glowing like a pebble just back from the rock polisher's after her day of beauty, stopped in her tracks. She leveled one of those frosty smiles that seemed more appropriate to a soap opera character than real life. It was as if I were suddenly coming face to face with Erica Kane. "Fun!" she told August. "Where did you go?"

"For hamburgers."

I was already in the throes of agony, so I decided I might as well fess up. "Spence took us to Twist's—that old place on Greenville Avenue. Remember?"

She frowned, though that forehead remained a conspicuously flat plane. "Twist's."

"It specializes in clogging the arteries of college students."

She rolled her eyes. "Spence *must* have been feeling nostalgic to go to a place like that. He's usually so careful these days." She walked over to the couch and inspected the bag of cheese puffs that August's hand was buried in.

"Really, Al," Pepper said, "I don't mind a little fun food. I don't want August to starve. But a little less grease might be called for, don't you think? I seem to recall putting grapes on Marta's shopping list."

"Sorry," I said.

August glanced up at me nervously, having sensed that I had just gotten in trouble.

Pepper shrugged. "Oh well. Never mind." She picked up the bag of chips, though. "Spence and August and I are having a big family dinner tonight. I suppose I can manage to get something green down her." *Her* was August, who looked a little less than enthusiastic now about the meal ahead. "Just make sure and have her ready by six on the dot. We have reservations."

"Someplace special?" I asked, feeling a tug of envy.

"Same-old same-old," she said. "The Mansion on Turtle Creek. We're going to discuss the *m-o-v-e*."

"Exciting!"

She laughed mirthlessly. "It's going to be a pain in the ass. But it'll be good to get out of this place for a while, I guess." She stared around her child's swank nursery as if it were a seedy tenement. Then she grinned at me—a sort of unsweetened-lemonade grimace. "And the change will make Phaedra jealous."

That was weird. She was talking about the move as if it were just going to be a sort of elongated vacation. I was about to ask a few nosy questions when I happened to see August staring at us with keen interest. I had no idea how well a three-and-a-half-year-old could collate information, but there was something going on behind those blue eyes that made me shut my mouth.

"So we won't need you tonight till we get back," Pepper told me.

"Oh, but . . ." I was confused. This morning she had been speaking to me almost like a pal. Now her voice was clipped, dismissive. It was her mistress-of-the-house voice.

"Actually, it's my night off," I reminded her. "I had something planned."

"My, you're a regular social butterfly." She sighed. "Well, I suppose it can't be helped."

As Pepper was turning to return to her room, I suddenly remembered something. "Oh! You haven't forgotten about that hundred and ten dollars, have you?"

Her face froze. "Hundred and ten dollars?"

"For the bathing suit. I put the receipt under your door . . ."

"I don't usually carry so much cash on me," she said icily. "I can write you a check."

"A check would be fine."

She nodded and turned to go again. This time she stopped herself. "I don't want to be critical, Al, but a hundred and ten dollars for a child's bathing suit is steep. You realize that, don't you?"

I blinked. "Yes, I know, but . . . she just seemed to like it . . ."

"It's *okay*," she said, as if exasperated with my self-serving excuses. "I just don't like to spoil her. You know how kids can grow up around here."

The memory of Pepper's Dude Ranch flashed through my mind. I knew how a couple of kids grew up around here, for sure. "Of course."

She turned on her heel.

August was remarkably compliant about taking a nap. I was worried if she didn't get some rest she would be cranky at the Mansion and I would be blamed. But apparently now that her daddy was home, August would do just about anything anyone told her to.

I stopped by the kitchen on my way back to my place, deciding to nab a Diet Pepsi from the fridge. Marta glared at me. "You better watch out, girl."

I have to say, Marta was probably thirty-eight, tops. But if you saw her face to face, something about her carried the authority to call me girl. I was annoyed, but I didn't sass back.

"It's okay." I refused to feel guilty about taking a Diet Pepsi so long as Pepper owed me that hundred and ten dollars. "It's just one measly can."

"I'm not talking about stealing colas. I'm talking about stealing husbands."

I was so startled that the can in my hand seemed to sense it.

When I popped open the tab, an arc of Diet Pepsi hissed out and spewed all over the spotlessly clean floor. I lunged for a sponge and started mopping it up. "What?"

"You know what I'm talking about. Lunch."

"What could I do? Spence wanted to have lunch with his daughter."

She put her hands on her hips. From my vantage point on the linoleum, it seemed that she was eyeing me as if I were something unbelievably low. Like a cockroach. "Spence? Even Marisol called him Mr. Smith."

I rolled my eyes. "Whatever!" I turned my attention to mopping up, but then something in what she said distracted me. It reminded me of what the vile Colby had said. "What do you mean—'*even* Marisol'?"

"You went to college. Figure it out for yourself." She laughed bitterly. "Marisol was trying to go to college, too. She was working to save money for community college. She had big hopes."

"So?" I asked. "I don't see what this has to do with anything. I call Spence by his name because I used to know him pretty well. But the key phrase there is *used to.* Now I just think he's a nice guy, that's all."

She practically spat. "Marisol thought he was nice, too. Now Marisol is cleaning motel rooms on the freeway."

"Wait, are you trying to tell me that she was *fired* because she *slept with Spence*?" Marta's eyes widened. "That's the nuttiest thing I've ever heard!" Not that I knew Marisol except from what little info people had told me about her, and maybe some stuff she had left behind. So basically all I knew was that she was a depressed romantic.

A little bell rang in my brain. *Why depressed?* Because of Spence?

I shook my head. Half the people in America were depressed, especially if you went by what that book said.

"You don't know Spence at all if you think that he would . . ."

I'm not sure why I swallowed the sentence. Maybe it was because the meaning behind that bug-eyed expression on Marta's face finally sank in, or because the bristly feeling on the back of my neck made me realize we were no longer alone.

Whatever. At the moment I was simply grateful that the words "screw the nanny" had not yet left my lips.

I stood, slowly, and turned. My hand nervously clenched, resulting in squeezing half the Diet Pepsi back onto the floor. "Oh, hi."

Pepper's blue eyes met mine and held. Far from seeming angry, she seemed simply to be enjoying my moment of writhing embarrassment. "I wanted to give you this," she said, handing me a folded up square of paper. "It's what we talked about."

In avoiding uttering the word *check*, it was as if she were implying how much more discreet she was than me. And given what had just taken place—two servants yacking about the sexual history of their employer—who could contradict her?

"Thanks," I said.

"I hope you have a good evening. If you can ever manage to pull yourself away from the gabfest." She eyed first me, then, more pointedly, Marta.

Marta turned away from me.

I scurried back to my apartment as quickly as my little legs would carry me. What an idiot! Babbling with Marta like two twenty-first-century refugees from *Upstairs, Downstairs*. I must have been out of my mind. Thank God I was free of this, at least for tonight. My answering machine was blinking. The first message was from my dad.

"It's just me, honey. I wanted to see how you were liking your new job. Give me a call this weekend."

How I was liking my new job. That was so like him, to frame the question in the positive. To ask whether I liked it at all wouldn't have occurred to him. His words both made me swell with love for him and dread calling him back, because I would have to work up some convincing positive spin on domestic servitude. No matter how things stood in my life, around Dad my demeanor tended to veer toward a squeaky smiley enthusiasm. *"You're marrying Darla the poodle groomer? That's soooo fantastic!"* I could never bear to see disappointment in his eyes.

The next call was from Nola. "Remember tonight, Al?"

Oh, shit. I ran over to look at my clock, which I kept by my bed, missing most of the message in the process. I was late—and Nola usually kept toddler hours. I was sort of hoping for a Calgon moment. Just a little time to myself. And maybe a cat-nap. Now I was going to have to rush, rush, rush to get both August and myself ready for our big nights. Also, I needed to run Pepper's money by the bank, pronto, before I started bouncing checks all over town.

Still, once I rearranged my brain a bit, I started getting excited about having an evening away from this place. Not that I was particularly looking forward to meeting Finn the do-gooder drip, but at least I could wear something fitted, without pockets. I could drink some wine and not even think about anything Disney for hours and hours.

Having washed and dressed August to the point that she was restaurant-ready, I quickly performed the same duty for myself before scooting out the door. I headed straight for my bank, where I waited in the drive-through line behind a man who had never seen an automated teller machine before, maybe never even seen a keypad. He squinted at the screen for an eternity, apparently perplexed, and when the time came that he finally decided to take decisive input action, his hand seemed to move in slow mo. The upshot was that by the time it was my turn, I was in such a damn hurry that I scrawled my signature and account number across what I soon discovered was a piece of note paper with the name and number of a divorce lawyer on it.

I blinked at the name written in Pepper's loopy writing for several moments. *Colby Cleiburn, Attorney.* It wasn't my check. It was the legal referral for my mother.

As if I would recommend Colby to anyone, for anything. Except maybe as a candidate for a mafia hit.

After I partially recovered from the shock of having no money to deposit, I drove directly to the liquor store, where I picked up two bottles of wine from the mark-down bin and wrote what I feared would end up being yet another a hot check.

When Nola finally opened the door for me, she looked at

me as though I was an alien being who had arrived on her doorstep out of the blue. "Oh, hi."

"Hi." I couldn't help noticing that there was no effort being made to show me through the door. I held up my bottles. "The boozin' nanny has arrived."

Her brow furrowed. "Didn't you get my message?"

"Um . . . message?" If there's one thing I've noticed, it's that people don't appreciate your not listening to every detail of their phone messages. Actually, I hadn't listened to much of hers at all, but I had assumed it was just the usual don't-forget-be-on-time blah blah blah stuff people like Nola always think they have to tell people like me. "Um, no. I left the apartment kind of early."

"Jason has the flu."

I jumped back a step. "Oh!"

"So does Steve. You probably shouldn't be here." I was practically spinning on my heel to run away when she stopped me. "I was just sending Finn out to a movie or something. He's so bored."

"Finn?" He was here when the whole house was sick? I would have been out of there like a shot.

"So this'll be perfect," she said. "The two of you can go have fun." On *have fun* she sent me a long wink. This had been a matchmaking dream of Nola's for a long time.

"Oh, but . . ." I didn't want to be rude, but I didn't even know this guy. Being around him with Nola and Steve was one thing, but this . . . this would be sort of like a date. "Where does that leave you? Stuck at home alone with your sick family."

"Don't worry about me. I'm used to having responsibilities."

"Sure, but . . ."

Just then, a man I could only assume was Finn poked his head around the door. He looked a lot like Steve, only with worse clothes. And Steve wasn't a fashion plate himself. But I doubt even he would have set off to the movies in paint-spattered pants, green Converse sneakers, and a stained and tattered Mr.

Bubble T-shirt. The T-shirt puzzled me; was he being ironic? Finn's hair was shorn almost to his scalp, like a monk's, and he wore a hoop in his lobe. I didn't even bother to check which ear it was, if that made any difference anymore. No self-respecting gay man would ever look like this.

"You must be Alison." He offered me his hand, which had some kind of Chinese character tattooed on it. "Nola's told me all about you." He was edging out the door, and seemed to pretty much take it for granted that we were going out together. "You don't mind driving, do you?"

"Finn doesn't have a license," Nola explained.

"I can drive, of course," he assured me, as if the way I was angling away from him had anything to do with his nonlegal status as a motorized vehicle operator. "I just choose not to, because I don't want to contribute to the gas-guzzling, petroleum-dependent car culture."

"That'll show 'em."

His eyes widened, and he drew back as if I had poked him with something sharp. Almost as if he'd never encountered sarcasm before. Surely that couldn't be right, though. I mean, the guy lived in New York City, which was the sarcasm capital of the world, right?

"You'd be surprised how much difference one person can make, Alison."

I sighed. It was going to be another long, long night.

"I liked that movie a lot, didn't you, Alison?"

Wouldn't you know it, Finn had chosen a teacher movie. Not a genre I'm particularly fond of. Granted, there wasn't an explosion in the whole thing, just a few gunshots when the Harvard-bound kid from the ghetto got in wrong with some of his old homeboys. I mean, it was a vast improvement on *In for the Kill.* But this was one of those movies where you sit down and watch ten minutes and get the creeping feeling you've seen it all before. As if you could predict every dramatic emotional scene right down to the red and gold autumn leaves quavering on the trees.

"It was okay," I said.

Finn looked hurt.

"Better than I expected," I added, looping my voice up to feign a positive response.

"You slept through some of the best parts."

The most boring sappy parts, he meant. But I have to say, I was grateful for them. It had felt great to get a little catnap. I actually came out of the theater refreshed. (Nothing like some stolen shut-eye to prepare you for the night of insomnia ahead.) "You want to go someplace and get a drink?" he asked.

I had been hoping Finn would want to call it a night. I was doubtful that we could actually keep a conversation going through a cup of coffee. "You don't think we should get back?" I asked. "Nola . . ."

He rolled his eyes. *Rolled them.* I hadn't thought him capable of looking so snide.

Maybe there was hope for him after all. "What?" I asked.

He seemed reluctant to dish the dirt on his sister-in-law. But only about five seconds of reluctant, it turned out. "Oh, you know Nola. She's in her element during times like this. Being in charge of sick people is like a big affirmation for her that she's the hypercompetent center of the universe."

Oh my God. This was my friend he was talking about. Which is what made the implied criticism so double plus satisfying.

Don't get me wrong. I liked Nola a lot. But is there anything more gratifying than finding out that another person has been cheesed off about someone for the exact same reason? I felt a sudden camaraderie with Finn.

"I know a great place for coffee," I said, taking his arm.

Over mocha sprinkled lattes Finn opened up some more. "I hope I didn't give you the wrong impression. I really love Nola."

I nodded like crazy. "Me, too."

"I'm so glad my brother found her."

"Of course."

"She just drives me nuts sometimes. It's as if she thinks I don't know how to live my life."

This was amazing. She always praised Finn to the skies, and yet she made him feel as if he didn't measure up. Just like she made me feel. Which made me wonder . . . was she also saying nice things about me behind my back? That would be freaky of her. Like being a bitch in reverse.

"I always want to tell her that I managed my life just fine without her input," he said.

I was forced to bite my tongue. I mean, sure he probably got through college and made a living. But he obviously could have used someone to tell him not to wear his Mr. Bubble T-shirt out with a girl. I was surprised Nola hadn't.

I guess she was busy being responsible.

"I always think she worries I'll finally hit rock bottom and she'll have to take me in as a permanent charity case," I said.

He smiled knowingly. "She's mentioned something to that effect."

Great. She *wasn't* saying nice things behind my back.

"But she said you have this terrific new job now," he added quickly. He frowned. "You're . . . a nanny?"

I nodded.

"I have a hard time picturing you as a nanny. Or anyone, really. I still think of nannies in terms of *The Sound of Music*. Is that what you do?"

"Sort of. I don't burst into song as much as Julie Andrews, of course."

When he smiled, I realized that Finn was actually pretty cute. Viggo Mortenson, emaciated. Why hadn't I noticed right away? He had really great eyes, and even that head was sort of intriguing. All that fuzz. What would it feel like to run my palm over the top of it?

I am not, was never, a shy person. If I'd really been curious, I would have reached over and rubbed my hand on his head as if it were a lucky Buddha belly. The truth was, no matter what I thought of Finn, there was a screen separating us. I just had that gut feeling that it didn't matter. It was as if I were in love with someone else and didn't have room to think of Finn seriously.

Not that I *was* in love with anyone else. Yet I couldn't help comparing him to Spence, just a little. When I'd sat across the table from Spence, I had felt nerved up, off balance. I'd experienced that stomach churning uneasiness that goes hand in glove with lust. With Finn I just felt a removed kind of curiosity, even if he did sort of look like Viggo.

"You must really love children," he said, probably uncomfortable with the way I was studying him like a zoology student would study a bug.

"Mm. With certain reservations."

"I work with teenagers."

That was my reservation. "That's what Nola told me. Troubled teens."

"Runaways, mostly. Street kids. We have a mission on the Lower East Side."

"That sounds extreme."

His brows raised. "It's so rewarding, some days it doesn't feel like work at all. Being around those kids, it makes me realize how lucky I've been. How pampered."

"But don't you ever have trouble with them?"

"Oh sure. Like, every day. But then we'll do something that'll make me realize that I'm coming at everything from a completely different perspective."

"Like what?"

"Well, last Christmas, for example. I took a bunch of the kids to get a tree for the shelter. The Christmas tree outfit in the parking lot down the street had donated a tree—we could have picked out anything. We could have gotten a tree to rival Rockefeller Center's if we'd felt like it. But those kids, they gravitated to every sad-sack spindly tree there was. When I talked to one of my coworkers about it, they said it's the same story every year. These kids, for all their swagger, empathize with the downtrodden. Even if it's just a tree."

That was sweet, in a sad way. In fact, there was something sweet and sad about Finn himself. Or maybe he just seemed sad to me, because he was obviously clinging tenaciously to his ideals. I dunno. Color me cynical. Peter Pan syndrome can take many forms, and it seemed to me that a guy living in modern American who was still spouting things like "one man can make a difference" had to be living in his own version of Neverland.

Spence would never say anything like that. And look at him! He had been out in the world, really out in the world. He had made himself a big success.

I suddenly wondered what it would be like to sleep with Spence again—a thought I had been consciously avoiding. But there it was. It had slipped right past my mental gatekeeper.

Clearly, I was losing my mind. I trained my brain on the subject at hand, and attempted a little flirtatious flattery. Just to prove to myself I didn't want to sleep with Spence *that* much.

"I admire someone who can work with teenagers. They're such a pain in the ass." Okay, it didn't come out quite like I intended.

His brow squeezed into a few ridges of lines. "Didn't Nola tell me you were a teacher once?"

What was up with her? Had she given this guy my entire life story? "I was a substitute teacher," I said, the way a person might confess to having been mugged. "It's not something I like to think about."

A brow arched toward his fuzzy scalp. "That bad?"

"I never had a lot of control. I think I lack physical authority." I swallowed. "I had a kid chase me down a hallway with a mop."

He blurted out a laugh. Probably he would have broken down into side-splitting cackles if he hadn't caught my glare. That sobered him up. A little.

"It was an *industrial* mop," I said, bristling. "Stolen from the janitor's closet."

His lips trembled toward a smirk, but he managed to keep it together. Just a slight titter escaped him.

Oh, sure, when you tell people that a kid chased you down the hall with a mop, it doesn't sound that traumatic. I mean, a mop, even an industrial mop, is not a lethal weapon. It doesn't have the dramatic power of an Uzi or a jagged-edged knife. Also, the fact that it was an eighth grader chasing me takes away from the dramatic power a bit. But have you taken a look at fifteen-year-olds lately? Have you heard their vocab?

Finn cleared his throat. "Wow . . . that must have been . . ."

"It was pretty awful, actually," I said. "It wasn't just the mop, it was what he said he was going to do with the mop. Cram it down my throat . . . and other places. Also, it was during lunch, so the hall was deserted."

"Oh." He frowned.

"Anyway, it was about as much of the blackboard jungle as I could take. I spent the next three months collecting unemployment and taking jujitsu."

He drew back. "No kidding? Are you . . . a black belt? Do they have those in jujitsu?"

"I didn't stick with it that long."

"That's great, though! You took adversity and turned it on its head."

Oh, brother. Another minute and he was going to start talking about making lemonade when life gives you lemons. "I became a paranoid nut, is what happened."

"Yeah, but you channeled it into something practical."

"It's not practical," I said. "Self-defense can only work if you've worked so hard at it that it's second nature. If someone comes at you out of the blue with a knife or a gun, it won't do you all that much good."

"I'd love to know how to do martial arts," he said. "Could you teach me?"

"Huh?"

"Just a throw or something."

"Here?" Was he nuts? It was practically empty and the lighting was low, but I was pretty sure somebody would notice if I started tossing my date around.

"Outside," he said, laughing.

"Oh, I . . ."

You had to hand it to the guy. He had enthusiasm to spare. Within minutes we were outside, with Finn facing me in a bandy crouch and spread arms—a position he must have learned from watching Jackie Chan movies.

"I don't feel good about this," I said. "I'm not an expert, by any stretch."

"Sure you are. This will be great for me in New York. I'll actually have a survival skill."

He seemed to need that. Finn was the type of guy who had miraculously not been mowed down by reality yet . . . one of those stubborn shoots of grass that the lawnmower blades miss. "Okay. We'll start with something simple. The point is to use your opponent's strength against him. So take it slow, and come at me from the side."

Eager as a puppy, he charged. My long-ago training kicked in and I hooked him just like my instructor had taught me. Finn flipped over my leg. He wasn't as heavy as I expected. Those baggy clothes probably disguised bones poking against skin.

The upshot was, when I turned around, Finn was lying on the ground. He had hit the curb where it met the grass. His body was motionless.

I ran over.

"Are you okay?"

He didn't respond.

Oh, shit. I've killed him. The next thought that occurred to me was, *Nola's never gonna let me live this down.*

Finn groaned and I fell to my knees next to him. Maybe he'd just had the wind knocked out of him. I hoped.

"Are you all right?" I asked. "Can you talk?"

He gargled something at me.

"*What?*"

"My . . . side . . ."

"Should I call an ambulance?" I asked. "We could take you to the emergency room."

That seemed to bring him around. "No!" he said. "God, no."

"But if you're hurt . . ."

"No insurance," he said. "I'll be okay. Just . . . help me to the car?"

"Okay, but maybe we shouldn't move you."

He laughed, then winced. "Are we going to get me there through levitation?"

I took sarcasm as a good sign. Or maybe an evening with me had just driven him to express hostility. That was a distinct possibility.

"I'll be fine," he said. "Give me a hand."

I wasn't so sure. But I was down with the no insurance problem. Yes, emergency rooms had to take anybody who came through their doors, but that didn't mean they wouldn't harass you until the day you died. (The day you finally had the good sense not to seek treatment you couldn't afford and died, that is.)

I half-dragged Finn back to the car and drove carefully back to Nola's. He was holding himself stiffly but seemed talkative enough. "When you said you weren't an expert, I thought you were just being modest."

"I'm never modest," I said. "I just don't have anything to brag about."

He laughed a little, and even though it came out as a forced wheeze, I was hoping that was a good omen. Maybe he was just bruised.

When we got to the house, the porch light was on. The front room's window curtain drew back, and I saw Nola first peer out at us then go bug-eyed at the way I helped Finn out of the passenger seat. Moments later she was skimming out in her practical but feminine nightgown and robe. Her sockless feet were jammed into sneakers. "What happened? Where have you been?"

"We had a . . . well, sort of an accident."

"An accident!" she screeched.

"Shh," Finn said as I dragged him along. "It's not that big a deal."

"Not a big deal!" Nola said as I handed him over to her. "Look at you—you can barely walk. Are you two drunk?"

It was all I could do to keep a straight face. She was like the mother of a wayward teenager—in fact, she would be the mother of a teenager someday. Maybe she was practicing on us. I felt like calling Jason out for a preview.

"We went out for coffee, and I started to give him a martial arts demonstration . . ."

She eyed me stonily. "In the middle of the night?"

"It's not even midnight."

"Where were you?"

"The parking lot of the coffee shop."

"A parking lot!"

"There was a little patch of grass," I explained.

"Oh, I give up!" she said, one arm akimbo. "You are hopeless. Now we'll have to go to the emergency room."

"I'm fine, Nola," Finn insisted, though honestly, as much as I could have wished otherwise, he didn't look so hot. "Don't blame Alison. We had a lot of fun."

Fun! Maybe his definition of that term was looser than mine. Mine didn't include anything that included pain.

Nola looked skeptical, too. "You'd better go inside and lie down."

"Yeah, I think so," he agreed.

I called after him, attempting at the last moment to inject some perkiness into my voice. "Bye, Finn—maybe I'll see you in New York soon!"

He pivoted awkwardly, still holding his side, and winced. "I'd like that," he said. Then he shut the door, leaving me alone. With Nola.

Nola in her responsible adult mode. My own parents had been so permissive, I didn't have much experience with this you've-got-some-'splainin'-to-do attitude. She withered me. The longer she stared at me, the smaller I became. "Honestly, Al! I'm so disappointed. I was really hoping you two would hit it off."

I snorted. "Then you got your wish. You might say I threw your brother-in-law for a loop." When she didn't respond, I added, "That was a joke."

She was not amused. "I should have known you would screw everything up."

"I didn't screw anything up. It was an accident. Even Finn said so."

"He would! Finn never says a negative word about anybody. For heaven's sake, Al, if you didn't want to go out with him, all you had to do was say so. Just say so flat out. You didn't have to nearly kill him. You don't have to do this passive-aggressive act all the time."

Passive-aggressive? "It was an accident!"

She folded her arms like a third-grade teacher. "You're *so* full of it. You're always letting things hit the crisis stage and then blaming somebody else."

Tell me honestly: Had I blamed anybody? Had I?

I was about to point out that saying something was an accident is the very opposite of placing blame, when one little word she'd tossed out stopped me in my mental tracks. "*Always?* When have I ever . . . ?"

She rolled her eyes. "Please. You're twenty-eight and your life has just stalled. Stalled. But have you ever *tried* to move forward? All these dead-end jobs . . ."

"The economy doesn't exactly favor people with liberal arts degrees right now . . ."

". . . that awful apartment you holed up in for months . . ."

"Because I had no money!"

"You could have asked your father at any time."

"I would never ask for money." She didn't understand. "My dad doesn't have much. And he gave me so much when I was young. If anything, I feel indebted to him."

"You're just doing the martyr thing."

I sighed. She was wrong, wrong, wrong, but she was wearing me down. "Anyway, it's different now. I have a job, I moved."

"Yes, after I practically had to spell it out for you that you had to take the job. For God's sake, Al, this is what I'm trying to tell you. If you want something, you have to reach for it. Take it. The same goes for what you don't want. Just say so. Going on dates to cover up the affair of that shrew you work for! I mean, that just said it all to me."

"Said what?" I asked.

"That you just have no backbone. You can't be forever waffling over decisions or tripping guys in parking lots or going around blaming a bankruptcy that happened ten years ago. Otherwise you'll never get a life, never get married, never find happiness. You'll just go on being this strange, abnormal person. What's okay for a twenty-six-year-old is *not very attractive* in a thirty-year-old woman."

Strange, she called me. Abnormal! "Has it ever occurred to you that I might not want to settle down and follow your template of happiness? Because if you don't mind my saying so, your marital bliss doesn't make me weak in the knees, Nola. I'm not dying to follow in your footsteps."

Her eyes flashed, and I knew then that I had just done something bad. Very bad. I had broken the rule. *Never insult anyone's husband, marriage, or children to her face.* And never insult Nola, period.

But the hell of it was, I was still restraining myself. Now that I had bitten back, there was more I wanted to say. Things like, *Did it ever occur to you that you would have more friends if you didn't treat everyone around you like a mental deficient?* Or, *What's it to you if I am single forever?*

"You'd better go home," she said after an extended frosty silence.

"Nola . . ."

She was not in a mood to reconcile. She lifted her chin. "Go," she commanded, casting me out of her life, which was, as we know, her idea of paradise.

What could I do? I went.

Chapter 12

I did not sleep well that night.

Accustomed as I was to Nola's telling me what the matter was with me, I had never before felt, so deep down, that she was so *right.* How did I know she was right? Because I lay in bed the entire night, staring at the ceiling, fuming about how wrong she was. In my head I told her where to get off about a million times. I mentally wrote my autobiography in a thoroughly sympathetic light, and wrote hers, too . . . showing her up for the bossy, priggish, controlling meanie that she was and always had been. The woman had probably emerged from the womb wagging a scolding finger at the doctors and nurses.

But the awful truth was that there were undeniable little germs of reason in all the things she said about me. I resented that more than anything.

I woke the next morning exhausted by my night of self-justification. Nothing can wear you out like defending your life to someone who's not even there. The worst part was, Nola would have been gratified to know that at least a little of what she had said had penetrated my thick skull. She'd won. I did need to be more assertive, I decided. To make a start, I decided to demand my money from Pepper.

I dressed hurriedly in a power-nanny outfit of linen shorts and a matching vest over a tidy knit top. As I stuffed some sandwich bags of Froot Loops into my pockets, I decided I wasn't going to take any shit from Pepper this time. I wasn't going to let the matter drop until I had that money, preferably in cash, in my hot little hands.

When I entered the house, I was immediately struck by the silence. I remembered, vaguely, the sounds of many cars coming and going as I came to consciousness this morning, and started wondering what that could have meant. I made my way to the kitchen to ask Marta what was up.

But in the kitchen, I didn't find Marta. Just Pepper, sitting at the table, sipping coffee. "Finally!" she said. "I thought I was going to have to go over to your place to roust you out of bed."

"I'm sorry," I said, "my alarm didn't go off."

The elaborate rolling of her Lancômed eyelids told me she wasn't buying that excuse. "Well, never mind. At least you're here now. Everything is a mess!"

"What's happened?"

"What *hasn't*?" she asked. "Spence has flown off to New York, and I'm going to follow him tomorrow."

"Tomorrow?" I squeaked.

You leave the house for one evening . . . That must have been some family powwow they'd had last night. I immediately wondered if Spence's hasty departure had anything to do with a personal conflict between them. Or the fact that he and I had had that little get-together at lunch yesterday. Maybe that's why he felt he had to leave . . .

Stop that!

"You'll need to move your stuff over to the spare room today," Pepper instructed, "so you can stay with August while I'm gone."

"August isn't going with you?"

She sputtered. "Apartment hunting will be difficult enough without a three-year-old. She's Pocahontas today, by the way. It's been driving me out of my mind."

Oh, God. Back to that.

I peered around the kitchen. "Where's Marta?"

"She isn't here anymore. We had to let her go."

My jaw nearly came unhinged. Let Marta go? How could she have done that? "Why?"

She sent me a cold stare.

Just then, a vision of yesterday afternoon occurred to me. Marta staring bug-eyed over my shoulder as I rattled on about family gossip—gossip about Spence sleeping with Marisol. The memory made me wince. Pepper had probably heard us talking for minutes before I knew she was there. But was that grounds for firing someone?

Apparently so.

Pepper gave me the official response. "Marta was becoming more irascible with every single day, and we just decided it was time to part company. Also, the move to New York would have left her here alone without much to do."

"But she was supposed to look after the house."

"We don't need a full-time employee for that," Pepper pointed out.

"But you'll need someone."

She huffed out a breath. "Maybe so, Al. I'll hire a service—or Spence will. About goddamned time he tended to something around here! I'm sick of handling *everything* by myself."

I nearly fainted. Everything? She handled nothing.

"The upshot is, Al, we need you now to fill in the cracks. Help keep the house clean, et cetera. I'm sure it can't be too much. Marta was so slack about everything! You don't have a problem with that, do you?"

What could I say? *No, I won't help?*

She didn't wait for my answer. "I knew you would be a good sport about it."

"Of course," I lied. "But . . ."

"But what?"

"I just worry about Marta. I hope I wasn't responsible for this."

Her eyelids batted in a stony blink. "Why?"

"Well, because . . . of yesterday . . ."

She continued to stare me down, as if daring me to mention the gossip about Marisol. Because that was what had precipitated Marta's being canned. There was no doubt in my mind about that. I felt like shit about it. The thought of quitting in protest flashed across my mind.

For about three seconds.

Who was I kidding? I wasn't about to give up my job now that I was on the brink of going to New York. Nor was I about to distance myself from the delicious temptation of Spence just when I was beginning to get a toehold in his thoughts. I wasn't that noble.

"I have no idea what you're talking about," Pepper said. "The bottom line is, Marta's gone, and we'll all need to pitch in to deal in her absence. Okay?"

I nodded.

"Good! But there's so much to do, and now I've got a manicure in just a few minutes! I've got a few things I want you to look into. 'Kay?"

"Of course . . ."

"I need you to line up movers and get estimates while I'm gone. Shipping *and* packing, natch. I'll let you know the big pieces that stay, and they'll need to fax the estimates to Spence's New York office. There are also a few other little things to do, like getting the pool drained. Nothing you can't handle."

"I don't know anything about pools," I said.

"Of course you don't," she said. "That's why you call the pool service and have someone else do it."

"Oh."

She fixed me with an impatient glare. "Really, Al, don't go dense on me. Even Marta was able to handle this sort of stuff."

It was only after Pepper had left for New York that I remembered the issue about my check had not been resolved.

I had always assumed Marta was a sort of institution in the house; she never seemed to be doing anything . . . or if she was, it seemed to be casual work. Running a feather duster over a few tables, wiping down a counter here or there. Issuing barbed comments intended to make me feel like an idiot. But once she was gone, I realized how false my assumption was. In her own quiet way, she must have been working like a Clydesdale.

The place was falling apart at the seams without her. For a house that seemed hermetically sealed and airtight, dust collected at an alarming rate. Dishes stacked up when I wasn't looking, even when it didn't seem that anyone had eaten anything, and grease formed on counters in a household where it appeared no one had consumed so much as an ounce of fat in decades. By the end of a week, I wanted to go beg her to come back. Or beg Pepper to beg her to come back.

That didn't happen, needless to say. I never heard from Marta again. I tried calling her at home, but she had a message machine, and she never returned my messages. What did I want from her anyway? Absolution, maybe. I wanted to be assured that she didn't blame me for being put out of work. Yet right or wrong, I'm sure she did blame me.

Another thing I wanted was advice. Unfortunately, Marta hadn't left a Rolodex behind. Apparently she had never written anything down, and just carried vital information around in her head like a covert CIA operative. Before Pepper left for New York City, she handed me a to-do list of all sorts of things I was to manage while she was gone. The exterminator. The plumber to fix a leak on an outside faucet. The lawn care company.

"Who do you use?" I asked her.

"Marta used to set up all of that. She must have the numbers written down somewhere."

But she didn't. Or maybe she had destroyed the evidence before she left. Perhaps it had all been part of her grand scheme. Code name: Operation Confuse the Idiot Who Inherits This Damn Job.

Nola wasn't returning my calls, but the day after Pepper left, I got a postcard with a drawing of Presbyterian Hospital on it.

Nola insisted on coming here, but the doctors said I just had bruised a rib. Enjoyed the coffee! Call me when you get to NYC. 555-0120. Finn.

At least someone forgave me. I was impressed that he had taken the time out of his emergency room visit to buy stationery to write a bread-and-butter note on. He scored major Emily Post points for that.

A few days after Pepper left, I was worn out from looking after August, a 2,800-square-foot house, and a pool (which, having been drained, I couldn't even enjoy). More than anything, I wanted to get out of there, so I called my dad and told him I was bringing him a surprise.

The surprise was August, and Dad was delighted.

August was thrilled about the road trip. I bought her a Dr. Seuss coloring book and a new set of crayons for the two-hour drive. She told me she had never been on a farm before, and practically went insane when I told her she would see dogs and a tractor.

My dad did give her the ride on his John Deere tractor, an old-fashioned thing, practically an antique. Darla made a big fuss over her, too, and luckily there were several friendly dogs at the groomer that day, so August got to spend part of the morning petting a recently groomed beagle named Lou.

While August was making friends in the canine world (and presumably with Darla) I tracked down my dad. He was participating in what had become his favorite activity since moving to the farm—weed whacking. He had bought one of those super brush mowers advertised on TV, and when I finally hunted him down, he gave me a demonstration of its expertise that itself would have made a good infomercial. When he was done, he seemed almost giddy to let me have a turn.

"Go ahead," he said, pushing me toward the bar, "it's not hard. Darla does it all the time. She loves it."

He really did seem to like his new toy, so I gamely mowed down some kudzu.

"Isn't that great?" he asked, running his hand lovingly along the handlebar. "Almost as easy as mowing Bermuda grass."

I allowed how it was, though never in my life had I mowed Bermuda or any other variety of grass. Had Dad forgotten the gardeners? The carefully clipped hedges around our old house that none of us had ever touched? In fact, this was the first time I had laid hands on an object designed to cut greenery.

"Maybe the little girl would like to try it," Dad suggested.

I shuddered. Pepper might not care too much about what August did, but chances were she expected her daughter to be in one piece when she got back from New York. I preferred to keep her away from anything motorized with large blades.

"I don't think weed mowing would be age appropriate." Dad hadn't been what you would call a hands-on parent. He was more the type who would wave at me through the patio window, scotch in hand, as I romped around the backyard by myself in the evenings. He had more important things on his mind—like keeping a business afloat.

"Oh." He looked disappointed. "I guess you're right."

"But thanks for being so nice to her, Dad. I know we descended on you without giving you and Darla much warning."

"That's okay!" he said. "Heck, you know I always enjoy seeing you. Wish you could make it down more often. I certainly don't need a warning to see my favorite person in all the world."

A wave of separation anxiety overtook me. I really didn't visit Dad enough. And now I would be moving to New York and would probably see him even less. I hadn't told him about the move yet, and now I wondered if I could. Or if I should even go at all.

How could I leave Dad out here in the middle of nowhere? I was his only family. Sure, he had Darla. But she was Darla. His late-midlife-crisis wife.

"I understand that you're busy," he added quickly. "That's a sweet girl you're taking care of."

I nodded.

His forehead crunched into a network of ridges. "But on the phone you said her name was April."

"August," I corrected. "It is. She's just Eloise for today."

"Is that right," my dad said, as if that were perfectly normal. "Well, I sure am glad you got such a good job, honey. I'm glad those Bramford Prep connections have paid off."

He made it sound as though I had been hired as a consultant to a Fortune 500 company. Only my dad would construe getting a nanny position from a high school classmate as really reaping the benefits of my connections. I squirmed, in part because I wanted to tell him to stop putting such a rosy spin on everything. It was irritating. And yet the statement was so deeply like him, so endearing in its way, I would have died before contradicting him. My poor dad. Was it any wonder he was glad to bow out of the business world?

"Naturally I wish you didn't have to work at all."

I laughed. "Oh, Dad!"

"No, I mean it. I wish I could do more for you."

"I don't mind working, it's finding the right job that's so taxing," I explained. "I like making money."

He shook his head, apparently trying to rattle those pre–Gloria Steinem years out of it. "You women, now."

"Now and for the past twenty years," I reminded him. "If I didn't work, what would I be?" *Pepper*, I thought enviously. I'd be having love affairs and mud wraps. Then I thought of someone else. "I'd be Mom."

"Would that be so bad?"

I remembered my missing mom. Dad apparently hadn't gotten wind of the scandal. The hell of it was, if I told him about the Bulgarian bendy woman, he wouldn't have even been gleeful. Just sad. Meanness just wasn't in him. He'd shake his head in disappointment over it. He still didn't blame Mom adequately for bailing out on us.

I felt such a surge of affection for him then, I gave him a big hug. For all his courtliness, he wasn't a huggy dad, really, but he squeezed me back.

Why wasn't I more like him? I wondered. If I was smart, I should have just told Pepper to forget the job and moved down to the farm and tried to soak up some of Dad's personality. And shed some of my own. Maybe that way I could turn myself into the type of woman who didn't dream of now married exboyfriends and bruise the ribs of peace-loving, do-gooder potential suitors.

For about five minutes I longed to snuggle back into the bosom of my family . . . or this fractured little corner of it. The farm wasn't home, exactly, but I was Daddy's girl enough to get misty eyed over the idea of packing my bags and moving into the spare room. And Dad needed me. I wasn't sure he was happy with Darla at all. How could he be? She wasn't part of our past; she had no idea. In her down home way, she was like Spence's Porsche. She was a consolation, but not what Dad had chosen originally. Not who he truly was.

"I'm happy things are coming together for you, Al."

Coming together? I was halfway in love with the guy I was in love with ten years before . . . and he was married. And technically, my boss. I had a job I could barely handle working for a woman who seemed, to put it politely, bipolar, and I was more broke now than when I had been unemployed. And now I was actually casting my lot by moving halfway across the continent with these people.

"Actually, I came down because I have more news for you," I said.

His face lit up. "Well good! Let's go in the house and call Darla over. I've got something I've been meaning to tell you, too."

"What?"

He chuckled. "Don't be so impatient. Let's go have some iced tea."

That was one great thing about Darla. She knew how to make sweet tea. Old-fashioned, full-sugar, crumble-your-tooth-enamel-on-contact sweet tea. There was always a jug of the stuff in the fridge.

We went inside and poured ourselves glasses. The mercury was stuck somewhere in the upper nineties, and it felt good to chug that cold sweet stuff. It was almost like iced syrup. After a quick phone call from Dad, Darla and August came in from the trailor for a break, smelling like dog shampoo.

"Seems like we've all got news, honey."

"Really?" Darla and I asked at the same time.

Darla's and my gazes collided. It always stunned me to hear Dad calling someone honey and have it not be me.

"Did you tell her already?" Darla's voice twanged with disappointment. "I told you we should wait till the doctor said . . ."

"I know, but she's here now, so let's just tell her."

That word *doctor* was like an ice cube down my back. My mouth turned up in a foolish grin. "Doctor? What's this?"

But I knew. I knew with a certainty that made me almost woozy with dread.

Darla and Dad were smiling like idiots now. It was Darla who finally said the words. "We're pregnant!"

Okay, a word about Darla. Basically, I like her. She is a fundamentally good person. I know I have been dismissive of her. I have called her leathery, weatherbeaten, and old. (Apparently she wasn't quite as old as I thought.) She just didn't seem like a great match for my dad, and I had never imagined her being, you know, fertile.

Suddenly the thought that this woman was going to give birth to what would be my half sibling, twenty-eight years my junior, made me seek out the nearest chair and sink into it.

"Isn't that something?" Dad asked.

I nodded vigorously.

"I still haven't been to the doctor," Darla said, "so it's only EPT official."

She and Dad laughed ruefully in that way that made me suspect there had been a nervous pregnancy-test bathroom scene in their recent past.

I downed the rest of my glass of tea in one slug, but I still couldn't get the *eeeeeeewwww!* out of my system. I tried hard. My dad was just in his fifties. Still, I admit I was a little freaked.

August regarded all of our faces. "What's pregnant?"

"It means that soon Alison's gonna have a little brother or sister to love on!" Darla exclaimed breathlessly.

August asked me through narrowed eyes. "Is that good?"

I was going to do my level best to pretend that it was, but Dad mercifully saved me from having to act at length. Maybe he sensed that my thespian skills were rusty.

"Didn't you say you had some news, Al?"

I had to cudgel my brains for a moment to come up with anything. *News? Me?* And then I remembered. New York! Thank God, I thought, forgetting that just a few moments ago I had wanted to move into Dad's spare room. The spare room would soon be occupied anyway.

"I'm going to New York with the Smiths," I announced. "We'll probably be leaving in a matter of weeks."

Dad's face sagged momentarily, but he was soon smiling again. "Why, that's terrific. You always did want to live up there. And don't you have a little friend in New York?"

"My best friend from college."

"Well that's terrific!" He meant it, too. He wasn't crushed at all.

Surprisingly, it was Darla who expressed the most distress. "Well, shoot! I hope you can come home sometime next February. I'm pretty sure that's when the baby'll be due. We've already decided we want to do a natural home birth, upstairs in the new sauna bathtub your daddy just had put in. It'd be awful if you missed out on that."

Just awful, I agreed.

Pepper returned from NYC without Spence. (Terrible but true: I made mental chalk marks every time I saw signs of the marriage eroding.) She did come back with pictures, however—fistfuls of snapshots of every square inch of the apartment she had rented. And what an apartment! Five bedrooms. Three and a half baths. Park views.

"It used to be Fred Astaire's apartment, when he lived in New York in the twenties," Pepper told me. "Did you know he lived there back then? I had no idea he was so old! But of course he would have to be, since he's dead."

I was naturally most interested in the room that was going to be mine. From the pictures, it wasn't quite as swank as the rest of the house. For instance, the one window did not have a park view. It had a brick-wall view. But it did have a private bath. And it was in New York. When I described it to Jess, she nearly fainted. "Are you kidding? Fifth Avenue?"

"That's what she said."

"And how big is it?"

"I think she said eighteen hundred square feet."

Jess let out an uncharacteristic stream of curses. "Eighteen hundred square feet? Do you know what you've landed in?"

"I'm just living there as an employee."

"Cotton—you've landed in cotton."

"It's not like my name's on the lease."

"Don't try to make me feel better," she said. "I've never even set foot in a place up there."

"Now you will. You can be my first visitor."

"I hope you don't get kicked out before then," she said, already looking for possible drawbacks.

"Now why would that happen?"

"Please. You know."

"Spence?" I asked. "Forget it. I haven't seen him at all since that one lunch. I think he's just confused. He's living, or not living, with a woman who sees him as a cash register. It's disgusting."

"So you're sympathetic to him."

"Not so sympathetic that I want to hop into bed with him."

"Yet."

"What?"

"Not so sympathetic yet."

"He wanted to move his family to New York so they'd be closer to him. And it's not like anything can happen when we're all crammed together in a little apartment."

She choked. "You don't know from little. Besides, you'd be surprised how much can go on in spite of people being crammed together. Or because of it."

"In this case, *nothing* is going to happen. I'm the nanny. This isn't a French movie, for heaven's sake."

"*Quel domage*. Your life could use some spicing up."

"Nola thinks just the opposite. She called me a wuss and predicted I would end up alone and strange."

"Uh-un. When?"

"After I bruised her brother-in-law's ribs." I filled her in on the details. "Nola was not pleased. I've got to make it up to her before I leave."

"Why?"

"Because she's a friend. For better or worse."

"She's such a bitch, though."

"Well, we all have our faults."

"You're too nice."

"No, I'm not. You should have seen me when my stepmother announced her pregnancy. I could hardly even pretend to be happy. I spent the entire drive back to Dallas gagging back sweet tea."

We bade each other good-bye using what was becoming our usual sign-off now. "Two weeks," I said.

"I'm jazzed about this. I really am, Al. We're going to have high times when you get here. Just two weeks!"

"Two weeks!"

I was expecting those two weeks to be nonstop activity, but this wasn't the case. I mean, an entire household was being transported halfway across the country. You'd think that would require frantic activity. But the days crept by, and Pepper was back to her usual schtick, hanging out with Phaedra and shopping. I accompanied August to play dates and swimming lessons.

There were no Bekins boxes anywhere. No precious items being carefully wrapped up.

When I asked Pepper about this, she stared at me stonily. "The movers are going to pack us up the day before the move. You know that."

I knew that because I had actually been the one to get movers over to give estimates. But I guess I hadn't understood what *packing* meant. Since most of my moves had been panicky gestures of downsizing, I had never been able to afford packers, or even movers. Tearing "man with a van" numbers off of coffee shop bulletin boards was more my speed.

"They'll pack everything?"

"Of course. None of us has to lift a finger. And that includes you, Al. Spence told me to make sure that your stuff is included in the move, too."

"Wow."

"I thought that was pretty nice of him," she said. "To single you out that way."

Was I paranoid, or was she looking at me funny?

"All you have to do is take some of these stickers . . ." She pulled out a plastic container of little adhesive colored dots, like people use at garage sales to mark prices. "Put a dot on the things you want packed up. Everything else stays."

The packers would come and box up or wrap everything marked by a sticker. The next morning, we were all flying out. The movers would be there that day, but since Marta was no longer there, Phaedra had promised to come over and oversee the movers.

"But you don't want me to leave anything here, do you?" I asked. Naturally, since the Smiths were keeping the Dallas house, they weren't taking everything. But I couldn't leave my things behind.

She frowned. "No, I guess not. But you better dot the garage apartment in any case, just to make sure."

Not having to lift a finger before a move sounded like heaven. No rooting around grocery-store loading docks searching for boxes. No spending days stumbling around those boxes once they were in your apartment. No inky hands from stuffing newspaper around every item you cared about, all the while knowing the next time you saw it, it would probably be broken into a million tiny pieces.

But come to find out, *not* doing all those things filled me with anxiety. Leaving everything unpacked was unnerving. By the designated packing day, the day before the move, I was a little nervous. I had dotted everything long ago. The garage apartment was a sea of dots. Now I couldn't wait to see all my stuff neatly boxed, taped, and marked.

On packing day, Pepper asked me to take August out and keep her out so that she wouldn't be underfoot, or freaked out by the sight of strangers rooting through her stuff and tossing it into boxes. I planned a big day with August—breakfast at her favorite pancake house, the zoo, and then the big summer Disney movie, which she had already seen but what the hell. She'd seen *The Little Mermaid* twelve times (and that was just since I'd been her nanny).

But it was too much. I knew that by the time we were stumbling toward the polar bear exhibit. The day was hot, we were full of pancakes, and temptations abounded. Cotton candy. Hot dogs. Little hats with antlers. August wore me out, and then realized she was worn out herself. I had to put her in the stroller and push her around. She promptly fell asleep, and I headed for the nearest coffee shop.

She was awake for the movie, but I fell asleep. Luckily, August was the kind of kid that would stare transfixed and speechless at a movie screen, so she didn't jump up and start running down the aisles screaming while I was out. Or at least, I'm pretty sure she didn't.

"Wait till you see the house," I told her as we were driving home. In the rearview, I saw her kicking toward the passenger seat. "You'll be all set for the big move! Isn't that exciting?"

I was using my overly perky adult voice, which made her tilt her head suspiciously. "What about Bink?"

Bink was the stuffed raccoon that she declared was her absolute favorite toy ever. She'd had him, in her words, "forever." It made me jealous for a time when forever was only four years.

"Bink's coming too!" I said. "You don't have to worry about him."

I parked the car in the garage and took August up to her room; sure enough, the place looked like a warehouse. Brown cardboard boxes with the moving-company logo were everywhere, with directions in big bold magic-markered letters. **Kitchen. Living Rm. Master B'rm.**

I felt like that old shoemaker after the elves had toiled all night. The packers had come and gone with such cool efficiency; I hadn't even seen them at work.

I dropped August off to marvel at her room, and then I skipped over to my apartment. I wondered what my boxes would say. **Nanny's Rm**?

I got my answer soon enough. *Nothing*. My boxes said nothing, because there were no boxes.

My rooms were exactly as I had left them. Nothing was packed. Dots mocked me.

I blinked hard for a few moments, perhaps thinking that I could pull a Samantha Stevens nose twitch and have all the stuff magically boxed up. Mostly, I think I was just in shock. I had a plane to catch the next morning at six-thirty am, and I was completely unready!

I flew back to the main house and found Pepper. Her eyes widened in alarm when she saw me. "Jeez Louise. What's the matter with you?"

"My stuff!" I was practically hyperventilating. "None of it got packed."

She tilted her head. "How is that possible?"

"I don't know! All my stuff is sitting there no different than it was this morning."

"But that's not possible," she said. "I told them, explicitly, that everything needed to be packed."

"And you reminded them about the garage apartment?"

"Of course." She tapped a long, coral nail against her chin. "At least, I'm pretty sure I did."

Pretty sure!

She shrugged. "Oh, well. It's lucky you don't have much stuff."

"But I have to do all my packing tonight!"

"So? You've barely unpacked from moving in here, I'll bet. I'm sure you'll have no trouble."

"But I've still got to feed August and get her supper, and a bath . . ."

She shot me a look that said, *and your point is?*

My point was, I was put out. But Pepper didn't get it. And then August started screeching because she couldn't find Bink. I spent the next hour of my life, a precious hour when I needed to be getting my butt over to the Safeway to fetch boxes so I could pack, actually *unpacking* already packed boxes in order to locate a stuffed raccoon.

By the time I did get the boxes and start packing, I was in a rage. Pepper had done this on purpose. There was no doubt in my mind. Okay, maybe a little doubt. She was forgetful, but the fact remained, *I* was the person who had been forgotten.

And now there was so much to do it felt beyond me. How could I possibly get packed in time to make a morning plane?

When my doorbell rang, I was tempted to ignore it. If it

was Pepper, I would just want to punch her lights out. If it was anybody else . . .

Who else could it be?

That was a sobering thought. All these years in Dallas, and this was my last night, and there was no one I wanted to go party with. The few friends I still kept up with, I'd called and said bye to over the phone. Earlier in the week I'd had drinks with a few old work buddies from my tech days.

I went to the door and was stunned to see Nola standing there. There were tears streaming down her face. "So you were just going to leave?" she burst out. "You weren't going to say good-bye to me?"

"Nola, I—"

I hadn't thought she would want to say good-bye to *me*. She hadn't answered my calls from a few weeks back. Of course, I'd only left four messages. She probably considered that an insufficient attempt at reconciliation on my part.

And yet here she was. I was amazed. And touched.

My chin started to tremble. "If I'd thought you wanted to see me . . ."

"Well of course! You're my . . ." She started to hiccup. ". . . My friend!"

At that, we fell on each other like two weepy drunks. "I'm sorry, Nola," I said when I could speak again without gulping. "I should've have been more careful with Finn."

She shook her head. "He liked you."

"He did?"

"That's what he said. I was surprised." She smiled. "Do you want to go have a drink somewhere?"

Oh my God. It had been years—pre-Jason, at least—since those words had issued from Nola's lips. I was ready to lunge for my purse . . . then I remembered. The boxes. "I can't!" I said. "I'm packing."

Her jaw dropped and she pushed past me across the threshold. Her eyes swept over the room in horror. I obviously had so far to go and so little time. "What happened?"

"They were supposed to pack me, but Pepper forgot to tell them."

"Forgot!"

Forgetting was not something Nola was prone to.

"Well . . ."

Her eyes narrowed on me and she wagged a finger in warning. "Mark my words, you need to watch your back with that woman."

"I know . . ."

"But never mind that now," she said. If she hadn't been wearing a T-shirt, she would have been rolling up her sleeves. "We have work to do."

I almost started bawling again. A friend in need was a friend indeed. "You're going to help me?"

"Only if you order a pizza."

I was already reaching for my phone.

By the time I wobbled onto the plane the next day, hurrying past first class where Pepper and August were already installed, sipping 7-Up and fiddling with their portable DVD players, and squeezed into my economy-class seat in row twenty-six, I thought I would be able to doze off the whole way to New York. But I was wrong. I was too excited to sleep.

I had done it. I was starting anew. I was leaving my past behind.

I wondered how soon I would be able to see Spence.

Chapter 13

For our reunion, Jess and I spent the whole afternoon together. It was so good to see her. It had been two years since she'd left Dallas, but she seemed just the same. She had always had an anemic Joyce Carol Oates look about her—pale skinned and dark haired, with big eyes magnified by wire-rimmed glasses—but in New York she didn't seem to stick out quite as much as she had in the land of suntans and big hair.

"I've always wanted to live in a hotel!" she exclaimed when we returned from our welcome to New York expedition. "Like Eloise. You're so lucky!"

"It's just temporary." I wasn't sure how lucky I actually felt, comparatively. The Smiths were on the fifteenth floor, in a luxury suite, and I was in a single on the second floor overlooking an alley. They got bathrobes. I was lucky to get extra towels. Then again, last night there had been a man sleeping on the sidewalk next to the dumpster outside, so I wasn't feeling too deprived.

Jess was in the bathroom now, inspecting the glass on the sink with approval. She tended to be comforted by things that were wrapped in plastic. She was probably the only person in the world who actually took the time to use the wax papery disposable toilet-seat covers provided in public bathrooms.

"Ooo, I love hotel sewing kits," she said, moving on to the

freebies. "Better than a chocolate on your pillow any day." She sighed, and looked for a moment like she might actually try to slip my shower cap into her purse. "This is the life."

"I'm not so sure. I was woken up at four o'clock by garbage trucks."

She dismissed my whining with a wave of her long, thin hand. "Pretty soon you won't notice garbage trucks any more than you notice stinky street smells. Which reminds me . . . I brought you something . . ." She started digging through her handbag, a large leather tote the size of carry-on luggage. In fact some airlines would have made her check it.

Finally, she produced a plastic Ziploc bag full of . . . full of . . .

I wasn't sure quite what it was full of. Even after I had inspected it. The contents looked like a bunch of rags.

"They're surgical masks."

I stared at them more closely. That's what they were, all right.

"For ozone-alert days," she explained. "Also, you should really wear them when you go out and you aren't sure about where you'll be. The air here is very iffy."

I pulled out a mask. It was one of the old-fashioned kind—with just a white patch of cotton with a string dangling off each corner. Dr. Kildare-style. It reminded me of TV newscasts of medical emergencies in Asia. "Jess. I can't wear this on the streets of New York. Everyone will think I've got SARS."

"Which is one of the reasons you should wear it!" She crossed her arms. "Notice how they like to make out like that disease hasn't ever really hit the U.S.?"

"Well, has it?" I asked her.

My credulity brought forth a skeptical harrumph. "Well, if you want to believe the medical community, the media, and the government . . . then no. But remember, it's in all their interests not to cause a panic."

I decided to accept my surgical masks with grace and changed the subject. "I can't wait till the movers get here with our stuff."

Jess fiddled with the air conditioner, I assume to adjust the temperature downward. New York was very warm just now. "Cooled air alone makes it worth putting up with that woman."

"Pepper's okay. I've recovered from the packing thing. When we got here she said I could pick my own decorating scheme for my room at the apartment."

She arched a brow at me. "Decorating scheme?"

"Well . . . she said I could choose my wall color."

"Al, she's going to buy you a can of paint. For that you don't have to put anger aside."

I shrugged. "I thought it was kind of her to ask for my input. It's more than some employers would do."

Jess continued to be unimpressed. "And what about that poor maid who got fired?"

Marta. That reminder caused a pang. As did the whole mystery of what had happened to Marisol. "I'll admit Pepper's erratic. But if she turns around and fires me, believe me, I won't cry."

Jess leveled an amused gaze on me. "And what kind of peace have you reached with Spence?"

I had to suppress a sigh of disappointment. A disappointment that I knew deep down I should be glad about. "I hardly ever bump into him, so it's no problem. I just saw him when he picked us up at the airport, and briefly in the hotel lobby this morning."

"Meaning that if you did see more of him, then it would be a problem," Jess guessed.

"I doubt it."

"But you're not sure."

"Come on, Jess. We're talking ancient history. We had one little moment at the restaurant in Dallas, but I think that was just because he was feeling nostalgic, and maybe a little depressed. The poor guy. He married Pepper when he was practically a kid. Twenty-two. I mean, most people can barely be considered sentient beings when they're twenty-two."

"Twenty-two is young. What do you think happened?"

"He said something about a false alarm . . ."

Her face went slack. "Isn't that awfully personal information to be telling to your nanny?"

"He told me because . . . well, because I knew him. It didn't feel indiscreet to me at the time."

I had to admit that it did a little now, though.

"So she trapped him."

"I don't know . . . I guess they were in love. It's not unheard of for people to fall in love at twenty-two. I was in love when I was twenty-two, too. With Barry Saddler, remember?"

Jess groaned. "A guitar player. You were out of your mind. That's my biggest don't-do now. Don't do musicians."

Jess had her own don't-do's, but instead of no-nos like staying away from comedy clubs, violent movies, and open-mike anything, her items were usually things like *don't go out again with anyone who mentions Foucault more than once on a first date.* A musician prohibition seemed entirely too broad, not to mention completely illogical.

"Jess, *you're* a musician."

"That's right. For me it's over-the-top gross, like incest. For you it's just going out of your way to date someone who is chronically underemployed, badly dressed, and who has a lifetime obsession with the sound created by plucking a string."

"Maybe that's why I haven't dated a musician since Barry," I said. "But that's what you do when you're twenty-two. You make mistakes."

"You didn't make your mistake legal, though." She gnawed her lower lip. "My guess is that Pepper didn't want to join the real world and decided to join the Junior League instead. Only you would think she'd try a little harder to hold on to her meal ticket."

"She's held on okay so far," I pointed out.

"Thanks to you and your phantom dating for her."

I still shuddered over that night with Colby. "Never again," I said. "Anyway, I honestly think she's turning over a new leaf. She's taking August to FAO Schwarz this afternoon. She hasn't done anything so mommylike since I've been working for her."

"Taking her daughter shopping—wow. Where can I nominate her for mother of the year?"

"Well, anyway, she's trying. And Spence is a busy man. And married."

"To a cheating shrew he's probably dying to be free of."

"And I'm not interested in dating anyway," I said.

"Everybody's interested."

"I'm acclimatizing."

"Oh!" Jess jumped up and lunged for her purse again. She dug into the depths and pulled out a Barnes and Noble sack and handed it to me. "Speaking of acclimatizing . . . a welcome-to-New-York gift," she said.

"You shouldn't have," I said. "The surgical masks alone were more than I expected . . ."

"*Open* it!"

I guess I was expecting something New Yorky. A book about the city, or the Zagat restaurant guide, or even a copy of *A Tree Grows in Brooklyn*. What I got instead was a thin book with a blue cover and the title in startling white letters. *Outwitting Head Lice*.

I studied it for a few moments, during which my scalp began to itch.

"So?" she asked. "Whattaya think?"

"I'm speechless."

She laughed. "It's for the subway. I've got one, too." She pulled another well-worn copy out of her tote. "Carry this book conspicuously on your person at all times on public transportation. You will always be able to get a seat, sometimes even have a whole row to yourself. Even at rush hour."

"I guess you don't have to worry about anyone hitting on you, either."

"Exactly. Or if they do, you know there's something *really* wrong with them."

"You're twisted, you know that?"

"Oh, and I made up a subway map circling all the stations to steer clear of, and which ones to avoid only at certain hours."

"Thank you," I said, accepting this from her as well. "And for the book, too. And the masks." Such bounty. It was almost overwhelming. "With a little practice, soon I'll be able to appear as mentally ill as you."

She hugged me on her way to the door. "That's what friends are for, Al."

Pepper's newest best friend was Alessandra, the wife of one of Spence's coworkers, who was an interior decorator and knew practically everybody in Manhattan worth knowing, according to Pepper. With Alessandra's help, Pepper was navigating the unfamiliar social (not to mention interior design) waters of Manhattan; she was in thrall.

Today we were meeting her at a paint store so I could pick my room color and Pepper could match a paint chip for the trim in her pantry.

"I went to this woman's house, and omigod, Al, you wouldn't believe it," Pepper said as we headed for the paint store. She was in one of her chummy moods that I was now suspicious of. "There was an actual Cezanne on her wall! One of those native women pictures in the Ralph Lauren colors. That's Cezanne, right?"

"Gauguin, I think."

"Really?" She didn't look convinced. "Well, anyway, it was the kind of thing that belongs in a museum. And do you know who was there?" She rattled off names of Lauder heiresses, third-tier television stars, and a discarded Trump wife, taking pains to inform me who was speaking to whom and what they were all wearing. She sounded like a Cindy Adams column. My brain was going numb.

During this time, I was navigating us and August in her stroller up Madison Avenue. August's stroller was really too small for her; yet she was not quite up to long walks around the city. I gazed with envy at other nannies dashing around with their huge jogging strollers and only half-listened to Pepper's tale of her new social whirl.

"I *can't wait* to call Phaedra! She's going to be positively green when I tell her about all this, especially when I mention this guy I ran into—Jonah Adams. He used to do crappy feature writing in Dallas, but he was so hot, Phaedra really had her thong in a wad over him."

"What does he do here?"

"Same thing. Crappy feature writing. I think he's with something called *New York Now*. There's so much to read here! I'm really having to readjust."

We were nearly flattened by a woman coming out of a salon and yapping on a cell phone. She was a perfect specimen of Manhattan: thoroughbred body encased in black fitted slacks, heels, and perfectly accessorized with scarf and sunglasses.

Pepper, who was wearing a great beige Halston outfit with a coral silk top, stopped in her tracks. "My God, do I feel like a hick!"

"What are you talking about?" I asked. "You look fantastic."

"Please! I'm all wrong. Alessandra told me I dressed like a Miami Beach pensioner. She said I need to drop the parakeet colors from my wardrobe." She stopped and gave herself a brutal assessment in a coffee-shop window. "She's so right, isn't she?"

"You look good."

"I'm gonna have to buy all new clothes," she said furiously. "It's so irritating. Honestly, sometimes I wish I were someone like you who didn't have to care about how I look. It would be so much simpler!"

As Pepper charged on down the sidewalk, I started tossing assessing glances at myself in the windows. The shorts and Rockport sandal combination was sort of schlumpy looking. Not that I could do much about it now. Unlike Pepper, I needed to be comfortable, and I didn't have the money to change my look even if I wanted to.

"Now I know Alessandra said this paint store was around here somewhere . . ."

We were in an area dominated by boutiques and little gourmet stores. It was hard to believe there would be anything so pedestrian as hardware sold in this vicinity. But a few moments later, Pepper let out a little Eureka gasp. "There!"

The store, called Colors, seemed bare, and not even particularly colorful. It was just a big room with pastel paneled walls and several tables set up with paint-chip cards and decorating books on them. The place was so silent that I was embarrassed by the slappy sounds my sandals made against the tile.

"Doesn't this look fun!" Pepper whispered.

A woman who reminded me of Mrs. Danvers from *Rebecca*, only not quite that friendly, floated over to help us.

"We're looking for a bedroom color," Pepper whispered to her.

"For your little girl's room?"

"No, for the nanny." She pointed to me.

"Oh, I see." Giving me a quick up and down, the woman swept aside some paint chip books left on the table and brought out another book. The budget book, no doubt. "You might find something you'll like among these samples." It took me a moment to realize that the flattening of her lips was meant to be a smile, or as much of a smile as she would bother with for the likes of me. "Was there some color or hue that you particularly wanted to match?" Mrs. Danvers asked Pepper.

Just then, the door opened and what appeared to be the world's tallest, thinnest, scariest-looking woman pushed through the door. Pepper turned. "Alessandra! Over here!"

As if we weren't the only people in the whole store.

Alessandra came slinking over. One up-and-down look was all it took for both her and me to know that we were natural antagonists. She couldn't have been a day over thirty-five, but she was so salon engineered that she managed to achieve the look of having had cosmetic surgery without having gone under the knife. Tanned, waxed, plucked, Botoxed, collagened . . . all she needed was a strapless gown and she'd be ready for the red carpet. The woman was *done*.

She terrified me, frankly. Women like this always did—they seemed to practice intimidation through cosmetic perfection. The look she leveled on me when Pepper introduced us affected me like biting down on tinfoil. It was hard to believe one little glance could contain so much disdain.

Alessandra immediately turned her back to me. "Now where are we?" she asked, looking at Mrs. Danvers.

The saleslady seemed to come alive. (Rebecca had arrived!) "I was asking your friend what color she was interested in."

"I'm leaving this entirely up to Alison," Pepper said.

"How nice!" Mrs. Danvers said, with a glance to Alessandra that clearly said, *What a dope.* The entire group turned back to me. "And what color interests you?"

Under their cold, pseudo-benevolent gazes, I felt as if I were shrinking. "I wanted something cheerful. Maybe yellow?"

Alessandra and Mrs. Danvers exchanged looks. "There are some nice cream tones in here . . ." the saleslady said.

"I was hoping for bright yellow."

Pepper rolled her eyes at her friend. "Parakeet color!"

"Is that bad for rooms, too?" I asked.

"Well . . ."

Apparently it was very, very bad. Somehow, after thirty minutes of badgering, of bringing out book after book, it was decided that my room would be painted something called willowed ecru. Alessandra told Pepper that it would go well with what Pepper had picked out for drapes. (With Alessandra's help.)

After that, I was left on my own as the group turned to the task of matching the color of the pantry cabinets. It seemed to take forever. Only August's impatient howling finally brought our visit to Colors to a conclusion.

"Okay, we're done," Pepper said, coming up to me.

Thank God. I felt like I had been through the same three paint chip books a million times. I now knew them as well as I knew *Miss Spider's Tea Party*.

I looked down at Pepper's hands. There was no bag, nor was she tucking a receipt into her billfold. No purchase had been made.

"You can go ahead and buy the willowed ecru and we can go home," she told me. "Alessandra decided that there's another place we should check to match the pantry color."

I stared at her.

I could buy it, she said. No one had mentioned a possible outlay of cash for my paint before this moment.

This was too much. "Pepper, you still owe me for the bathing suit."

She blinked at me as if I had suddenly lost my marbles. "What bathing suit?"

I lowered my voice. I didn't want Alessandra . . . not to mention Mrs. Danvers . . . to think I was a cheapskate. "The mermaid bathing suit."

A laugh escaped her. "Oh, I forgot all about that!"

No kidding. "It was a hundred and ten dollars. I don't want to whine, but I don't have a lot of money in my checking account right now."

In fact I still hadn't worked up the nerve to go to a new bank and open a local account. Maybe with my next paycheck. Transferring my piddling balance from Dallas seemed too pathetic to make a special trip. I wasn't sure my ego was up to seeing a bank clerk smirk.

"And you ask me about this money now? *Now?*" The chumminess of our walk over evaporated completely.

Her petulant little voice made me want to scream. "Yes, *now*. Because you're asking me to spend more money *now*."

"*I'm* asking you? Oh for heaven's—" An agonized sigh came out of her. "Well, okay, I'll write you a check this afternoon."

"But the paint . . ."

She emitted a haughty snort. "Al, it *is* your room. I let you pick out your own color."

"Willowed ecru?" I asked. "If I'd known I was footing the bill for this I would have insisted on yellow."

"It *is* yellow." She tossed up her hands in a theatrical manner that hadn't improved since our *Picnic* days. "You said you *liked* it. My God, you act like I'm some sort of tyrant!"

By now, Alessandra had returned to her side, and even Mrs. Danvers floated back over. "Is there some problem?"

"I don't think you're a tyrant," I said, answering Pepper. Which was true. *Bitch* was the word I would have used at that moment.

"She doesn't want to pay?" Alessandra asked. She looked flabbergasted, and appalled. As if I were the world's biggest ingrate.

Pepper let out a huff. "Forget it! Let's get out the parakeet colors again and start over."

Screw it, I thought. What difference did it make? It wasn't even my apartment. And I was sick to death of being in that store. "The willowed ecru will be great. I'll take a gallon."

The saleslady's face puckered in disdain. "We sell that selection by the quart."

"Why not sell it by the ounce, like perfume?" I shot back.

Everyone glared at me.

"Okay, four quarts."

"Four!" Pepper exclaimed.

"That's a gallon," I translated for her. Bramford Prep wasn't big on math. Or anything useful, really.

The bill for my four quarts of willowed ecru was seventy-eight dollars and change. I was still quivering from forking over such an outrageous sum for four cans of ugly wall color when we got back to the hotel.

"You'll have to bust ass to get your room painted before the movers arrive," Pepper said.

The Smith furniture had been in storage awaiting the last decorative touches Pepper wanted to perform on the apartment. But the painters had been discharged, apparently, and now the movers were going to be coming early the next week. Which meant I really did need to hurry.

Damn. I hated painting.

My spirits were buoyed when I got back to my room and found the phone-message light blinking. Maybe Jess would be able to make me laugh.

But the message wasn't from Jess, who would of course have called my cell. It was from Finn.

This was a surprise. I wasn't sure what to think about Finn. I wasn't interested in him romantically, but then maybe I was being presumptuous. What were the chances he would have any romantic interest in a woman who had bruised his rib?

I was dithering over whether I should call him back, and

whether calling back too soon would make me look (a) interested in him, or (b) like I had no life, when the phone rang. I jumped for it.

"Hi!" It was Finn.

Even though I had just been thinking about him, I hadn't expected him to be the one calling. I took a moment to mentally readjust. When I didn't answer right away, he said, "I called again too soon, didn't I? I was worried about that . . ."

"No, no," I said. "I'm sorry, I was just in the middle of . . ." *Of deciding whether I should avoid you.*

"I couldn't decide whether calling you again would make it look like I was too eager or something. Or like I didn't have a life."

I laughed. There was something refreshing about a guy who wore his angst on his sleeve, especially when his angst was so close to my own. "How are you?"

"Doin' okay." He still had a trace of his Texas drawl, but just a trace. He actually had a nice phone voice. "Good as new, really. I don't squeal when I sit down anymore."

"That's . . . great."

"It's progress. Anyway, I wanted to call back to tell you that I wasn't just calling to say hello, like I said in that message before. I want to take you out to dinner."

The way he said *dinner* sounded like *date* and that made me nervous. It wasn't just Finn, even though we didn't seem in the least bit compatible, really. There was also the problem of Nola. We had made up after the first Finn disaster. But I wasn't sure our friendship could stand long distance and an ill-fated romance with her favorite in-law. "I'm not sure about that," I said, casting about wildly for excuses. "We're still at the hotel, and the move is the day after tomorrow . . . I really don't have much time to myself."

"You must have *some* time," he said.

"I'm a nanny."

"Even nannies get time off," he said. "Even Julie Andrews supernannies."

I began to question whether persistence was really that great a quality.

"Any time is great for me," he said. "You need to get stuff for your room? I know some thrift stores . . ."

My room. I groaned. "That's another reason I have no time. I have to paint my room."

"Cool! I'm a whiz at painting," he said.

"It gives me a backache. And a headache. That fresh paint smell."

"I love that smell!" he chimed in. "It's the smell of new beginnings."

It was gee-whiz statements like that that made me wonder if Finn had been the kind of kid who looked forward to going to the dentist so he could read the newest issue of *Highlights* magazine.

"When do you want to do it?" he asked. "Tomorrow?"

"Look, I would hate to put you to this trouble."

"It's no trouble. Besides, you're paying for it."

I hoped he was kidding. I was already down seventy-eight bucks on this project.

"Get three orders of Chinese delivered for noon tomorrow," he instructed.

"Three?"

"Order something for yourself, too, if you're hungry," he added.

"Does painting give you that much of an appetite?"

"Just wait. Moo-shu chicken turns me into a regular painting dervish. I'll have your room painted in an hour."

"An hour?"

"As long as you tape off first."

I hated taping. But what the hell. I figured the less painting I could get away with in this lifetime, the better.

Besides, I could always ask Jess over to help me with taping everything off.

August was having a hard time adjusting to New York, the hotel, the heat. She hated it all—especially after Spence had to fly to London. (A business trip that, conveniently, coincided with the move from the hotel to the apartment.) I had to admit that I felt let down, too, to the point where I was drooping around the hotel like a junior high kid who just learned the guy she has a crush on wasn't on the bus that morning. Without the hope of seeing Spence, even to have him say hi to me as he was scurrying out the door to work, I felt listless. And I was much more susceptible to August's demands. Forget reading aloud. I let her order pay-per-view movies and have soda out of the minibar.

But sometimes even this wasn't enough. "I want ice!" she whined at me when we got back from the park that afternoon and I had let her nab a Sprite from the little fridge. (Pepper wasn't there.) It had seemed like too much of an effort to scrounge up dollar bills and go across the hall to the vending room.

"It's already cold," I pointed out to her.

Her eyes filled up with tears, and I picked up the bucket. So much for not going across the hall. "Sit on the bed. I'll be right back."

She climbed up on the bed and commenced bouncing. Pepper would have had a fit—but oh, well. The kid needed exercise.

I trudged across the hall to the ice room, which also housed two vending machines. It was odd, I thought as I scooped up my bucket of cubes, how even swank hotels have these Holiday Inn–type places for soda pop machines. Maybe there is no way to make vending machines seem upscale.

Outside the elevater dinged; I then heard the doors swoosh open and Pepper and Alessandra's voices echoing down the hall. My first instinct was to dash across the hall before they rounded the corner and tell August to stop jumping on the bed. Then I heard my name. I flattened against the door and tried to block out the humming of the Coke machines.

"You have to put your foot down with people like that," Alessandra was saying, "or else they'll walk all over you."

"I know it, believe me. I just had to fire my housekeeper in Dallas. She just acted like she knew *everything*."

"If I were you I would have given her the boot right there in Colors."

Wait. Was she talking about me? About giving *me* the boot?

"Shh!" No doubt Pepper was making elaborate pointing gestures at the hotel suite.

Wrong door, ladies.

"I would definitely keep my eye on her," Alessandra said, her voice lowering to a fervent whisper.

"What do you think I've been doing?"

I stiffened.

"Smart girl!" Alessandra hissed approvingly. "I hope you have a nanny cam."

I craned my head as far out as I dared.

"Spence doesn't believe in them."

A burst of laughter blasted through the hall. "Oh for heaven's . . . and what did you tell me about *him*? No wonder!"

What *did* she tell her about him?

"I think, if anything, Spence just feels sorry for Al."

Felt sorry for me? Was she kidding?

Apparently Alessandra was as incredulous as I was. "Are you kidding?"

"You would never believe it, but we all went to school together. She was super-wealthy but then her family went broke. Broke-broke. Lost *everything*. A friend back in Dallas said she saw her in a supermarket checkout line and she couldn't even pay for a little basket of groceries! Even I felt sorry for her then."

Oh, God. The ramen noodles. My face felt so hot I wanted to plunge it into the ice bucket. *I had been the object of Pepper's pity?*

"And believe me," Pepper whispered confidentially. "She was never one of my favorite people in school. A complete know-it-all!"

"All the more reason for a nanny cam!" Alessandra insisted. "People like that never lose their sense of entitlement. She might even think she's entitled to your husband. Spence wouldn't even have to know, and it would give you peace of mind."

"Oh, I have peace of mind. Believe me. If he strays, he's toast."

I was practically quaking. How could she possibly talk like that—as if she were the long-suffering wife. The saint. What kind of hold did she have over him?

"Well, I would still want to protect myself, if I were you," Alessandra went on. "She looks shifty to me."

Shifty!

"And pushy. Believe me, you'll have trouble with her."

Pepper laughed. "Oh, I can handle it. I always have. As far as adversaries go, she's strictly in the Wile E. Coyote category."

I heard the key card swipe. The door clicked open and shut.

My muscles were beginning to cramp up from being frozen in a crouch, but even though Pepper and Alessandra were gone I didn't want to straighten up. Somehow, I was going to have to cross that hall and pretend I hadn't heard anything. Which was going to be difficult, since I probably looked like a box of ACME Dynamite had just exploded in my face.

"Is Finn cute?" Jess asked me as we set up our little Chinese buffet. My room was tiny—ten by twelve, but it had a window and ornate crown molding. I hadn't lived in a room with crown molding since my parents had sold the house in Highland Park. Even that small detail felt validating . . . except these days it was hard to feel good about anything. I kept hearing Pepper and Alessandra's voices hissing in that hallway.

"If I were casting the New Testament, he'd be the perfect John the Baptist. Only with an almost shaved head."

"Almost?" she asked.

"It's that odd length—somewhere between a burr and razor stubble."

Amazingly, this description did not seem to deter Jess's enthusiasm. Which surprised me. I hadn't expected her to look on this as a meet-up. Actually, I hadn't expected Jess would want to stay for the painting at all. Paint fumes might give me a headache, but things like that practically gave her a heart attack. Fresh paint was one item on Jess's long list of things not yet admitted by the U.S. government but strongly suspected by her to be carcinogens. The whole apartment smelled like fresh paint right now.

Which is why she was strapping on her surgical mask as soon as she walked into the apartment.

"He's a social worker," I warned.

"So?"

"So I would imagine that would be right up there with musician in your book."

"Is he employed?"

"Yeah, he works with homeless teens on the Lower East Side."

"Well, if he's employed he's one up on most of the musicians I know."

When Finn arrived, I understood why he'd wanted the copious amounts of Chinese food. He brought helpers.

They were a scruffy lot, and when I saw them coming into Pepper's immaculate, huge, pastel apartment, I admit I felt a wave of anxiety. One kid had more tattoos than an NBA starting player. Another wore the nastiest-looking dreadlocks I'd ever seen. And the third had no hair at all. His specialty was piercing—and almost exclusively in places that looked the most painful. In his ear cartilage. His eyebrows. Three hoops in his nose. They all wore baggy black T-shirts featuring rock bands whose names I did not recognize. These were worn untucked over even baggier jeans with wide frayed legs. These outfits had to be hotter than hell, but these were the kind of boys who looked like they would relish discomfort, especially if it achieved a look that made everyone around them even more uncomfortable.

Jess and I were uncomfortable. I wasn't flashing back to my subbing days, but close. Of course, if we were looking at them like alien beings, it was nothing compared to the stares they were leveling on Jess, with her glasses poking over her mask. Yet it wasn't her appearance that seemed to wig them out so much as her demeanor.

Jess had turned into an unrecognizable being even to me. Suddenly she was the hostess with the mostest. Imagine a chirping cross between a waitress at TGI Friday's and the social director on *The Love Boat* and that would fall way short of the vim she exhibited.

"More kung pao shrimp, anyone?" she asked, skipping around the circle of huddled people with a takeout container that was within easy reach of everyone. She lavished special attention on Finn, and even dropped a plastic tub of plum sauce on him. We had to put his fuzzy head under the sink to get it all out.

I was stunned. I kept looking around at the others' reactions, but no one else knew her, and they just seemed to think this was her. Or maybe they expected a woman who looked like a kook to act like one.

Or maybe they were just teenagers and we were off their radar anyway.

The guys fell on the food as if it had been forever since they had eaten. (Maybe it had.) I remembered that these guys were homeless and offered to order more for them, if they wanted it.

The tattooed one eyed me levelly. "Maybe you should wait to see what we do to your place first."

Do to my place? That had a menacing sound to it. "What do you mean?"

One of the kids smiled, revealing a gold tooth. "Only paint we've ever used is the kind in spray cans."

"Oh," I said.

Finn smiled at me and finished off a moo shu pancake. He was in remarkably good spirits for a man with sticky hair. Though I couldn't help noticing that he leaned away from Jess whenever she hovered near him, which was often. "Well! Guess we should get to work."

When I broke out the dainty little cans of paint the guys gaped in amazement. Dreadlocks actually jumped back. He looked like he wanted to shield his eyes. "What is that?"

"It's puke green," bald kid said.

"It's *ecru,*" Adolphe said.

"It's festering-wound green."

"No—it's the color of the cafeteria trays in juvie prison."

How I would have loved Alessandra to hear that.

"It's puke," the bald kid insisted.

"Yeah."

"Yeah."

Strangely enough, I felt depressed. They were right. It *was* puke. "I wanted yellow," I explained. "Bright yellow."

"Man, this isn't even close!"

"I know. My boss talked me out of the bright yellow."

"Al has assertiveness issues," Jess said, swooping in with a two-liter bottle of Coke. "More to drink, anyone?"

They all stared at me like I was pathetic.

Finn shot me a worried look, then rubbed his hands together. "Okay, guys. Time to cover Al's walls in puke. She didn't buy you lunch so you could just sit around, you know."

I'd found a little stepladder for the high spots, and Finn took it. "I'll do the tops," he said. The ceilings were eleven foot.

None of the boys seemed to be listening to him. I felt a moment of worry when I saw him climb the ladder, but I let it go. I didn't want to badger him. He was doing me a favor.

"Would you like a Coke, Finn?" Jess singsonged at him, as if he were in any position to sip on soda pop right now.

"No, thanks."

"That's good," she said. "Coke is terrible for you. It's poison, really."

"I'll have one," the guy with the dreadlocks told her.

Jess jumped. "Oh! Okay."

Painting and consuming beverages at the same time didn't strike me as a good idea. Jess hopped between paint cans and plastic trays to get to the guy with the dreads. On the way back, once, she stepped on a paint tray and fell.

Fell into Finn's ladder.

I knew what was going to happen, but I couldn't look. I just listened. There followed more grunts, *oofs*, and splat sounds than in the conclusion of most episodes of *Batman*. When I finally worked up the nerve to open my eyes, Finn was on the ground, staring at the ceiling, and Jess was kind of rolling on her side. Her legs and one side of her shorts were covered in puke-colored paint.

She pulled off her surgical mask. "I think you'd better call an ambulance."

Chapter 14

"Do you think he likes me?" Jess asked me.

We were in the emergency waiting room of New York Hospital, which, Jess had hastened to remind us, was the hospital where Andy Warhol died. Nothing dire had happened to Jess, however. After taking an X-ray the doctors had said that she was just suffering from a minor bruise to her tailbone. But as Jess said, that wasn't exactly great news. "I mean, I play cello. You sort of need your tailbone for that."

It was a matter I had never given much thought. But even so, I was a little more worried about Finn. There was an egg-sized bump on his head that had seemed to get bigger during the nail-biting cab ride to the emergency room.

I was so amazed how wrong everything had gone, I had a hard time concentrating on what Jess was saying to me. She'd been asking me about someone. "Who?"

"What do you mean, who?" she asked. "Finn, of course. Don't you think he liked me?"

Was she out of her mind? "Oh . . . I'm not sure," I said, hedging diplomatically.

"Because I think he's really cute, and I caught him staring at me a few times."

Everyone had been staring at her. "All I noticed was that he mostly seemed interested in getting the job done."

She sighed. "I think he's really, really nice. I mean, don't you think it was just so great of him to bring those kids over?"

"Mm."

"They really seemed to interact well with Finn, didn't you think?"

"I didn't really notice." I was worried about those kids. I'd wanted to send them home while we were at the emergency room, but they had insisted on finishing the job.

"He seems great with kids." She looked dreamily in the direction of a man clutching his stomach.

How could she have a crush on Finn? They'd only just met! And they had both come out of the hour's meeting with physical trauma.

Poor Finn. Maybe he was cursed or something.

"I think I'll invite him to the quartet's next concert," Jess said, nibbling thoughtfully on her lip. "I think he'd like that, don't you? We're doing Berlioz."

"A little Berlioz never hurt anybody."

Jess looked as if I'd just tossed her the bridal bouquet. "Exactly! I'm gonna ask him. I'm psyched."

"Mm."

"You should find someone, too, Al, you really should." I opened my mouth to respond, but she cut me off. "I know, I know. You're still acclimatizing or whatever. But at some point, you need to get back in the swing or you're just going to be playing Jane Eyre to Spence's Rochester for the rest of your life."

"Please stop saying that. I'm not Jane Eyre. I'm not Maria Von Trapp."

"Well, whenever you're ready. I'm sure I could find somebody for you. I know lots of people . . . though they aren't necessarily people anyone else would want to know."

"Thanks, but . . ."

"I should thank you. I owe you for introducing me to such a great guy."

We turned back to wait in silence, me frowning and her smiling beatifically toward the door they had taken Finn through.

Finn came out of the incident with a concussion and a positive attitude. "Could have been worse," were his first words upon emerging from the treatment room. Jess hustled him into a cab, insisting on carrying him home.

"Since we're both going downtown," she said. "You can walk, can't you, Al?"

I was a little miffed about being shut out of the taxi—plus I was concerned for Finn. And not just because of his concussion. I had never seen Jess like this.

But I did need to get back to the apartment anyway to assess the damage. I was worried about the floor; the last time I had seen it, it was splattered in willowed ecru. I needed to fix it before Pepper saw it; otherwise she was probably going to have me pay for sanding down and refinishing the wood.

And she still hadn't paid me my hundred and ten dollars; plus I'd had to shell out for the paint.

There was no getting around it. This job was costing me.

I expected the apartment to be empty, but the moment I let myself in, Pepper swooped down on me like a hawk on a field mouse. Her screeching voice made very able talons. "*Finally!* Where the hell have you been? I was calling you and calling—and then I realized that every time I dialed your number, a phone was ringing in your bedroom!"

In my hurry to get everybody to the hospital, I'd forgotten my phone. "Sorry. I had to take a friend to the hospital. There was a little accident while we were painting. . . ."

"You're telling me! Al, you left three hooligans in the apartment! I almost fainted. I thought I was going to be killed."

I hadn't considered that Pepper might run into the guys while they were painting. I hadn't expected her at the apartment at all. It was Sunday, my day off, so I thought she would be out with August. "I didn't know you would be here," I said.

"I was in the neighborhood, and I bought this cute stuffed animal for August, so I thought I would bring it by so it would be here when we move." She pointed to a stuffed monkey sitting on the mantel, which, to tell the truth, was not that cute. It seemed like something you would win at the state fair for throwing darts at balloons. A cheap, demonic-looking monkey.

And this from a woman who had grown up with two Steiff pandas!

"Cute!" I said. "She'll love it."

"Never mind the monkey, Al, who were those hoodlums?"

"They aren't hoodlums. They're underprivileged kids from a homeless shelter."

She gasped. "A *homeless* shelter? You asked *homeless* people into my house?"

Guess I should have known that appealing to her sense of pity would get me nowhere. "A friend of mine works there."

"Oh, great! This is who you hang out with in New York? Thugs? What if I'd had August with me?"

"They weren't *thugs*. Believe me, my friend wouldn't have invited them to help if he didn't absolutely trust them."

That argument cut no ice with Pepper. "Honestly, Al, I thought I could trust you. I didn't ask you for references because I knew you were a BP girl. But if you're going to pull stunts like this . . ." She clucked angrily. "I had to call the police!"

"Wait—whoa." My legs felt rubbery. "The police?"

"I thought they were intruders! I had to hold them in your room with my mace keychain until the cops got here."

"You pulled a keychain on them?" I couldn't quite picture it.

"It's a good thing August wasn't with me!" She shook her head. "Thank God I managed to find a babysitter for August."

"August is with a babysitter?" I squeaked.

She stiffened. "Of course. Did you think I left her alone?"

"No, but . . ." One measly day she had to entertain her kid, and she couldn't? Just amazing.

"Well, what would have happened if she had been with me?" Pepper asked.

"*Nothing* would have happened." I was still horrified at the idea of Finn's helpers being dragged off to the pokey. "They're just kids. And I told Lou they were up here."

"Who is Lou?"

"The doorman—he saw them. I told him they were in the apartment."

"Well I didn't speak to the doorman," Pepper said. "And

I'm not sure I trust the doorman anyway. Who told you that you could leave strange men in the apartment?"

"They were painters. You've had painters up here a lot unattended."

"Painters that came *recommended.* Painters who were *licensed and bonded.*" Her eyes narrowed. "Who was this person who fell? Is he going to sue?"

"No, no. It wasn't like that." I wanted to argue with her, I very dearly did. But I was in a panic about the guys. "What did the police do?"

"*Do?* They took the thugs away."

"They weren't thugs," I repeated, wanting to strangle her. "What precinct?"

"How the Heloise should I know, Al? For that matter, how would *you* know?"

She was right. I didn't know. I just knew I had to find them. I turned on my heel and headed for the door.

"Where are you going?"

I stopped. "I'm going to look for them."

Wrong answer. Pepper's face was beet red. "Don't you want to see what they did?"

That question gave me pause. I hadn't thought they would do anything but finish up painting. Now I remembered the angst that had jangled through me when the one kid had told me I should hold back on offering seconds *until I saw what they did to the place.*

Oh, God.

Pepper frog-marched me back to have a look-see. When we arrived at my room, she flung open the door and flipped on the ceiling light with a dramatic flourish.

"*Look!*"

For a moment I couldn't speak. A big smile spread across my face, which I quickly remembered to cover. Pepper was so upset she was vibrating.

The room was completely clean. The floor was unmarred. And the walls were yellow. *Yellow* yellow. Bright yellow. The color of daffodils, of sunshine. Of parakeets.

I ran around the streets till I could find the local police precinct. The cop at the front desk only half-listened as I blurted out my story.

"Those kids are long gone," he said.

"Gone?" I gulped. I imagined Ryker's Island.

"We didn't hold them."

My heart leapt. "You didn't?"

"No—their story seemed right enough. The officer said they had painted the room, so he couldn't see the harm."

"No, they did a good job," I said. "They even bought new paint!" As if this guy cared.

"The officer who made the call said that lady in the apartment was crazy, though. He tried to hustle those kids out fast."

To save them from Pepper. I was beginning to think we all needed someone to save us from her.

"I just work for her." It was easier than explaining to the man that we had grown up together, but I was absolutely not like her.

I was back at the hotel when I got hold of Finn. I wanted to see if he knew whether the guys were okay. "Did the police treat them badly?"

"Not as badly as that shrew you work for."

"I'm sorry. I should have left her a message or something that there would be strangers in the house . . ."

"It's like she thought they were crooks!" Finn exclaimed, clearly baffled. "Anyone looking at them can tell they're all good guys."

Anyone whose brain had been taken over by Father Flanagan do-goodiness, I thought. But I didn't say anything. Those kids had pissed off my nemesis. Plus they had painted my room glorious, rebellious yellow. I owed them. "Did you hear what they did?"

Finn chuckled. "Yeah."

"They must have bought the paint the moment we stepped out the door."

"They did."

"But how? Where did they get the money?"

"One of them picked my pocket and took it from my wallet."

"Oh." I cleared my throat. "Well, it was an incredible gesture. Aside from the theft angle."

"They're good kids."

Finn was the kind of guy you would really want testifying for you at your sentencing hearing.

"Are *you* okay?" I asked him.

"Just a headache. I'm waiting for the drugs they gave me to kick in. I'm sorry if I sound irritable."

He was sorry? "You're the most calm irritable person I've ever spoken to."

"I had fun today," he said.

I had to knock my hand against my ear to make sure I was hearing correctly. "Fun?"

"Well . . . the part before the hospital."

"I seem to be bad for your health."

He laughed. "I'll give you the opportunity to finish me off. How about doing something this weekend?"

The question took me by surprise. After sending him to the hospital for the second time, I hadn't imagined that Finn would want to talk to me, much less see me again.

And then there was Jess. I didn't want to poach on territory she had fenced off for herself. "Maybe we should wait till you feel better."

"I'm pretty sure I'll be over my headache by next weekend," he said.

"Well, I'd have to check my schedule." When the words were out, I realized how lame they sounded.

Finn did, too. "Oh. I see."

I cringed. The sad undercurrent in his voice made me suddenly want to change my mind. But that wouldn't be right, either. Not if Jess was really interested in him. "What I meant to say is, I'm just not sure . . ."

He cut me off. "I'll give you a buzz later. Maybe you'll be surer."

The trouble was, I was worried about it being a surer *no*. I'd always thought persistence was an admirable quality in a guy. Now I wondered. Finn was like the mirror opposite of Weebils, those little toys I used to have with the egg-shaped bottoms. Finn could fall down, but he just didn't wobble.

"I wanna go home!" August whined at me when we were coming out of the planetarium later that week.

A planetarium in not a good place to take a fretful child, by the way. I liked it because it was cool inside and I could sit on my ass and stare at constellations, but August was one three-and-a-half-year-old who wasn't into astronomy. Go figure.

Unfortunately, when August said home, she meant Dallas. "I want my Pooh room," she said as we trudged across the park with her towards home. "I want to go to the pool."

The pool? My teeth were grinding, but I tried to reason with her. "There are pools here. We'll find one for you."

"I want to go today!"

"Maybe not today . . ."

The apples in her cheeks mutated into angry red streaks and I knew I was in trouble. I tried to hurry us along, but crossing the park takes longer than you would think by looking at it on the map, especially when the person you're walking with is roughly the size of a garden gnome. I thought about hailing a cab, but my money was tight and I wasn't sure Pepper would ever reimburse me for anything now that I had disobeyed her on the matter of wall color.

I loved my room though. Whatever headaches defying Pepper brought me in the long run, it was worth it.

"*Why* can't I go to the pool?" August asked. Suddenly she was Mark Spitz.

"We'll talk to your mom about it as soon as we get home."

When we arrived back at the apartment, I was sweaty but feeling pleased with myself on the whole. August had not erupted into her usual afternoon Krakatoa tantrum. Now if I could coax her into a nap, I'd have a little down time.

As I opened the apartment door, I heard an odd sound.

Singing. And it sounded like Pepper singing, croaking out a tuneless version of "On Broadway" in a room somewhere. I stopped in the foyer. I had never heard Pepper sing before.

And from the tuneless warble floating toward me, it would be okay if I never did again.

At the sound of the front door shutting, the sound stopped. Pepper popped her head out of August's room at the back of the hallway and shot us a manic grin.

"Come look what I got you!" she shouted to August. Magic words to any kid (any adult, too).

August ran for her room. It was painted in lavender with white furnishings and a lilac blossom–painted chair rail. A room fit for a princess. Pepper told me that she was going for a maturer look for August.

August hated it.

On the white eyelet bedspread, which was half-covered with August's stuffed animals, were laid out several little dance ensembles. Tiny tap shoes. A pink leotard. Another little leotard with a tuxedo pattern knit into the fabric at the top. Black and pink and white tights.

August gaped. "What's that?"

"They're dance clothes, silly-billy," Pepper said in the voice she used when she wanted to sound extravagantly chummy with her daughter. "They're for you. And I got some too! 'Cause you know why?"

August eyed her warily. "Why?"

"Because this afternoon I went and enrolled us in Tappin' with Your Toddler."

"What's that?"

"It's dancing, beetle bug. We're going to have so much fun!"

At the prospect of such intense mother-daughter togetherness, August reacted just as I would have. She started whimpering. "I want to go to the pool!"

Pepper's arms went stiff. "The pool? You don't even like the pool!"

"Yes I do. I like it when Alson takes me."

Pepper glared at me.

"Why don't you have a nap, August?" I turned to Pepper and mouthed silently, *"She's getting a little cranky."*

Pepper spun on her heel and marched out of the room.

"She's just fussy," I explained when I joined her in the kitchen.

Lumi, the Smiths' new cook, disappeared the moment I came in. She was so shy, it was as though she were trying not to be caught working. Or maybe she had learned that the domestic who lasted the longest was she who made the fewest waves.

"She didn't like the planetarium. I shouldn't have taken her there."

Pepper sniffed. "I would think you'd have better sense . . . although I'm beginning to wonder." She was never going to let me forget the fact that I had endangered her life.

"I'm sure she'll enjoy tap class when she gets started," I said.

"She'd better. The only reason I'm doing this is for her. Things are so crazy here. It's a whole new world. Alessandra said I needed to enroll August in this preschool called Central Park Play—she said that if you didn't you were basically sinking your child's future. But I went over to Central Park Play this afternoon and the woman who runs it practically laughed in my face. *Laughed!* I'm serious. I've never been so humiliated. She told me that they had a waiting list as long as a city block . . . for the class of 2008! How can they have a four-year waiting list for a preschool when most of the kids who go there aren't even four years old yet?"

It did seem odd.

"They must be signing up kids based on their sonograms!" Pepper grumbled. "Of course I went crying to Alessandra . . . though honestly, she had to know that I would have trouble. Don't you think she could have warned me?"

"What did she say?"

"She acted like I was an airhead. Said I was going to have to pull strings, and the only way to do that was to get August in with some kids whose families have influence. Otherwise I'll just never get her into a good Montessori, and apparently if that happens we can just write off the Dalton School and who knows what all. Pepper will end up going to some public school hell—PS one zillion and three."

"It can't be as serious as all that."

"Ha! You have no idea. I looked into the eyes of that Central Park Play woman and it was like I was talking to the high priestess of preschools. She frightened me."

"So there are important people in the tap class?" I asked. "That's odd. Tap class sounds sort of . . ."

"*Seedy*," Pepper finished for me. "I know. Show-businessy—and Alessandra did mention Sarah Jessica Parker. If one famous person does something, there's this stampede. A real herd mentality. It's sick." She sighed. "I hope that tap school lets me in. They've *got to*. I'll die if they don't."

"I'm sure they will."

"But that daughter of mine—what an ingrate! Sometimes I think we need to take her to a psychiatrist. Alessandra seems to think so."

I gasped. "August? No way!"

"She's so *negative*," Pepper complained. "It's a real problem. She just *resists* everything. She won't even use her correct name half the time."

"But that's just her . . ."

"What would you know about it?" Pepper snapped at me. "Are you a child psychology expert?"

"Well, no, but . . ."

"*But she's just a little girl*," Pepper said, mimicking my unspoken thoughts. "That's what Spencer always says. But what does he know, either, I'd like to ask. *I'm* a mother. I think I know a little more about children than him or you."

I made a grunting noise.

She stared at me and then pushed back from the kitchen table. "I have a waxing appointment, thank God. I'm going crazy cooped up in here." She turned back to me from the doorway. "Oh, Al—there's some dry cleaning down the street. You can pick it up while August is taking her nap."

I bit my lip. I wonder if ordering me to run her errands was in the way of taking Alessandra's advice not to let me get away with too much. "Okay."

Her right eyebrow arched in challenge. "Is there a problem?"

I guessed it was too late to start talking about what was and wasn't in my job description. "No, no problem," I said.

It's hard to put your foot down when someone is already stepping on your toes.

Just when I thought New York was as uncomfortable as it could be, along came August. (The month, not the child.) We were having a heatwave. By afternoon each day, heat had twice baked all the cement and stone in town and withered most people. I was accustomed to Dallas, which was hotter than New York would ever be. But people in Dallas had figured out how to function in the summers with minimal contact with untreated air.

I would find myself ducking into delis just to stand next to the ice-laden salad bars. I would open freezer doors and find myself paralyzed with indecision between frozen fruit bar flavors. Suddenly *raspberry or coconut* demanded ten minutes of mental debate.

But it wasn't just the weather wearing me down. I began to question whether coming to New York had been such a great decision. I had hoped my life would blossom the moment I stepped foot on the Gotham pavement. I had expected the twenty-four-hour party person section of my life to begin, full of excitement and men. I had conveniently forgotten that I would be working, and that I would mostly be seen by toddlers and other nannies. On the few occasions I had managed to catch the eye of something male, the guy's glance would drop to the sticky little hand clasped in mine and he would scurry away as if for dear life.

Back when I was a Dallas insomniac, I would stay up nights angsting about feeling stuck in a rut. I had thought I needed to do something drastic to get unstuck. Now that I was a New

York insomniac, however, I angsted that my life was now forever glued to the handles of August's stroller.

In one moment of three am madness, I decided that the best decision would be to simply go home. The next day, however, a legal-sized envelope was waiting for me in the mail. It was a copy of my stepmother's sonogram, a shadowy bunch of blotches in which I could barely make out a head and maybe a foot. Attached to the picture with a paper clip was the scribbled note, *A big first hello to Big Al from her little sis, D'Ann!!!*

It's humbling to acknowledge the moment of intense sibling rivalry I felt toward that mimeographed sonogram. And that name! *D'Ann?* What kind of name was that for my half sister? And what was with the contraction? Shouldn't it at least be spelled Deanne? I felt vaguely slighted that no one had solicited my opinion in this very important matter.

D'Ann!

D'Ann, who would be growing up with my kind old dad, who would actually have time now to lavish on a daughter. He would become one of those middle-aged men who would expound at length about how he never realized what a joy parenthood was until the second time around. I, that other daughter, the daughter of unrealized joy, would fade in significance. He probably saw his obligations to me as all over anyway. If I ever did manage to get married, Dad would offer me some cash in lieu of the trouble of having to walk me down the aisle at a wedding. I would become—was already—D'Ann's big sis. Big Al. Grr.

The one positive thing happening was that August was beginning to adjust. She had discovered a playground not far from the apartment, and she was willing to brave the heat and crowded sidewalks to get there.

One day, as we were leaving the building to visit her new favorite spot, Spence was coming in. I practically choked. It was the first I'd spotted him since he had come back the day before.

"Just who I wanted to see!" he exclaimed, taking us both in.

He means August, I assured myself. He'd probably missed her like crazy while he was in London.

"Daddy!" August screamed, arms outstretched. "Come to the park."

I started to remind August, in my best nanny voice, that Daddy was a busy man. But to my surprise, Spence agreed. "Excellent idea! How did you know that was exactly where I wanted to go?"

"I guessed!" August shouted. She grabbed his hand and started tugging.

Without missing a beat, Spence fell into step next to us. Almost as if this was actually what he'd intended.

"This is the life, isn't it?" he asked me.

I mumbled a general agreement, though I wasn't sure quite what he meant. New York? Staggering wealth? Withering summer heat? It was hard to disagree with someone in such transparent good spirits, however. As we walked along, he really did look like he had the world on a string.

In order to steer us around an oncoming dog walker with eight canines on a leash, he put his hand on my elbow. That simple touch felt like a thousand volts of electricity going straight through me. I gulped and stumbled along dumbly for half a block, then managed to wriggle away after we had crossed Fifth into the park.

I'm walking down the street in New York City with Spence, I kept telling myself. Marveling. It was like a dream.

"I can't tell you how glad I am to have you here," Spence told me when we were sitting on a bench.

"Oh . . ." August was tentatively approaching a sandbox, and while I was trying to keep my eye on her, at the same time I couldn't quite manage to look away from Spence.

"Not just for me," he said. "Though God knows you've acted on me like a drug."

That seemed a bit much, especially when Pepper had said that Spence just felt pity for me. "Depressant or stimulant?"

He laughed. "Stimulant, definitely. You always could lift my spirits, Al."

Belatedly, I realized I shouldn't have used any variation on the word stimulate. I fought off a blush with sarcasm. It wasn't hard. *He thinks you're a pity case*, I reminded myself. "Right. I'm an inspiration."

"I'm serious," he said. "I always think back on those months we went out as some of the best times of my life. I know it sounds corny, but sometimes maybe your first love is the strongest."

I was about to melt into a little puddle right there on the bench, but then I thought about Jess singing "The First Cut Is the Deepest." Nothing like having your life compared to a Rod Stewart song to sober you up. "It certainly didn't seem to be very strong when you dumped me," I couldn't help reminding him.

"Dumped *you*!" he exclaimed.

I cleared my throat. I should have kept my yap shut. "Not that I'm bitter or anything."

He laughed incredulously. "I should think not. As I recall, you were the one who dumped me."

That was so wrong, for a moment I could just sputter wordlessly.

"Okay, maybe not technically," he admitted. "But you were always keeping me at arm's length. That's how you were with everyone. You were so busy, so sure of yourself. What did you need me for?"

"Me, sure of myself?" That had to be a joke.

"More than I was."

"You didn't think I was a know-it-all?" I asked.

"No! I thought you were fantastic. And then came Pepper," he said, withdrawing into memory. It was as if he were talking to himself. "She tried out for that play because of me, she told me. And she kept inviting me out while you were busy."

"I thought you were too naive to see what was going on."

"Are you kidding? I saw, and I was flattered. Do you remember that she even applied to Vanderbilt because I was going there? That seemed like such an extravagant gesture, I was bowled over by her. I couldn't imagine a person doing such a thing for me. You—"

He cut himself off, but the implication was so clear. *You*

wouldn't have. What would he have said if I admitted that I'd tried and failed?

"I never knew how Pepper got in," I said.

"Her aunt was on the Board of Regents. Serious strings were pulled."

I never had a chance.

He appeared still in wonder at it all. "I mean, Pepper was a little dynamo. Still is. But she really seemed to need me back then. Whose ego could resist that?"

That was it, then. I had never been attentive enough, complimentary enough.

"Oh, we were in love," Spence went on. "I know that. Especially in college. But I wonder occasionally about her motives. Sometimes I think I'm just a meal ticket to her."

As I chewed it all over, I could feel Spence's gaze studying me. Finally I looked over. I shouldn't have. My heart did a flip.

He wasn't looking at me with pity. Unless his pity was easily confused with lust.

This is exactly the kind of situation I had been patting myself on the back for avoiding. I had managed to stay out of temptation's reach . . . for a few weeks. Well, actually it had just been days, since Spence had been gone most of the time.

"God, I was crazy about you!" he exclaimed.

I dragged my gaze away and yelled at August, who was doing a tightrope walk around the railroad ties of the sandbox. "Be careful!" I called out, even though the only danger she was in was of falling six inches. I, on the other hand, seemed in much graver danger.

"Do you remember that locket I gave you for Valentine's?" Spence asked. "Do you still have it?"

"I never throw anything away," I said.

I even had my rejection letter from Vanderbilt . . . proof that *I* had loved him as much as Pepper had . . . if he'd just stuck with me a little longer.

"I angsted for weeks over that silly locket." He smiled indulgently over his younger self. "I don't think I've worried so much about any present since."

Certainly not over anything he'd given Pepper, was the implied message.

It was suddenly hard to get a good gulp of air. "Don't you need to get back to work?" I asked him, checking my wrist for a nonexistent watch.

"Nah." He laughed and inadvertently patted my thigh, where his hand just happened to come to a resting point. "I don't actually work anyway, didn't you know that?"

But just then, he reached for his ringing cell with his free hand. The other one was still a lump on my leg. I was torn between the urge to jump off the bench or to leave his hand there and see what happened. The latter was a bad impulse, I knew. Very bad.

"Uh-huh," he said into the phone. "Damn it, Frank, are you kidding? Please tell me you're kidding." He rolled his eyes at me, then fluttered his fingers playfully against my leg. I nearly lost it. I shot off the bench and made a circle around August, who was up to her knees in sand.

"Uh-huh . . . well, talk to Janine. Honestly. She's the expert on this." He hung up and studied me for a moment. "I remember worrying about the inscription on your locket."

I was amazed by the way he could stop thinking about a phone call that had just taken place; he could do a mental turn on a dime. "But there isn't an inscription."

"I know. My mom advised against it. I wanted to put something like 'Forevermore . . .' but she said you would think that was too corny."

My heart did a little flip. He'd wanted to write that? How sweet!

What was sad was that I *would* have thought it was too corny.

" 'Remember, Spence,' Mom told me, 'This is Al. She's so sensible!' Mom knew you better than I did, I guess. You always said we wouldn't last forever."

Yeah, but I thought we'd last longer than six months . . .

And maybe we would have. If only Pepper hadn't come along and stolen him.

"Well, maybe nothing lasts." He sighed regretfully.

That sigh made me wonder if he was thinking about our ill-fated high school romance . . . or his marriage. At any rate, wistful regret sounded safer than what we had been heading toward before that phone call. I sat down on the bench again, but this time a more cautious distance apart.

"I sure am glad you're with me now, Al," he said, clasping his hand against my shoulder. (So much for caution.) "I'm trying to hold things together, I really am."

I swallowed. I wondered how his holding my shoulder could hold together his marriage. "I'm glad," I said. "For August's sake . . ."

He nodded. "That's exactly it. For August." He sighed again. "It doesn't seem like much of a marriage, does it, when you have to say you're just staying together for the child?"

"Oh, I . . ."

"But I'm trying, God knows." His gaze burned into me. "I guess you know Pepper hasn't exactly been faithful."

My face felt fiery.

"Believe me, it's not a secret. Things haven't been good between us for a long time. It's hardly been a marriage at all."

Jesus. I wasn't sure I wanted to hear much more. Did "hardly a marriage at all" refer to their sex life?

Come to think of it, I wanted to hear *everything*.

He laughed, making me jump. "Listen to me moping! As if I'm not a lucky sonofabitch in every other respect. Loneliness isn't the worst thing that can happen to a man, is it?"

The question broke my heart. He was *lonely*? The sweet guy I knew in high school, who had been so cute and escorted me around town all those months, was a cuckolded husband in a miserable marriage at the age of twenty-eight? The thought made me sick. It made me want to throttle Pepper.

I shook my head. I felt numb. I felt dangerously close to offering myself as a solution to his loneliness.

"Right. Well!" He sniffed, and for a moment I could swear there were tears in his eyes. "Oh! I almost forgot . . ." He reached into his jacket and pulled out a little bag from Barney's. "I got you something."

I protested, but he shut me up.

"It's nothing. Just some perfume. I seem to remember you like Chanel."

He'd bought me a little bottle, which, since it was real perfume and not *eau de* anything, was probably the most expensive gift a guy had given me since . . . well, since Spence had given me that locket.

"Everybody likes Chanel," I said.

"Not Pepper," he said quickly, as if this were another black mark against her character. "She likes something different every year. I can't keep up."

The woman was evil. She didn't even like good solid smells.

"Well . . . thank you."

He smiled and gave my shoulder another squeeze. "I just want you to know how much it means to me to have you here right now. I think the prospect of seeing your face at the end of the day is all that's keeping despair at bay for me right now."

"Oh . . ."

That didn't sound like he pitied me. Nor was Chanel a pity present. *Why had I believed Pepper?*

His phone rang. "Right!" he barked. "Okay, I'm on my way back now." He hung up. "Thanks for spending time with me, Al."

"Oh—"

"Talking to you always makes me feel better," he said, getting up. He stood and took my hand in some sort of formal good-bye gesture. "I hope we'll be able to talk more soon."

As I watched him stride over to August and give her a good-bye kiss, I felt weak-kneed even though I was still sitting down. When he was gone, I sat immobile for a long time, just running my hand over my cellophane-wrapped box of Chanel.

He remembered my perfume after all these years . . .

After a moment of practically falling into a swoon, I straightened. *Oh, God.* This was nuts. And so, so wrong.

I dug my own phone out of my handbag and dialed Jess at work. Her job was to answer the phones, and I was grateful when she picked up after just one ring.

"Al, whassup?"

"I need a man," I told her.

Chapter 15

"Anyone will do," I told Jess later that afternoon.

I had managed to grab a few hours while Pepper was taking August to their first tap class, and Jess had weaseled out of work by saying she had an emergency. (Wasn't it true?) She worked on Wall Street so we met in the Village, at the Magnolia Café, where hipsters stood in line to consume sickeningly sweet cupcakes, the old-fashioned kind with bright buttercream icing with sprinkles. Jess was one of those thin people who seemed to be able to eat any amount of disgustingly unhealthy food and remain bony and frail looking. I sometimes wondered if she ate at all when no one was looking.

"Are you going to call Finn?" she asked.

I detected a catch in her throat. She seemed really obsessed with him. "Believe me," I assured her, "the state I'm in, I need a man I don't have to worry about putting in the hospital all the time."

She nodded. "Anyway, he seems like he would be more compatible with a more purely artistic type."

"Say . . . a cellist?"

She squirmed girlishly.

Enough about Finn already, I wanted to tell her. "That would be great. Look, do you know anyone I could meet? You were right. I've got to start going out again or I'll go crazy."

"Spence putting the moves on you?" she guessed. "Or is it worse? *'Reader, I slept with him.'* "

"No!" I said. Then, "We just talked."

"Uh-oh. Talk is more dangerous than moves."

I remembered the feeling of his large hand clamped down on my leg. "Nothing happened except a little touching and—"

"Wait!" Jess said, stuffing a bite of lemon cupcake in her mouth. "Touching *is* the moves."

"But it was innocent, almost inadvertent. We were sort of reminiscing . . ."

I filled her in on what he had said, about how he was trying to save his marriage, and how he had felt about me all those years ago. Before I knew it, fifteen minutes had gone by, and I was again considering offering myself to Spence as a love slave.

"Hold on, Al. You're telling me this guy, this prince charming of yours, let *his mother* talk him out of putting an inscription on your locket? That's pretty weak. And acting like the martyr, telling you about how hard he's trying to save his marriage! You said the guy was hardly home two days the whole time you were in Dallas."

"It was only a month . . ." But she was right. It sounded feeble. "I just need to get my mind off this whole situation. Whatever Spence and I had—it was just this high school thing—and it's *so over.* I was okay with that ten years ago, so why am I having a hard time accepting it now?"

"Because ten years ago he dumped you, and now he has you dangling."

"I'm not dangling. And he hasn't done anything."

"He gave you perfume."

"That was just . . ." I stopped short.

Come to think about it, what on earth had he been thinking? Perfume? That was a romantic gift, not something you would give your nanny.

"Okay. I have this friend, Troy," Jess began cautiously. "He's an actor."

Actor. I sighed. "Has he ever been in *Picnic*?"

She squinted at me. "What are you talking about?"

I shook my head. "Never mind. More to the point . . . is he straight?"

"Of course!" She paused, then added, "I'm pretty sure."

I groaned.

"Or, actually, I would consider him sort of asexual right now."

"Jess! You are not selling this person very well."

"It's just a phase. He's had a sort of tough couple of months."

"Oh." I frowned. A year. "You're saying he's been asexual for a couple of months?"

"Right."

I rolled my eyes. "For heaven's sake. By that criteria, I'm asexual, too."

"I would make a distinction there," Jess said. "Troy sort of dropped out of the dating game, while you've been trying to get laid, but haven't managed to find anybody."

"Thanks for being so precise." With friends like mine I never had to worry about getting a big head. My ego was a Swiss cheese of puncture holes.

"To tell you the truth, I hesitated to tell you about Troy," Jess said. "I've had sort of a crush on him for a while. Not that I would ever fess up to him. We've been friends for a long time, but it's always been in the back of my mind, you know?"

I knew what she meant. He was her friend-boy, her designated unrequited love. She was keeping him in reserve, so that if the stars ever aligned just so, maybe when they were both forty, they would look at each other and have one of those *When-Harry-Met-Sally* moments.

"So why tell me now?"

She blushed. "Well, to be honest, now that I have Finn, I covet Troy less."

I gaped at her in astonishment. She and Finn were an item already? I'd just spoken to her the afternoon before and she hadn't mentioned a thing. "You and Finn went out and you didn't tell me?"

She waved a napkin. "No, we haven't gone out yet, exactly . . . but I asked him out for coffee last night."

"What happened?"

"He said he had to do his laundry."

That didn't sound good. Then again, I was a great laundry procrastinator myself and knew what happened when the dirty clothes pile reached critical mass. You either had to face up to Maytag or face social exile. "Did you ask him to your concert?"

Her face lit up. "Yes, and he seemed really enthusiastic. He said he'd have to check to see how busy he was that week."

It was hard not to let my doubts show. Maybe Jess was just a poor reporter, but these did not sound like the words of a man bursting with plans for a big romance.

"Anyway, I'll sound Troy out this evening and see if he's up for a little matchmaking. Could be just what he needs right now."

Something about her description of this guy wasn't putting me in hearts and flowers mood. "Has he had a nervous breakdown or something?"

"No, no, nothing like that. Just a string of bad luck. His girlfriend left him, his dog died . . ."

That sounded depressing, all right. I felt myself slumping in my chair, despite the sugar high from the three cupcakes.

Obviously, the best solution would be more sugar.

"I think I'll pick up some cupcakes to take home. Nothing makes August happier than food in primary colors."

"I'll let you know about Troy," Jess said.

The subway was crowded on the way home; I'd inadvertently bumbled into early rush hour. The local was too packed to even dream of getting a seat. Just as an experiment, however, I dug *Outwitting Head Lice* out of my shoulder bag and perused a few pages while I clung unsteadily to an overhead strap. Within a few moments, I noticed I had a bite. A seated man in a suit reading *Who Moved My Cheese?* glanced up to see what I was reading. He squinted. When he digested the title, his gaze darted quickly back to his own book.

Moments later, before we had even reached a station, his seat was empty.

Maybe Jess wasn't crazy after all.

I returned to the apartment, stopping on my way up to give the doorman, Lou, a cupcake. Lou was a sweet old lug, a marine who saw duty in the early days of Vietnam who now donned the gray uniform of apartment gatekeeper and greeted me each morning with a rueful smile and a wry salute.

When I deposited the sky blue cupcake on the podium that served as his headquarters, he arched a bushy brow at me. "Am I supposed to eat that?"

"It's delicious. Believe me, I just had three of them. I'm still buzzing."

"I was expecting you to buzz in earlier," Lou told me. "You had a visitor."

How could I have a visitor? I didn't know anybody. "Did they leave their name?"

"Yeah, but I can't remember it. Something odd. An older lady—quite a looker. I called upstairs and Mrs. Smith said to send her up."

I sent the elevator a suspicious glance. "Is she still up there?"

"Unless she left by way of the fire escape, but I doubt that happened. Those weren't exactly hiking boots she was wearing."

I worried all the way up to the fourth floor. For a person who never had trouble with the law and wasn't raised Catholic, I had a surprisingly overdeveloped sense of guilt. The first thing that occurred to me when Lou told me about the mysterious visitor was that I had finally been found out. (That house I had toilet-papered in high school . . . that unpaid parking ticket in Portland, Oregon . . . that lie I'd told a guy I wanted to impress about having read *The Brothers Karamazov* when I'd actually given up after forty-six pages . . .) Obviously the authorities had come for me.

But then the specifics of what he said began to sink in. Odd name. Older lady. Good looker. The vague details sounded a lot like my . . .

It couldn't be, I assured myself. I hadn't heard from her in over a month. No one had. My checkup calls to the Ritz had yielded nothing.

Asked for me but Pepper let her up . . . Why would Pepper let just anyone asking for me up to the apartment? Unless it was someone she recognized, or knew . . .

Could it be?

By the time I stumbled out of the elevator and over to the door, my heart was palpitating irregularly and a line of sweat had broken out on my upper lip. My hand felt slippery as I tried to work my key into the deadbolt. When I swung open the door, there she was. My mother. Grinning. Arms outstretched. She had obviously planted herself there—my big surprise—the moment she'd heard the elevator.

She flung her arms wide, as if to say "Ta-da!"

"Mom!" I managed to make my voice sound pleasantly surprised, I think, even though a boulder of dread had taken up residence in my sternum.

"Here I am!" she announced.

"What are you doing here?" I asked, exchanging a brief hug with her that she turned into a full-body, emotional long-lost-parent squeeze. She pulled away, sniffling dramatically.

I could see why Lou had called her a good looker. The last time I had seen her she'd been blond, but now her hair was auburn and was worn shoulder length and loosely permed. Her clothes were amazing—a stylish pencil skirt topped with cool layers of silk and tailored linen in tones of cream and blue. Looking at her, I became more certain than ever that fashion sense was one of those things that skips generations. A filmy scarf was loosely tied at her throat, disguising what she always said was her worst feature—"*My skinny neck!*" she would complain, craning her head and distending her ballet dancer's build until I wanted to strangle her by that skinny neck.

Sorry, but a too-skinny anything is hard for me to sympathize with.

Pepper popped into view, clutching her own handbag. "Doesn't your mom look *fantastic*?"

"Sure does."

Mom demurred. "It's just my new outfit, is all. And maybe my new divorce!" She tossed her head back for a long, throaty laugh.

Pepper cackled along with her.

"What are you doing here?" I asked.

She grabbed my arm. "Now, I intended to tell you all about that at the Plaza."

"You're staying at the Plaza?"

"No, I'm taking y'all there for a drink."

Pepper did have an expectant look, and August, I finally noticed, was sitting in her stroller, half asleep.

"All of us?" I asked.

"Did you know that little August has never been there?" Mom asked, as if this were a scandalous lack of life experience for a three-and-a-half-year-old. "I have to remedy that."

The whole situation was making me uneasy. How long had she been in the apartment . . . and what had she been saying? What had happened to Murph and the bendy woman? Why was she in New York?

"I bought cupcakes," I said, not certain I was up to the whole Plaza atmosphere. "We could have coffee here . . ."

"We've had coffee, waiting for you," Mom said, squeezing my arm. "Poor Pepper made several pots of it. She ran herself ragged waiting on me."

(I assumed Lumi could contradict that statement. My mother had always had an extravagant way of talking.)

"Besides," she said, "If I'm going to waste calories on carbs, let it be a cocktail, not some nasty cupcake." She swatted me playfully on the hips, like we were schoolgirls. "Cupcakes! I'm surprised at you!"

Actually, I suddenly felt like a schoolgirl—a stammering mess embarrassed by her mother. I hadn't had this want-to-sink-through-the-floor feeling with quite such intensity since . . . well, probably since the last time I had seen Mom. It had been a while.

"C'mon," Pepper said, brushing past us. "I've got an errand to run. It's right on our way."

They left me to assume my natural place behind August's stroller.

"I thought I'd never see my daughter pushing a buggy!" Mom joked as we waited for the elevator.

Ha, ha.

Mom and Pepper remained a few steps ahead of me as we walked down the street. They were chattering away like old buds.

"Is she really your mommy?" August asked me.

I nodded. *See?* I wanted to say, *You don't have it so bad.*

The errand Pepper had to run turned out to be a trip to a furrier on Fifty-seventh Street.

The idea of buying a coat—and a fur of all things—in the middle of August floored me. Here I had barely been surviving the heat of the day, and Pepper had been dreaming of insulation against a cold that I could only dream of.

The store was another barren place with whispering salesmen. One got the feeling you had to know a secret password to actually view the bulk of the merchandise. There were a few coats exhibited on hangers, and my mother kept running toward them, gasping and clutching at their furry sleeves with Marilyn Monroe–like ecstasy. I hung back a bit inspecting things a bit more coolly. Some of the fur didn't even look like fur; a few coats on display featured fur that had been sheared down, dyed bright colors, and sewn into patchwork designs. Definitely not your grandmother's fur coat, although there were plenty of those on display, too.

Mom was equally pleased by them all.

"Look at this, Alison!" she said, holding up one of the patchwork coats for my inspection. "I would think you'd *love* something like this. It's sort of got that hippy-dippy look about it."

My eyes hadn't rolled so dramatically since I was twenty. "Right, Mom. I'm a hippie."

She chuckled. "You know what I mean. They're so *unusual.*"

"It doesn't matter anyway, because I'm poor. I couldn't afford anything here even if it was to my taste, which it isn't."

"You, poor?" Mom laughed. "You're doing great. Look where you're living! My poor little rich girl on Fifth Avenue!"

I put my hands on my hips. "I'm a nanny. A domestic. Do you know what that means?"

She waved off that little inconvenient detail. "Now don't go getting all Karl Marxy on me, Alison. Pepper's so nice! So much better than that mousy little violinist you used to hang around with."

"I'm still friends with Jess," I replied. "She lives here, which is part of the reason I took this job to begin with. And she doesn't play violin, she plays cello. She is my friend, and Pepper is my employer."

"Well I'm sure you could make *more* friends if you weren't so prickly all the time!"

"Prickly!" I practically shrieked.

I couldn't believe we were arguing already. I couldn't believe that we were here together, period. That she had just appeared out of the blue, without explanation, was something I was still trying to wrap my mind around. "Mom, what happened in Paris? You called once and then you disappeared. Where is Murph?"

"He's back in Houston. He's started divorce proceedings." She sounded less happy about it than she had earlier, when she was joking with Pepper.

"I'm sorry," I said. That explained what she was doing in New York. "I can see why you wouldn't want to move back right away."

"I'm never going back," she declared.

Houston probably was too small for her now; all those Mrs. Murphs past and present running around in it. "You mean you're moving back to Dallas?"

"Oh, no. I wouldn't like that, either. Dallas seems like a different lifetime."

"Well, then . . ."

She grinned. "I'm going to live here."

"Here?"

"Why not? I heart New York! Besides, I want to be with my family."

My brow was tensing into deep trenches of lines. I could feel a headache coming on. "Is Aunt Brenda living here? I thought she and her husband lived in Rhode Island."

"Brenda!" Mom laughed. She and her sister had never been close. "I was talking about *you*! You're my family, honey."

For some reason, that thought hadn't occurred to me.

Mom . . . me . . . together at last. This took a few moments to absorb.

As it did sink in I wanted to bury my head in the nearest silver fox and weep. Good grief. Everything in my life felt unsettled, and now my prodigal mother was waltzing into my world again after a ten-year absence. No doubt she would suck me emotionally dry and then waltz out again as soon as she could get her hooks into another millionaire.

Pepper came out to model her coat. "What do you think?"

Mom clapped her hands together. She was positively entranced. "Sable! Oh, it's gorgeous! Absolutely gorgeous."

Pepper had not chosen one of the modern fur-that-doesn't-look-like-fur creations. Instead, she had taken the other road at a gallop, picking out a coat an old movie star might have worn. Gene Tierney, perhaps. It was a calf-length sable, rich deep brown, and I had to admit, it was amazing to look at. It screamed rich.

Mom practically had tears in her eyes. "It's so pretty. I can't remember when I've seen such a beautiful thing. It must cost a fortune!"

Pepper put her fingers to her lips. "*Sh.* It's eighteen thousand dollars."

I was afraid I was going to pass out.

"It's a birthday present from Spencer. Isn't that sweet?"

I reeled over to a rack of mink jackets and took a few deep breaths. Spence was buying Pepper a coat for her birthday that cost more than I would earn in a year? Was he mad?

Or was this what he considered trying to hold on to his marriage?

"I'm having the sleeves taken up, but what do you think about the length?" She twisted to show us the back.

"Don't cut off a centimeter," Mom advised her. "Don't you dare."

Pepper stared at herself critically in the mirror, then smiled. "I don't think I will."

Mom shook her head. "If I had a coat like that, I'd think I'd died and gone to heaven. I wouldn't want another thing in the world."

Pepper stopped smiling. "People never stop wanting more, no matter what they have."

"Yes, I suppose that's true," my mother said. Then she laughed. "But it's better to want more when you've got too much than wanting it when you've got nothing!"

Pepper laughed along with her.

"I'm going to wait outside," I blurted out. I had to escape. "August is getting fussy."

She wasn't. She hadn't made a peep the whole time we'd been in the store. It was shameless of me to use her that way, but I didn't care. Jealousy was slashing at me with Norman Bates ferocity. Spence didn't *love* Pepper. He was just trying to save his marriage . . . which everyone knew was simply a way of saying that he was sure to dump her sooner or later.

Right?

By the time we got to the Palm Court, everyone was ready to be refortified. I had planned on just getting a cup of tea but opted instead for a double martini.

"How did you find me?" I asked Mom.

She clucked her tongue. "I had to call your father."

Pepper leaned forward. She seemed to be enjoying this visit with my mom entirely too much. "Didn't you just hear from your dad the other day, Al? I thought I noticed something he had sent you . . ."

"Oh, yeah."

Everyone looked expectant, but I really didn't want to go into this subject right now. I half-suspected Pepper was already laughing at us, not with us.

"It was a really large envelope," Pepper told Mom. "I worried it was something legal . . ."

Mom looked startled.

I heaved a sigh. I couldn't keep it a secret forever. "Darla's having a baby. They sent me a copy of the sonogram."

Mom's lips flattened into a straight red line. "I knew she was expecting, of course. Your father just couldn't keep his lips buttoned about that." She shook her head. "I don't know if I approve of this sending out of fetus pictures."

"Everybody does it," I said, suddenly feeling the need to defend Darla.

"I didn't," Pepper said.

Mom tilted her head thoughtfully. "And I'm not *entirely* certain that if I were a fetus, I would even want people taking pictures of me. Being stuck in a womb doesn't really afford you the opportunity to look your best."

"Well, they already have her named, so maybe they're just feeling ahead of the game," I said.

Everyone jumped on that tidbit. "What name have they chosen?"

"D'Ann." When Pepper and Mom frowned, I had to spell it for them. And then I couldn't help expressing my exasperation with it. "What kind of name is that?"

"I think it's white trash for Diane," my mom said, tossing back the last drops of a vodka martini. She turned to August and smiled. "How old are you, sweetheart?"

August sipped shyly at her lemonade as she considered whether she actually wanted to answer. "Three."

"Almost four," Pepper corrected.

"Four!" Mom exclaimed.

"Her birthday is next month." Pepper shifted in her seat, revving up for a big reveal. "I'm so psyched. I've got the greatest idea for a party for her!"

I looked up from my vat of booze. This would probably be important to me in the long run. "What?"

"A western theme!" she said excitedly. "I got the idea in tap class. Suddenly I saw August and myself, up on a stage. We're wearing little cowgirl outfits, like Dale Evans."

I choked on my martini olive. Was she yanking my chain?

You couldn't tell it by looking at her. She seemed sincerely caught up in her big vision. "I want to rent Central Park—some part of it, anyhow—and have ponies and cowboy clowns and all sorts of stuff! Won't that be fun?"

"Fabulous!" Mom said.

I narrowed my eyes at my mom. This wasn't ringing any bells?

Pepper, wound up, started gesticulating. "And I want to have a big banner with old-west lettering that says 'August's Dude Ranch.' Won't that be cute?"

I gaped at her. Was she seriously trying to mess with my head? I turned to my mom. She had to remember *that.*

But mom was just smiling enthusiastically.

"I've got our Tappin' with Your Toddler teacher to work up a routine for us," Pepper said. "We're going to do a little dance to 'Buttons and Bows.' Won't that be cute?"

"Adorable!" Mom exclaimed. She grinned at August, who, to her credit, was looking a little guarded about these plans. "You'll be a hit!"

"I don't like dancing," August said.

"Of course you do," Pepper said. "Wait till you see the little outfits I'm going to get for us!"

"I don't want to." August's face was taking on that sweaty fretful look that usually augured rough seas ahead.

"Alison will help you. Won't you, Alison?"

I nodded, numb. "Of course."

"Alison's a whiz at stage stuff!" Pepper's lips curved up in a smile. This was one of her few references ever to our theatrical past . . . or our past, period.

But I suddenly had the unsettling feeling that this was all about our past.

Mom paid our check and walked out with us. Pepper wanted to catch a cab home. "I think I'll walk back to my hotel," Mom said when the others had gotten in the cab and I was about to follow. I had thought we would drop her off, but she insisted on going on foot. "It's not far, and this city just gives me such energy!"

Better than that yucky old Paris, I guessed.

"Will I see you soon?" she asked me. I could tell that there was something on her mind.

"Of course," I said, worried that I had been less than gracious to her. For one moment I tried to shake off the resentment she seemed to whip up in me whenever I was around her and act like a grown-up. "Just say when. I get Sundays off, and Thursday nights."

"That does sound like servitude—positively Victorian!" She laughed. "Does the master of the house have a mad wife in the attic?"

I rolled my eyes. The *Jane Eyre* cracks really did get old. "The master of the house is Spence Smith, Mom. You remember Spence."

"Of course! He was so cute. Too bad you didn't marry him—then you'd be getting that fabulous fur coat."

"I don't want a coat." I just wanted Spence. But I wouldn't tell her that.

She trilled her fingers at me. "I'll give you a buzz, sweetheart. Stay fluffed!"

She turned and flitted away, her long scarf flapping behind her like a flag, and I sank into the taxi.

"I love your mom!" Pepper exclaimed. "She is soooo cool. It must change everything, being raised by someone like her."

I nodded grimly as I shut the door. "It certainly does."

Chapter 16

My room needed some decorative touches, so I decided to meet Finn in Chelsea that Sunday morning for the flea markets. Since the painting fiasco, we'd only spoken on the phone a few times. I was amazed how game he was to go shopping with me, considering the fact that our past two outings hadn't exactly ended favorably for him. No matter what, this time I was determined that no ill should befall him.

The strange thing was, he seemed equally concerned about me. "You look awful," he said when I came up out of the subway where we had agreed to meet.

I felt, as I did most mornings, like some creature that had just clawed its way up from the ooze, but I hadn't expected anyone to call me on it.

"We'd better stop for coffee," he said, steering me toward a bagel store. "And food. You need sustenance."

We ordered breakfast, then sat down and stared at all the other people going to the flea market. Usually I would be panicked at the idea of other people finding bargains intended for me before I could get to them, but this morning I felt very mellow. It had to be Finn and his comfortingly Zen-like presence. Astonishing how someone in a tattered tie-dyed T-shirt and Teva sandals could have such a soothing effect on me.

"Is everything okay?" he asked.

"I didn't sleep last night." He looked alarmed. "It's okay. I never sleep."

"Never sleeping isn't okay. Have you tried chamomile tea?"

That made me laugh. "That's Insomnia 101. I've graduated beyond that now. Believe me, I've tried everything."

"I read a story in the *Utne Reader* that said most sleep disturbances are caused by chronic worry."

(Duh.)

"So what's bothering you?" he asked.

What wasn't! I really didn't think I should be talking about my problems with someone who was essentially still a stranger, but he had such a reassuring voice, like a shrink. "I thought when I moved here that I would be starting fresh, but it feels like I've just lugged all my problems two thousand miles. I've got the same nut-job for an employer, only now she's apparently planning a birthday party that's an exact re-creation of one she had when she was five that I ruined. Doesn't that seem weird to you? I mean *weird* weird, as in almost psychotic."

"You're probably misremembering. It probably wasn't that bad. How could you have ruined a birthday party?"

I told him about Pepper's Dude Ranch, and as the story unfolded, his face slackened until, by the end, when I was dragged away in my itchy dress in shame, his mouth was in full fly-catching mode. "Now she's planning a party exactly like that one, right down to the corny banner and the Dale Evans costumes. And she's acting like we've all had our memories erased, but she remembers. I know she remembers."

"Okay, that's a little strange," he said.

"And my mother was right there when Pepper was telling us this, and she didn't say a thing! It's as if *she* doesn't remember, either."

He leaned forward, squinting at me. "Your mother? Is she visiting you?"

I let out a long sigh. "She's *living* here . . . or so she says. That's another problem! Do you realize I've been in New York for weeks and practically everyone I've met is from Texas?"

"It's a city of immigrants."

"Okay, but for once I'd like to meet an immigrant from somewhere exotic, like Ohio." I sighed and took another swig of coffee. "Just out of the blue, the minute I finally relocate to New York, Mom decides to move here, too. She just popped up!" I shook my head and gave him a rundown of the history of my mother, and what had happened the day we'd all gone to the Plaza. "It wasn't until after I had gotten into the cab that I remembered that she hadn't told me where she was living, or given me her phone number. That's so typical of her. She tends to create chaos and disappear."

"What do you resent her for more, creating the chaos, or disappearing?"

I frowned at him. "You really need to watch that."

"Watch what?"

"Sounding like a school psychologist."

He laughed ruefully into his coffee cup. "I'm sorry."

"Anyway, we didn't come here for psychoanalysis, we came for the shopping. Let's go."

"All right," he said. "But if you ever need to vent, I'm always available."

Out in the flea markets, it was a post–*Antiques Roadshow* world. Every seller of used anything was convinced he possessed hidden treasure. I found a guy selling his rusty shovels for thirty dollars apiece. Not that I was in the market for shovels. I wasn't sure what I was looking for. But it was depressing to think that even used junk being hocked in empty parking lots was now beyond my budget.

After much scouring, I came upon a black-and-white photograph of a circus performer from the early 1900s. She wore what was probably considered back then to be a daring costume—a sleeveless wool dress with a skirt that came just below her knees. A full three inches of leg encased in baggy tights was showing between her hem and the tops of her buttoned boots. On her shoulder were two parrots. Perched on her arm was a tiny monkey. Yet the young woman looked as deadly serious as one of those old tintypes of pioneers.

"You think she ever had doubts about the way her life was going?" I wondered aloud.

Finn seemed as in awe of the picture as I was. "She looks like she's having serious doubts right there. I wonder what she did with those birds?"

"And that monkey," I said. "I'll bet her act had a great name, like 'Amazing Mabel and her Menagerie.' "

It was tempting to buy Mabel, but she was a little pricey, so I kept going. I found a bud vase in the shape of Felix the Cat for five dollars, which was more suited to my pocketbook. And my taste, I feared. I was spending so much time around August, my taste was reverting to a toddler's.

After paying, Finn and I headed back for the subway.

"You didn't find anything," I noted.

Finn shrugged. "I was sort of along for the ride. Where are you headed now?"

"The apartment. I'm hoping to catch a nap and decompress before the week starts again."

A worried look crossed Finn's face. "Jess told me the guy you're working for is sort of a lech."

I bristled. It was one thing to bad-mouth him to me . . . "He is not. He's my old boyfriend."

Finn's blue eyes registered astonishment. "Isn't that awkward?"

"Well, a little," I admitted. "Another part of my troubled past that seems to have creeped after me."

We were at the point where we were going to have to cross the street to get to our respective subway platforms. He was going downtown and I was going up.

"Thanks for coming out with me," I told him. "You've been great. If you ever need someone to play Dr. Freud for you, I'll do my best."

"How about now?"

I squinted at him against the sunlight. He looked depressed. "Is something wrong?"

"I want to ask you to go to Jess's concert, but I'm getting the feeling that wouldn't be kosher." He shifted, then combed a hand through his practically nonexistent hair. "I mean, I'm getting the feeling that Jess . . ."

"Considers you her date," I finished for him.

"Well, yes."

"You're right. She does."

His shoulders rounded. I could feel his disappointment and was equal parts amazed and embarrassed. When was the last time I'd disappointed a guy? Had I ever?

But I also felt a sharp pang of dread for the disappointment Jess obviously had in store. She was so psyched about going out with him, so sure he was the one for her.

But maybe she wouldn't be disappointed. Maybe if they just gave it time . . .

"I couldn't have accepted your invitation anyway," I told him. "I'm already going with someone else." Which was true. Jess had set me up on a blind date that night with her designated unrequited object of love, Troy.

"Going with?" he asked, obviously worried I was using the term in its junior high school sense.

"To the concert," I clarified.

He let out his breath. "Just to the concert." He reached out for my hand. "Right?"

Oh, God. I tried to think fast. But at the same time, a shot of adrenaline rushed through me, rendering me incapable of rational thought. In one instant, I looked at Finn's lips and thought, *I wonder what it would be like to kiss him.* But even as the question crossed my mind, I felt vaguely guilty.

Yet towards whom? Troy, a guy I hadn't even met yet? Spence?

There was no denying Finn was strangely handsome there in the stark sunlight of noon, looking so nervous-hopeful that I felt my heart breaking a little, even though we weren't at all right for each other. We had different worldviews. Plus I worried that he was a much better person than I was.

I yanked on my hand, but he held it firm. "I like you, Al," he said. "I can't seem to help myself."

My lips trembled into a smile. "I guess that means you've been trying."

His breath gushed out. "So hard! You wouldn't believe. I worry I'm a masochist or something. I mean, I know we've joked about this, but bad things seem to happen to me when you're around. You've been hazardous to my health."

"Not today, at least," I said.

"Not yet," he said. "But I have the feeling you're about to tell me that you just want to be friends, and that's worse than a concussion any day."

I nodded. "A lot of my friends seem to feel that way."

At least I managed to make him smile. "That's not what I meant."

"I know." I had to look away for a moment. Why was everything always so screwed up? Why were guys always married to someone else or coveted by someone else or just all wrong for me?

"I'm sorry," I said. "Jess is my friend, and—"

"I'm not interested in Jess." He spoke matter-of-factly, without the slightest bit of petulance.

"It wouldn't work out." I swallowed and managed to retrieve my hand. "You're a lot nicer than I am, Finn."

"Not true," he said. "Especially not at this moment."

I had no idea what he meant, and I wasn't sure I wanted to know. Maybe irritation made him want to bean me on the head with a brick.

"I'll see you at the concert." I turned on my heel and descended into the subway.

"Al!"

I stopped and turned. He was standing at the top of the stairs. "I didn't mean what I said. Being your friend is much better than a concussion."

As compliments went, it wasn't what I would call robust. But I had to take what I could get.

"Thanks."

"I'll call you."

We waved in parting and I stumbled down into the bowels of the subway. Sleep. That's what I wanted more than anything right now. As the train racketed its way up to the Upper East Side, I could almost feel myself slipping into oblivion already.

Sometimes I got more rest thinking about sleep than I did while actually sleeping.

I crawled home, let myself in, and was relieved when I discovered the apartment was silent. Spence had gone to Dallas and I supposed he still wasn't back yet. I poured myself a glass of juice and padded down the hall. When I passed August's room, I was surprised to find her door closed. It was usually open, unless she was in it. I cracked it open and peeked in. Sure enough, August was conked out on her bed, her arm flung over her eyes like a diva on her fainting couch.

I closed the door, curious. Maybe Pepper was taking a nap somewhere, too. But her bedroom door had been wide open, the room clearly empty. Surely she wouldn't have left August alone, I fumed as I headed for my room. Surely—

I opened my door, which I always kept shut, and found myself staring at a man's bare ass. In my bed! Actually, from that vantage point I could see a man's naked butt and a tangle of legs, two of which I assumed belonged to Pepper. Those were her clothes strewn across my floor.

Goldilocks, the pornographic version.

For a few moments I felt physically incapable of doing anything more than standing stock still. And gawking. Hollywood obviously was selling the world a bill of goods; in real life there wasn't anything appealing about watching two people having sex. I assumed whoever this was in my bed was a pretty fine specimen of manhood (as for his actual manhood, I couldn't vouch—wrong angle) yet from where I was standing his backside was an unsavory display of jiggling white flesh punctuated with surprising tufts of Cro-Magnon man butt-fur.

I didn't feel like I had stumbled into a Hollywood movie so much as one of those raunchy paperback books we used to pass around in sixth grade. *In the Nanny's Room*, this one might have been called.

I decided the best course of action would be simply to get the hell out of there, but when I reached back to grab the doorknob again, my bag with the Felix bud vase in it clunked against the door frame.

The butt jiggling ceased. In unison, two faces turned back towards me, eyes owl wide. Pepper gaped at me, then flung her head back against the pillow. "Shit!" she cried. There was relief in her voice, though. *I thought we had been caught*, her tone implied.

As if being caught by me was no big deal.

"Sorry!" I mumbled, shutting the door.

I scurried back to the kitchen with my juice, which I poured down the sink. I wasn't thirsty. I was too mad. I stood with my hands braced against the granite counters, breathing hard. How could she do that in my room? With August sleeping two doors down! Why?

Moments later, I heard my door open and clothes and footsteps scurrying toward me. "Al!" she said, still yanking up the side zipper of her pants. "What are you doing home? I thought you were on a date!"

"I was just out with a friend."

"Right, with some guy, you said." She shook her head. "Not that I planned anything. It just happened. Jonah just came over for coffee, and one thing led to another . . ."

Jonah, the crappy journalist that Phaedra was so wild about. Another Texas transplant.

"How did it lead to my room?"

"I was telling him about that hideous color and he wanted to see it. And then he sort of pulled me down onto the bed . . ."

I held my hand palm out like a pedestrian traffic cop. "I don't need to hear the rest. I saw it." I wondered if I should tell her about his Cro-Magnon butt, but I decided that was, given the circumstances, a triviality. "August was taking a nap two rooms away."

"She didn't hear anything," Pepper said.

"How do you know?"

"She sleeps like a rock! Anyway, she's fine. I just peeked in on her."

"But what about . . ." *Spence* my mind screamed, but I didn't want to sound as if he were foremost in my mind. ". . . your marriage?"

She snorted. "It's safe, believe me. Journalists barely have money for a shoeshine."

In that case, I supposed they really lacked funds for ass electrolysis. She made it sound as if, had he been rich, there might have been some danger. Which was so twisted.

"But Spence . . ."

"His plane isn't due till late this afternoon," she said.

"He could have come home early."

Her eyes flashed. "What are you, the morality police all of a sudden? What's it to you?"

I have a feeling my mouth was opening and closing like a beached fish. What was it to me? I should have been glad, actually, to have Spence catch her and her crap journalist in flagrante; I should have relished the prospect of a bust up. In fact, I should have been jumping up and down and yelling *I'm gonna tell!*

The trouble was August. I wanted to shake Pepper, just shake her. Didn't she realize what she had? Did she realize how many people would kill for what she had?

How *I* would kill for what she had?

But somehow, I couldn't bring myself to tell her exactly what kind of an idiot she was. Instead, out of the blue, I blurted, "I just changed my sheets two days ago!"

She blinked at me, then bent over laughing. "Oh, for heaven's sake. Is that what you're so cranked about? I'll get Lumi to change them for you."

"It's Sunday," I reminded her. Both Lumi and I had Sundays off.

"Tomorrow then."

Tomorrow?

"Oh!" Pepper said, as if our conversation were already beginning to bore her. "Your mother called."

The events of the past fifteen minutes had filled my thoughts; I had to shake my head to free a little room for my mother to squeeze in up there. "Mom?"

"She wanted to talk to you. It sounded urgent."

"She called *you*?"

"She called me when you didn't pick up your phone."

I hadn't even carried my phone with me that morning.

I sank down onto a chrome stool. A mother crisis was all I needed. And then a deviously comforting thought occurred to me. "She didn't give me her number. I don't have it."

"Yes, she did," Pepper said, running over to the message pad by the phone. "She gave it to me."

I eyed the number warily. "718?" I asked. "That's Brooklyn."

Pepper lifted her shoulders. "That's the number she gave me."

Now I was curious. What was my mother doing in Brooklyn? "Could you grab my phone for me?" I asked. "It's in my room."

"It's okay," she said. "Jonah's in the shower."

I hurried back and snatched the phone off my bedside table, noting my rumpled bedcovers with dismay, then scuttled out of the apartment as soon as I could. Maybe I could visit Mom until I cooled off a little.

"Alison darling!" she exclaimed after picking up. "I guessed you were out whooping it up with your friends and wouldn't get back to me."

"I wasn't exactly whooping." *My employer, on the other hand . . .*

Mom laughed a husky laugh. "Now you don't have to play dour daughter all the time. I was young once, too, you know."

"Was there something you wanted?" I asked.

"I wanted to see you, of course, if you have time. As I always do."

"Right, Mom. You're always pining away for your only child." Even as the sarcastic words escaped me, I regretted them. Why did I get so churlish with her? Snappish words just seemed to bubble up from me whenever we were together, even on the phone.

Finn would probably have a Dr. Phil explanation for that.

"The truth is, I need your advice," she said.

"Advice," I repeated. "*My* advice?" That would be a first.

"I've got a problem, and it's right up your alley."

"Where are you?" I asked.

She gave me an address . . . and sure enough, it was in Brooklyn.

I didn't speak for a moment. "What's the matter?" she asked.

"Brooklyn, Mom?" It was hard for me to believe that my mom had even found Brooklyn. I had never been there myself, but it did not sound like the proper borough for Margery Bell Tripton.

"It's Prospect Heights, darling. Just gorgeous! Wait till you see. Just take the F train on the metro."

"Subway," I said.

"What?"

"It's called the subway here."

I could sense her nose wrinkling. "I don't like that name, do you? It sounds so coarse, so . . ."

"Sandwichy?"

It took forty-five minutes to get to Mom's place, if you factor in my getting turned around on the street for five blocks before I realized my mistake. I could see what she meant by gorgeous. There was something wonderful about the beautiful old stone apartment buildings along the avenue my mom lived on, but it was a faded kind of beautiful. No matter what she said, this was not a glamour spot.

When she buzzed me into her building, I walked up three flights of stairs and wound up in a narrow hallway; in the apartment next to Mom's, I could hear a television blaring ESPN through the door. I was still staring at the loud person's door when Mom opened hers. "Alison! Come in."

"Doesn't that noise bug you?" I asked, gesturing with my thumb to the next door.

She didn't even follow with a glance. "That? Oh no, I hardly notice it."

There was no way you could not notice it. The place sounded like a sports bar.

"Don't you look grand!"

Mom was prone to exaggeration. I was still in the khaki shorts and sleeveless cotton shirt I'd worn to the flea market, and I hadn't so much as brushed my hair since early this morning. "Thanks," I said. "You, too."

She was wearing a bright red suit with a white silk shell underneath. "This is what I wanted to talk to you about."

I didn't exactly hear her at first because I was busy scoping out her apartment. Now that the door was shut, the noise from next door wasn't as bad, I noticed. Nothing like thick walls. The bones of the building were good; but the off-white paint job was so old it yellowed to the color of dog tooth tartar. It was also smaller than I had expected.

Mom's apartment was bigger than Jess's little efficiency, but I still wanted to suck in my breath. The living room/kitchenette, the tiny bath and bedroom were all visible from the doorway. The place seemed small even though it was empty. There was practically no furniture. Just a mattress on a metal bedframe in the bedroom; two folding chairs and a drop-leaf table next to the kitchen; and an armchair next to a television set on the floor.

My mom was almost fifty. This was not how I wanted to be living when I was fifty.

"What do you think?" she asked.

"It's . . ." I couldn't think of a complimentary word at first. "It's classic."

She clapped her hands together. "I knew you would see it that way. You always had such a spirit of adventure!" It was one of those moments when I didn't recognize the person Mom was describing as me. Adventurous? I was the girl who at age ten had called home from summer camp in tears because my bunk didn't have box springs.

"You haven't said anything about the outfit yet," Mom said, turning slowly for me.

"You look nice."

"Would you hire me?"

I frowned. "For what?"

"I have an interview at Bloomingdale's."

My chin probably dropped to my stomach. She was going to *work*? My mother didn't do work. As far as I could recall, she'd never had a paying job. She had gone straight from college graduation to her wedding. Maybe there had been a few months in there when she was free . . . but she certainly hadn't used them up *working*.

"Bloomingdale's?" I asked, incredulous.

"Well don't sound so shocked, Miss Snooty-Pants! A person has to earn her living. Do you think this outfit is too dressy for a woman interviewing for a salesclerk position?"

"Sales?" I shook my head. "Retail is brutal, Mom. And badly paying. Don't you think you'd be happier working in an office?"

Her nose scrunched. "I don't think so. You know how I love stores! Besides, what would I do in a boring old office? I can't even type. Now tell me what you think," she said quickly, very focused on the fashion challenge of her upcoming interview. "Too red? Too dressy?"

It was so dressy, she probably looked better than most of the women who ever went into Bloomingdale's.

Bloomingdale's. That was what I was still attempting to absorb. I was trying to wrap my mind around the idea of my mom selling panty hose.

"I think the key is not to be too much better dressed than the person you'll be interviewing with," I said.

"But I don't know who that will be."

"Think off the rack."

She held out the arms of her suit, which I was pretty sure was a designer outfit she'd picked up in Paris. "This is off the rack. I went into Yves St. Laurent and—"

"A *cheap* rack, Mom," I said. "Off the Ann Taylor sales rack. Off the TJ Maxx rack."

Her face went still as she thought for a moment, then she lifted a hand. "I think I have just the thing."

Skeptical that the words TJ Maxx could have run any bells in her head, I followed Mom into her bedroom, where I discovered the only place not sparsely furnished in her apartment: her closet. The rod was crammed with hangers and all manner of impractical shoes lined up obediently beneath, toes pointed outward, ready to go. A day of sales clerking in any of those shoes, and her feet would be killing her.

I tried to tell myself that this was cosmic payback for a life of careless luxury. Poetic justice for the woman who'd abandoned her life when it turned not-so-cushy.

But when push came to shove, I felt outraged. This is what *my* life should have looked like, not hers. This simply wasn't the life to which she was accustomed. "What about Murph?" I burst out. "Doesn't he owe you something?"

Her face briefly became a mass of tiny lines, like crazing on an old vase. "Oh . . ." She brightened, and the lines vanished. "I don't want to bother him!"

"Mom—he's your husband."

"Was," she corrected.

"He owes you alimony, doesn't he?"

"Actually . . ."

I groaned. "Oh, Mom. Did you sign some sort of a prenup?"

"A draconian prenup!" she said, bursting with relief that I had guessed. "You remember how awful Murph's first divorce was, sweetie. That crazy bitch just wanted to take him for everything he was worth. Naturally I agreed to say that I wasn't going to soak him like she had. But I thought Murph and I would last forever. Truly, I had forgotten all about the prenup till he ran off with his Bulgarian acrobat."

"Oh, Mom."

"Now, it's not as bad as all that," she said with forced brightness. "I couldn't have soaked Murph like his first wife did, anyway. The oil business isn't as profitable as it used to be, you know. Already we were having to make little economies."

"Is that what he told you when he abandoned you at the Ritz?"

"Actually, he didn't say anything. It was two days before I finally realized he was gone."

"He must owe you something."

"Yes, I'm supposed to get a payment, but I can't seem to squeeze it out of him at the moment. His assets need to liquefy, or some such nonsense. Oil—you'd think it would all be liquid already."

"How are you getting by?" I asked. "Where did you get money to rent the apartment?"

By way of an answer, she held up her hands. It took me a moment to notice that her fingers were bare. Even the third finger on her left hand. "Murph might not have had the best taste, but what he did have was an eye for resale value."

She seemed awfully calm about having hocked all her jewelry. She loved her jewelry! Yet she was trying to make light of it all, which was all the more depressing. And maddening.

She gave my arm a fortifying squeeze. "Can you stay and have some coffee?"

"Oh, I . . ." My instinct was to refuse, but I couldn't get the words out. I didn't particularly want to go home to Madame Bovary's. After this morning, I didn't want to spend time with Jess, who would be twittering about her (hopeless, I now knew) crush on Finn. And I didn't have any other friends in New York.

"Please?" Mom asked. "I need your advice on filling in those gaps on my résumé."

Gaps? Her work history was nothing but one big gap. From a personnel office perspective, her whole life to this day had been the Grand Canyon of frittered time. Over coffee, I tried to help her list volunteer activities (most over a decade old) that might point up her people and organizing skills. But even after an hour of working on it, I didn't feel very hopeful.

Mom was excited, though. "This is terrific! I have a lot now to bs that woman about tomorrow. Then I'll go to a printer and get this copied up for the next time I have to do this. Which hopefully won't be for a long, long time."

As least she was feeling optimistic.

"Just think," she said. "I'll be in your neighborhood! We can lunch together."

"I lunch at eleven o'clock, with August."

Mom sighed wistfully. "I hope I love my job as much as you do yours."

"I'm not sure . . ."

She swatted my hand. "What aren't you sure about? You're living in paradise with fabulous Pepper to work for!"

"Don't you think fabulous Pepper is just a trifle strange?" I asked.

"No . . . why?"

"Don't you remember what she was saying about her daughter's birthday party? *August's Dude Ranch?* That doesn't bring back memories?"

Mom's eyes looked vacant. "Should it?"

"Mom, you don't remember Pepper's fifth birthday party? You were there. There was a huge sign: Pepper's Dude Ranch!"

From the anxious look in her eye, she obviously thought I was going round the bend. "So?"

"It was the party where I got in trouble for tossing horse poo at my hostess."

Her eyes widened. "You threw horse shit at Maggie McClintock?"

"No, Mom—at *Pepper.*" Was I the only person in the world with a memory of this incident? "I threw horse shit at Pepper and got her Dale Evans dress dirty. How can you not remember this? You were furious."

"Oh now, I doubt that," she said.

I sighed in frustration. "And now Pepper is talking about staging another of these parties. A replica, almost. And I'll be there. Don't you think that's odd?"

"I think it's perfectly natural. She wants to reproduce a memorable party from her childhood for her own daughter."

"But the party wasn't memorable," I said, "except that I ruined it."

"Well, I'm sure that's all water beneath the bridge now."

I wasn't. By the time I left Mom's, I felt certifiably paranoid.

My state of mind was not helped by the fact that on the subway back I was menaced by a guy with rheumy eyes and a demented smile. He started staring at me when I got on, and then kept moving a few seats closer at every stop. When I switched trains, he followed, which was creepy. He didn't say anything to me, either. Just sort of smacked his lips. No one else on the train seemed to notice, maddeningly. I felt defenseless; I hadn't even brought *Outwitting Head Lice*. (Though, in this particular case, I doubt that would have been much of a deterrent. He already looked like he had vermin aplenty.)

Still, it reminded me not to leave home without it again.

The amazing thing was, when I skittered off the train at West Fourth Street, tossing nervous glances behind me like a girl in a noir movie, he hadn't followed me. Probably he had found someone else to bother. I had just been a blip in a long day of harassing folk.

I was miles from where I needed to be, but I still didn't feel like going back to the apartment. I dreaded what I would find there. Probably Jonah would be gone, but what next? Family night? I don't think I could stomach that, either.

I wanted to call Jess, but I wasn't sure I was up to hearing her chirp on about all her hopes for her upcoming date with Finn.

That left one person in New York that I knew. I pulled out my phone. Finn answered immediately.

"It's me," I said. "Would you be up for dinner? I can't face going home."

"Why not?"

"I'll explain when I see you. I'll pick something up and cook for you, how about that?" It would suit both our budgets, at least.

"Wow—that sounds terrific."

"Only because you've never had my cooking," I warned. "Do you have a microwave?"

"No, I don't trust them."

Oh, brother. Maybe he and Jess were a match made in heaven after all. "That cuts down on the culinary possibilities. Your choice just narrowed down to PB and Js or spaghetti."

"Spaghetti," he said.

"I'll be right over."

Finn's place was an efficiency on the Lower East Side. When I took a gander at his kitchen(ette), it struck me that it was just as well that he didn't trust microwaves, since he didn't have room for one. A body barely had to move in there at all, except to squeeze in sideways between the fridge and the tiny range, essentially making yourself the meat in an appliance sandwich. The rest of the apartment was also small, but he had managed to stuff a lot into it. He had a couch *and* a futon bed, with a coffee table separating them. The apartment was guy clean—everything was picked up, but there was an inch of dust on everything but his bicycle, his TV remote, and his hackey sack.

In honor of my stopping by, he had changed into a clean T-shirt. It practically reeked of laundry soap, which made me realize that just friends or not, he wanted to impress me. Regrettably, the shirt had a big green Gumby on it.

"Nice apartment," I said.

He looked pleased. "It took me a while to find just the right place. I've got a view of the Manhattan Bridge."

I aimed a squint towards the window. I didn't see anything but a closed-up laundry across First Avenue.

"You have to stand on a chair," he explained. "But at night it's a real knockout."

"I'll bet," I said. "Especially if you fall off the chair."

He smiled and held up a hand. "Just a sec!"

He crossed the room and started rooting around in his closet. "I got you something today." When he came back over, he was holding something that was wrapped in a D'Agostino grocery bag. "I guess you already know what it is."

I shook my head. I had no idea.

"Open it!" he said excitedly.

I pulled a flat object out of the paper bag and came face to face with Mabel and her menagerie. I laughed. "You shouldn't have done this!"

"Why not? She belongs with you."

I looked at her again. That hideous outfit and the baggy stockings. That grim, somehow dazed look on her face that said *How the hell did I wind up here?* She seemed like a kindred spirit, suddenly.

"You're right," I said. "I think she does."

Finn smiled. "You sounded kind of down when you called earlier, so I ran to the deli and bought dessert. An Entenmann's cake—I hope you don't think that's gross. I got the raspberry-filled kind."

At the mention of one of my favorite junk comfort foods, my heart pitter-patted shamefully. "With powdered sugar?"

"Of course."

Forget Mabel. Maybe Finn was my kindred spirit.

Chapter 17

Here was a surprise: Troy was hot.

Troublingly hot.

I don't usually have an inferiority complex or anything about my looks around guys. I mean, I'm not overly self-confident by any means. I'm not pencil thin, I'm not beautiful. Sometimes that works in my favor, though. I am utterly approachable. I don't have extraordinary height, or flamboyant fashion sense, or even a standoffish catwalk pout that would mark me as intimidating. Which is good, because when you look so completely average, you can't afford to scare anyone away. Yet I've never felt compelled to make myself over to snare some Adonis who otherwise wouldn't spare me a glance. Makeover stories always gave me pause—you know, the ones where some poor geekette miraculously loses twenty pounds, dolls herself up, and wins the heart of the captain of the football team. That always sounded like way too much effort for a guy who was, in all probability, a vain jerk.

But when I opened the door and found Troy standing there, I'll admit I felt a moment of panic. *Too gorgeous.* He was beautiful in an all-American blond, blue-eyed young Robert Redford way. It threw me. Jess had said a lot about Troy and about what he'd been through in the past year (the girlfriend and the dead dog) and his personality (depressed), but she had somehow omitted the fact that the man was a babe.

How could she have forgotten to mention this?

Troy was even better looking than Spence, which was one aspect of his hottieness that did give me a glimmer of hope. Perhaps Spence could be displaced from my thoughts through the sheer force of Troy's GQ cover-readiness.

I was glad that I had decided to wear my red dress, which was sort of like my little black dress, only red felt dressier, somehow. Or flashier, at least. Troy was just wearing black slacks and a short-sleeved shirt, which was far from formal, but I felt like I had some catching up to do, looks-wise.

"I'm sorry, I hope I'm not too early," he said.

"No, you're right on time," I assured him.

"I don't wear a watch anymore. I can't stand to have time tick-tick-ticking away on my wrist." Despite his boy-next-door looks, his voice had an I'm-off-my-Paxil droop to it.

"I tend to get nervous when I don't know what time it is," I said.

"I used to be that way." He lifted his shoulders. "Time just doesn't seem to matter to me now."

I grinned, as if by showing as many teeth as possible I could buoy his mood. Another way to compensate was to adopt Florence Henderson pep-speak, which to my horror I proceeded to do. "Well! I certainly want to be on time tonight! I haven't heard Jess play in ages."

"We should have plenty of time . . ."

"Fantastic!" I chirped. "I really want to get a good seat."

The Hoboken String Quartet was performing in a church on the Lower East Side. As promised, the evening was heavy on the Berlioz. They sounded great, though as I watched Troy slumping next to me in our pew, I wished that the program could have featured something a little peppier.

One time I glanced over at him and caught sight of Finn sitting at the end of our pew. He was checking out Troy, too, but when he caught my eye he smiled. I smiled back. We'd had a good time at his apartment the night I'd made him dinner, which had seemed to put us on normal footing for the first time. The evening ended without a trip to the emergency room. The curse had been lifted.

After the concert, Jess joined us all in the audience, lugging her cello case, which was bigger than she was. In her long black dress, she looked incredibly slim and elegant. Her dress accented her white skin and dark hair without making her look too Morticia-like.

"Thanks for coming."

I assumed that comment was meant for all of us, but it was hard to tell. She only had eyes for Finn. In fact, she had grabbed his arm and seemed to be latched on for the duration.

"What did you think?" she asked him.

"You guys were great," Finn said.

I agreed, even though I knew my opinion was probably not the one she cared about.

Troy also agreed that the concert was excellent.

After that, we spent a few minutes standing in a circle with awkward smiles on our faces.

"Well!" Jess said. She was staring pointedly at Troy and me. "I guess you guys want to get going . . ."

Troy and I exchanged glances. Neither of us seemed to have the inclination to move at all. I had enjoyed a breather from the effort I'd expended trying to keep the conversation going on the way downtown. I'd been hoping for a group situation to help me out for the rest of the night, actually.

Finn's eyes sought mine. He sounded desperate. "I thought we could all have dinner together . . ."

Jess wacked him playfully on the arm. "Don't be silly. They're on a *d-a-t-e*."

Troy was finally roused to action. "Sure—I thought we could grab a bite. Thai food okay?"

Maybe he and Jess had consulted each other and decided d-a-t-e was his cue to lead me away so she and Finn could be alone.

Finn and I exchanged regretful glances, like two friends who had been picked for different playground teams. I know I was disappointed. I also felt a little bad about leaving Finn, frankly; not once on Sunday night had he expressed hope that he and Jess would hit it off.

But he was a big boy. Besides, he barely knew Jess. Deep down I believed they might click if he gave her half a chance.

I was a bit more skeptical about my chances of clicking with Troy, but I was willing to give it the old college try. I had no complaints in the looks department; it was just getting conversation out of him that was wearing me down to a nub. We trudged in silence all the way to the Thai restaurant.

"I admit I don't know that much about classical music," I said when we were installed at a table, "but I think Jess is really talented, don't you?"

He nodded.

"Of course, I'm strictly an I-know-what-I-like person when it comes to music," I said.

He chewed on a fish cake.

"Unfortunately. I should try to listen and learn more," I added.

"Yeah, me too."

By the time we finished our appetizers, we were out of small talk and I was beginning to get seriously worried. This is what I hated about dating. The pulling-teeth conversations with people you probably would never sit down with ever again.

I cast about desperately for some topic that might interest Troy. Then I remembered he was an actor. "So tell me about yourself," I said.

"I'm a boring subject, I'm afraid."

Despite the protest, I knew from the telltale gleam in his blue eyes that my conversational metal detector had hit ore. "Jess didn't fill me in on details," I said. "You were a theater major in college?"

"Oberlin," he said.

"Isn't that in Ohio?" I asked, excited. Someone not from Texas. My dream had come true.

This could be a good omen.

He looked suspicious. "Yeah . . . is there something wrong with that?"

"No—it's fantastic! Tell me more."

The floodgates opened. I got his entire résumé. What he'd done in college. What he'd done after college. Straw-hat auditions, regional theater, small parts on television. The time he'd met Sidney Pollack. By the time he was telling me about playing in a *Guys and Dolls* road company, he was actually animated. I can't say that I was too interested in the stories of various cast members or what a reviewer in Seattle had said about his performance, but I did feel proud that I had managed to get him out of the dumps, at least momentarily.

We lingered over tea so he could tell me about an independent film he had just shot in New Jersey. I was impressed. In fact, I was impressed by his entire career, which, if not a clear moonshot toward fame and fortune and his name in lights, at least was steady. It sounded like he was always working. I would have thought that most actors in his position would feel pretty good.

"When can I see this movie?" I asked him.

"It's one of those things that might show up on cable someday. Maybe. I think the director was going to try to take the film to Sundance next year, but personally I think he's dreaming."

After dinner, I was gratified to see that Troy had perked up to the point that he didn't want the evening to end. I allowed optimism to take over. *Could this possibly be it?* I wondered. Forty years from now, would we be sitting in our rocking chairs, withered hands clasped, rehashing this evening?

I was lost before I found you, he would tell me. *Remember? I had that awful year, and then you came along . . .*

"How about coffee?" he asked. "I've got an espresso machine in my apartment."

Maybe espresso machines were the new bachelor lure, like etchings were in the old days, but "Come up and see my espresso machine" was a new one on me. I was always a sucker for good coffee.

And I have to admit, I wasn't averse to the idea of making out with Troy. He was the closest thing to an Adonis I had ever been out with. You'd think he'd have to beat women away with clubs. It was peculiar that a guy this good looking could be wandering around unclaimed.

His apartment was in Chelsea, on a block dominated by fur warehouses. I was expecting, hoping, that he would have a cool open loft, but it turned out that his apartment was a loft that had long ago been chopped up into efficiencies. His was bigger than Finn's, but not by much. The main difference was that he had an almost full-sized kitchen.

"This is terrific," I said, already Manhattanite enough to be duly impressed by such luxury.

"I know," he said. "I was amazed at my luck when I found it."

His espresso machine took up about half the counter space, but I could see why he would give it such prominence. The man could whip up a mean latte.

"What are you doing now?" I asked him, continuing the conversation from the restaurant. He seemed happiest when he could talk about himself.

He smiled ruefully. "I'm what we call 'at liberty.' But I've been going on a lot of auditions. I think I'm going to be in a Mountain Dew commercial, which would be incredible luck. The residuals on something like that can save an actor's bacon."

We retired to the futon and sipped coffee. Continuing in chatterbox mode, he told me about the commercials he'd done. I nodded and smiled and told myself that I obviously had a hidden talent for cheering up depressive types—or at least getting them over the hump to a manic phase. I was the Saint-John's-wort of women.

Troy put his coffee down. "This is going to sound nuts, but would you mind if I kissed you?"

I smiled. "I don't think I've ever been asked before. I like that. It makes me feel very Victorian and proper."

He waggled his brows. "Promise not to swoon?"

I promised, but to tell you the truth, I did feel all fluttery. I was coming off a long dry spell, so I was as eager for this kiss as a thoroughbred pawing at the starting gate. And Troy was a good kisser—nothing too aggressive, but not passive, either. It was better than I expected, and when he pressed me back against an oversized pillow, I put up no objections.

Going well, I thought. Beyond the usual worries about how my Scope was holding up (I'd swished in the bathroom of the Thai restaurant) and whether it was really unwise to sleep with someone on a first date, I was enjoying myself. Of course, a few doubts crept into my thoughts. Namely, how could I be this lucky?

He was an employed actor . . . good looking . . . a great kisser . . .

Why didn't this guy have ten girls lined up at his door?

These women worried me more and more. It was almost as if I could feel their presence . . . or absence. As if they were watching us.

And then, from the corner of my eye, I did catch someone watching us.

While our mouths were still locked, I did a double take and then stared for a moment before I realized that they were eyes—a small dog's protuberant eyes.

There was no dog here, though. I would have seen a dog. A dog would have met us at the door.

But wait, Jess had mentioned a dog. A dead dog.

I yanked my mouth away from his so I could give this matter my full attention. Sure enough, a Boston terrier stared up at us. A taxidermied Boston terrier.

I shrieked and bolted upright, sending Troy flying off the futon.

"What's the matter?"

He had to ask? I was panting now, mesmerized by the dog. I was surprised I hadn't noticed it before, although it was sort of hidden next to a bookshelf. I had heard of people doing this—Roy Rogers and Trigger popped immediately to mind—and always thought it seemed borderline sad. Now it felt creepy.

"That's just MuuMuu," Troy said. "My dog. She died seven and a half months ago."

I bet he could name the exact number of days.

"Does she bother you?" he asked. "I know it's sort of unusual . . ."

"No, no," I lied, trying to cover my discomfort. "I just hadn't expected it. Those eyes . . ."

He nodded. "Aren't they lifelike? They did an amazing job on her. She looks so alive I sometimes find myself talking to her before I realize that she's . . . well, that she's not really there anymore."

Since graduating from college, I had been out with a lot of guys. Guys with all sorts of weird baggage, guys with drug habits, guys who still lived at home and didn't want to leave their parents. I'd even dated a guy once who was also fanatically devoted to his dog, a golden retriever named Luther. This guy never wanted to eat out because he liked to share meals with Luther. That had been a little weird, not to mention dietetically constricting—but Luther had been alive.

I didn't want to be mean, but Troy's having a stuffed Boston terrier in his tiny apartment, and talking to it, seemed like a bad sign to me. It seemed like a sign that he needed to be talking to a *therapist*, not a dog.

"She's really cute," I said, swallowing.

He looked at MuuMuu and dissolved into a smile. "Isn't she?" His eyes teared up.

I needed to get out of there, I decided. I liked sensitive guys. But you could even take sensitivity too far.

As I fled into the night, after claiming a headache that really did seem on the verge of becoming a reality, I wondered why Jess hadn't told me about MuuMuu. Of course, she hadn't told me Troy was so good looking, either. Maybe she hoped that movie star looks would cancel out a dead dog.

The next day I had to run errands for Pepper. By the time I dragged home special soap from a boutique on the other side of town, *and* her dry cleaning, I was already feeling put upon. Then Lumi started following me around the apartment.

"Where's August?" she asked.

I shrugged. "I'm not sure. Dancing class, I guess."

"Weren't you supposed to pick her up?"

This was the most Lumi had said to me in all our weeks of working together. "Pepper has her."

Doubt spread across her face. In fact, I could tell that she knew that was absolutely not the case. "I think Mrs. Smith wanted for you to pick her up."

"But Pepper's with her. They take the class together."

Lumi shook her head. "She left you a note."

"A note?" I asked.

"It's in your room," she said. "On your bed."

For heaven's sake! I ran to my room, and sure enough, there was a sheet of white linen note paper with PMS written in calligraphic scrollwork at the top. Had anyone ever had more appropriate initials?

Gone this afternoon. Please pick up August at 4. Dinner and bedtime as usual.

I frowned. Four o'clock? It was almost four now!

I hit the ground running and jumped in a cab. But I was still late getting to the midtown studio where Tappin' with Your Toddler was located.

At the moment the rehearsal room was full of twenty eight-year-old girls in pink leotards and half as many mothers who looked none too pleased to have their lesson interrupted by a straggler from the last class. At my intrusion, the instructress punched the off button on a CD player, bringing Tchaikovsky to an abrupt end, and glowered at me. I guess she wanted to make sure no one missed a word when she put me in my place.

August looked very small slumped against the wall. She had been forgotten and she knew it. When she finally caught sight of me, she jumped up, adorably stubby in her black leotard with the tux top, and flew at me. She locked onto my legs for dear life. "Alson! I hate it here!"

"Where is Mrs. Smith?" the instructress asked, looking as if she had no intention of letting August go with me.

"It's okay," I said. "I'm the nanny."

"It is not okay," the woman snapped back. "This is a mother-daughter class, not a drop-off daycare center. I told Mrs. Smith that before."

Pepper had dropped her off here before? This was news to me. And here I had given Pepper credit for going to three whole lessons with August.

"Let's go!" August cried. "I'm tired!"

"Don't forget her rehearsal music," the dance teacher said, handing me a cassette.

Barely balancing because August was both entwined around my knees and trying to yank me towards the door, I had trouble fiddling with my purse. I was nervous from all the people staring at me, and angry at Pepper for putting me in this position. My bag slipped off my shoulder and fell to the ground. A lipstick spilled out, as did *Outwitting Head Lice*.

That cover. The letters looked so bold in relief. Several mothers who were sitting against the wall leaned forward in disbelief at the title. Horror crossed a few of their faces. I noticed a few of them staring at August. At August's head.

Idiots. Did it never occur to them that someone might just want to read about head lice? After I chased down my lipstick, which had rolled under a folding chair, I snatched the book up and tossed it back in my purse.

"I'm sorry to have interrupted," I said. "It won't happen again."

August and I scooted out as fast as possible.

"I hate dancing," August said, stumping along angrily beside me. I tried to flag down a cab, but it was getting late in the afternoon now and I didn't see one free. And if I did manage to get one, I feared it was going to take it ages to crawl back uptown. I started looking for bus stops.

"Where's Mommy?" August asked when we stopped at the corner to wait. In the distance I could see the top of a bus rumbling slowly uptown toward us.

"Um, I don't know exactly . . ."

"Where's Daddy?"

"I don't know that either, Augie."

Her brow pinched. "Do you know anything?"

I laughed. "I know that a bus is a block away now."

She gasped. "How?"

I lifted her up. "See, there it is."

On the bus August entertained herself with one of her running games of Whatsit, in which she pointed to something out the window and asked "What's that?" and I had to tell her. She could do this for hours at a stretch. Its appeal for me was that I got to be the expert, even if it was only explaining parking meters to someone who was three.

It was after five when we got home. Lumi would be gone, back to her home in Queens, and I would take over the kitchen to make August's dinner. I was fully expecting an empty apartment, or Pepper back from whatever errand had sent her scampering off this afternoon, but instead, it was Spence who was home. At five. That was a jaw dropper. Spence was never home before seven.

He usually wasn't home, period.

He had even removed his suit coat and tie and looked like he was settling in for a relaxing evening at home. August was ecstatic. "Daddy!"

"Hey, kiddo!" he said.

"I hate dancing," she told him as he lifted her up for a hug.

He looked over at me and winked. "You just haven't found the right partner yet."

I scuttled toward the kitchen to start rustling up something for dinner. Soup and sandwiches, I was thinking.

Spence followed me in a few minutes later. "Fun day?"

"Oh . . ." I shrugged. "It was long, at least."

I tilted my head. I could hear August's television. She was Wiggle dancing. Spence grinned. "I had to remind her that all dancing wasn't bad. I wouldn't want her to be a wallflower during those exciting mixers in high school."

Another vague reference to our past. I hunted through stacked cans of Progresso soup for something August would find acceptable and tried hard not to think about how close Spence was standing to me.

"Where's Pepper?" I asked.

"Gone," he said.

I froze. "Gone?"

"She and Alessandra went to an overnight spa in Connecticut."

A likely story. The flimsiness of it, and the fact that Spence seemed to have bought it hook, line, and sinker, made me shift uncomfortably from foot to foot. "Okay, so . . ."

He grinned. "So it's just the two of us tonight, Al."

"You mean the three of us," I said.

His brows lifted.

"You, me, and August," I reminded him.

"Of course," he agreed. "August is coming, too."

"Where?"

"To dinner."

I folded my arms, ready to retort that I was making dinner, in case he hadn't noticed, when his phone rang.

He snapped it out of his pocket. "Hello?" It was obviously a business call, because he turned away and started mumbling in a work voice. I dangled off to one side, half-listening to one side of a discussion of the opening of markets in Europe. Business never stopped, I guessed. There was always money to be made somewhere.

When he hung up he turned to me expectantly. "You were about to say?"

I had mentally lost my place. "I'm making soup."

His gaze alighted on the can of minestrone I had picked out and his brow furrowed. "That's dinner?"

"For August," I said.

"You look all done in," he said. "Let me take you out. We can talk over old times by ourselves. I've been looking forward to that opportunity."

So had I. Which is why I was so hesitant.

"August isn't restaurant ready," I said. "Neither am I. And we're both liable to be fussy."

"Don't worry about that," he said. "Go freshen up and I'll take care of Augie. It's early enough that I don't think we'll need reservations anywhere."

I tilted my head. He seemed so eager, like he was really looking forward to it. What could be the harm? "Okay . . ."

"Good!" he patted my shoulder, sending me on my way.

I would like to say that I kept a level head and put on sensible clothes and didn't even dare think of this as anything other than an employer-employee dinner. I wish I could say that no untoward romantic thoughts crossed my mind. That I didn't stand under a hot shower daydreaming what it would be like if Spence kissed me.

If I ever needed confirmation that I had my mom's blood running through my veins, I had it now. Ever since my failed date with Troy, I had been wondering what was wrong with me. I couldn't seem to have a normal date with a guy. Or maybe I couldn't find a normal guy to date. Or maybe it was me who wasn't normal. Whatever. More and more, I was dreaming of Spence, and dabbling in moral relativism.

For instance . . . when you compared it to all the other things going on in the world, what was wrong with a little adultery?

As my mother had told me so long ago, we all do things we're not proud of. I was only human . . .

And anyway, August would be with us. That should temper any dangerous impulses we were tempted to follow through on. Fortified by the assurance that we would have a three-and-a-half-year old providing a wall of Jericho for us, I went ahead and put on my black dress, since the red one was still at the cleaners, and slipped on higher than usual black heels (Spence rated stilettos, even if he was technically off-limits), and splashed myself in Chanel like a finch in a birdbath.

By the time I emerged from my room I was too dolled up to fool anyone. Spence whistled when he saw me. "You look beautiful, Al. A knockout!"

"Stop," I said, attempting a hard-boiled insouciance. "You'll make me blush."

He chuckled. "Same old Al."

"You were expecting someone else?"

"No, you'll do." His eyes twinkled. I swear.

I was tempted to say something corny, like *you'll do, too, mister*, but I held my tongue. I looked toward the front door. "Is August ready?"

He bit his lower lip a little, his face twisting in concern. "Actually, I decided to call a sitter."

"A sitter!" He was going to call a babysitter so he could go out with his nanny? "Why?"

He smiled a little guiltily. "I wanted to relax tonight, and I remembered what you said about August and restaurants. Besides, I was in the mood for sushi . . . not one of my daughter's favorites, as you know."

"Uh-huh," I said, not believing a word of it. I couldn't imagine that he had ever taken August to a sushi joint; no one would be that dumb. Besides, he was staring at my legs.

"Don't worry," he said. "The girl coming over is the daughter of my secretary. She lives just a few blocks away and babysits for a lot of the guys at work, so she comes highly recommended."

"We could have just ordered takeout," I said.

"And then I would have missed your looking like this," he said as the doorbell rang. He grinned at me. "I promised her a twenty-dollar tip if she could make it in half an hour."

As I told the girl, Rebecca, where everything was, introduced her to August, and listened to August's wails of bitter protest at being left behind, I told myself that none of this was my doing. Spence was the culprit. August was his daughter, and this was his house. Could I help it if he wanted to take me out for a bite to talk about old times? Was that a crime?

Still, I sneaked back into my room and put on a thin cotton sweater, part of a twin set. It made me feel less vampy.

When I came back out, Spence frowned.

"I was cold," I explained.

"It was eighty degrees out, last I checked."

"You know how it is when the sun goes down," I said, looking him square in those eyes that had featured so prominently in my dreams lately. "The temp can change quickly."

I think he understood. He said no more and he gave me the knight in shining armor treatment on the way to the restaurant—whisking ahead to open doors, handing me into the cab and then scooting a safe distance away himself, taking my elbow to help me sidestep a puddle of what looked like vomit on the sidewalk. A perfect gentleman. Best of all, he kept talk going so I didn't feel compelled to jabber idiotically. And he was so handsome, so snappily groomed and put together that I caught a few women on the street doing double takes to look at him. He had jackpot written all over him.

Except for that wedding ring, of course.

We went to a Japanese place, much more upscale than any sushi joint I had ever been to. The first thing he did was order sake for both of us.

"I shouldn't," I said.

"Sure you should." When he saw my stern nanny look, he smiled. "You're through for the day. By the time we get home, Rebecca will have August tucked away in bed."

"You seem pretty sure of that fact. Makes me wonder how much time you've spent with your daughter lately."

Sometimes I wish there were a way to zap ill-considered words before they fly out of my mouth. I needed one right then. Spence reacted to my quip with a slight turn of the head and a wounded expression.

"Not enough," he said, shaking his head. "Not enough."

"Well . . ." I racked my brains trying to think of something comforting to say to him. He was an absentee dad, almost, but after all, he was keeping his family going. Keeping me going, when it came right down to it. I couldn't imagine having the responsibility for so many people. Most days it seemed I could barely take care of myself. "You're busy with work."

"Which reminds me." He pulled his phone out of his pocket and switched it off. Then he winked at me playfully. "I'm all yours."

"Wow. I rate a no-phone dinner?" I had to fan myself to keep from fainting. "You must *really* feel nostalgic."

"Are you kidding? For weeks I've been wanting to talk about the old Bramford Prep Rep days. Not many people in my life know what a skilled tragedian I am."

The sake was delivered to our table and quickly imbibed. I don't remember ordering, or what we ate particularly. My memory of that meal is snorting with laughter over Spence's recounting of those dull and sometimes frantic rehearsals for *Antigone.* He had incredible recall—he could remember the name of poor Alice Burlingham, a freshman playing a Greek soldier who had a moth fly into her helmet one night. Despite my hisses from the wings for her to exit, she had stood at twitchy attention upstage throughout the third act, looking like a sentry with Tourette's syndrome.

He could remember my arguing with Ms. Crouch—truly the Ed Wood of high school drama directors. Such as when I told her that we needed to weight down the papier-mâché pillars so they didn't sway violently every time someone walked across the stage. And later, when I argued that no matter how earnestly intended, nobody would want to read her program notes comparing Antigone to Anita Hill. (Which, no matter what your political persuasion, didn't make sense anyway.) And that plastic shower flip-flops, even when slathered in brown Kiwi shoe polish and modified with laces, did *not* look like Greek sandals.

He remembered us as a couple, and the places we'd gone. Parties I'd forgotten were brought back to me, and the fact that I'd hated *Wayne's World*. He remembered the moment we met, and that we'd had to yell over Madonna singing "La Isla Bonita."

"I can't believe you remember that!" I exclaimed.

"Why wouldn't I?" he asked. "I remember everything about that night—watching you while I was dancing with what's-her-name."

Poor Larissa. "You don't remember everything, obviously," I joked.

He smiled. "Just the important things. I remember your face . . ." He rolled his eyes ruefully. ". . . laughing at me. You told me I was the worst dancer you'd ever seen, and that you were impressed."

"I told you that you looked like John Cusack."

He nodded. "Which I realized later was a lie. You were just trying to get me to try out for that awful play. But by the time it dawned on me that I was being duped, I didn't care, because doing the play was an excuse to see you."

"You did look like John Cusack," I said. "Sort of."

"You knocked me out that night. But after we talked you wandered off and started mingling with other guys. I figured out that you were trying to get *them* to audition for that stupid play, too. So I went to each and every one you talked to and told them that the drama director of your school had caught a guy who was in the previous year's play kissing a girl backstage and had called his school and gotten him suspended."

My mouth dropped open. "And they believed you?"

He sent me a sly smile. "Did anyone else call you back?"

I had never suspected. "You toad!"

He chortled gleefully. "You were such an operator, so wrapped up in trying to scam all those gullible fellows, I couldn't resist you. Or resist undermining you."

I laughed, remembering. I *had* been manic that night; looking back on it, it was hard to believe that person had been me. It was probably the closest I'd ever come to being a live wire. That was the other thing about Spence: he didn't just remember us, he remembered *me*, the way I used to be before my life went kerblooey on me.

"That was probably the happiest I've been," I said. "I had no idea that there would be trouble ahead. I assumed that there were nothing but good times from then on."

"Everybody assumes that as a teenager," Spence said, downing another sake. "Then you grow up."

I thought of Pepper, with her unlined brow, her clear eyes never clouded with worry. Yes, she was married, yes, she had a child; but in a lot of ways it seemed like *she* had never grown up. Sometimes August seemed more levelheaded than Pepper.

"Is something wrong?" Spence asked.

I shook my head. "No. I was just thinking about August. She's got so much ahead, so many hurdles."

"She shouldn't have hurdles at her age. Pepper and I were arguing about that just the other day."

I couldn't help myself. I craned forward with interest. *Arguing?* I definitely wanted to hear about this.

"She has so much baggage she wants to foist off on August," Spence huffed. "First it was the psychiatrist. For a three-year-old! Then she wanted to have some crazy birthday party for her that was just like she had when she was a kid. You know—the one where you two had your infamous dustup."

He remembered! I could have wept with gratitude. I leaned back in my chair, limp with relief. "I'm so glad you said that! I thought I was going crazy."

"Pepper will make crazies out of all of us," he said. "Believe you me, I heard her talking about August's Dude Ranch and I put the kibosh on that, fast. Especially when I heard she wanted to dress you up as a cow."

"A *cow?*" I exclaimed. Heads swiveled to stare at me. I was a little drunk, I'll admit.

He nodded. "I told her to forget it. I told her that she could rent a clown for the afternoon, and that would be enough. I can't stand these people who try to relive their glory days through their kids."

My admiration knew no bounds. I wanted to stand up and applaud. And then there was the other thing . . . he'd rescued me. Again.

We were in the backseat of the cab home maybe half a minute before we started kissing. I'm not talking a little shy peck. We seemed to come together in an explosion, tangling together, our lips bruising in their eagerness. I didn't have time to feel guilt, or even conflicted. I just felt lust. I'd wanted this so badly, for so long, and so, obviously, had he.

In no time we were home, and we managed to tear ourselves away from each other long enough to pay the driver, walk through the lobby and make chitchat with Lou, then wait for the elevator while standing a respectable foot or so apart. But the moment the elevator doors closed on us, we were going at each other again like love-starved beasts, like reuniting lovers. There was something so familiar yet unfamiliar about the way he tasted, about the way he held me. It was intoxicating.

I felt something like pain when we broke apart to go into the apartment. Spence sent Rebecca home in a cab with a fistful of loot. I stood in a daze, unsure of what would happen the moment Rebecca disappeared. Unsure even of what I wanted to happen.

I decided to look in on August, which was bound to be sobering. But her room was empty. I made a mad dash around the apartment, my heart beating wildly as I imagined weird kidnapping scenarios.

But I found her almost immediately, asleep on Spence and Pepper's bed.

I sighed. Spence and Pepper's bed. *That* was what was sobering.

Instead of gathering up August, who looked utterly peaceful, I decided to bring her a stuffed toy or two. In her room, I was gathering up a few of her favorite Little Mermaid plush toys when Spence came in. "Where's August?"

"You're going to have company tonight," I informed him. "And I don't mean me."

He smiled, even though he looked disappointed. "Al . . ."

I shook my head. "Please don't tell me that you don't know what got into you. Maybe it was the sake—"

He stepped closer to me. "But I *do* know. You got into me, fueled by memories I've been trying like hell to keep at bay for weeks. Alcohol didn't do that." He chuckled. "Just Al."

I groaned, but not because what he said was so goofy. I groaned because it was goofy and it made me want him all over again. "Oh, Spence."

He took one more step forward and held my head in his two hands. Then he bent down and kissed me again, gently at first, and then more hungrily. Desire for him slammed through me. It would have been so easy to relent. I fully intended to. What was the use of fighting it? I wanted him; I was pretty sure I even loved him.

I burrowed closer to him, lifting my hands up to hold his shoulders. That's when I realized I had a stuffed crab in one hand and a stuffed flounder in the other. I groaned at my stupidity.

"What's the matter?" Spence murmured.

"August," I said.

"You said she's asleep . . ."

I stepped back, practically panting. "There's no guarantee she'll stay that way."

His face was red, and he seemed as out of breath as I felt. "Damn," The look behind his eyes told me he was still looking for a solution to the dilemma.

But I knew there wasn't a solution. Not a good one, at least.

"Good night," I said.

"Al . . ."

I didn't stop to listen. I practically ran out of the room and didn't stop till I was across the hall safely installed in my own room. I flung myself across my bed, my heart pounding, my body still keyed up. Frustration shot through me like a punishment.

I wouldn't get a wink of sleep for hours, I knew, so I caved in to a bad impulse. I wasn't sure whether it would be therapeutic or masochistic, but since it was inevitable, it didn't matter. I lay on my bed, clutching the crab and the flounder, closed my eyes, and relived every moment of the night up to that point. Over and over again.

Chapter 18

"I'm never speaking to you again, Al. This is the end."

I had only been half awake when I reached for my phone, so it took me a second to recognize Jess's voice. My eyelids squealed in protest as I glanced over at the clock. It was only 7:18. How could I have made people angry at me so early?

There was that phrase. *The end.* That sounded . . . well, it sounded bad.

"What's wrong?"

Jess clucked over the phone. "Are you kidding me? Is this some kind of innocent act?"

"I can't act," I said. "I'm not even awake yet."

"Oh, right. Little Miss Insomniac! Stays up all night pacing the floor over her problems but meanwhile doesn't care that she's"—her voice broke and she barely managed to croak out—"*ruined . . . my . . . life!*"

As I lay back against my pillow, staring at the ceiling, listening to Jess weeping, I wondered what the hell I could have done. I didn't remember anything . . .

And then it came back to me. I'd kissed Spence. The memory of it slammed into my gut, and heat flushed through me. That had been bad.

But Jess couldn't know about that. Nor did I think it would cause her to stop speaking to me.

"Jess. Back up." At the very least she needed to speak to me long enough that I could talk her off the ledge. "I don't know what you're talking about."

She sucked in a breath. "Finn!"

"Finn? What's wrong with Finn?"

"Nothing. Except that he doesn't like me."

"I'm sure that's not true." Finn didn't seem to dislike anybody.

She snuffled. "Oh, well, sure, he *likes* me. He told me that the other night after the concert. He said he *liked* me, he just didn't like me *that way*. Do you know how humiliating that was?"

"Oh, God. I'm sorry."

"And then I was stupid enough to ask if there was someone else, and he got this moony look on his face and he said yes. *You*."

I was awake now. "Me?"

"Al, why didn't you tell me you guys had been seeing each other? Why didn't you stop me?"

"We haven't been seeing each other," I said.

She laughed bitterly. "He said you guys went shopping together Sunday, and then you came back to his apartment that night and cooked for him."

"That was nothing. Honestly."

"Cooking for a guy is *nothing*? I've never heard of you cooking for any guy. I didn't even know you could cook."

"I can't. That's why it was nothing. I just boiled linguini and made a quick garlic and olive oil sauce."

"Listen to you—Julia Child."

"Jess, it was nothing. It meant nothing."

"Maybe to you, but it certainly meant something to Finn. He's practically in love with you, and you don't even want him."

"It just wouldn't be doable," I said.

"Why? What's wrong with him?"

"He wears Mr. Bubble T-shirts."

"That's *cute*! You would realize it if you weren't so obsessed with that rich, married jerk."

"Spence is not a jerk."

"See?" she asked. "See? You make excuses for him. He's your own Mr. Rochester."

"He's not," I said, but I could feel another wave of heat creeping into my cheeks. He was. I was a nanny and I was hot for my employer and he was married. I was in the Jane Eyre snare. My only hope now was for Pepper to burn down the apartment building.

"I swear to you," I said, "I thought Finn and I were just friends. We even talked about it."

"Maybe you talked, but he's still hoping."

I didn't know what to say. It wasn't as if I had mind control over Finn. "I'm sorry, Jess."

"Well."

"Let's have lunch today. I'd have to bring August, but—"

"I can't today," she said tersely. "I promised to visit Troy at the hospital."

"Hospital!" I exclaimed. "What happened?"

"You tell me. You were the last person to see him before he checked himself in for severe depression."

My heart sank. "Poor guy. But you have to admit, he needed help."

"Apparently after you got through with him, he did."

Oh, God. Did I really do that much damage? "It was the dog," I admitted. "It freaked me out."

"I told you about the dog."

"You didn't tell me he was stuffed!"

The line crackled a moment with unspoken tension. "I barely recognize you," she said. "You were never like this before."

"Like what?"

"Choosy!"

I couldn't help it. I laughed.

"It's not funny," Jess insisted.

"No it isn't, I know that," I said, sobering quickly.

"You're unrepentant," she said, disappointed.

"I'm just surprised, Jess."

"Because your mind is on the married guy."

I couldn't deny it.

She took a deep breath. "You know what's going to happen next, don't you? You're going to rush headlong into something awful and then you're going to feel shocked when it goes wrong. Your friends will have warned you, but that won't matter. It will feel like a slap in the face anyway. You'll be miserable, possibly homeless, eating stale boxed grocery-store donuts in some skank hotel room, wondering what to do next . . . and who will you turn to?"

That bit about the donuts made me nervous. "Why do they have to be stale?"

"What?"

"Can't I have fresh deep-fried Krispy Kremes?"

"Never mind the donuts!" she said. "You'll turn to the friends who warned you, that's who. *We'll* have to pick up your shattered little pieces."

"But you won't be speaking to me anymore," I reminded her. "This is the end."

There was a frustrated pause. "Nobody gets off that easy," she said. Then she slammed down the phone.

As a wakeup call, the conversation with Jess worked pretty well. I knew that if I lay there for even three minutes I wouldn't be able to pry myself out of bed for the entire day. I would start thinking about what Jess had said, and how right she probably was, and how I was a walking disaster, an emotional Typhoid Mary, and that if I had any decency I would banish myself to a remote, uninhabited island so I would contaminate the world no more . . .

Well. I certainly didn't want those thoughts to creep up on me, so I hopped out of bed, knocking Disney plush toys to the floor, and took a bracing hot shower. A new beginning, that's what I needed. Obviously, I had been saying this for some time now. Taking the nanny job was supposed to be a fresh start. Moving to New York was also going to be a fresh start. But I realized now that those were just the superficials. What I needed to change was *me*. I needed to become someone who looked at situations square in the eye, problems included, and acted accordingly.

For instance, I had known this job would be problematic. Yet I'd taken it. That had been a mistake.

I had known that going out with Spence last night would be a big no-no. Yet I had rationalized. *What harm could one little dinner do? We were just going to talk . . .*

Nonsense. Foolishness.

By the time I had finished shampooing my hair, scrubbing my scalp with strong, punishing vigor, I vowed I would make changes. Significant changes. Henceforth, I would be strong in my resolve, forthright in my dealings with people, and much more sensitive and tactful. I was going to be Joan of Arc, Katharine Hepburn, and Gandhi rolled into one. I stepped out of the shower, wrapped myself in towels, and stepped back into my room.

Where I ran smack into Spence.

I let out a surprised bleat and he covered my mouth with a kiss.

I ended the kiss immediately. (Okay, after three minutes.)

(Five, tops.)

"Stop," I said, tearing my lips away from his before they could get stuck. "What are you doing here?"

"I was waiting . . . I didn't want to wake August."

Remembering that I was supposed to be channeling Katharine Hepburn, I leveled a skeptical glare on him. He was dressed for work. Some men look to die for in business suits, and unfortunately he was one of them. "You think you would have woken her by waiting for me in the kitchen?"

"I wanted to talk to you in private. I can't let things stand as they were last night . . ."

"Last night was a big mistake."

He shook his head. "I don't think so."

"Spence, you're married! We're in your apartment that you share with your wife. Your *child.* That doesn't mean anything to you?"

"Situations can change."

Those words vibrated through me like a strike against a tuning fork. I was practically humming. Was he saying he was going to leave his home, and August? He would give all that up . . . *for me?*

I stared at him for a long moment, overwhelmed.

He stepped forward. "Al . . ."

I held my palms out. "Don't say anything more. Don't. Not here, now."

"Then when?" he asked. "When can we really be together?"

I gulped. Was he trying to suggest we get a hotel room on my next day off? I just didn't get it. I knew he wasn't that kind of person, but I couldn't imagine what else he could mean.

Before I could speak, he turned suddenly, and flipped open his phone. "Yeah," he said. "Okay. Good. And Chet?"

My mind raced. I needed to think of an adequate response, quick. For a moment I squeezed my eyes closed and tried again to channel Joan, Katharine, and Mahatma . . . but let's face it. That never works unless you're a certified lunatic or a movie star. And it's hard to think when someone next to you is having a loud conversation involving nothing but monosyllables with a guy named Chet.

"*Lost them?*" Spence exclaimed. I jumped. "How?"

He rolled his eyes at me. He was tapping his foot impatiently.

"Okay. Think. I'll be there pronto."

He hung up and I opened my mouth to say something about waiting, the value of time, and restraint, but he stepped forward before I could get a word out.

"I gotta go. The office. You know."

"Oh . . ."

He gave me a kiss on the forehead. "This isn't over though. I want you to spend the day thinking about us."

Did he think I could possibly think about anything else?

I dithered around most of the morning, trying to convince a cranky August that she really did need to get out of her pajamas. God knows I would have been just as happy to have stayed in mine. But there were appearances to keep up. I didn't know when Pepper was coming home, and every time I heard a sound in the world outside the apartment, I tensed.

I felt guilty for drinking her orange juice, for eating her organic faux Wheaties, for kissing her husband.

Midmorning, my phone rang. It was Mom. "I wanted to know if you could have lunch with me," she said.

"I'm working today."

"So am I!"

My unspoken shock traveled across the wireless universe.

"Isn't it wonderful?" she asked. "I punched in at eight-thirty this morning and already I feel like an old hand."

"So your interview went well?" I asked.

"Oh, it was a snap! That woman didn't know what hit her."

"I guess not. Well, look, I guess we could meet at a diner or something . . ."

"That's all right, I brought my lunch. Just pack something. We can meet at the park, on the benches near the zoo."

I have to admit, it was hard to imagine my mom eating lunch on a park bench. But I couldn't envision her even packing a lunch, or for that matter, making a sandwich. Life thus far had shielded her from things like sliced bread.

She seemed cheerful enough, though. "See you at twelve-thirty?"

"Okay."

"Be on time," she said. "I have to be back at one-fifteen on the dot."

I promised that I would be punctual, and I was. August and I went deli shopping for our lunch, and we got there early.

August was chewing her way into her favorite, cheese on a kaiser roll as big as her head, when Mom walked up. Briskly. She had a brown bag, and she took out a sandwich consisting of some kind of cold cut on wheat, with a snack-sized bag of Lays potato chips on the side.

"Aren't you overdoing the proletariat thing, Mom?" I asked.

She looked offended. "It's delicious. Have you ever had bologna?"

"Not since I was in sixth grade, but yeah, I'd call myself lunch meat savvy."

Tomato slices were spilling out of August's sandwich, and I tried to catch them.

"How's your job? For that matter, what's your job?"

"Terrific!" she exclaimed. "I absolutely love it. You know, I think I might have been born for retail. This might sound like shameless braggadocio, but I have a natural flair for it. You should have seen me this morning, saving some poor deluded woman from buying a C-cup!"

"A bra?"

"I'm in lingerie," Mom said. "The poor thing! If you could have seen her. She was a double D at least, but she was squeezing herself into something smaller and just spilling over in all directions. Her entire bust line was outlined with a lip of fat, like a piecrust or something. Some people have no self-awareness."

I made a grunting noise. It struck me that my mother would be my nightmare of a saleswoman.

"But the beautiful thing was, I took that woman in hand and really helped her. I've never thought about it before, but being a salesclerk is really important work. You can provide essential humanitarian aide to people."

Mom was probably the first person Bloomingdale's had ever turned into a humanitarian. "It's good you like your job," I said.

"My feet hurt," she said, rubbing the toes of one foot against the heel of the other. "So much standing! But to complain about that would just be whining."

August tugged on my sleeve. "Can I go sit in the grass?"

I frowned. "You haven't finished your sandwich." It was a knee-jerk reaction to her complaint. If we stayed in that park until ten pm, she would never be able to finish that sandwich.

"I want to sit in the grass," she insisted. "It's like a yard!"

She had Central Park a block from her house now, but she still missed her yard. "Okay."

We watched her skip off three feet and collapse onto a square of grass, the condition of which I tried not to think about. This was a popular corridor for dog walking. August, blissfully unaware of my worries, started making grass angels. I was glad that I was not in charge of her laundry. Of course, soon I might not be in charge of her at all. I might have to quit. Or be fired. That thought brought a quick kick to my gut.

Or maybe I would be her stepmom.

That thought practically stopped my heart.

Mom finished her sandwich and started munching thoughtfully on her chips. After a moment I was disturbed to realize that she was staring at my bust. "What size are you?"

"I'm a B, and I'm fine."

She waggled her brows with uncertainty. "Even we B girls can start sagging prematurely if we don't watch out."

How could it be that talking about underwear with your mother was just as embarrassing and irritating at twenty-eight as it was when you were twelve?

"Are you still doing the exercises I showed you?"

Was she kidding? She had demonstrated Jack La Lanne arm exercises for me one afternoon in a rare spurt of motherly concern for my flat chest. I had been ten.

"Women go to gyms now, Mom. They lift weights."

"Do *you?*" She stared doubtfully at the bread-dough arms sticking out of my sleeveless top.

"Well, no," I allowed. "Not now. I can't afford a gym."

Pepper belonged to a gym, of course. I wondered if I married Spence whether I would be able to live a life of leisure . . . or if I would even want to.

Oh, God. Listen to me! I was regressing into a someday-my-prince-will-come state of mind that I hadn't indulged in since I was thirteen. (All right, twenty-five, maybe.)

I must have let out a moan of despair, because Mom's lips twisted into a frown. "What's the matter?"

I closed my noodle container. It was no use trying to eat. "I'm just a mess." Looking into her eyes, it occurred to me that of all the people on earth, she knew exactly what it was like to be in exactly the mess I was in. "Mom, when you left Dad . . . I mean . . . when you met Murph, did you make a conscious decision to do what you did, or did you just get swept up in something?"

"Oh! Let me think." She ate a chip and ruminated for a long minute, almost as if she had never thought much about this before. "Well, I think I would have to choose the swept-up option. I met Murph and he was so fun. Where your father was so dour—gracious, he'd become a real pill!—Murph was flirty and enjoyed throwing his money around. And it had been ages since I'd had fun, and a friend to laugh with. *That* was it. We were good friends, in a way that your father and I weren't. Not quite. There's a big difference between meeting someone when you're forty and meeting someone when you're twenty-one."

"Or eighteen," I said, realization dawning.

She frowned. "Are you all right?"

Maybe I really wouldn't be busting up a marriage. (As Spence kept reminding me, it was barely one anyway.) Maybe I was just stepping into a marriage in its final stages of decay.

My heart thumped optimistically.

Mom was looking at me funny. "Did I help?"

Help? Good God. This was pathetic, I realized. I was sitting on a park bench with my mom, asking for homewrecking advice. I needed to have my head examined.

I lifted my shoulders in a casual shrug.

"I love talking this way—makes me feel all momsy-womsy!" She crumpled up her bag. "I wish we could gab all afternoon, but it's back to the salt mines for me. You're so lucky not to be working!"

"I am working," I reminded her.

She laughed. "Taking care of that sweet girl? That's not work."

That sweet girl had been gathering up little bits of trash and was inspecting a discarded foil condom wrapper. I jumped off the bench. "Okay, Aug—enough trash collecting."

"I'll see you soon, hon," my mom said, hopping up. "We'll do lunch again."

"Okay," I said, watching her stride away with something like awe. She seemed so cheerful, so unflappable. But she always had been. I suppose I thought that since she had never had to deal with adversity that she would be incapable of coping if her life ever became difficult. Now I had to revise my opinion a little.

August had a play date at two, so we headed that way. While she hobnobbed with her contemporaries, I went down the street and drank coffee and tried to make sense of what was going on in my life.

According to Mom, I was on easy street. But she was twisted, so her opinion didn't count.

According to Finn, I was A-okay. Finn was such a nice guy, though, his opinion didn't count, either.

Spence thought I was great, but he was trying to get me in the sack, so his opinion really didn't count.

According to Jess, I had turned into a superficial, callous bitch. That was harsh, but I had to admit, she made a strong argument.

What was I going to do? I couldn't go on living with Spence and Pepper. I just couldn't.

Well, I could. I could tell Spence that we were going nowhere. The trouble was that I had told him that, in so many words. He just hadn't listened.

Yet how could I just pick up and leave? And go where? At that moment, since I had finally received my first paycheck, and made a few payments on my credit cards, I had approximately eight hundred dollars in my checking account, which was a lot more than I'd had in a checking account for a long, long time. But in terms of trying to live in New York, it wouldn't support me for a week. And unlike Mom, I didn't have any jewelry to hock.

When I picked up August, I wasn't any closer to deciding what to do, though I knew if I was going to quit working for Pepper I would have to give her notice. Several weeks, at least. I just couldn't run out on August. There needed to be a smooth transition, so they could replace me with a new nanny.

A new nanny.

Strange as it was, I felt staggered at the idea of not seeing August anymore. Which was weird, since I'd spent a good many days that summer dreaming of the day when I would be able to escape nannydom, and not be subject to the mercurial emotions of a three-and-a-half-year-old. I wanted to be able to walk out my door in the morning with a tiny handbag instead of a tote bag full of snacks, activities, and Huggies pull-ups in case of emergency. I imagined myself being reborn into the world, unfettered by baggies of Froot Loops, juice boxes, and moist towelettes.

Now all I could see was that I would be so alone. How would I stand it? What would my days be like?

After her play date, August wanted ice cream, so we stopped in a deli for a Dove bar. (Just to be companionable, I got one, too.) They were cold, messy, and scrumptious, and we were still finishing up when we got back to the apartment.

The moment I walked in, I felt a difference in the air. Was Pepper back already? Or had Spence come back early, to ambush me? Or maybe it was just Lumi.

"Hello?" I called, uncertain. "Anybody home?"

"Anybody home?" August parroted.

In retrospect, I see that this was the last moment of normal I had for a long, long time. It was the moment before the deer jumps in front of your car, or the piano drops on your head. One moment I was carefully gnawing on that awkward bottom of Dove bar, calling out to see who was in the apartment, and the next Pepper was flying out of her room and headed towards me with fists clenched at her sides, a human tornado in pedal pushers and slappy sherbet green sandals.

I went deathly pale, I'm sure. *She knew.* I knew she knew. The jig was up. Somehow she had found out about Spence kissing me, and now my goose was cooked. Confrontation was never my strong suit.

She looked like she was going to start yelling at me, but around mid hallway she screeched to a halt, goggling at the Dove bar that was dripping in August's hand.

"*What are you eating?*" she yelled.

August quivered.

"What are you eating!" she demanded again.

She was definitely having a *no wire hangers!* moment.

I answered, uneasily, for both of us. "Dove bars?"

"I can see that!" she snapped. "I can see that very plainly. August, go to your room."

August, predictably, started to fall apart. Her face turned red and her eyes squinched. "Mommy . . ."

"*Now*, August. Give me your ice cream and go to your room."

"It's my fault," I jumped in. "I thought it would be a treat . . ."

"It's not a treat, it's an indulgence, and August is plenty old to know that she's not supposed to snack before dinner." She rounded on August again, her finger wagging. "You're turning four in two weeks, young lady! You need to start acting like it!"

August started howling. (Much like a four-year-old, I thought.) But Mommie Dearest simply removed the ice cream from her hand and gave her a shove toward her room. "Go take a nap."

As I watched August run, hysterical, to her room, I felt stunned. And guilty. And mad. This wasn't about ice cream. It was about me.

"Please don't take this out on August," I said. "I—"

She cut me off the moment August's door slammed shut. "I could kill you!"

My mouth dropped open, but the logical word that should have come out—*why?*—lodged in my throat. I knew why. I just wanted to put off having my transgression spoken aloud for as long as possible.

She shook her head in disgust, pivoted on her sandal heel, and flapped angrily toward the kitchen. I fell in after her, madly trying to cobble together excuses. Scraps of rationalization popped into my head. *Mistake . . . carried away . . . mad, passionate nostalgia . . .*

Nothing made any sense. What were acceptable excuses for kissing someone else's husband?

Pepper dropped the remainders of August's Dove bar down the garbage disposal, wooden stick and all.

Instinct kicked in. That Popsicle stick would play havoc with the disposal. "You shouldn't—"

"I know that!" Pepper hollered at me. "You think I don't know how a garbage disposal works?"

I tossed my Dove bar in, too, suddenly wishing the firing squad would just go ahead and shoot. She flipped the switch and we listen to the machine angrily chewing wood. "Look, Pepper, if I did anything . . ."

She howled. "*If? If?* The first thing I heard when I got home was that damn message!"

I frowned, confused. "Message?"

"From Connie Shearer."

This wasn't becoming any clearer. "Who?"

"The dance teacher!"

My mind grappled foggily with this new information. How could the dance teacher have seen Spence kissing me? What was this about? "I don't understand."

Pepper was so angry, she was practically twitching. "First off, she said you were nearly thirty minutes late picking up August. *Thirty minutes!*"

She was yelling at me about *dance lessons*? About being late? I had to balance myself against the counter to keep from collapsing in relief. "I didn't know I was supposed to pick up August. I didn't get back until . . ."

"Well *of course* you're supposed to pick her up. That's your job! Connie was fit to be tied."

"I'm sorry . . ."

"*Sorry?* Connie said she was going to have to excuse August from Tappin' with Your Toddler from now on because the other mothers had lodged a complaint!"

"Because I was late picking her up?"

"No—because they think she has lice!" Pepper nearly screamed. "They said you were carrying around books on lice, and so they naturally all assumed that August—"

"Oh, for heaven's sake . . ." I muttered.

"Apparently they all spent the morning up in Harlem where there's some woman who's a famous nitpicker. Have you ever heard of such a thing?"

"No, but . . ."

"Oh, I let her have it," Pepper declared. "I told that Connie woman that August had never had lice in her life. Never even got mosquito bites. I said the bug hasn't been born that's been on that child!"

"It's all a misunderstanding," I said. "A stupid screw-up on their part. I was just carrying around the book—it was a present from a friend."

Pepper crossed her arms. "A present."

I dug into my bag and produced *Outwitting Head Lice*. "See? I've been carrying it for weeks. It's great if you're on the subway and it's crowded . . ."

Pepper narrowed her eyes on me. "And you want me to believe that?" She cackled. "You must think I just hatched!"

"No, I—"

I frowned. Why wouldn't she believe it? She obviously didn't think I had a head lice problem, or she wouldn't even let me in her kitchen. So she had to think I had some other motivation for carrying this book to the dance lesson.

"You think I don't see what's happening here?"

I froze. She *did* know about Spence. I waited for the ax to fall.

"You're just trying to undermine my party."

This was another curveball. I angled my head. "What party?"

"August's party," she said. "You've got to be crazy if you think I couldn't see through your sabotage We were going to do the routine to 'Buttons and Bows,' but you *couldn't stand* the fact that you weren't going to be the center of attention."

If she had actually been at that spa, they must have been handing out crack. "That's the nuttiest thing I've ever heard."

"Oh sure, act all innocent." She oozed disgust. "You don't think I saw the look in your eye when I was telling you and your mother about the dude ranch party? You should have seen yourself! You've probably spent all the time since trying to think of ways you could ruin this party just like you ruined my birthday party when I was five."

Okay. Now I understood. I'd been waiting a lifetime for that incident to be regurgitated at me, and here it was. Only now, when it was finally happening, she didn't even sound justified; she sounded demented. "Pepper, I swear to you. I was not trying to undermine anything."

"So you just happened to get August kicked out of the school where we were going to learn our dance routine?"

This was too much. "I didn't get her kicked out—not on purpose. Anyway, how were you going to learn a dance routine in two weeks? You've already skipped the last two classes to go have a tryst with your sleazy journalist friend."

Her face went slack. But she wasn't sputtering out any denials, I noticed.

"Besides," I went on, "if you listened to your daughter at all, you would know that she hates dancing. Hates it. She doesn't even give a damn about the party, either. She's never mentioned it."

Pepper sneered. "Listen to you, lecturing me. You're just jealous!"

"How?"

"Because you're not a mother." She laughed that out-of-control mad laugh of hers. "You're just another pathetic single twenty-something. Oh, but give a single woman charge of a kid for three months, and suddenly she's Doctor Spock!"

"I'm not jealous," I said.

"Yes, you are. You have been from the first, ever since I plucked you out of that pathetic apartment in Dallas and offered you this job. And probably even before that, because I got Spence and you lost him. This is your way of getting petty, petty revenge."

She must have stuck the pin in the right place in the voodoo doll, because I practically squealed in outrage. I'm ashamed to say that, more than anything else, it was the mention of my crappy apartment that pushed me over the edge. I thought she'd been too drunk to notice. It was one thing to be unloved and childless, but to be poor really stung. "Well at least I'm not so petty as to make my nemesis wear a cow suit."

Her body fell motionless. "Who told you about that?"

"Spence."

"When?"

"Last night. He also told me that he was against the whole dude ranch party in the first place and tried to talk you out of it."

"Sounds like you two did a lot of talking," she said.

She was coming too close to the sweet spot for my comfort. "Oh, never mind. This is ridiculous!" I turned to walk away, but after a few steps outside the kitchen I nearly smacked right into Spence, who was strolling through the door with a cellophane-wrapped bundle of yellow roses. His face blanched when he saw me, I think because he spotted Pepper screeching up right behind me.

"Hi, hon," he said, speaking over my head.

She planted her hands on her hips. "Who are the roses for, your girlfriend?"

His frantic gaze searched mine, but I rolled my eyes to indicate she was whistling in the dark.

"They're for you," he said, handing the flowers to Pepper.

She smacked them back against his chest. "Well I don't want them!"

She ran back to their bedroom and slammed the door.

Spence raised his brows in puzzlement.

"It's about the party," I explained in a whisper. "She doesn't know."

"Oh, thank God," he muttered.

I'll admit, I recoiled at that. Did he mean he *didn't want* her to know? Ever?

"Where's August?" he asked.

"She's in her room . . . upset . . ."

"Okay, I see. I'll handle this," he said.

He marched bravely back to face his wife and daughter.

I slinked to my room and shut the door. Though August's room was across the hall, I could hear Spence talking to her—her high, outraged tones alternating with his deep, comforting ones. Then, after about five minutes, that door opened and closed and he doubled back to his and Pepper's room. I don't know what I expected. Probably that they wouldn't come out again for an hour or so, and that when they did, there would be steely silence between them as there often was.

What happened instead was the battle of the century. Shrieking voices penetrated the thick prewar walls, as did the sounds of angry footsteps and, on more than one occasion, objects being thrown. I felt like a child in one of those old after-school specials, cowering in her room as she listened to her parents arguing. I could only imagine what August felt.

I grabbed up the stuffed crab and flounder from last night,

tiptoed across the way, and slipped into her room. She was lying across her bed, burrowed in stuffed animals. I added two more to the pile. "I forgot to give these back to you, Aug."

She glared up at me, her chin wrinkled from the effort not to cry.

"I'm sorry about the ice cream," I said. "It's gonna be okay. I told your mom that it was my idea. You didn't do anything wrong."

She started crying and snuffling, and for a moment I just gave her a hug. What could I say that would make sense to a three-year-old? The real explanation—that parents could be as irrational as children—wasn't even all that comforting, if you were the one who was going to be at the irrational adult's mercy for the next fourteen years.

I left her with her eyes closed, buried in fake fur, and crept back across the hall. The adults were still at it. Every time I heard Pepper shriek, I felt angry all over again. Jealous, she'd called me! And thinking that I would undermine her child's birthday party out of some leftover fit of pique—that was really too much. Really.

I wondered what Spence was saying to her. Was my name being mentioned? The few words I could pick out—I'll admit that my ear was pressed against my door at this point—were maddenly neutral.

"*Me!*" Pepper shouted.

". . . *at the airport!*" Spence boomed a few moments later.

The bit about an airport made no sense to me. Though I suppose I couldn't be expected to pick up on every reference in someone else's marital spat.

I did pick out Pepper's shrill voice tossing the word *nanny* in his face, which sent me scurrying guiltily back to perch on my bed.

Somehow, in the midst of all this, my guilt dissipated somewhat. To have such bizarre accusations come at me from left field had made me forget that Pepper had a legitimate beef against me, if she cared to poke around enough to find it. But then again, who was *she* to talk? She had been carrying on with

Colby, and then Jonah, and would no doubt keep on being a serial adultress until someone stopped her. Why not me?

Spence deserved better than this shrill nutcase of a wife.

When the screaming abated and then started up again after about forty-five minutes, I started packing. Spence walked in on me as I was filling my second suitcase.

"What are you doing?" he asked.

He had to ask? "Leaving."

He held my shoulders. "Don't leave. Please. Not yet."

"But—"

"Stay and watch August?" he asked.

"Here?"

"Of course here."

I gaped at him. "And where will you be?"

"Our company has an apartment. I can probably go there. If not, I'll check into a hotel."

"You're leaving?" My voice was very nearly a squeak. "*Leaving* leaving?"

He heaved a long-suffering sigh. I couldn't say that I blamed him. He probably hadn't expected to walk in on a daytime soap opera. "I don't want to live this way anymore. I don't have to."

"No, you don't. Had you ever?"

He brushed a hand over his head. "Maybe at some point I felt trapped—because Pepper's dad gave me a great job right out of college. I still work for the same company. I felt I owed Mr. McClintock."

"You mean you stayed married for your in-laws?" I asked. "That's a switch!"

"They're good people. They've been nice to me." He sighed again, as if he couldn't bear to think of anyone being nice to him now. "I'll call you, okay?"

Acute separation anxiety set in; my chest squeezed in panic. "How can I stay here?"

"I explained that you weren't out to get her, and that there's nothing to her suspicions about us."

"Oh." But there *was* something to her suspicions about us. Wasn't there?

He smiled at me. "I know. I lied."

Relief gushed out of me, even as a tiny backflow of doubt seeped in. I wasn't sure how glad I should be that the man I wanted was a confessed fibber.

"Everything will work out," he promised.

And I believed him. He sounded so sure. And he was leaving her!

"Sleep tight," he said, about to duck out the door.

"Wait!" I said.

He stopped.

I tilted my head. "Were those yellow roses really for Pepper?"

"What do you think?" he asked, winking.

It was all the answer I needed. I smiled as the door shut, then backed up and sank onto my bed.

But after five minutes of staring at the ceiling, I realized it really hadn't been much of an answer at all.

Chapter 19

The next two days were agony. The apartment fell silent. Pepper was barricaded in her room. She didn't come out at all during daylight, and only a few times at night did I hear her stir.

I should have been relieved that I didn't have to face her, but I wasn't. There was no relief in those days. Not seeing her became just as nerve-racking as the prospect of having her screech at me again.

Spence had insisted that she had bought the idea that I was not plotting against her, and that her suspicions about him and me were completely off the wall. But in that case, what reason had he given her for leaving? I didn't know, because Spence and I exchanged only a few furtive conversations on the phone, usually when he was fairly certain I would be out of the apartment. A typical one:

"Has she come out yet?"

"No."

"Not even to eat?"

He sounded concerned, which made my heart stop beating momentarily. Did he still care so much about her? Then I reminded myself that it was a good thing that he worried whether his wife was starving to death.

"How's August?"

"She's holding up." One upside to having a mother who

treats you with benign neglect is that you get used to neglect. "Yesterday she told me that she hates it when her mommy gets one of her headaches. I guess that's what she thinks is going on."

"That's probably what Pepper told her the last time."

"Last time?" I asked, alarmed. No one had told me there had been a last time.

"The last time she pulled something like this," he explained. "So childish of her! She's always going over the top."

I would hang up from these conferences thinking, *how else is a person supposed to react when her marriage ends?* Even a cheating, irritable shrew like Pepper could be forgiven for being a tad upset when the father of her child left her.

Jess called me, too. It was good to hear from her, to know that she really hadn't given up on me, but I couldn't confide in her. She would be completely negative, tell me to bail, to never see Spence again. That might be good advice from her perspective, but from mine it was not an option. I did have to give her an excuse why I couldn't go to the movies with her, though.

"Things aren't going so great right now," I explained.

"Uh-oh. Pepper knows you're lusting after her husband." I should have known it would be hard to hide what was going on from her. "She doesn't have you tied up in a closet so she can torture you, does she?"

"How did you know?" I asked. "We're just taking a torture coffee break now."

"So you're okay?" she asked. "You've been so evasive."

"Spence has left Pepper," I said. "But it's not about me."

Jess hooted. "He left and it's not about you? What was it about, irreconcilable differences over how they squeeze the toothpaste tube?"

"It's complicated."

"Darn tootin' it's complicated. You need to get out of there. Fast."

"I can't. I have to take care of August. Besides, Spence says leaving suddenly now would just make her suspicious."

"Al . . . you think she's not going to figure this out?"

That was a good point.

"I repeat: You need to bail out."

See? I knew she'd react like this.

"I don't want to abandon August. Pepper doesn't seem stable."

"That's some knight-in-shining-armor you've got. He goes to ground and leaves you to handle the fallout."

"He couldn't stay here."

"So why should you?"

She didn't understand. But she'd never liked Spence. Actually, she'd never met him. But she never liked the idea of him, not even in college when I would occasionally—after a few beers, say—wax nostalgic for the high school sweetie who had dumped me cold.

I decided I shouldn't talk to Jess again till this was all cleared up. Finn also called, but I didn't pick up. And I didn't return his call.

It's amazing the things you can learn to live with, especially when you cut yourself off from the people who will tell you that you are wrong. I spent three days wandering around the apartment, taking August to the playground, and the swimming pool, and coming back to a woman barricaded in her bedroom. Where-upon I would read stories to August, or watch videos, or go chat with Lumi. Lumi and I almost bonded during this time. At first she didn't understand what was going on in the apartment; and I felt fortunate to be an insider who could really give her the skinny. (The bowdlerized myself-as-the-innocent-bystander skinny.)

During the day I could convince myself that I *was* innocent—heroic, even. I could pretend that this really didn't have anything to do with me, that I was just the nanny, taking care of my charge under difficult circumstances. I became the über-nanny, in fact, taking August on educational outings, reading her entire library to her from beginning to end, fixing her nutritious smoothies. I bought *Wee Sing in French* out of my own pocket, and even sang through it once with her. I felt like Julie Andrews on steroids.

Nights were different. When I was all alone, my confidence wavered. I would sit up in bed thinking about Spence, wondering how long it would be before we were, officially, a couple. I worried that people would condemn us, so I began to go through a list of people who had done what we were doing, if not worse, compiling a who's who of famous adulterers. Practically all the presidents I admired were famous cheaters, I realized. Writers were comforting to think about, too. Those literary types were all randy—even the women. Even the painfully plain George Eliot had stolen a woman's husband; did that stop people from reading *Middlemarch*? And in Hollywood you could practically lob a brick at random and come up with an adulterer or two. Humphrey Bogart had been married when he started courting Lauren Bacall . . . and look how that had turned out. A real love story.

And didn't Robin Williams marry his kids' nanny?

Meanwhile, I wondered what Spence was doing. Why didn't he call me more? Everything was so unresolved between us. I felt passive, just waiting for his go-ahead. And what was I going to go ahead and do? Announce to Pepper I was taking her husband and walk out? Or just say nothing and flee?

But by the time my eyes came blearily awake the next morning, I would have forgotten the torment of the night before, and I would manage to get through the day as if things were almost normal.

Then the cavalry arrived.

I should have guessed something big was afoot, because all of a sudden Pepper appeared again. She came flying out of her room one morning, dressed in beige slacks with a black shirt, very subdued for her. Yet there was a brittle edge to her. Her eyes were glassy and distracted looking as she started barking orders at everyone. "Al, I made August a hair appointment for today. I want you to take her there and make sure they don't butcher her bangs like they did the last time. She'll have birthday pictures coming up. And make sure she's tidy this afternoon. No rolling around in the dirt, or whatever it is you two usually do. Oh, and Lumi, I want the apartment to look really nice. We're having company."

"Who?" I asked.

"Alessandra. And Phaedra is flying in."

"Oh." Oh God, I meant. Then, remembering myself, I piped up, "Great!"

"Could one of you make sure we have plenty of sparkling water, Diet Coke, salad fixings, and gin in the house? Healthy food. And maybe some Pringles. And we'll need bagels for breakfast . . ." She paused and blew out her breath. "Well, use common sense. We just don't want anyone to get hungry, dehydrated, or sober." She laughed.

Even though we were secret adversaries, seeing her up and swinging again brought me a momentary burst of fellow feeling for her. I had to suppress the urge to clap her on the back and shout *You go, girl!*

Just so long as she didn't go at me . . .

"What's the matter, Al?" she asked, snapping her fingers in my face. "You're in a daze. Chop, chop!"

"Are you okay?" I asked.

A mistake.

She drew back defensively. "What do you mean?"

I stammered something about how I hadn't seen her for a while, so I didn't know . . .

She spoke through gritted teeth. "Spence has flown the coop, in case you haven't noticed, but good riddance! I suspect he'll come crawling back again when he gets tired of whoever he's found to stroke his pathetic ego for him this time . . ."

I could feel myself shrinking.

". . . but just let him try it! I'm fed up this time."

She was fed up. That was rich. Whenever Pepper got mad she made it seem like she was the victim, the aggrieved one.

And what did she mean by *this time*?

"Let his squeeze of the moment deal with his patronizing absenteeism for a while," she raved. "See how long it takes her to realize her Prince Charming is nothing more than an ear attached to a phone!"

Oh, I loved that. It was all I could do not to shake her. She was blaming him for having to talk on the phone—to conduct the business that kept them all afloat? No wonder Spence was fed up!

The smile she aimed at me looked as if it just might crack

her face. "So in answer to your question, Al, everything's fine. Just *fine*. And pretty soon it's going to be better."

And with that, she stamped out.

Pretty soon it's going to be better. Those words sounded ominous.

There was a lot to do, so I didn't get Spence on the horn to inform him that his wife was on the warpath. Every time I called his office, he was at a meeting, or lunch. Lumi was up to her eyeballs in housework, so I ran to Food Emporium to do some speed-shopping. Then I ran to the liquor store and bought one of everything. Then it was time for August's hair appointment, which wasn't at just any ol' salon, but the expensive one where Pepper had been getting hers done. I had to talk the stylist, Gervaise, out of giving August red highlights, so I didn't consider my hour there a complete waste of time.

August was mesmerized by her glorious new reflection in the passing windows, so it felt like it took an hour to walk the twelve blocks home. It may have. When we got there, Pepper and Phaedra were already installed at the dining room table, drinking. Alessandra was there, too. I was struck at once how much she looked like Phaedra, only taller and even more angular. X-treme Phaedra. The three of them sitting there made an intimidating triumvirate. They were so tan, so pointy, so sharply made up, the rest of the world seemed like it was in soft focus.

While they all made a big fuss over August's haircut, I slipped into the kitchen. Lumi and I exchanged sympathetic glances. I was going to say something snide—and impolitic—when Phaedra slithered up behind me.

"Al! Isn't it terrible?" she asked, as if we were alone. Lumi might as well have been invisible.

"Awful," I agreed.

She shook her head, and I could have sworn she was watching my reaction with eagle eyes. Maybe I was just being paranoid. "I thought they would last forever."

She had? Between Spence being gone ninety percent of the time and Pepper leaving her boy toys strewn about like abandoned roller skates, I wouldn't have given them six months.

"I mean, they've always been together," Phaedra said. "Always."

Right. Ever since she stole him from me. Shaking my head, I mewed, "I know it!"

"Men are shameless. Thank God there are a few good ones, like Colby."

"Colby?" I gulped. Colby, I remembered suddenly, was a divorce lawyer.

"That's why I'm here. He sent me up with some great ideas for things Pepper should do."

"Like what?" I asked.

She smiled that frosty smile of hers. "Just things."

I was not invited to the divorce-planning pow wow, naturally. I took August back to her room and read some Pooh stories to her. She wanted to watch a video, but I was trying to catch snatches of conversation coming through the living room. Mostly I just heard their voices when they were laughing, which gave me no useful information. During a quiet stretch, I darted out of August's room and went to the bathroom nearest the dining room. I put my ear to the door.

". . . Colby said the best thing is some kind of evidence of abuse, or anger."

"Oh, right!"

"You never know—besides, something might look like it. He suggests checking security cameras, nanny cams, and deposing household help."

"I don't think Spence even knows Lumi exists . . . yet."

"Al?" someone whispered. I tensed.

"Puh-leez!"

They all laughed.

What did that mean?

"But nanny cams . . . that's not a bad idea. I haven't checked since I got back."

I could see myself in the bathroom mirror, and my forehead was so pinched that my eyebrows almost met. *Nanny cam?* She told me she didn't do nanny cams! What's more, I hadn't seen one.

Not that I had anything to worry about on that score. August and I had always managed to settle our differences using non-violent means. The only thing I had done to be ashamed of was kissing Spence . . .

My heart thumped like a gerbil's. Where would she have put a nanny cam? In the kitchen? In my room? In August's room?

August's room. Where Spence and I had been necking. Oh, God. Oh, God.

I streaked back to August's room. She was still sitting with a picture book on her lap. I immediately started scanning her shelves. What did a nanny cam look like? I couldn't see anything that looked the least bit camera-like. Though of course I knew they hid them. In books, electronics, in stuffed animals . . . I glanced at the bed, which was piled with stuffed toys. They were strewn on her mattress, and lined up on the shelf that served as a headboard. What was I supposed to do, start ripping all of August's toys apart in front of her?

I kept expecting Pepper and company to bust in. I felt nauseous with nerves.

"What's the matter, Alson?" August asked.

"Nothing!" I was probably grinning manically at the poor thing. "How about a video?"

"I want another story," she said.

"Videos are stories."

"I want you to read me a story."

"I can't right now, sweetie." I needed to talk to Spence. I wondered if this would be an okay time to call him. The clock read 5:35.

But of course it would be a waste of time to call him. Time was of the essence.

Time.

I zeroed in on the clock again; my hair stood on end. For the life of me, I couldn't remember there being a digital clock in August's room before. Maybe I just never noticed it. But then why would there be a clock there at all? August couldn't tell time, even digital time.

The clock was long and flat. Just about the size of a videotape, as a matter of fact.

I fell on the clock like a halfback tackling a football. I

yanked the cord out of the wall and started running for the door.

"What are you doing?" August yelled after me.

"Clock's broken. Gotta fix it!"

It was only about a fifteen foot journey to my room, but by the time I got there I had the sweats. I threw myself on the bed and started inspecting the clock with shaky fingers. Sure enough, I found an opening on the bottom. I struggled to slide the right piece of plastic out, but with the help of some nail scissors it finally popped loose.

Revealing the standard battery cavity that you find on every clock like this one. It was empty.

I slumped on the bed, feeling foolish. There were footsteps outside my door, and I tensed, hoping no one would come in and find me guiltily dismantling electronics.

When the hallway was silent again, I tiptoed back across to August's room. "All fixed!" I said brightly.

As I was plugging it back in I looked over and saw August was crying, silently. "What's wrong?"

"Aunt Phaedra took my monkey!"

"Your . . ." I looked at the headboard shelf, where part of her menagerie resided. The ugly monkey, the one Pepper had given her right after they moved, was gone.

I stumbled to my feet, trying to think fast. If the camera had been on the bed, then . . .

It would have had a perfect view of us kissing in the middle of the room.

I had just run out of time.

Oh, God. Oh, God. My whole body was jittering. What was I going to do?

The voice that answered me didn't belong to the Almighty, it belonged to Jess. *Get out of there*, she had said.

I sprang to my feet. Then I looked over at August, staring at me with wide, teary eyes. I froze. Could I just run out on her?

But if I said good-bye, she would get hysterical.

And this wasn't good-bye. Not really. I would see her again, often. We would be together a lot.

I slipped out of the room, then sprinted across the hall, dragged a suitcase out from under my bed, and started stuffing everything into it that I could in thirty seconds. Clothes, CDs, books, jewelry, shoes. I tossed in Mildred and her menagerie. I had to sit on the case to close it, and even then my bathrobe belt was trailing out one side. It didn't matter. My hands were trembling too frantically to fix it.

I grabbed my purse and flew down the hallway. Flew. I'm not sure if anyone saw me. Everyone was congregated in the living room. They would have had to look fast.

Down in the lobby, Lou laughed when he saw me struggle out of the elevator. "Going on a trip?" he asked as I skittered by.

I groaned. "My whole life is a trip."

Spence was staying at a hotel, but I wasn't sure which one. I tracked him down at his office, which was in the Wall Street district. Since it was rush hour, it might as well have been the moon. The cab took an eternity worming its way downtown, but I was too distraught to strap-hang. My blood was racing as if I had just chugged three lattes. It felt as if dogs were nipping at my heels, and I had to resist the temptation to flick frightened glances behind me through the back window, as if I actually expected Pepper and company to be bearing down on me.

But halfway there, I started getting angry. Nanny cams? How dare she tape me? Especially after she had told me that she wouldn't, that bitch. There was no telling how many surveillance cameras were around that place. They might have been in every room, for all I knew. Did she think I was going to hurt August . . . or steal the silver? That made me angrier than anything. I was a fellow BP girl, dammit. If she couldn't trust me, who in the hell did she trust?

Of course, as it turned out, she *couldn't* trust me.

But there was no way for her to have known that until she stooped to spying.

When I got to Spence's building, I practically had to promise lifelong sexual bondage to the security guard to even get him to call up to Spence's floor, and when word was delivered that I could come up, he still seemed to mistrust me.

Maybe he thought I had a bomb in my suitcase along with my flannel bathrobe.

Spence practically yanked me off the elevator the moment the doors slid open. "What are you doing here?" he hissed as he dragged me back to his office. All the cubicles we walked past were empty; there were lights glowing from under the doors of just a few offices. Somewhere, I heard the sound of a vacuum sweeper. Still, Spence seemed awfully determined to whisk me out of sight as soon as he could.

As soon as he shut the door behind me, my brittle nerves finally snapped. After all, I was working for him, too. He bore some responsibility for this. "*Nanny cam?*" I exclaimed.

He frowned at me.

"A surveillance camera generally used on domestic staff," I explained. "Maybe you've heard of them?"

"I've heard of them . . ."

"Well your wife had one. Has. In her possession."

His mouth formed an O of understanding.

I nodded. "Uh-huh, and it's got pictures of us on it."

His eyes bugged. "How do you know?"

"Because she took it out of August's bedroom just an hour ago! She and her friends are probably freeze framing images as we speak to find the best angle to use in the divorce suit."

"How do you know it's got pictures of us?" he asked.

"It was at the perfect angle," I said.

"But was there a tape going at the time?"

I stopped. For the first moment in the past hour I felt as if I was able to take a real breath. "I don't know."

He went around his desk and plopped down into his leather chair. He steepled his fingers and nodded at me to sit down in the guest chair, which I did, wordlessly.

"I hope you don't think I condone spying on people," he said.

I waggled my head from side to side. "No—I'm sorry I lost my temper. I was just so frazzled . . ."

He laughed and tilted a glance over at the suitcase. "Seems you left the apartment in a hurry."

"I know, I'm sorry. I didn't intend to bug out this way. I

mean, of course I wasn't going to stay there forever, but I wanted a smooth transition . . ." I felt like I was gabbling pointlessly, and anyway, Spence had stopped listening. He had that frown on again.

"We've got to find out what was on that nanny cam."

"How?"

His brows arched. "I suppose I could hire someone . . ."

"To break into your apartment and steal the tape?" I asked, my voice looping up. I couldn't believe I was involved in anything like this. I was a normal person. I never gave surveillance cameras a thought. That stuff was for spy movies and convenience stores. Now we were talking about private detectives. Revulsion and utter fascination warred in me.

He shook his head. "Thing is, Pepper's not stupid. If she's looked at that tape, she already knows what she has or doesn't have. And if she has something, she's not going to let it out of her sight. But if that's the case, and she really has something, I think we'll hear fairly soon."

"Why?"

"Because I know her. She won't be able to resist crowing about it."

I thought back. "I'm not so sure. I think Pepper is more patient than we know. From what I could gather, she had waited twenty-three years to get me into a cow suit to pay me back for her fifth birthday party."

His eyes narrowed. "But she still wouldn't let the tape out of her sight."

"No."

"If there is anything on it," Spence said. "I'm willing to bet there isn't. It would be too much of a coincidence. She would have had to set the timer to be going exactly when we were in the room."

He was right. It did seem like a long shot. "Unless she had Lumi changing the tape for her while she was gone."

Spence snorted. "Pepper, trust her maid?"

He had a point. If Pepper didn't trust me, she sure as hell wouldn't trust Lumi.

He leaned back, rubbing his hands together. "She doesn't have us."

"You don't think so?"

"Time will tell, of course," he said. "But I'd say the odds were probably ninety-ten in our favor."

Ninety-ten. Those were pretty good odds. Those were almost condom-used-correctly odds.

My spirits surged—but just as soon plummeted back down to basement level. "But she does have us."

"How so?"

I pointed to my suitcase. "I cut and ran at the very moment anyone mentioned nanny cam."

"Coincidence," he said. "You got a new job opportunity and felt you had to jump on it."

"So fast that I couldn't even take the time to take all my clothes, or leave her a note?"

His lips turned down. "I know. I'll tell her you were freaked out from being yelled at by her and couldn't take it anymore. I'll say you had a nervous breakdown, or something."

That wouldn't be far from wrong. "But we'll be seen together," I pointed out.

"We're old friends."

"Is that all?" I asked.

He grinned. "Let's go out and celebrate your freedom. You're a nanny no more."

That did sound good. At the same time, however, I felt a moment of queasiness. Somewhere in an apartment on Fifth Avenue, August was probably wondering what had happened to me.

"What's the matter?"

"August," I said.

His lips turned down. "Pepper will find someone else," he said. "And you'll still see August a lot. We both will."

There was something about Spence. When he spoke, his words were vocal Prozac. No wonder he'd made so much money. He had the ability to make me think everything was going to be okay, even when all evidence pointed to the contrary. For instance, there was the little problem of my now being jobless and homeless.

My suitcase was there to remind me, even if Spence was doing his best to make me forget. "You're still worried, aren't you?"

"Well . . ."

He got up. "Eat first," he said. "Then worry."

"If I'm worried, I can't eat."

He came around the desk and gallantly took my arm. "That's what cocktails are for." He grinned and picked up my suitcase with his free hand and pointed it towards the door with his arm outstretched. "To Oz?"

I laughed. He did have a little crazy scarecrow optimism in his eyes just then. I had been so focused on my own survival that I hadn't really stopped to think about what my fleeing the apartment would mean to him. We actually were starting out on a journey together. "To Oz!"

We practically skipped out of his office, forgetting that Oz had turned out to be bogus.

We dropped off my stuff at Spence's hotel and went to a Greek restaurant uptown. After we first sat down, I kept tossing nervous glances over my shoulder, which drove Spence crazy.

"What's the matter?" he finally asked.

I bent guiltily towards him. "Aren't you worried that someone will see us?"

"Who?"

"Someone you know . . ."

He laughed. He was calmer than he had been at the office. "Relax. The people I know and like wouldn't make a big deal of my having dinner with a woman friend, and as for the people I don't like, I don't give a shit about their opinions anyway."

I blinked. Why couldn't I be like that?

"Feel better?" he asked.

I nodded.

"Good, let's order drinks."

And I must say, my troubles seemed to slip from me like fat clothes falling off the body of a woman who had just lost one hundred pounds. Spence ordered a vodka tonic for me, and then another, and then kept the food and booze coming until I achieved a sort of Spring Break of the brain. Most of all, Spence made me laugh. I laughed in that giddy, stomach-achey way that I hadn't experienced since I left college. He was a low-key cutup. He could do impressions of people that could almost fly on *Late Night* . . . or at least they seemed that way after three vodkas.

He could even do Phaedra and perfectly mime the way she would flip her Cleopatra hair over her shoulder. I chortled my way through a three-course meal that probably cost more than I usually spent on food in a month. Then Spence was paying the bill and leading me out of the restaurant and hailing a cab.

"Wait," I said, slapping a hand on his outstretched arm. "Where am I going?"

"With me," he said. "To my hotel."

"But after I get my suitcase . . . where do I go?"

He bent down and kissed my lips gently. "Why go anywhere?"

The yellow cab wasn't built that could get us to that hotel room fast enough. We necked in the backseat, held hands through the hotel lobby, necked in the elevator, then fell through the hotel door and became a tangle of arms and legs as soon as the door shut behind us.

I had thought a lot about Spence in the past ten years. I had fantasized about him. But as we collapsed on the bed, everything about him seemed as unfamiliar as it was familiar. The way he felt was different—a far cry from his sweaty teenagery self of a decade ago. He seemed fleshed out, more solid. I couldn't help running my hands over him, trying to detect the differences, as if I'd found a lost artifact from my youth.

Yet he was still so Spencelike. What was it? He was the kind of guy who could rip your shirt off and not make it feel aggressive.

I had expected awkwardness, but there was none. We weren't even tentative. Maybe those vodkas helped, but after the initial exploration, we frolicked on the king-sized bed like long-lost playmates. We even cuddled like longtime lovers afterwards, with him kissing my head sweetly and me twirling my finger through that tantalizing thatch of chest hair I had forgotten about completely.

"I can't believe we found each other again," he said, with real wonder in his voice that exactly mirrored my own.

"Took us a while."

"But that's what will make it all worthwhile," he said. "Maybe it's better to rediscover what you loved and lost. That way you'll know better than to take it for granted."

Message: Lesson learned.

I snuggled as close to him as I could possibly get, which led to more frolics, which seemed to do Spence in completely. He had barely rolled off of me before he was snoring contentedly away.

I sighed and turned off the light, fully expecting to doze off myself.

But before my eyes could close, I found myself staring up at the barely visible light fixture in the middle of the room. My mind started going over everything that had happened that day, until I was certain that my old friend insomnia had followed me to the hotel room.

Oddly, out of all that had happened, what stuck in my head in that dark room was an offhand comment Spence had made. *"You're a nanny no more."*

Which begged the question . . . so what was I?

Chapter 20

The next few days were maybe the happiest of my life. Spence and I were inseparable. He even called in sick to work one day. We stayed in bed half the day, then went shopping at Barney's. I couldn't afford a pair of socks from there, but Spence was feeling flush with love. He wanted to buy me everything—shoes, clothes, lingerie, makeup, jewelry. He was spending money like a sultan, and I was his one-woman harem.

Much as I was enjoying the novelty of being a pampered adult, I tried to rein him in. Sort of. "You can't do this," I said when he insisted I try on a new pair of boots.

"Why not?" he asked. He was already sagging under the weight of shopping bags, and looked perfectly content. "If I don't spend it on you, Pepper will get it all."

That answer made me flinch. Not that I minded the mention of his wife. We talked about Pepper often, wondering, like guilty children who had skipped school, what was going on at the apartment. It was the reference to the upcoming legal battle that got me. The idea that I was going to be the horse-faced Camilla in the middle of their divorce.

I was going to be my mom.

But since I was going to be my mom, I relented and let him get me the boots.

After one day of suspense, Spence had called Pepper to tell

her that he had spoken to me. I, of course, was standing right next to him, hanging on to every word.

"She said she just thought the atmosphere was too tense at the apartment," Spence told Pepper—the story we had agreed on. "Yes, I think it was irresponsible, too . . . absolutely . . ." He twirled a lock of my hair around his finger. "I think she got wigged out after you yelled at her."

He grinned at me.

I shook my head. He was so bad.

"I know you didn't." He paused. "No, I don't know where she is. She probably went to stay with her mom until she could find somewhere permanent, but that's just a guess."

His side of the conversation turned more stilted as they obviously began discussing August. He turned away, as if this were none of my business.

Which, much as it killed me to admit, it wasn't. This fact was just beginning to dawn on me. August had been my charge for a few months, but I had no more claim on her. And in fact, after the fallout ahead and after Pepper had finished reeducating her, she would probably look on me as her adversary. The dreaded stepmom.

After a few more minutes of increasingly hostile monosyllables, Spence snapped his Nokia shut. He looked delighted with himself. "No mention of the nanny cam."

"No hints of vengeance?"

He shook his head. "I really don't think she suspects that you're here with me. She was saying that you had some friend down in the village . . ."

"Jess," I said.

"Right. She said you were probably down there."

I hadn't called Jess yet to tell her what had happened. At the moment I didn't trust myself not to sound too smug with her. She had been so sure Spence was leading me down the garden path. *Au contraire!* By the weekend I felt like we were a permanent item. Spence started turning on his cell phone again and taking business calls, which was irritating but nothing I couldn't deal with. He loved his work; it was important to him.

Wasn't it the goal of every relationship to go about your business and assume that the other person will understand and be there for you? Some churlish girlfriends might call this *taking me for granted.* Not I. I called it companionability.

I only hoped that I could find something to do that I enjoyed half so much as Spence enjoyed his work. On one day, I even said so.

He snorted. "Half as much would be just about not at all."

This was a surprise. "You must like your work," I said. "You're at it all the time. All the travel . . ."

He rolled his eyes. "I wanted to get away, mostly. As for working all the time—who would pay for everything if I didn't work? Don't women ever think about that?"

I frowned. "You're accusing me of not worrying about money?"

"I'm not accusing . . ." He shook his head. "I'm sorry. I shouldn't lump you into a category. A lot of these guys I work with, though, they have these wives that work. You know, at *nonprofits.* Or at *magazines.* In the *arts.* Little vanity jobs they can wear like accessories over their husbands' incomes."

I was about to reply that these were jobs that were often most suited to women's interests and lives. And that it really wasn't as easy to break into business and earn six-figure salaries as he might think . . . especially if your family wasn't rich and your father-in-law wasn't the biggest investment banker in Dallas.

In other words, I was about to throw a lit match into the gas tank.

But I didn't. And Spence, no doubt seeing my face twisting into a sort of feminazi contortion, held up a hand, palm out. "Don't get me wrong. Those jobs are worthy. You know I like the arts. It's just . . ." He sighed, but let the argument trail off. "And then there's Pepper! She never even considered working. For her, getting a pedicure is activity enough to justify her day. I make a lot of money, but even so I was barely keeping up with what Pepper managed to spend. Did she tell you about that coat I was giving her as an early birthday present?"

I gulped. "The sable? I saw it!"

"The thing cost a small fortune. Enough to feed a Central American village for a decade."

"Why did you give it to her, then?"

"I didn't! She bought it herself, then posed the early birthday idea, and what was I going to do at that point, tell her no? After she'd had it altered?"

"That's what Ricky Ricardo would have done," I said.

He chortled. "Yeah, and spanked her. But I caved in. I guess that's the difference between me and Ricky Ricardo."

"That and the fact that you don't play conga drums. Otherwise you're like Twinkies."

He drummed his fingers on the hotel room desk. "I should be able to take the coat back, since we're going to be separated by her birthday anyway."

"Why don't you?" I asked.

He smiled, but shook his head. "She picked it up already."

"So go get it and take it back to the store."

He squinted at me. "Steal it?"

"Why not? It's your money. You could put that money into a trust fund, or—"

"Or give you the coat."

I shook my head. "That wouldn't be me at all. That's the kind of thing my mom would like."

"So I'll give it to your mom," he said, as casually as if we were speaking about a bottle of wine. "I always liked her."

I laughed. "She'd love you forever."

"And it would drive Pepper up a tree," he said gleefully. "So when do we do it?"

I gaped at him. "Do what?"

"Steal the coat."

"Spence, are you nuts?"

I didn't think he really wanted to give the coat to my mom, but he did seem intent on the idea of stealing it back from Pepper.

"Maybe. Or maybe I just want to let Pepper know that her days of yanking my chain are over."

Oh dear. I wasn't at all sure about this idea, but Spence had a gleam in his eye.

On Sunday, we staged a stakeout.

At a coffee shop near the apartment, we started monitoring the comings and goings of Pepper and company. At first espionage made us giddy, and we giggled behind our newspapers and dark glasses.

After an hour, the only glimpse we got of Pepper and Phaedra was of them walking out under the awning and then hailing a cab. "Where are they going?" Spence wondered, ducking behind his *Village Voice* as the taxi sped past.

"I don't know, but we'd better hurry."

"Hold on."

A woman appeared, leading August out by the hand. August's brow was pinched and fretful. They turned and went towards the crosswalk to the park.

I had to restrain myself from hopping out of my seat. If I hadn't, Spence would have. "Wait," he whispered, as if August would be able to hear us from a half a block away, and with a wall of glass between us. "Wait till they're out of sight."

"But I don't want them to get out of sight," I said. "That strange woman has August!"

"She's the new nanny," he said.

I didn't like the looks of her. She looked too young. And too blond.

"How could Pepper have found a nanny that fast?" I asked. "Did she call McNannies, or Nannies to Go?"

"Calm down, Al. The woman seemed perfectly respectable."

"But did you see August? She looked miserable!"

"She's a three-year-old. They pout."

"She's almost four," I said. "Less than two weeks from now."

He leveled a hostile look at me. The first all week . . . all summer, in fact. "I know when my daughter's birthday is, Al."

"I know, but . . ." God, he was right. What was wrong with me? I acted like no one could take care of August except me, but really, how qualified had I been to take care of her? They could have picked a name at random from the phone book and come up with a person more experienced with kids than I was.

"Okay," Spence said, craning his head to watch them disappear from view, "Let's do it!"

We dashed across the street. Spence was so into it that I half expected to see him running serpentine. We were needlessly breathless by the time we made it into the lobby.

Lou's eyes widened when he saw me. His face broke into a smile. "Hey, you! I've been wondering what happened to you."

"Oh, I had to leave," I said.

"Yeah, that's what the Missus told me." He cast a squinty glance up at Spence, registering who he was. When Lou turned his gaze back to me, he wasn't smiling anymore. The message was clear. I was a Jezebel. "Anyways," he went on, "the day after you went tearing out of here, Mrs. Smith came down and told me that if I was to see you, I was to give you this." He pulled out a small envelope with an address on it and handed it to me.

When I shook the contents of the envelope into my hand, a key came out. I frowned, then turned the envelope over again. The name of the town in the address on the little envelope was White Plains, New York. "What is this?"

"Key to a storage locker. On account of that's where your stuff is."

"She hauled all my stuff to White Plains?" I asked, my voice quaking with indignation. White Plains was . . . well, I didn't know where it was. I knew it wasn't in New York City, though.

Lou scratched his head. "Yeah, I thought it was odd. I offered to let her store a few boxes down in the basement, but she was having none of it. Said this would work just as well."

I glared at Spence. I didn't feel a bit bad about stealing Pepper's coat now.

"Thanks," he said. "We're just going up for a few moments."

Lou hefted himself off his stool. "Beg pardon, but Mrs. Smith left instructions not to let missy here up into the apartment."

"It's my apartment," Spence said. "Alison is my guest."

"Mrs. Smith won't like this," Lou said.

Spence breathed out an impatient sigh and began digging through his wallet for hush money.

"It's okay," I said quickly. "I'll stay down here."

Spence put a fifty on Lou's podium. "Here. You never saw us."

"Okay," Lou said, pocketing the cash with a shrug. "It's all the same to me."

In the elevator, Spence looked pissed off. "Who does that guy think he is?"

He obviously didn't even know Lou's name. "He's the doorman. He's just doing his job."

"Sure he is. I'll bet he's on the take from everybody."

The old Spence, I thought as I watched the numbers above the doors blinking in succession as we climbed, *would have liked Lou.* Or at least he would have appreciated what a character he was.

The old Spence wouldn't sneer at wives of corporate executives working at nonprofits.

They were just brief observations, yet I felt a little traitorous for marking them. The old Spence had been eighteen. He hadn't been to college, had never held a real job or shouldered responsibilities, hadn't been married for ten years. Who on earth wouldn't change, sometimes radically, over a decade? The amazing thing was how much like his old self he still was. *I* was probably the one who had changed more.

Maybe knowing someone from their teens was a little like having known someone while on vacation. Sure, senior year had had its stresses, but looking back they were so minor, so diminutive when compared to the problems you had to face as an adult. We had always been in a place apart from the real world. Now we would have to get to know each when it wasn't all sunshine and good times.

Even the past week had seemed unreal, now that I stopped to consider it.

The doors slid open and we let ourselves into the apartment. It felt different, somehow. I was struck again by how new everything felt. It still had that new-paint smell.

"We shouldn't stay here long, obviously," Spence said. "I'll just run and grab the coat."

He did run. I, meanwhile, strolled around, taking a last look. An outsider would never guess that this was a household fraying from the center. The place was immaculate. Even August's room was perfectly tidy, with just her *Little Mermaid* video cover on the floor. I wondered if she was back to watching that movie over and over. I wondered if she was back to not letting people call her by her real name. I wondered, with a sharp pang, whether this wasn't all a huge fuck-up.

I wandered across the hall to my room. I knew my stuff wouldn't be there. What I wasn't prepared for was a complete transformation.

After getting a peek at the room, I pushed on the door and let it swing open all the way. Then, just to make sure I wasn't seeing things, I switched on the ceiling light.

Unbelievable!

Spence was by my side in a flash, hefting a huge bandbox, presumably with the fur in it. "Turn off the light and let's go." He was still in rushed, spy mode.

"Look at that!" I exclaimed. "What a lunatic!"

His face was a blank as he stared around the tiny bedroom. "What's the matter?"

"She's painted the walls willowed ecru."

Monday morning I woke up in my usual bleary-eyed fashion, only something was different. On the painful road to wakefulness I had heard the wakeup call from the front desk, and the shower running, and Spence talking into his phone at regular intervals. Now Spence was looming over me in a suit, holding a briefcase.

"I've got to go," he said, leaning down to kiss me on the cheek. "Have a good day. What are your plans?"

I had no plans. I felt a hitch in my chest at having to face an entire day alone. "I'm not sure. I guess I need to decide what to do with my life."

"Make sure you include me in," he said.

I smiled. "I'll take you into consideration. But what I really need to think about is—"

Spence held up one hand and grabbed his phone with the other. "Hello? Yeah . . . okay. Well hold on, I'm on my way." He snapped the phone shut.

Someday she'll realize that her Prince Charming is just an ear attached to a phone . . .

I rubbed my temples. Pepper had invaded my head.

"Sorry, gotta run," Spence said on his way out the door. "Order yourself some coffee from room service—you look like you need it."

"I didn't sleep well."

"No kidding. You toss and turn all night. You need to do something about that!"

I sank back down against the pillows, but didn't let myself fall asleep again. Today was the first day of the rest of my life. It sounded like something Finn would come out with, but it was true nonetheless. Time to get my ducks in a row.

I took a long hot shower, but dressed quickly in my new Barney's clothes, spritzed myself liberally with Chanel, and left the hotel by ten. Which was still an early-bird hour, to my way of thinking. Plenty of time yet to get the worm.

This is what I was going to do: I was going to go to a newsstand and buy papers, then settle myself down in a coffee shop somewhere and go through the employment ads. I had no intention of leeching off Spence. I was even going to look into apartments, since he hadn't mentioned anything about our living situation yet.

This is what actually happened: I walked five blocks to a newsstand near a Starbucks to get a *Times* and ended up gaping goggle-eyed at the stack of *New York Now*. Because I was on the cover. *Me*. The tabloid was practically a big newsprint square, and yours truly was taking up the whole front page. There was a grainy shot of me kissing Spence—though Spence was almost too blurry to make out clearly. Then there was another shot of me, full face, smirking. That one really made me recoil. My hair was a mess, and I looked like I had ten chins.

Oh, but it was me.

At first I really thought I was seeing things. Or that this was some elaborate practical joke. I mean, there were important things happening all over the world. Like wars. And famine. And horrible, grisly murders. There were people involved in serious financial shenanigans that would affect the future of millions. I was even pretty sure there was a hurricane or two out there somewhere, threatening all manner of destruction.

So what was I doing on the front page of a major newspaper of the biggest city in the country?

The headline, if you could call it that, shouted, *NAUGHTY NANNY!* NANNY CAMS SHAKING UP FAMILIES IN NYC. PAGE 3.

Were they trying to pass this off as news? With shaking hands, I snatched up the paper and turned to page three. The moment I saw the byline, I understood all. The article chronicling marital infidelity, class war, and general distrust on the Upper East Side was written by none other than Jonah Adams. Old fur butt.

"This idn't a library, lady," the newsstand guy barked at me.

I flicked him an irritated glance and then dug seventy-five cents out of my purse. He took it, squinted at me, then tossed another glance at the stack of papers. "Hey, wait a minute . . ."

I began backing away.

"Aren't you . . . ?"

He turned to the people who had bottlenecked behind me. "That's the lady! The naughty nanny, right there!"

From the excitement in his tone, you'd think he had just spotted Julia Roberts.

It was only five blocks to the hotel, but my legs didn't feel as if they would be able to support me for five feet. I wobbled to the curb in my uncomfortable new boots and stuck my arm out for a cab. "Taxi!"

Meanwhile the guy behind me was still shouting to anyone who would listen. "That's *her!* I know it's her!"

This is the thing about New York City—when you really need a cab, there are no cabs. I did finally see one speeding from a block away, and I started snapping my fingers. That was the moment when the arc of spit landed on my cheek.

"*Slut!*"

I rounded on the woman in her suit and her shopping bag, but I was too stunned for words. Anyway, how was I supposed to respond? "*Am not!*" With my dignity already under assault . . . obliterated, actually . . . I wasn't going to stoop to schoolyard type exchanges.

Besides, she bustled off before I could think of anything appropriately scathing.

The cab mercifully screeched to a stop in front of me and I fell into it. Through the window, I could still see the newsstand guy pointing and grinning, and a crowd on the street staring at me with openly curious faces as the cab pulled away. I felt like the bearded lady at a freak show.

In the cab I scanned the paper. The article was awful. A complete hack job of trumped-up social commentary to rationalize a sensational picture on the front page. There were statistics about divorce, and statistics about nannies, and interviews with owners of surveillance stores saying that yes, nanny cams sold pretty briskly. The article named me, and Spence, though it conveniently referred to Pepper only as "the aggrieved wife." It had to be the world's slowest news day, or this never could have made the front page.

I yanked my phone from my bag and saw that I had several messages. All from Spence. I called him once I got back to the hotel.

"Where the hell have you been?" he shouted into the phone. "I've been trying to reach you."

"I forgot to turn my ringer back on after the movie last night," I explained.

"Al, what is the point of paying for a cell phone if you are always leaving it behind, or turning the ringer off?"

I didn't know how to respond. I hadn't expected a lecture on my lax cellular phone habits.

"Never mind," he said. "Did you see that thing?"

"Yes. Just now. What should I do?"

"I don't know, but what *I* should do is wring that bitch's neck."

"I had already forgotten about the nanny cam."

"She was just waiting to spring this on us," he growled,

along with a few choice expletives. "I don't know what she thinks this is going to get her."

"Revenge," I said.

"Bullshit! I was feeling guilty before, but now I'm just mad as hell."

"You were feeling guilty?" I asked.

"Well, of course. I'm still married, you know."

"I know."

"Word's already gotten out at the office. People have been covering their chortles all morning."

"I got spat on."

"Christ!"

"I'm at the hotel," I told him. "I'll probably stay here."

"I'll be there tonight," he said.

"Tonight?" I squeaked.

An impatient sigh chuffed across the line. "I've got to work," he explained. "Besides, if we let this affect us, she wins. And I'm not going to let her win. Believe me."

I lay on the bed, feeling uneasy. It's strange to be in a newspaper, to be so exposed and misrepresented. That little slice of your life taken all out of context, blown out of proportion. To all the world I was the naughty nanny, but I wasn't even a nanny anymore. And I had resisted being naughty for so long, it just didn't seem fair. If I had known someone was going to do a smear job on me, I would have misbehaved earlier, and more spectacularly.

Within ten minutes of my hanging up the phone on Spence, Jess called.

"Oh my God!" she exclaimed the moment she heard my voice. "Where are you?"

"At an undisclosed location."

"Do you need help? What's happening?"

"I'm lying on a hotel bed. Nothing is happening, except that thousands of New York office workers are probably laughing about me by the water cooler."

"That close-up of you was terrible."

"Jess—it's all terrible."

"I know. I know. Do you have any protection?"

"What do you mean?"

"Weaponry."

I laughed. "Do you think Pepper's going to come and bust down my door?"

"I wouldn't put it past her."

Come to think of it, neither would I. But I wasn't ready to go pick up an AK-47 just yet. "I'll be fine."

"Do you need someplace to stay?"

"No, Spence is taking good care of me. I'm living in the lap of luxury."

"In exile, you mean. He's completely embroiled you in his mess."

"Not his fault."

"It *is* his fault, Al. It's his crazy wife that did this to you. It's not going to get better, either."

"I had something to do with all of this, too," I told her. "Why do you always have to be so negative?"

She snorted. "Right, and you're Pollyanna."

"If you had finally found the love of your life, do you think I would call you predicting doom and gloom?"

"I would hope you'd remind me that the love of my life is the same guy who dumped me once before."

"When we were kids!" I said. "That was years and years ago."

"Ten years. And has he improved? Would you want to be treated like he's treated Pepper?"

"What has he ever done to her?" I let out a sigh. "Never mind! God—it's like you want me to fail."

She sputtered. "I don't want you to fail. I just don't want you to crash and burn."

I let out a strangled sigh. "Look, I'll be fine. Just fine. I'm *happy!*"

That last word came out pitifully strained; for an awkward moment silence crackled over the line.

"Okay, okay. I'm glad you're happy. But if you need a place to crash, remember there's four square feet of space here with your name on it."

"Thanks."

I hung up, feeling almost worse than before. Why had I argued with Jess? She was on my side, and yet I reacted to her every word like a cat on its back.

I tried to close my eyes, but I couldn't relax. I hadn't thought about Pepper showing up at the hotel, but now that Jess mentioned it, it was a distinct possibility. My paranoia kicked up a notch.

The next time the phone rang, it was Finn. "I saw the paper," he said. "Are you okay?"

"Fine." I didn't want to start grousing with him as I had with Jess.

"Where are you?" he asked.

"A hotel."

"With him?"

I sighed. "His name is Spencer Smith. Didn't you read the article?"

"Oh. So it's true?"

He sounded wounded, like a little boy who'd just realized there was no Santa Claus.

"It's mostly true." There was no answer. "Finn?"

"Look . . . I think you should get out of there," he said. "I don't think this is how you want your life to proceed."

I sat up, getting angry again. "Why would you think that?"

"Because you're a kind person, deep down. You don't want to live your life that way."

"What way?" I asked, exasperated. Why did my friends have such a problem with this? "Happy? Feeling wanted? What does my being a kind person—even if it's just deep down—have to do with my falling in love?"

"It should have everything to do with it, Al."

His condescending tone made me bristle. Like I really needed this Alan Alda throwback's criticism right now. "Don't worry about me," I told him. "I'll get along just fine."

"All right," he said doubtfully, "but if you aren't getting along so well, there's room here if you need a place."

We exchanged a few more words before hanging up.

The next time the phone rang, I picked it up with less enthusiasm. What other friend could I snap at today?

It was Nola. "Oh my God, Al—Finn just called. He's so worried about you!"

I was ready this time. I laughed. (Gaily, as they would have said in the old days.) "Oh, that Finn. He's such a worry-wart. I'm fine. There was a little thing in a newspaper—no big deal, really—but aside from that, I've never been happier."

"He said you were shacked up with that guy."

"Spence. I told you about him. We were high school sweethearts."

Nola didn't seem to be buying my sunshine on the dewdrops tone. "I worried you would get into a mess like this! And now there's Finn, too."

"Finn?"

"I think he's in love with you," she said. "Isn't that terrible?"

Love? That sounded extreme. "I'm sure he's not, Nola. We don't know each other all that well . . . and we're not that compatible . . ."

"How well do you know this Spencer person?" she asked. "Do you really know him at all? I assume you can't, since up until a few days ago he was married to someone else."

"We were in high school together."

"High school!" she exclaimed. "You can't tell anything about people from high school. People aren't even human then."

"That's not true!" I argued. "I'll bet you were the same person then that you are now."

"Well, of course . . ." she said. "But were you?"

My ears felt like they were buzzing. I *was* the same person back then—just a little more so. Richer. More superficial. More arrogant. And, unfortunately, more self-confidant.

"You don't want him," she said. "You're just trying to get back to that earlier version of yourself, back when you were . . ."

"Less of a loser?" I asked. Inside, I was quaking. *Was she right?* But she couldn't be. She was just angry because I was with Spence, not Finn.

Finn was in love with me?

"We're just seeing how it goes," I mumbled.

"Sounds like it's going great so far." I started to blurt out something in my defense, but she cut me off with a sharp sigh.

"I don't want to fight with you, Al. If you need to get the hell away from that place, just remember you can always come back here and stay."

So for once, all my friends were unanimous. I was making a huge mistake, and when I realized it I was welcome to crawl back to any of them and eat crow. Unfortunately, the more they scolded, the less I felt like seeing them, much less staying with them.

And I wouldn't need to. Because they were wrong about Spence. I was sure of that. Everything was going to work out fine.

I must have drifted off to sleep that afternoon, because I didn't wake up until Spence came through the door. "Have you been here the whole time?" he asked as I rubbed my eyes.

My body felt leaden. "Uh-huh."

He shook his head. "I wish *I* could have slept all day! I'm ready to pass out."

"Have you eaten?" I asked.

"Yeah, I grabbed something on the way back here."

A lump formed in my throat. He stopped . . . instead of waiting to have dinner with me? My stomach was rumbling hungrily; I had thought we'd eat together.

"Did you hear from Pepper?" I asked.

He struggled to yank off his necktie. "No, but let's not talk about that, okay? I would like to be in a Pepper-free zone for once."

I understood where he was coming from, but I had waited all day to blow off steam, and now I felt cheated. I wanted to talk about how I was feeling, but Spence just wanted to forget about it all. In the end, we spent the evening watching Pay-per-View movies in our room and not talking much. It was a relief to turn out the lights and have sex—that was some way of communicating, at least. But afterwards I lay awake for a long time, wondering how long I could hang out in a hotel.

The next day was a repeat of the day before, only no one called me. I told myself that I really didn't want to talk if everyone was going to be so judgmental. Still . . . where was everybody? Where was my mom? Hadn't she seen the newspaper?

That night Spence and I went out to dinner. I think he sensed that I had felt abandoned the night before . . . and besides, he didn't want me snacking from the minibar anymore. (He might be rich, but he had a laudable frugality in some matters.)

Over the main course, I told him I was probably going to start looking for an apartment soon.

He put down his fork. "For yourself?"

"Don't you think I should? I don't want to live in a hotel room forever. It doesn't seem real."

"Okay, but I hope you'll be looking for something big enough for two."

"For you and me?" I asked.

"Of course. I just assumed we'd be moving into a place together, didn't you?"

The words, which might have made me flush with pleasure over the weekend, now struck me as presumptuous. "We never talked about it."

"Sure, but I just took it for granted . . ." He smiled. "We're a couple now. Even the newspapers agree."

I twirled some pasta around my fork.

"Don't you want to?" he asked. "You could have carte blanche, you know. Wherever you want to live—condo, loft, townhouse. House hunt to your heart's content."

"Wouldn't you want to be in on it?" I asked.

"I just thought since you're unemployed . . ." he said. "After all, I've got work. I'm so busy. I'll probably have to run out of town on business while you're looking."

I tilted my head. I had thought he would stop traveling so much now. "That's right."

"You have to be ready to jump on these things," he said. "Finding a place to live in this city is a full-time job, almost."

For a moment I had a flash of Spence in ten years, saying snarkily to someone, "*She acted as if finding that damn apartment was a full-time job!*"

He leaned across the table. "Is everything all right?" He took my hand. "You look pale."

I shook my head to clear it. "Everything's fine." It was. I was just letting other people's doubts infiltrate my brain. Which is just what they wanted, no doubt.

I smiled. There was nothing like holding hands with your lover in a candlelit Italian restaurant. This really was how I wanted to live my life. *Sorry, Finn.*

We went back to the hotel and made love, and I told myself that all was well. I would start apartment hunting the very next day.

"I don't want a place that's too big," I said.

Spence, who was lying back with his eyes closed, squeezed my hand. "That's good. Whatever you want."

"Of course we'll need a place big enough to have a room for August," I said, aware that I was only being half-listened to. "But I would like a place cozy enough that I could take care of it myself. I'm not the greatest at dealing with servants."

Spence smirked. "Believe me, you couldn't be worse than Pepper. She was always getting pissy about the help."

"No kidding! I couldn't believe the way she fired Marta," I huffed. "And all for an innocent little innuendo."

Spence opened one eye and looked at me. "What did Marta say?"

Didn't he know? I shifted uncomfortably. "Oh, she just mentioned that Marisol had lost her job because Pepper was jealous of her. Pepper overheard us talking."

"I wondered what had happened to Marta!" Spence shook his head. "Pepper always made too much of the Marisol thing."

I nodded.

Then, slowly, it seemed as someone had attached an intravenous cold-water drip to my arm. The Marisol *thing*?

"So there was a *thing*?"

He breathed out, as if he were about to drift off to sleep. "Huh?"

"You actually did have an affair with Marisol?"

He opened his eyes again with obvious reluctance. "It wasn't an affair. We weren't in love or anything like that. It just happened."

I gawped at him.

"Look, you know what my marriage has been," Spence says. "You've seen it, warts and all."

Not all the warts, apparently. I had assumed—foolishly, perhaps—that Spence was the wronged party. All the warts I had noticed were Pepper's. Because she was the one I had been focused on. Because Spence was never home.

What had Pepper called it? *Paternalistic absenteeism.*

"Knowing what you know, can you honestly blame me?" he asked. "I mean, Marisol practically threw herself at me."

And now she was cleaning hotel rooms on the interstate, Marta had said. She'd been saving up to go to college. She had wanted to start a new life for herself, and she had gone off track.

I could understand that.

"It doesn't matter who threw themselves at whom," I argued. "It's cheating. It's adultery."

He laughed. "What do you think this is?"

Chapter 21

Reader, I didn't marry him.

I didn't even come close. My infatuation for Spence Smith lasted eleven years, then died in less than a week. Pepper would always say I stole her husband, but the truth was, I tried to return him promptly, even before seven days were up. In the world of retail, that would have been a quick turnaround. Hardly enough to damage the goods at all.

Had we re-met at a different time, under different circumstances, things might have been different. But after I learned about Marisol, I didn't think I would ever be able to get over the fear that he was a serial nanny-seducer. I didn't think I would ever be able to get the grainy pictures of us caught by the nanny cam out of my head, either. We would always be tainted by that. And I realized that I would not have been a great stepmother to August; from the beginning, I had not done what was best for her.

For instance, busting up her already shaky home had definitely not been in her best interest.

From whatever angle I looked at it, I had behaved very badly. But when you have made a terrible mistake, and you realize it, what do you do next? I couldn't turn myself in. Well . . . maybe I could have. I could have knocked on Pepper's door and . . . and said what? *"I'm* soooo *sorry I took Spence . . . Here, have him back—just slightly used."*

Years ago, in the heat of her own marital fiasco, my mother had given me some lame rationale for breaking up our family. "The heart has its reasons," she had said, or some such nonsense. I lambasted her for it at the time. But as I sneaked away from Spence's hotel room that night after he confessed about Marisol and then calmly turned over to go to sleep, I wanted to find my mom and tell her that maybe her words hadn't been so idiotic after all. Maybe there was just enough of a grain of truth in what she'd been trying to tell me all those years ago that I owed her an apology, or at least an ounce of understanding.

Late at night, it can take forever to get to Brooklyn. I was tempted to call Jess or Finn and crash at one of their places, but I had been so snotty to them. They had every right to be smug, to tell me they told me so, or even to withdraw their offers of sanctuary. (Besides, Mom had more room.) It was past one when I dragged my suitcase up the stoop of my mother's apartment and buzzed on her door.

And buzzed.

It took her forever to answer, and when she did, it was just with the faintest of greetings. Not her usual faux-fab tone.

I climbed up the stairs and was completely out of breath when I saw her—but what I saw took what little breath I had away. I had come here thinking I was having the biggest crisis in New York City. Not so. My mom looked like she was about to die.

Seriously about to die.

I rushed forward to catch her before she fell; she looked that ill. "Mom, what's the matter?"

"I don't know. I think I have the flu."

"How long have you felt this way?"

"A couple of days."

Oh, God. I put my shoulder under her arm and walked her to the couch. She looked white, yet she had a fever. "Are you nauseous?"

"I've been throwing up. I think I want to go back to bed."

I had the feeling that if she did that she would never wake up again. "Mom, I'm calling a cab. We're going to the emergency room."

She shook her head, but I ignored her. I called the cab, then went about getting her things together. I threw a nightgown and a change of underwear into a paper bag, along with some of her toiletries. When the cab arrived, I had to ask the driver to help me get her down the stairs. He practically carried her. Mom was so out of it she wasn't even able to be indignant.

The cab felt like it was traveling in slow motion. I had no idea where we were going, or what the best hospital in New York was. When we arrived at an emergency room, where I expected the usual eternal emergency-room wait, the triage nurse took my mom's vital signs and immediately asked an orderly to whisk her back to see a doctor. They obviously thought she didn't have a moment to spare.

The diagnosis was appendicitis, as acute as it came. I filled out reams of forms and consents, and she was hauled off to surgery immediately. I went back to the waiting room and sat in a funk, praying she would make it. Appendectomies were just routine, right? The only good thing I can say for waiting there was that it seemed like the first time in weeks that I had thought about someone other than myself.

Finally, a doctor came out to see me. "Mrs. Tripton is doing fine so far. She's in recovery and should be awake in a few hours. When we move her to her room you can sit with her there."

By the time I finally got to see her, I was stunned to look out the window of her semiprivate room and see daylight. I hadn't been paying attention to time. Mom was sleeping, so I didn't disturb her, but I did decide to slip out and call Bloomingdale's so I could inform them she would be out for a while. Also, I needed to check what kind of insurance Mom had. I hadn't known what company to write down on the forms.

"I'm sorry to hear about your mother," the woman in personnel told me. "Give her our best. But I can't help you with your insurance questions. Mrs. Tripton no longer works with us."

"No longer . . . ?"

"As of last week."

"Last week?" I said. "But she just started working last week! Did she quit?"

"I'm sorry, I'm not at liberty to discuss past employees."

After the conversation ended, I sagged back against the wall. What had happened? Had she been fired from her new job? Why hadn't she called me?

Why hadn't I called her, to check up?

The surgery was going to cost a lot. I hoped Murph still had her covered. If he didn't, I intended to put the squeeze on him until he coughed up enough to cover her hospital bill.

Mom's eyes finally blinked open around nine. When she saw me she smiled at me beatifically. "My Al! There you are! Don't you look awful!"

I held her hand. It felt as if a huge lump were clogging my throat.

"You look like a ghoul," she said.

I squeezed her hand. "I didn't get my beauty sleep."

I thought engaging in a little lighthearted banter might make her feel better, but instead her eyes teared up. "Oh, honey."

"Mom, what's the matter?"

"I don't know why I called you a ghoul! You're beautiful."

"Forget it."

"I've been terrible to you, haven't I?"

"No—Mom, no."

Her head was moving like a bobble-head doll's. "Yes, I know I have. I've hardly been a mother to you at all. No wonder you turned out so weird."

"You've been fine. That's what I was coming to tell you last night . . ."

She frowned. "Last night? Were you there?"

It was then that I realized she might be a little out of it. No telling what they were giving her for pain. "I went to your apartment and found you sick. But you're fine now, the doctors say."

"I don't feel fine." She bit her lip. "And the expense. Al, I don't have insurance! Bloomingdale's fired me."

I pretended to be surprised. "But you were doing so well!"

"Just for one morning," she confessed. "For one morning I was employee of the year! I was going to set the lingerie world on fire. Then my feet started hurting and these annoying women kept coming in and I ended up tossing a pair of tap pants in an eighty-year-old woman's face."

I covered my mouth. I wasn't sure if I wanted to laugh or cry, but I didn't want her to see me doing either. "It's okay, Mom. Don't worry about that now. We all have our moments."

"But what am I going to do next?"

What were either of us going to do?

"Believe me," I said. "There are other eight-dollar-an-hour jobs. You'll get by." We both would.

"I wish I had been better to you. I wish . . ."

"I'm the one who should apologize, Mom. What have I done for you?"

When I looked into her eyes, tired as they were, I had the comfortable sensation of looking into my own face, older. "You didn't have to do anything, Al. You're my daughter."

I could hardly speak. "I love you, Mom."

She dabbed her eye with her sheet. "Are hospitals awful? They always make people so sickeningly emotional."

I nodded.

She fell asleep again, and I was at loose ends. I wished there was just one nice thing I could do for her. I supposed I could go buy her flowers. But there was only one thing that I could think of that she wanted that I could give her.

I headed out. At the subway, I called Spence. His secretary answered and told me he was in a meeting. She took a message from me about my mom being in the hospital in Brooklyn, and that I would call him back. I headed for the hotel.

He had told me he couldn't return the sable. In a joking way, he had even told me I could give it to my mom. I only intended to give it to her for a little bit—it would be a pick-me-up for her, like a bunch of carnations. She loved beautiful things.

And as luck would have it, I still had the key card to Spence's hotel room in my purse. There had been no big dramatics when I had snuck out the night before, so it was questionable whether he had even realized that I had left him yet.

I went back to the hotel and tried the coat on. It was a little snug, but it looked fabulous. As I vogued before the bathroom mirror, the room's phone rang. I picked up the bathroom extension automatically. "Hello?"

There was no sound on the other end. I frowned.

"Hello?"

I don't know why, but my first thought was, *Pepper.* She was spying on me.

But the other party hung up after another second, and I decided that I really needed to get my paranoia under control. It was probably just a wrong number.

Because I had spent the night in a chair, I decided to freshen up a bit. I jumped in the shower, and afterwards decided to help myself to a few hotel freebies, which went into my purse along with select items from the mini-bar that would carry me through another day at the hospital. (Technically theft, I know . . .)

Then I picked up the coat box and my purse and left the room.

As the door was clicking shut behind me, two policemen approached me. "Alison Bell?"

The cop who had said my name had a Joe Friday tone. It was the kind of voice that said, *you are so screwed.*

"Yes?" My own voice was a nervous squeak.

"We need you to come with us down to the station."

"What?" Defensiveness kicked in. "That's ridiculous! What for?"

"On the matter of a theft of the sable coat belonging to Mrs. Spencer Smith."

So that *had* been Pepper on the phone. She had probably been calling often and waiting for me to pick up to know when to sic the police on me for stealing her damn coat. Which just showed how nuts she was.

"But that's—"

My voice died. After all, it was hard to argue my innocence

when my hands were leaving sweaty prints all over the box containing the stolen loot.

I didn't have to go to jail. I never had to leave the precinct waiting area. While I was there, I had a taste of my fifteen minutes of fame, since there was a reporter around who recognized me as the Naughty Nanny. While I waited for Spence to get his butt over and clear this all up, I gave the *Post* guy an exclusive. The next day, buried in the local news, was a decent picture of me, Marilyn Monroe-ing it up in the sable coat. The shout lines read:

HUSBAND THIEF OR REAL THIEF?
"NO THIEF AT ALL!" INSISTS NANNY.

You get the idea.

I was actually treated pretty well. The police didn't like being used in these kinds of marital disputes. Obviously, they had bigger problems. Plus a couple of cops recognized me from the day Pepper had them drag away the homeless kids who were painting her apartment, so when I explained that this was just more of her madness, they were sympathetic and whispered something in the ear of the officer in charge of my case. He seemed inclined just to let me go . . . until he ran a check on my Texas driver's license, which divulged the fact that I had bounced five checks in Dallas during the month of July.

Oops.

When I tried to blame *that* on Pepper, too, and her refusal to reimburse me for a child's sparkly green bathing suit, I saw that I had stretched his patience. His eyes glazed over. I was stuck waiting for Spence.

I cooled my heels in a hallway, watching an interesting cross-section of the population of New York pass by. I drank a Sprite I had pilfered from Spence's mini-bar. About an hour after I got there, I wandered off in search of a ladies' room and a quiet place to make a phone call. Jess wasn't answering the phone at her office, but I left an SOS message for her.

When I came out of the bathroom, I nearly ran smack into Pepper. She was carrying the box with the reclaimed coat in it, and she seemed as surprised to see me as I was to see her. Her look of surprise made me bristle, since she was the one responsible for my being there in the first place. Did she think I didn't know that?

"Did you think they had dragged me off to Sing-Sing already?" I asked her by way of greeting. It was friendlier than what I wanted to do, which was punch her in her button nose.

She shifted the coat box to her other hip. "Well! I didn't think they'd let thieves loose."

That really made my blood boil. "I didn't steal your coat and you know it." She had to be aware that Spence had taken it. "Why would I even want it?"

She raised her brows coolly. "I don't know . . . why would you? Maybe because you seem to covet everything I have."

"I wasn't going to steal it."

"The police said you were even seen trying to leave the hotel with it."

"I was just borrowing it!"

She practically singsonged, "Poor little innocent Al. Never responsible for anything. Not even when she almost broke my neck."

If only I had, I seethed. "That was an accident."

"Oh, bullshit." She let out a mirthless chuckle. "Next you'll be trying to say that you just accidentally ended up with my husband."

I felt myself quaking from somewhere deep inside, as if an angry core was in danger of erupting. Even though this part of the hallway was deserted, I did not want to have a public scene.

"I don't want to talk about this," I said, trying to pass her.

She grabbed my arm and I winced. The fingers digging into my flesh were amazingly strong, and the anger in those blue eyes of hers was startling. "Of course you don't!" she said. "Because you know there's no excuse for stealing another woman's husband."

I didn't even want her damn husband, but I wasn't going to give her the satisfaction of knowing that. "That's rich, coming from you, Pepper. You've been about as faithful as a stray cat to Spence. You were doing a bang-up job busting up your own marriage before I ever came on the scene."

"You don't know a thing about it," she said.

"I know that you don't appreciate Spence. I wonder if you ever have."

"Of course I have! *You* were the one who didn't appreciate him all those years ago. You were all wrapped up in yourself to see that you had the greatest guy in the whole city at your feet. By the time I showed him a little affection he was so grateful it was pathetic!"

I yanked my arm back and crossed my arms over my chest, partly to keep her from grabbing me again but mostly to prevent myself from strangling her. "And why did you show him affection? Why did you suddenly develop this interest in my boyfriend?"

She blared out a laugh. "Because I couldn't stand you! You always thought you were such hot shit—you had been trying to show me up ever since that birthday party!"

Now we were getting somewhere, I thought. The birthday party!

"You were the one who started it."

Her mouth dropped. "Was *I* the one who was tossing feces at other children, Al? Was I?"

She had a point there.

"You're pathetic, you know that?" I said. "Holding some kind of a sick grudge all those years!"

"You're a fine one to talk! You obviously pined after Spence for a decade. It certainly didn't take you long to try to steal him once you found him again."

"I did not try to steal him," I repeated.

"I guess you just ended up sleeping with him by chance then!" she screeched. "Seducing him in his *own daughter's* bedroom! I swear I've never in all my life been as disgusted as I was when I saw that tape!" Her voice quavered self-righteously. "As a mother, it made me ill."

I hated her then. Really hated her. I hated her all the more because she had videotaped evidence. Anything I said in my own defense would sound lame, and she knew it. So she was playing mommy martyr, and hamming it up. She even swished her hair around a little as she had in her old Madge days.

All those years passed before my eyes, full of indignities and outrages: The barbs. The way she'd stolen my part in the play, stolen my boyfriend, hired me and then subjected me to her little jibes and indignities, the way she had fired Marta and even poor motel-room-cleaning Marisol, and made me a partner in crime by twisting my arm to go out with Colby. I remembered the bathing suit that never got paid for, my bounced checks, the unpacked boxes, the expensive thimble-sized quarts of ugly paint, and all my stuff sitting in storage in White Plains.

And then I thought about August, and I really feared I was going to have a stroke.

I could see people on benches down the hall craning to see us. A few men in blue were poking their heads out of their offices. I didn't care.

"You know what, Pepper? I don't care about your feelings as a mother. Half the time it makes me ill that you *are* a mother."

She tossed her head. "That's because you can't stand that I have something you don't."

"No, it's because I've had to watch you in action. You've got nothing but time, and you give none of it to August."

"We give her *everything*," she shot back.

"Except what she wants, which is a tiny part of your day. But you're too busy shopping and hanging out with your friends and screwing your boy toys to give a damn what she wants. Whenever you do notice her, it's usually just to criticize what she's eating, or to say that she's too negative. Well who wouldn't be, living where she's grown up! And here's a tip, *Peps*—it's not August who needs a psychiatrist, it's *you!*"

She stared at me, her face turning redder and redder, and then she lifted her head and pronounced, "You're just jealous."

I wanted to tear my hair out; or better yet, hers. She just didn't get it.

"Look, you can think whatever you want about me. I don't care."

She sneered.

"But for God's sake," I said, "couldn't you at least be decent to your kid? Maybe listen to her every once in a while and not fly off the handle just because she eats a Dove Bar?"

"You don't know anything about being a parent!" she said.

"I know that in twenty years you'll have a grown-up on your hands—an interesting person you might want to know—but by then it might be too late because she won't want anything to do with you. These little explosions you have probably mean nothing to you, but they're all she sees of you. They wound her."

Her eyes narrowed to angry slits. Maybe what I was saying hit home, because when she spoke, it was with a quiet rage I'd never heard her use. "You will *never* work as a nanny in this town again. Not in this entire country, if I can help it."

"Well here's a news flash—I don't want to. I can't stand to see the way people like you treat their kids. It's sick. People like you should have to take out special breeding licenses to minimize the number of kids whose heads you can fuck up in one lifetime!"

Okay. Maybe I went just a weensy bit too far. I knew it immediately when I suddenly noticed that Pepper wasn't screeching back at me. She wasn't even looking at me. Instead, she was staring at a spot just over my shoulder, and smirking. The hairs on the back of my neck stood on end, and I turned to see just who had heard that last outburst.

It was Spence. His face was white, and he was looking at me as if I were some kind of a monster.

"Nice girlfriend you found for yourself!" Pepper said, moving toward him. She tossed a glare at me as she brushed past. "Is that the kind of language you use in front of my child?"

I rolled my eyes.

"Look," Spence said, obviously at a loss for how to deal with this situation. "This isn't the place to have this discussion."

"You're right!" Pepper screeched back at him. "The right place to have it is in court, and that's where I'll see both of you!"

"Pepper!" he called after her.

She marched out, shoulders rigid, head high. The clicking of her heels was audible after she had disappeared.

He pivoted back to me, a harassed expression on his face. "For God's sake, what did you do?"

"I just gave her a piece of my mind," I said. "She had it coming."

Shaking his head, he took my arm and started pulling me toward the entrance. "I don't need this crap right now," he muttered. "Everything's nuts at work, I'm probably going to have to leave for Hong Kong again in a few days, and now you're at war with my wife."

"I don't think I harmed her. Her hide is as impenetrable as a Bradley fighting vehicle." We were passing the office. "Wait," I said, "I can't just leave."

"Yes you can. I sprang you," he said. "Though why you had to leave with Pepper's coat . . ."

I couldn't believe it. "Pepper sent them to the hotel room, Spence. Because she knew I was there. She called to spy on me. They would have nabbed me anyway."

"Okay, but did you have to be so out of line with her, Al?"

Out of line? Did he think I was still a servant?

"You can leave me here," I said when we reached the top of the stoop outside the police building.

"Don't you want to go back to the hotel . . . or have lunch?" He glanced at his watch. "I don't have much time, just a few minutes before I have to get back, but since I came all this way . . ."

"I left the hotel," I told him.

He looked flabbergasted. "You were just there."

"Just to get . . ." I shook my head, thinking of my ill-fated attempt to cheer up my mom. "Well, I picked up a few things. But I left the Barney's clothes you gave me. I wouldn't feel right taking them."

"Well what am I going to do with them?" he asked angrily. Then he sagged a little in frustration. "What's the matter with you? What's happened? Last night everything was fine."

"No, it wasn't. You were just able to go to sleep and forget about it."

"What, because I told you about Marisol? Am I supposed to stay up all night apologizing to you for something that happened months ago?"

"I don't know. Sometimes insomnia can be useful. It gives you time to think things through. Does *anything* keep you up, Spence?"

"Like what?"

"Well, did it ever bother you that your wife was so unhappy she would grasp at any kind of escapism, including pointless affairs? Did that ever keep you up at night?"

"What, you're making excuses for her now?"

"It's not all black and white." Not like I thought it was when I was nineteen. "And have you ever lost sleep over the fact that you never see your daughter, who basically thinks you hung the moon. Don't you realize what you have there?"

He went rigid. "Of course I do."

"Then *show* her something besides your backside walking out the door for once. Take the damn phone away from your ear and talk to her, play with her."

He rolled his eyes. "Oh, for heaven's sake!" He shook his head. "I've got to go. Something has obviously affected your reason."

"I'm being perfectly reasonable," I said. "You just don't want to hear that you've been an ass. I know I didn't."

He gave me an impatient look, like I was a Jehovah's Witness who had knocked on his door. "I'll talk to you tonight."

"No, you won't," I told him, and I meant it. I saw Finn and Jess getting out of a cab. It looked like the marines had landed just in time. "I'm going to be staying with friends."

I spent that night at Finn's. Mom was doing better and offered me her apartment for as long as I needed it, but Finn and Jess didn't like the idea of me rattling around a strange apartment in Brooklyn by myself. And I must say I welcomed the company.

Neither of them so much as uttered an I-told-you-so. They were great. They brought me comfort food and hot tea, basically treating me as if I were an invalid getting over a fever. And maybe I was.

Finn made up the futon for me and volunteered to sleep on the couch. "You might as well take the futon," I said after Jess had gone home. "I never sleep."

"Maybe tonight you'll get lucky."

I shot him a look.

"Platonically," he piped up quickly. "Sleepwise, I mean."

I doubted it. Even as I drifted off to sleep, I fully expected to wake up shortly. And truly, it felt as if just a few minutes had passed when my eyes were blinking open and Finn was standing next to the bed.

"Rise and shine," he said.

I sat up slowly and stretched. "What time is it?"

"Eight thirty."

I twisted to gape at the rays of sun pouring through the tiny window of the apartment. The couch across the room was made up, its sheets in a neatly folded pile. Morning. Sure enough, I had slept from about twelve thirty to eight thirty. Eight hours of *z*'s—like a normal person. What had happened? Was this miracle due to the fact that I had had almost no sleep the night before, or did Finn give off some kind of magical sleep-inducing vibes?

He handed me a big mug of coffee with milk and sugar, then perched on the edge of the futon. "That's how you like it, right?"

"How did you remember?" I asked him.

"Our first date was for coffee."

I shook my head. "I would think you'd want to forget that night."

"Oh, no. I remember everything about it. From the very moment we met. You showed up late. Nola was in such a state because everyone was sick, and she wanted me to get out from underfoot. But then you didn't look like you particularly wanted to go to a movie . . ."

"You were wearing a Mr. Bubble T-shirt, with a tear in it."

He laughed. "I could tell you hated it. I wanted to go back and change, but I was dying to get out of that house."

"And then I broke your rib." I hummed a bar of "Memories."

"Bruised." He sighed. "Well, it was memorable. And you seemed like such a singular person, and so kind, in a way, but not syrupy. In a no-nonsense unsentimental way."

"But I *am* sentimental," I said. "When I meet a person I always wonder if we'll know each other in fifty years, and if so, whether we'll remember that first moment."

"I hope we'll know each other that long." He grinned. "You know, I think I'll retire my Mr. Bubble shirt and bring it out every so often to remind you."

I put my hand on his, and squeezed it. "I assure you right now, you won't need to remind me. In fifty years, even in a hundred, I will still remember that Mr. Bubble shirt."

He looked at me questioningly, then caught my drift. An adorable, rueful smile came over his face. "On second thought, maybe I should just give it to the homeless shelter."

I nodded my approval and took a sip of his coffee, which was maybe the best cup of coffee I'd ever had in my life. Wouldn't you know . . . on the one morning I didn't really need it.

Still, good coffee . . . a full night's sleep . . . agreement to dispose of objectionable garments . . .

Finn definitely had qualities I hadn't appreciated at first.

"Do you like comedy clubs?" I asked.

He looked startled. "Uh . . . not really."

"Action movies?"

He shook his head. "I abhor violence."

Naturally. I took a deep breath. This was the sensitive one. "Have you ever participated in an open-mike venue involving folk music or poetry?"

"No." He frowned. "That is . . . well, when I was a senior in high school I wrote this thing for a class, and—"

I shuddered, and held out my hand to stop him. "Say no more."

He looked alarmed. "Is something wrong?"

I nodded. "High school. I'm thinking it's better just to forget about all that." I waved my hand over him like a high priestess. "You are officially absolved of your amateur poetry sins."

He bowed. "Thank you, O Great One."

Great One. I liked the sound of that.

Maybe it was time to rethink my dating criteria in positive terms, I thought, looking at Finn (who really did resemble Viggo Mortenson). I had missed all of his good qualities for so long. From now on, I decided, I would think in terms of *shoulds*, not *don'ts.*

Should be kind. Check!

Should love flea markets. Check!

Should make a blood-pumping cup of coffee. Check!

Should make me glad I am not living a pampered life of leisure in a luxury apartment on the Upper East Side . . .

"What are you thinking about?" he asked.

I let out a wistful sigh. "Just how some standards are too much for any mere mortal to live up to."

Nevertheless, maybe this was doable after all.

Epilogue

Darla's doctor persuaded her that a hospital would be a safer place to have a baby than the sauna tub on the farm, which was probably a good thing since Darla ended up having a cesarian.

A few weeks after the birth, Finn and I flew back to Texas for family visits. He came out with me to the farm for my first meeting with my new little sister. D'Ann was starting life with a hefty set of lungs and, as I predicted, a dad who doted on her every coo and burp. Dad confessed he had already run through fourteen disposable cameras—practically one for every day she had been alive. Finn added to the growing pile of documentary evidence of her existence by bringing along a camera, too.

"What do you think of your little sister, Al?" Darla asked me.

At that moment, D'Ann was clutching one of my fingers with a strength that surprised me. She had a fluffy thatch of black hair and large blue eyes that seemed to fix in astonishment at everything she looked at. Right now they were fixed on me, and I have to admit, any sibling rivalry pretty much evaporated on the spot.

"She's adorable—and strong!" If two weeks was any indication, she'd be out handling Dad's industrial strength weed whacker in no time.

"Yeah, she's gonna be a sturdy little thing. They always are in my family."

I hadn't given a lot of thought to Darla's family before, but suddenly I felt connected to them through this tiny little baby. I even felt closer to Darla, and over the weekend found myself becoming increasingly absorbed in her updates on the itchiness of her scar, her fatigue, and the difficulties of breast feeding.

"I tell you what, Al," she said as D'Ann helped herself to some lunch. "Givin' birth is just half the battle. I don't know what I'd do if I didn't have your daddy doing eighty percent of the work around here."

Dad was doing a lot, and he was actually competent at it all. It was as if he had found his niche. Maybe the wrong Bell had become a nanny.

I wasn't a nanny anymore, of course. At the moment I was working in production at a teen magazine, which was more to my liking. It was hard to take yourself too seriously when your day was spent surrounded by adults concerned with the best blemish remedies and the cultural impact of the Olsen twins.

Finn was still doing social work, and probably always would. Right after Christmas, we had taken a big leap and rented an apartment in Brooklyn together, not far from my mom's place. (But not too close, either.) It wasn't luxurious, but it was bigger than anyplace we could find in Manhattan. It was our funky love nest, full of cheap furniture and flea market finds, but it fit us. We were a perfect couple: his optimism and earnestness no longer grated on me, but seemed a perfect offset to my slightly darker worldview.

My mom finally got her alimony so her worries were over. What she had described as a draconian prenup actually reaped a pretty sizable income. Even a tiny percentage of a fortune can be a fortune, I guess. But she had still found another job working at the gift store at the Frick Museum, and at night she was taking classes. She wanted to become a travel agent. "Think of all the help I could be to people!" she told me when I expressed surprise at this. "I've been everywhere!"

I guess she was right. I hadn't really thought of my mom as the helping type, but she seemed to have turned over a new leaf. I was surrounded by people with good impulses now, which couldn't be a bad thing. Even Jess was less pessimistic than she used to be since she had officially allowed herself to fall in love with Troy. They had bonded during her visits to the psychiatric hospital. She and his doctor had even convinced him that it would be best if he buried MuuMuu.

Maybe all this positive energy was wearing off on me, because when I left from that weekend with my dad, Darla, and D'Ann, I actually felt hopeful. Even the prospect of spending the next two days with Nola did not dampen my spirits. For months she had been pestering Finn and me about getting married. Finn was very pro-marriage, too, which could make for some awkward moments. I didn't want to be a wet rag, but what I had seen of marriage close up had not been pleasant. Really, to ask my opinion on it would have been akin to asking a cardiologist about the advisability of taking up a two-pack-a-day smoking habit.

But maybe it wasn't all bad.

"What are you thinking about?" Finn asked me as we drove back to Dallas.

He was always asking me what I was thinking.

"I was thinking that Dad and Darla seemed so happy. I guess they always have been, and I just didn't notice."

"Because you were uneasy about them," Finn guessed.

"Right."

"See?" he asked. "Occasionally these marriages work out."

And occasionally they didn't.

I had run into Lumi on the number six train in early January, and she told me that although the Smiths had patched up their marriage after my departure, the union had since dissolved again and Pepper was alone in the apartment. Spence paid weekly duty visits to August, who perversely seemed to believe that divorce meant she got to spend more time with Daddy.

I still shuddered when I looked back on my days with the Smiths.

"I can't believe you would even want to marry a woman with a shady past," I said shaking my head.

He laughed. "I'll prove it to you. When we get back to

Dallas, let's get on the Internet, find the cheapest fair to Las Vegas, and go."

He made it sound so simple that a sudden excitement shot through me.

Could we? I wondered.

"Nola would be pissed that we cut her visit short," I worried aloud.

"Are you kidding? She'd be thrilled. I don't think she's been too happy with us anyway since we brought Jason that bongo drum." He waggled his brows at me challengingly. "What do you say?"

"I say it would be really impulsive."

"But fun, right?"

I nodded. I was swayed. "But a fun trip isn't exactly grounds for marriage."

We were about to pass a rest area on the highway, and Finn swerved into the exit lane.

"What are you doing?" I asked.

He pulled to a stop. Then he turned to me and took my hands in his. He was a hand-holdin' fool. "I'm giving you grounds . . . like the fact that I love you, have loved you from the moment I first laid eyes on you, and that I intend to love you for as long as we both shall live whether we go to Las Vegas or not." He kissed me. "How do you like those grounds?"

I felt a little dizzy, but I had to admit, "Those are pretty appealing grounds."

He sent me one of his heartbreaking, hopeful smiles. There were probably a million corny clichés rattling around in his adorable head just then.

"To Vegas?" he asked.

I only angsted for about half a second longer, which had to be a record for me. Then I laughed.

Why not?

"I'll take that as a yes," Finn said, gunning it for the highway.